A Roc… Mou…ain Christmas

A Rocky Mountain Christmas

William W. Johnstone

with J. A. Johnstone

PINNACLE BOOKS
Kensington Publishing Corp.
www.kensingtonbooks.com

PINNACLE BOOKS are published by

Kensington Publishing Corp.
119 West 40th Street
New York, NY 10018

PUBLISHER'S NOTE
Following the death of William W. Johnstone, the Johnstone family is working with a carefully selected writer to organize and complete Mr. Johnstone's outlines and many unfinished manuscripts to create additional novels in all of his series like The Last Gunfighter, Mountain Man, and Eagles, among others. This novel was inspired by Mr. Johnstone's superb storytelling.

ISBN-13: 978-0-7860-4162-6
ISBN-10: 0-7860-4162-5

First printing: November 2012
Eleventh printing: December 2017

19 18 17 16 15 14 13 12 11

Printed in the United States of America

First electronic edition: November 2012

ISBN-13: 978-0-7860-3243-3
ISBN-10: 0-7860-3243-X

Prologue

Lambert Field, St. Louis, Missouri—
December 20, 1961

Rebecca Daniels Robison awaited her flight in the comfort of the Admiral's Lounge. A huge Christmas tree sparkled with blinking lights and shining ornaments and Christmas music played softly over the lounge speakers. Rebecca was reading the newspaper when she was approached by a very attractive young woman.

"Ambassador Robison? My name is Margaret Chambers, and I'm a reporter for the *St. Louis Globe-Democrat.* I wonder if you would consent to an interview?"

"Why would you want to interview me, dear? I'm no longer an ambassador."

"No, but you are still active on the international scene, and a recent poll put you as the country's most admired woman."

"Nonsense, my dear. Eleanor Roosevelt is the most admired woman."

Margaret laughed. "You came in second, and Mrs. Roosevelt doesn't count. She's been the most admired woman for the last thirteen years."

"And rightly so," Rebecca said. "She has certainly been most gracious to me, over the years."

A voice came over the intercom. "Attention passengers, all flights are on temporary hold until the runways can be cleared of snow."

"I was about to say there wouldn't be time for an interview," Rebecca said. "But it appears that my flight has been delayed, so I would be happy to talk to you. I suppose you want to hear about my time as ambassador to Greece."

"No, ma'am," Margaret said. "I'm doing a story for our special Christmas edition. I understand you once had a most harrowing Christmas experience when you were a child."

"Harrowing? Yes, I suppose it was, though that's not exactly the word I would use. But it was also the most uplifting experience of my life."

"Could you share that story with our readers?"

"How much do you know about that incident?"

"Hardly anything. Just that you've been very reluctant to discuss it in all these years and that you've turned down every request for it. Your father was a U.S. Senator then . . ."

"A state senator in Colorado," Rebecca corrected.

"Yes, thank you. According to what little information exists, you and your family were on a train going from Pueblo to Red Cliff, Colorado, during a blizzard."

"That's correct. But that is only part of the story. If I told you everything, I'm afraid you would have a very difficult time believing it. Which is why I have never told the story before."

Margaret held her little narrow reporter's pad on her knee and raised her pencil, poised to take notes. "Why don't you try me? I would love to hear the entire story."

"Margaret, is it?"

"Yes ma'am."

"Well, since my plane is delayed, Margaret, I will tell you the whole story of that Christmas so long ago. I'm almost eighty years old and don't much care if people think I'm a crazy old lady or not. I guess now is as good a time as any to finally tell it. "

"Thank you, Ambassador Robison."

"Let's sit down, Margaret. And please, no questions until I am done."

Chapter One

New Orleans, Louisiana—July 9, 1889

The *Delta Mist* was moored to the bank, running parallel with Tchoupitoulas Street. Matt Jensen showed his ticket to the purser, then boarded the vessel, a packet boat that made the run between St. Louis and New Orleans and back again. Instead of going directly to his stateroom, he stopped at the rail of the texas deck, looking back toward the city of New Orleans, at the flower-bedecked iron-work trellises and balconies, and the belles of New Orleans strolling the streets in butterfly-bright dresses under colorful parasols.

Of all the cities he had visited, New Orleans was one of the most unique. Although it was an American city, it retained much of its French heritage, and although it was a Southern city, it had its own unique culture, making it stand apart from other cities of the South. Aromas of food, flowers, and a "perfume" distinctive only to New Orleans wafted toward the boat. Music, interspersed with laughter—loud guffaws of men and high trills of women—came from a riverfront bar on Tchoupitoulas Street.

The captain of the boat stood on the lower deck, frequently pulling out his pocket watch to check the time. It was obvious he was waiting for someone, and whoever it was, was late, contributing to an increasing agitation.

Matt watched a cab approach the river, the horse in a rapid trot, then pull to a stop at the river's edge. A woman got out, handed a bill to the driver, and hurried across the gangplank and on to the boat.

"Uncle, I'm so sorry. I was shopping and lost track of the time," the woman apologized.

"Jenny, I can't hold up the entire boat because my niece can't keep track of the time," the captain said.

From his spot on the texas deck, Matt was able to examine the woman rather closely. She was an exceptionally pretty woman with red hair, a peaches-and-cream complexion, blue eyes, and prominent cheekbones. If one had asked her about her lips, she might suggest they were a bit too full.

"Mr. Peabody!" the captain called.

"Aye, sir," answered one of the other officers.

"Away all lines. Pull in the gangplank."

Matt maintained his position at the rail on the texas deck, watching as the boat crew performed the ordered tasks. Captain Lee had reached the wheelhouse, and once the boat was free of its restraints, a signal was sent to the engine room. Smoke belched from the twin, fluted chimneys and the stern wheel began to turn, pushing the boat away from the bank and into the middle of the Mississippi River. The boat turned upstream, and the great red and yellow paddle wheel began spinning rapidly, leaving behind it a long, frothing wake.

Jenny Lee worked for her uncle as a hostess in the Grand Salon of the *Delta Mist.* It was her duty to see to the comfort and needs of the passengers who came into the Grand Salon. She also arranged friendly games of whist, checkers, and even poker for the passengers who wanted to participate.

Over the past two days, the boat had been averaging twelve miles per hour and was approaching Memphis, 704 miles by river from New Orleans. She was passing pleasantries with some of the passengers when a loud, angry voice got the attention of everyone in the salon.

"No man is that lucky! You have to be cheating!"

The speaker was standing at one of the tables, and the object of his anger and the subject of his charge was Matt Jensen.

Unlike the angry man, Matt was composed as he sat across the table.

Not so the other two players who, at the outburst, had stood up and backed away from the table so quickly they knocked over their chairs.

For a long moment there was absolute silence in the Grand Salon, with nothing to be heard but the sound of the engine, the slap of the stern paddle, and the whisper of water rushing by the keel.

"Mister, nobody cheats me and gets away with it," the man addressed his hostility toward Matt.

"You're out of line, Holman." Dr. Gunter was one of the other players at the table. "Nobody has been cheating at this table."

"The hell there ain't nobody been cheatin'! I ain't won a hand in the last hour. And he's won the most of 'em." Holman reached for the money piled up in the middle of the table. "I'm just goin' to take this pot to make up for it."

"That's not your pot." Jay Miller, a lawyer from St. Louis, was the fourth player at the table.

"Yeah? Well, we'll just see whose pot it is," Holman said contemptuously as he started to put the money in his hat.

"Leave the money on the table, Holman." Those were the first words Matt had spoken since being challenged.

"The hell I will. This money is mine, and I'm takin' it with me."

Jenny hurried over to the table. "Mr. Holman, please. You are creating a disturbance, and your behavior is making the passengers uneasy."

"Yeah? Well, to hell with the passengers. What kind of boat is this, anyway, that you allow cheaters in the games?"

"I wasn't cheating," Matt pointed out dryly.

"Mr. Jensen is tellin' the truth, Miss Lee." Dr. Gunter pointed toward Matt. "He wasn't cheatin'."

"What do you say, Mr. Miller?" Jenny asked the third man.

"I've played a lot of cards in my day, and I think I can tell when someone is cheating. I don't believe he was."

Jenny looked back at the angry gambler. "These gentlemen don't agree with you."

"Of course they don't. They are probably in on it. I wouldn't be surprised if they all get together later on and divide up the money. *My* money." Once again, he leaned over the pile of money on the table. "Like I said, I'll be taking this pot."

"Miss Lee, I've played cards with Mr. Jensen," declared a passenger who wasn't currently in the game. "I've never known him to be anything but honest."

"Same here," another put in. "I wasn't in this game, but I've played a few hands with him since we left New Orleans, and I found him to be an honest man. If these two gentlemen who were in the game say he wasn't cheating, then I would be inclined to believe them."

"Mr. Holman, that makes four people who say Mr. Jensen wasn't cheating. When you play cards for money, you are accepting the possibility of losing. The only thing protecting the game is the honesty, integrity, and honor of the players."

"You!" Holman pointed at Jenny. "You are in on it too, aren't you? You are all in it together."

"Look. We were in the same game as you. You think we would take up for him if he was cheating? Hell, we lost money, too," Miller said.

"Yeah, well, neither one of you lost as much money as I did."

"That's because neither of them is as bad at cards as you are," Matt gracelessly pointed out.

"What do you mean, I'm a bad player? Why, I'm as good at cards as any man."

"No, you aren't," Matt insisted. "You can't run a bluff and you raise bets in games of stud when the cards you have showing prove you are beaten. You should find some other game of chance and give up poker."

Jenny turned to Matt. "Mr. Jensen, I believe the pot is yours." She reached for the money to slide it across the table toward him, but Holman pushed her away from the table so hard that she fell.

He pointed down at her. "Keep your hands off my money. Like I said, I'm takin' this pot, and there's nobody here who can stop me."

Matt and another passenger helped her up. "Thank you for interceding, Miss Lee, but I think you had better let me handle this now."

"Ha!" the angry gambler cried. "You are going to handle this? What do you plan to do?"

"Oh, I'll do whatever it takes." Matt's calm, almost expressionless reply surprised the angry man.

The shock showed in his face, but was quickly replaced by an evil smile. He stepped away from the table and flipped his jacket back, showing an ivory-handled pistol in a tooled-leather holster.

"Mister, maybe it's time that I tell you who I am. My name ain't John Holman like I been sayin'. My actual name is Quince Justin Holmes, only some folks call me Quick Justice Holmes because I tend to make my own justice, if you know what I mean."

"Quick Justice Holmes," A passenger repeated in awe. "That's Quick Justice?"

"This is gettin' downright dangerous," another said.

"What do you say now?" Holmes asked.

"I say the same thing I've been saying. You aren't getting that pot," Matt said resolutely.

"It won't matter none to you whether I get the pot or not, 'cause you ain't goin' to be around to see it," Holmes said, his voice menacing.

"Does this mean you are inviting me to the dance?" Matt asked, still calm.

Holmes laughed. "Yeah, you might say that. I'll even let you make the first move."

Despite his offer, his hand was already dipping for his pistol, even as he was speaking. He smiled as he realized his draw had caught Matt by surprise. But the smile left his face when he saw Matt's draw.

To the witnesses, it appeared Matt and Holmes fired at the same time. But in actuality, Matt fired just a split second sooner and the impact of his bullet took Holmes off his aim. Holmes's bullet whizzed by Matt's ear and punched through the glass of one of the windows of the Grand Salon.

"I'll be damned! I've been kilt!" Holmes cried as he staggered back from the blow of the bullet.

"You could have prevented it at any time," Matt uttered.

Holmes dropped his gun and clamped his hand

over the wound in his chest. Blood spilled through his fingers, and he opened his hand to look at it before he collapsed.

Matt returned his pistol to his holster. Looking over toward Jenny, he saw a horrified expression on her face. "I'm sorry about this, Miss Lee."

"No," she replied in a small voice. "You . . . had no choice."

The boat put in at Memphis, and a coroner's inquest was held. The hearing lasted less than an hour. Enough witnesses testified that Quince Justin Holmes instigated the shooting and a decision was quickly reached.

Quince Justin Holmes died as a result of a .44 ball, which was energized to terrible effect by a pistol held by Matthew Jensen. This hearing concludes that Mr. Jensen was put in danger of his life when Holmes drew and fired at him. It is the finding of this hearing that this was a case of justifiable homicide and no charges are to be filed against Mr. Jensen.

Matt was welcomed back aboard the *Delta Mist* by those who had witnessed the shooting, as well as those who had only heard about it. He apologized to the boat captain for having been involved in the incident.

"Nonsense," Captain Lee replied. "Why, you've made the *Delta Mist* famous. People will want to take the boat where the infamous Quick Justice Holmes was killed. To say nothing of the fact that he was killed by Matt Jensen. You are truly one of America's best known shootists, as well known for your honesty and goodness of heart as you are for your prowess with a pistol."

"Hear, hear!" someone called, and the others cheered and applauded.

For the next 575 miles, the distance by river from Memphis to St. Louis, passengers vied for the opportunity to visit with Matt, or better, to play poker with him. His luck wasn't always as good as it had been during the trip from New Orleans to Memphis. By the time the boat docked up against the riverbank in the Gateway City, he had no more money with him than he had when he left New Orleans.

Jenny Lee stood by the gangplank, telling the passengers good-bye as they left the boat and thanking them for choosing the *Delta Mist.*

"Mr. Jensen, I do hope you travel with us again. You managed to make this trip"—she paused midsentence and smiled broadly—"most interesting."

"Perhaps a little too interesting," Matt suggested as he took the hand she had offered him.

Chapter Two

At sea—September 23, 1890

The ship was the *American Eagle*, a four-masted clipper in the Pacific trade. As much canvas as could be spread gleamed a brilliant white in the sunshine, and the ship was lifting, falling, and gently moving from side to side as it plowed over the long, rolling swells of the Pacific. The propelling wind, spilling from the sails, emitted a soft, whispering sigh as the boat heeled.

The helmsman stood at the wheel, his legs spread slightly as he held the ship on its course. Working sailors moved about the deck, tightening a line here, loosening one there, providing the exact tension on the rigging and angle on the sheets to maintain maximum speed. Some sailors were holystoning the deck, while others were manning the bilge pumps.

Twenty-four-year-old Luke Shardeen stood on the leeward side on the quarterdeck, his big hands resting lightly on the railing. From the age of seventeen he had been at sea, rising from an able-bodied seaman to first officer. His dark hair blew in the wind as his brown eyes examined the barometer for the third time in the last thirty minutes. There was no doubt it was falling, and that could only presage bad weather. Shrugging his broad shoulders, he left the quarterdeck and tapped on the door of the captain's cabin.

"Yes?" the captain called.

"Captain, permission to enter?"

"Come in, Mr. Shardeen."

Luke stepped into the cabin, which was as large as all the other officers' quarters combined. Captain Cutter was bent over the chart table with a compass and a protractor.

"Captain, the barometer has fallen rather significantly in the last half hour. I've no doubt but that a storm is coming."

"Do you have any idea how fast we are going, Mr. Shardeen?"

"It would only be a guess."

"We are doing nineteen knots, Mr. Shardeen. Nineteen knots," Captain Cutter said. "It's my belief that if we can maintain this pace, we'll outrun the storm."

"We won't be able to maintain this pace, Captain, if we rig the storm sails."

"I have no intention of rigging the storm sails. Certainly not until it is an absolute necessity."

"Very good, Captain." Luke withdrew from the captain's cabin and returned to the quarterdeck.

"Mr. Shardeen," the bosun called. "Will we be taking in the sail, sir?"

Luke shook his head. "Not yet."

He looked out over the water. The sea was no longer blue, but dirty gray and swirling with white-caps. It was the kind of sea referred to by sailors as "green water" and so rough the ship dropped into a trough and took green water over the entire deck as it started back up.

Shortly, the storm was on them, with wind and rain so heavy it was impossible to distinguish the rain from the spindrift.

"Captain, we have to strike sail!" Luke shouted above the noise of the gale.

"Aye, do so," Captain Cutter agreed.

Luke sent men aloft to strike sail, praying that no one would be tossed off by the bucking ship.

The masts were stripped of all canvas without losing anyone, but the storm continued to build. By mid-morning, it was a full-blown typhoon. Fifteen-foot waves crashed against the side of the 210-foot-long ship. The *American Eagle* was in imminent danger of foundering.

"Captain, we have to head her into the wind!" Luke Shardeen shouted.

"No. Even without sail we're still making head-way," Captain Cutter shouted back.

"If we don't do it, we'll likely lose the ship!"

"I'm the captain of this vessel, Mr. Shardeen.

And as long as I am captain, we'll sail the course I've set for her."

"Aye, aye, sir."

The huge waves continued to crash against the side of the ship and the rolling steepened, going over as far as forty-five degrees to starboard. It hung for so long the sailors had sure and certain fear it would continue to roll until it capsized.

Below deck in the mess, cabinet doors swung open and plates, cups, and bowls fell to the floor, crashing against the starboard.

"Everyone to port side!" Luke shouted through a megaphone and, though the sailors found it difficult to climb up the slanted deck, their combined weight helped bring the ship back from the brink of disaster.

When the ship rolled back, the dishes tumbled to port, breaking into smaller and smaller shards until there was nothing left but a jumbled collection of bits and pieces of what had once been the ship's crockery.

Above deck the yardarms were free of sail except for the spanker sail, which had been left rigged, and was now no more than tattered strips of canvas, flapping ineffectively in the ninety-mile-per-hour winds.

Captain Cutter was standing on the quarterdeck when a huge wave burst over the side of the ship. He and three sailors were swept off the deck, into the sea.

"Cap'n overboard!" someone shouted, and Luke

ordered the helmsman to turn into the wind. That kept the ship in place and stopped the terrible rolling, but it began to pitch up, then down, by forty-five degrees. Luke put the men to the rails to search for those who had been washed overboard. They found and recovered two of the sailors, but there was no sign of the third sailor or the captain.

By late afternoon the storm had abated, and Luke ordered the ship to remain in place to continue the search. For the next two days, in calm winds and a placid sea, they searched for the captain and the missing sailor, but found no sign of either of them. Finally, Luke ordered the ship to continue on its original course.

They raised San Francisco twenty-three days later.

A tugboat met them in the Bay, a seaman shot a line up to them, and, with all sail gone, they were towed to the docks, where they dropped anchor. As soon as the ship was made fast by large hawsers, a ladder was lowered for the officers and a gangplank was used by the men to offload their cargo of tea.

Luke sat in the outer office of the headquarters for the Pacific Shipping Company. The walls were decorated with lithographs of the company's ships, including one of the *American Eagle.* Beside each ship was a photograph of its captain. Emile Cutter's face, stern and dignified in his white beard, was alongside the picture of the ship Luke had just left.

"Captain Shardeen, Mr. Buckner will see you now," a clerk said.

Luke wasn't a captain, but he figured the clerk didn't know that or had called him "Captain" because he had assumed command of the ship to bring it home.

Although Richard Buckner's shipping empire had made him a millionaire, he had never been to sea. Nevertheless, his office was a nautical showplace, replete with model ships, polished bells engraved with the names of the ships from which they came, and the complete reconstruction of a helm, with wheel and compass.

Buckner was a man of average height, but in comparison to Luke's six-foot-four-inch frame, he seemed short. He greeted Luke with an extended hand. "Mr. Shardeen, you are to be congratulated, sir, for an excellent job of bringing the ship back safely. Please, tell me what happened."

Luke told about the storm, and how a huge wave hit them broadside, washing the captain and three other sailors overboard. Luke made no mention of the argument he'd had with Captain Cutter about bringing the ship into the wind.

"We rescued two of the sailors right away and stayed on station for two days, but we never found Captain Cutter or Seaman Bostic."

"Thank you. I'm sure that Mrs. Cutter will be comforted to know exactly what happened and will be grateful for the effort the entire ship showed in trying to rescue her husband."

"I wish we had been successful."

"Yes, well, such things are in the hands of God. Now, Mr. Shardeen, if you would, there are some reports you need to fill out. After you are finished, please come back into the office. I have something I want to discuss with you."

"Aye, sir." Luke normally didn't use *aye* except when he was at sea, but he knew Buckner enjoyed being addressed in such a manner.

As he was filling out the reports, Luke was given a stack of letters that had been held for him until the ship's return. One of them was from a lawyer's office in Pueblo, Colorado. He had never been to Pueblo, Colorado, and as far as he was aware, didn't know anyone there. Tapping the envelope on the edge of the table, he wondered why he would be the recipient of a letter from a Pueblo lawyer. His curiosity was such that he interrupted the paperwork in order to read the letter.

1 February 1890

Dear Mr. Shardeen:

It is with sadness that I report to you the death of your Uncle Frank Luke, who passed away on the 5th of August from an infirmity of the heart.

As you were his only living relative, you are the sole beneficiary of his will, in which he leaves you the following items:

18,000 acres of land
A four room house

All the furniture therein
A bunkhouse
A barn
1500 head of cattle
20 horses with saddles and tack
$1017.56 (remaining after all final expenses)

In order to claim your inheritance, you must present yourself at the Pueblo courthouse on or before November 1st, 1890.

Sincerely,
Tom Murchison
Attorney at Law

The letter came as a complete surprise. Luke had not seen his uncle Frank in over ten years, had no idea he'd lived in Colorado, or that he even had anything valuable to leave in a will. And he'd left everything to him!

Conflicting emotions quickly rose in Luke—elation over what appeared to be a rather substantial inheritance and guilt because not only had he not seen his uncle Frank, he had corresponded with him only three or four times in the last ten years.

Setting the letter aside, he finished the paperwork and returned to Mr. Buckner's office as requested.

"Mr. Shardeen," Buckner said. "With the unfortunate death of Captain Cutter, we have to find a new captain for the *American Eagle*. You know the ship and the men, and you brought her successfully through a terrible storm. I would like for you to be her new captain."

Had this offer been made to Luke one month earlier—or even one hour earlier—he would have accepted it immediately. But the letter from Tom Murchison had changed all that.

"I thank you for the offer, Mr. Buckner. I am extremely flattered by it." Luke took a deep breath before plunging on. "But I believe I will leave the sea for a while. I'll be submitting my resignation today."

"What?" Buckner replied in shocked surprise. "You can't be serious! Mr. Shardeen, this is the opportunity of a lifetime. How can you possibly pass it up?"

"Simple. Until today, I had no anchor. But now"—Luke held up his letter—"I am a man of property and can no longer afford to sail all over the world."

"Are you absolutely positive of that? If you are, we will have to promote someone else to captain."

"I am positive."

"Very well. The company will hate to lose you, Mr. Shardeen. You have been a good officer. If ever you wish to return to the sea, please, come see us first."

"I will do so," Luke promised.

Chapter Three

New Orleans—October 5

Nate McCoy boarded the *Delta Mist* and immediately entered the Grand Salon, interested in getting into a game of poker. He dressed well, had impeccable manners, and seemed able to get along with everyone. He was also the most handsome man Jenny had ever seen.

For the next two days, she watched him as he played, though she stood on the far side of the salon so nobody could see that she was watching him.

As evening fell, she took a quick break from her duties and she leaned on the railing of the texas deck, looking down at the great stern wheel, its paddles spilling water as they emerged from the river.

A man spoke to her. "You have been watching me."

Turning toward the speaker, Jenny saw Nate McCoy. "I'm supposed to watch people in the salon. That is my job."

"You're not watching me as part of your job. You're watching me for the same reason I'm watching you."

"Oh? And why is that?"

"I think you know why that is," McCoy quipped.

Jenny was lost from that moment, falling head over heels in love with him.

Three months later, On January 3, 1891, they were married.

Jenny learned quickly that marrying Nate McCoy was the biggest mistake she had ever made. Although he'd told her he was a broker who dealt with "other people's money," that was an extremely broad interpretation of his actual profession. McCoy was a professional gambler, and not an honest one.

Caught cheating on the *Delta Mist*, he was barred from taking passage on that or any of the passenger boats that plied the Mississippi. When he left the boats Jenny left with him, and for the next eighteen months, her life with McCoy became little more than running from town to town just ahead of a lynch mob.

"Why do you cheat?" Jenny asked her husband.

"Why do I cheat? Isn't it obvious? I cheat to make money. Where do you think we get the food we eat? The expensive clothes you wear? How do we pay for the fine hotel rooms? From my winnings, that's where. The odds of winning are not good enough for all that unless I give myself an edge. And that is exactly what I do, my dear. I give myself an edge."

"By cheating."

"You call it cheating, I call it increasing the odds."

"When you were caught cheating on the boats you were barred from taking any further passage on them. But if you are caught cheating in a saloon or a gambling house, the consequences could be much more severe. You could be killed."

"Ahh, it does my heart good to know my darling wife is frightened for me," Nate said sarcastically.

"Nate, why don't we make a living doing something else? I have an education. I could teach school." Jenny made that offer, even though she knew most schools had a provision in their contract that the teachers they hire be unwed.

"Assuming you could get around the obstacle of being married, what would you propose that I do, my dear? Become a store clerk perhaps?"

"Why not? It would be honest work. And we could settle down somewhere and have a real home like ordinary people."

"Like *ordinary* people," McCoy repeated, emphasizing the word.

"Yes."

"And this real home, no doubt, will have a white picket fence? Perhaps some flowers that you care for so tenderly? Maybe even a brat or two running around?"

"I-I wouldn't call them brats," Jenny mumbled, hurt by his sarcastic response.

"Yes. Well, my dear, as for your rather tedious dream, I am not *ordinary,* as you know."

"Yes," Jenny said, the dream now dead. "How well I know."

Colorado Springs, Colorado

Two days after that very conversation, Jenny and Nate had breakfast in the hotel dining room.

"I've never seen a town that had so many people who were ripe for the plucking. Why, I wouldn't be surprised if we didn't get out of here with between a thousand and fifteen hundred dollars."

"Nate, please be careful."

"Oh, don't you worry about that, my dear. I've been doing this for a long time. I know how to take care of myself." McCoy stood and left Jenny to return to their room alone.

Jenny tried to concentrate on the book in her hand, but her thoughts kept interrupting. Nate had been gone for over four hours, and it wasn't like him to be gone so long. He had told her they would have lunch together, but it was nearly one o'clock and he hadn't come back to the hotel room yet.

Feeling an overwhelming sense of foreboding, Jenny put the book aside and walked to the window, looking down onto the street below. When there was a knock at the door she gasped. She knew something was wrong. Nate wouldn't knock.

Turning away from the window, she took a sharp breath, and with trembling hands, crossed over to open the door. The man standing in the hallway was wearing the badge of a deputy city marshal.

"Mrs. McCoy?"

"Is he dead?" Jenny asked in a quiet and resigned voice.

If the deputy was shocked by her question, he didn't show it. "Yes, ma'am, I'm afraid he is."

"What happened?"

"I'm told he was caught with an ace up his sleeve. There was an altercation, your husband went for a gun, and he was shot."

"That isn't possible."

"Mrs. McCoy, are you saying your husband didn't cheat?"

"No, he cheated all right. But it isn't possible that he went for a gun. He never carried one."

"To be truthful with you, Mrs. McCoy, it doesn't matter whether he had a gun or not. There was a bitter argument precipitated by your husband, and the man who shot him believed McCoy was going for a gun. The belief that his life was threatened is all it takes to justify shooting your husband."

"Where is he now?"

"The undertaker has him. Will you be paying for his final expenses or will the city pay?"

"You mean the city would pay?"

"A plain pine box and a hole in the ground. I'm afraid there is nothing comforting about a city-financed burying."

"I'll go see the undertaker," Jenny said. "Perhaps we can come to an accommodation of sorts."

Learning that the undertaker's business was next door to the hardware store, Jenny left the hotel and walked down to see him. Surprised to see a rather substantial knot of people standing around in front of the undertaker's building, she wondered why they were there.

As soon as she arrived, she saw what was holding their attention. There, in an open casket, she saw her husband. His arms were folded across his chest, and he was holding a hand of cards. A hand-lettered sign read A CHEATING GAMBLER'S FATE.

"I'll bet all five of them cards is aces," a man in the crowd said, causing several others to laugh.

Jenny went into the establishment where she was met by a tall, gaunt man in a black suit, white shirt, and black string tie.

"Yes, ma'am. Is there something I can do for you?"

"There certainly is. You can remove my husband from that horrid display in the window," Jenny answered pointedly.

"Your husband? You mean the gambler?"

"Yes, Nate McCoy. He is—was—my husband. And what you are doing, displaying him like that, is disgraceful. I thought morticians were supposed to show respect for the dead and their families."

"I-I beg your pardon, madam. I wasn't aware the deceased was married, and I was especially unaware he had any family in Colorado Springs. Of course, I will remove the remains at once."

"Why would you do such a thing, anyway?"

"I thought the city would be responsible for burying him. They pay so little I don't even break even on the cost of the services I provide. Displaying his body in such a way draws people to satisfy their curiosity, morbid though it may be. And that is good publicity for my business."

"I will pay for his funeral," Jenny promised.

"Yes, ma'am. Will you want a church service and a minister in attendance during the committal?"

"I will."

"What is your denomination?" the undertaker asked.

"I am not particular."

"And how soon do you want the funeral?"

"As quickly as it can be arranged." Jenny opened her reticule and withdrew the roll of money Nate had won in the last city. It was to be his seed money for his next gambling operation. "How much will this cost?"

The undertaker looked at the wad of money and licked his lips. "I think, uh, one hundred and fifty dollars should cover everything."

"Yes, I should hope so," Jenny said, counting out the money.

"Yes, ma'am. Leave everything to me. I'll take care of all the details."

"How soon can we do this?"

"Oh, I'm quite sure we can arrange it for you as early as tomorrow."

"Today would be better, but if it is to be tomorrow, then that will have to do."

"Where are you staying, madam?"

"I am staying at the Dunn Hotel."

"I will get word to you when the arrangements have been made."

"Thank you."

The only people present for the church service the next morning were Jenny, the preacher, and the mortician. The preacher knew nothing about Nate McCoy, so instead of preaching a funeral service, he merely reread the sermon he had given the previous Sunday.

An additional person was present for the graveside committal. The gravedigger stood off at a respectful distance, leaning on his spade and smoking a pipe as he waited for the opportunity to close the grave so he could draw his fee, then go have a drink.

The committal service was short, consisting only of a single prayer, during which the preacher called him Ned, instead of Nate. The moment the preacher said amen, the gravedigger sauntered over and he and the mortician lowered the pine box into the ground.

As she walked away from the open grave, Jenny could hear the *thump, thump* as dirt landed on the pine box.

Leaving the cemetery, Jenny went directly to the railroad depot. "What time is the next train?" she asked the ticket agent.

"The next train to where, madam?" the ticket agent replied with a long-suffering sigh.

"I don't care where it is going as long as it is the next train."

"The southbound is due in about half an hour."

"I want a ticket on that train."

"Where to, madam?"

"Where is it going?"

"Pueblo, Salt Creek, Walsenburg . . ."

"Pueblo," Jenny said.

"Yes, ma'am." The ticket agent made out the ticket, stamped it with a rubber stamp, then handed it to her.

"That will be eight dollars."

"Thank you." Jenny handed him the money.

When the train rolled into the depot twenty-six minutes later, Jenny boarded it and found an empty seat, purposely choosing not to sit by the window. She had no wish for a last look at the town where all her fears had culminated. Though she would never admit it, even to herself, it was also where she'd gained freedom from a marriage that never should have been.

CHAPTER FOUR

Pueblo, Colorado—April 1893

The thirty-three children of Jenny's fifth grade class were gathered for a photo in front of the steps leading up to the school. Students in the first row sat on the ground with their hands folded across their laps. Those in the second row sat on a long, low bench, and the third and fourth rows were standing on ascending steps.

"Now, if the teacher would just sit beside her class." The photographer had a long mustache that curled up at each end. His camera, a big box affair, was sitting on a tripod in front of the class.

Jenny sat on a chair alongside the class, her hands folded across her lap just as she had instructed the children.

"Now, nobody move until I say so." The photographer put his hand on the shutter latch. "See the honey up in the tree, I wish you would bring some to me," he said in a monotone voice. "There. Now you can move."

"I can move," one of the boys on the front row exclaimed, and he pulled the hair of the girl beside him.

"Ouch!"

"Danny," Jenny scolded. "All right, children, school is dismissed. Don't forget your homework."

"Yea!" one of the boys shouted and the class, which had been so motionless a moment earlier, scattered like leaves before a wind.

Jenny picked up her chair and carried it back into her classroom. The principal and the superintendent of schools were waiting for her.

"Mr. Gray, Mr. Twitty?" she said, obviously surprised to see them.

"Miss McCoy, or should I say Mrs. McCoy?" The expression on Twitty's face was grim.

"I'm not married." Jenny paused for a moment. "I'm a widow."

"You were married to Nate McCoy, were you not?" Twitty asked.

"Yes, I was."

"It has come to our attention that Nate McCoy was a gambler of, let us say, questionable ethics. And, while you were married, you followed him from gambling den to gambling den. Is that correct?"

Jenny looked down. "Yes," she said quietly.

"I'm sorry to have to tell you this, Mrs. McCoy. The school board has asked for your dismissal."

"On what grounds?" Jenny asked.

"Moral turpitude."

"What? But I . . ."

"Please take your things and leave," Mr. Gray said.

"My class?"

"They are no longer your class. We have already hired a replacement teacher," Mr. Twitty informed her.

"Can't I at least finish the year? We've only one month to go. For the children's sake, don't you think it would be better for them to keep the same teacher until the end of the year?"

"Good-bye, Mrs. McCoy," Gray said coldly.

Jenny fought hard to keep the tears from welling up in her eyes. She stood and turned away from them, determined not to let them see her cry. She walked into the cloakroom, removed her coat, and left the schoolroom. There was nothing else she wanted to take from there.

Red Cliff, Colorado—July 8

The sign out front of the store read RAFFERTY'S GROCERY. One of three, it stood at the very edge of town. Michael Santelli stepped into the little store, and a bell attached to the top of the door announced his entry.

"Yes, sir, what can I do for you?" Mr. Rafferty asked. Mrs. Rafferty looked up from sweeping the floor and smiled.

Santelli took a quick glance around. Seeing nobody else in the store, he pulled his gun and pointed it at the shopkeeper. "You can give me all your money. That's what you can do for me."

"Yes, sir," Rafferty said nervously. "Just don't be

getting trigger happy there." He opened his cash drawer, took out thirty dollars, and handed it across the counter.

Santelli counted it quickly, then looked up at Rafferty, his face twisted in anger. "What is this?" he demanded.

"You said give you all my money. That's what I did. This is all the money I have."

"Thirty dollars? Do you expect me to believe that all you have is thirty dollars?"

"That *is* all I have," Rafferty said. "We deposited yesterday's receipts in the bank last night. I always start the morning with just enough money to make change."

"You're lyin'!" Santelli pointed his pistol at Mrs. Rafferty. "You better come up with more money fast, or I'll shoot the woman."

"Please, I don't have any more money!" Rafferty shouted desperately.

"I warned you." Santelli grabbed Mrs. Rafferty, pulled the hammer back on his pistol, and held it to her head.

With a shout of anger, Rafferty climbed over the counter toward him.

Santelli shot him, then turned his pistol back toward Mrs. Rafferty and shot her. Quickly, he went behind the counter and looked through the cash box, but found no more money. With a shout of rage, he picked up the cash box and threw it into a glass display case, smashing the case into pieces.

That done, and with no more money than the

thirty dollars Rafferty had given him in the first place, Santelli left the store, mounted his horse, and rode away.

Sixty-seven-year-old Burt Rowe witnessed the entire thing from the back of the store. Santelli hadn't seen him when he looked around. But Rowe recognized the gunman, Santelli, having seen him before.

As soon as he was certain Santelli was gone, Rowe stepped out in front of the store and began shouting at the top of his lungs. "Help! Help! Murder! The Raffertys have been robbed and murdered!"

Within moments the store was filled with townspeople, including the sheriff and deputy sheriff.

"You are sure it was Santelli?" the sheriff asked Rowe.

"I'm absolutely positive," Rowe said. "I've seen him before."

"When he left here, which way did he go?"

"I seen him heading south, but that don't mean he kept going that way. By the way, he only got thirty dollars."

"Thirty dollars?" the sheriff asked incredulously. "You mean he murdered Mr. and Mrs. Rafferty for no more than thirty dollars?"

"Yes, sir," Rowe said. "I know that's all he got, 'cause I heard 'em talkin' about it."

"What are you going to do about it, Sheriff?" one of the townspeople asked. "Mr. and Mrs. Rafferty were two of the finest people in the world. We can't let that animal get away with this."

"He won't get away," the sheriff promised. "I'll get the word out to other sheriffs and city marshals. We'll get him, and when we do, we'll bring him right back here to hang. I promise you that."

One week later Michael Santelli rode into the town of Kiowa, Colorado, sizing it up as he went along the main street. The little town was made up of whipsawed lumber shacks with unpainted, splitting wood turning gray in the sun. A sign over the door of one rather substantial-looking brick building identified it as the BANK OF KIOWA. Still angered by the slim pickings from Rafferty's Grocery, Santelli figured the bank might offer some promise for a bigger payoff.

So far, he had over five thousand dollars he'd stolen from a bank in Greeley and hidden in the bottom of an old abandoned well near Gunnison. His plan was to put together enough money to buy a saloon in Texas. The idea of owning a saloon appealed to him—unlimited access to whiskey and beer. And the whores working for him would be available to him anytime he wanted them. But he figured he would need at least ten thousand dollars . . . to set himself up for the rest of his life.

Santelli was a wanted man. There was so much money on his head every bounty hunter in the state was looking for him. The sooner he was able to put together enough money to get out of Colorado, the better it would be. Once he got to Texas, he would be a model citizen. He smiled. He might even run for mayor.

Santelli rode up to the hitching rail in front of the Silver Nugget Saloon, dismounted, and patted his tan duster a few times, sending up puffs of gray-white dust before he walked inside. The saloon was busy, but he found a quiet place by the end of the bar. When the bartender moved over to him, Santelli ordered a beer, then stood there nursing it as he began to formulate a plan for robbing the bank.

Matt Jensen stood at the opposite end of the bar with both hands wrapped around a mug of beer. Something seemed familiar about the man who had just come in, but he couldn't place him. Studying the man's reflection in the mirror behind the bar, he took in his average height and weight and unkempt black hair. He had dark, obsidian eyes and a purple scar starting just below his left eye and disappearing in a scraggly beard.

The scar helped Matt make the identification. He had seen drawings and read descriptions of the outlaw Michael Santelli and just that morning had heard that Santelli had killed a grocer and his wife for no more reason than that they didn't have as much money in their cash box as he thought they should have.

Matt was neither a lawman nor a bounty hunter, but he didn't plan to let Santelli walk away. Before he could make any move, Deputy Sheriff Ben Mason came into the saloon, and Matt decided to wait and see how things played out.

He had met the deputy earlier, when he first rode into town, learning about Santelli's latest atrocity at the same time. Matt and Deputy Mason were about the same age, and Matt respected the lawman's dedication to duty.

When Mason saw Santelli standing at the bar, he stopped and stared for a long moment until he was sure it was the wanted outlaw.

"Santelli," Mason called out. "Michael Santelli."

Matt saw the way Santelli reacted, stiffening at the bar, but not turning around. The reaction gave him away, and Matt knew his first impulse had been right. The man was Santelli.

"You are Santelli, aren't you? Michael Santelli?" Mason asked. The lawman's voice was loud and authoritative.

Everyone in the saloon recognized the challenge implied in its timbre. All conversations ceased, and drinkers at the bar backed away so there was nothing but clear space between the lawman and Santelli. Even the bartender left his position behind the bar.

Matt stood in place at the opposite end of the bar, watching Santelli with intense interest as the drama began to unfold.

Santelli looked up, studying the lawman's reflection in the mirror, but he didn't turn around. "Lawman, I'm afraid you've got me mixed up with somebody else."

"No, I don't think so," Mason said confidently. "I know who you are. You are a bank robber and a murderer, and you are under arrest."

Not until that moment did Santelli turn to face the lawman, and he did so with a slow and assured nonchalance. "It looks like I can't fool you, can I?" he said as a frightening smile curled across his lips. "What are you, anyway? A city marshal? A sheriff?"

"I'm a deputy sheriff. Mason is the name."

"Well, now, Deputy Mason, you think you've got yourself a big prize, don't you? You're right. I am Michael Santelli, but there's not a thing you are going to be able to do about it. Because the truth is, mister, you have just bitten off more than you can chew. If you make a move toward your gun, I'll kill you right where you stand."

"And then I'll kill you." Matt added his voice to the conversation for the first time.

Santelli was startled to hear a new challenge from his left, and he turned his head quickly to see Matt standing away from the bar, facing him. Like Mason and Santelli, Matt had not drawn his pistol.

"Who asked you to butt into this?" Santelli asked.

"Nobody asked me. But I met Deputy Mason earlier today, and I found him to be a fine, upstanding gentleman. I don't plan to stand here and watch you shoot him."

"Thank you, Mr. Jensen," Mason said. "I appreciate your help."

Santelli's face, which had been coldly impassive, suddenly grew animated. His skin whitened and a line of perspiration beaded on his upper lip. "Jensen?" he said nervously. "Is that your name?"

"Matt Jensen, yes."

"You fellas seem to have me at a disadvantage, two of you to my one."

"I would say that is a smart observation, Santelli," Matt said.

"Take your gun out of your holster, using only your thumb and finger," Mason ordered.

Santelli reached for his pistol, then suddenly wrapped his entire hand around the pistol butt.

Seeing that, Matt made a lightning draw of his pistol, pulling the hammer back as he brought his gun to bear. The sound of the sear engaging the cylinder made a loud clicking noise.

Hearing it, Santelli jerked his hand away from his gun and held it, empty, out in front of him, imploring Matt not to shoot. "No, no! I ain't goin' to draw! I ain't goin' to draw!' he shouted. Holding his left hand up in the air as a signal of surrender, Santelli's right hand removed his pistol from the holster, using his thumb and forefinger as the deputy had directed.

"Now, lay your pistol on the floor and kick it over here," Mason ordered.

Santelli did as he was directed.

"I'll help you march him down to jail," Matt said.

"Thanks."

"Did you see that draw?" someone asked, the quiet voice reflecting his awe. "I ain't never seen nothin' like that."

"Didn't you hear who that is?" another asked. "That's Matt Jensen.

Deputy Mason put Santelli in handcuffs, then he and Matt walked the prisoner down to the jailhouse. Three minutes later, the cell door clanked loudly as it closed on him.

"Jensen," Santelli called out as Matt started to leave.

Matt turned to him.

"I have a feeling me 'n you are going to meet again, someday."

Matt nodded, but said nothing.

Chapter Five

Pueblo—August 4

Jenny was getting desperate. She had not been able to find a job, and she was nearly out of money. She'd paid her rent for August, but if she didn't find employment soon, she would have to give up her room. Sitting at her desk, she was writing a letter to her uncle, begging his forgiveness and pleading to be allowed to come back to work for him.

She was agonizing over the letter she didn't want to write when there was a knock at the door. Answering it, she saw a very pretty, elegant woman in her early fifties.

Jenny recognized her. Adele Summers was the proprietor of the Colorado Social Club, a house of prostitution.

"Miss Summers," Jenny said, surprised to see her. "What can I do for you?"

"I hope it is something I can do for you," Adele replied. "I've heard of your problem, and how the school board, a bunch of ninnies, fired you. I would like for you to come work for me, and I will pay you three times more money than you were making teaching school."

"Oh, Miss Summers, uh, I thank you, I really do. But I don't think I could do something like—"

"Hear me out before you reply. It isn't what you think."

"Oh?"

"I'm not asking you to be a prostitute," Adele said. "Not for a minute. I don't know what you know about the Social Club, but it isn't your ordinary house of prostitution. We have a very high-classed clientele. I would want you to meet our clients when they arrive, and for those clients who would enjoy such a thing, spend a little time with them, talking to them, having a drink with them, and making them feel welcome. That's all."

Jenny thought back to her time working in the grand salon on the *Delta Mist* and smiled. That was exactly what she did then. "You mean you want me to be a hostess."

"Yes!" Adele replied with a wide smile. "Yes, that is exactly what you would be. You would be a hostess and nothing more."

Kiowa, Colorado—November 11

A rather short, beady-eyed man with a red, splotchy face and thin blond hair dismounted in front of the Kiowa Jail. Tying his horse at the hitching rail, he went inside. Three men were in the front, two of them in conversation. The third sat behind a desk in the far corner of the room. The sign on his desk read ADAM CARTER—SHERIFF—ELBERT COUNTY.

"Can I help you?" one of the two deputies asked.

"You've got my brother in jail. I want to visit him."

"What's your name?"

"Ward, Bob Ward."

The deputy shook his head. "We don't have anyone by that name in jail."

"You've got Michael Santelli here, don't you?"

"Yes."

"That's my brother."

"Your brother?"

"We have the same mother. We don't have the same father."

Sheriff Carter looked up. "Ward? Isn't there some paper out on you, Ward?"

"Not 'ny more, Sheriff. I was let out of prison two months ago. You can check."

"All right. Mason, let him see his brother."

"Take your pistol belt off and lay it on the desk," Deputy Mason said.

Ward did as directed, then he was thoroughly searched for any hidden weapon.

"He's clean," informed the deputy who searched him.

"I'll take him back," Mason said.

"Deputy, is there someplace we can talk in private?"

"What do you want to talk in private for?"

"My brother's goin' to be hung, ain't he?"

"Yes."

"Well, then, we may have some private, family things to talk about."

Mason looked at his boss. "What about it, Sheriff?"

"Has Durham sobered up?" Sheriff Carter asked.

"Yes, sir, I'm sure he has." Mason chuckled. "He probably has a pretty bad headache, though."

"He's the only other prisoner we have right now. Turn him loose. That'll give Ward and Santelli the whole place alone."

"Come with me," Mason said.

Mason took the keys into the back of the building, while Ward followed close behind. Eight cells made up the back of the jail, four on either side of a center aisle. Mason opened the door to one of the cells. "Let's go, Durham."

Durham was lying on the bunk. "It ain't time for me to be turned out yet."

"You're getting out early."

"Damn. Can't you let a man sleep it off?"

"Let's go," Mason repeated.

Grumbling, Durham got up and plodded out of the cell.

"I'll give you half an hour," Mason said to Ward as he pushed Durham to the front. He closed the door to the cell area, leaving Ward and Santelli alone.

"Well. My brother has come to see me. I'm touched."

"They tell me you're goin' to hang," Ward said.

"That's what the judge said at my trial."

"So, look, I was thinkin'. I mean if you're goin' to hang anyway, why don't you tell me where the money is that you took from the bank in Greeley?"

"What makes you think I've got any of that money left?"

"I know you do. I just don't know how much."

"It's a little over five thousand dollars. I was plannin' on gettin' enough money to go to Texas and buy a saloon." Santelli shrugged.

"Yeah, that's a good idea. It's too bad you can't do it. So, look, why don't you tell me where the money is, and I'll buy a saloon and I'll name it after you."

"What do you mean, you'll name it after me?"

"Well, I mean you'll be dead. So it's only right that if I buy a saloon with your money, that I name it after you."

"What makes you think you're going to have my money?"

"Well why not, Michael? Like I said, you'll be dead. What good is that money goin' to do you, when you're dead? You may as well tell me where it is. 'Cause when you think about it, me 'n you is the only kin either one of us has got."

"Get me out of here, and I'll tell you where the money is."

"How am I s'posed to do that? There's only one way out of this building, and it's through the front door. There's a sheriff and two deputies up there with guns, and maybe you didn't notice, but they took my gun away from me before they would let me come back here."

"They're takin' me to Red Cliff to hang," Santelli said. "That's a long way, by train. Figure out some way to get me off the train."

"I don't think I can do it by myself. It's goin' to take three or four people to do somethin' like that."

"Then hire them. Promise 'em five hundred dollars each. That'll leave three thousand for me 'n you to split, half and half."

"Fifteen hundred sure ain't like five thousand," Ward said.

"How much money do you have now?"

"I don't know. About forty dollars, I reckon."

"Fifteen hundred is a lot more than forty," Santelli pointed out.

"Yeah. Yeah, I guess you're right. All right, I'll find some people to help me."

Santelli smiled, then walked back over to his bunk and lay down, with his hands laced behind his head. "Thanks for the visit, Bob."

"All right. Uh, listen. Just in case somethin' goes wrong, don't you think you ought to tell me where the money is? I mean, just in case."

"It's up to you to make certain that nothing goes wrong."

Ward stood outside the cell for a moment longer, frustrated that it didn't go as he had planned. But at least he saw a way of getting fifteen hundred dollars, and it had been a long time since he had had that kind of money.

"I've got a friend I was in the pen with. I'll get him to help."

"You do that," Santelli said in a dismissive tone. It was obvious that, as far as he was concerned, the visit with his brother was over.

Ward walked back out front, then looked toward the desk where he had put his pistol. "Where's my gun?"

Mason walked over to a cabinet, opened it, then handed it to him.

"Thanks."

"You'll need these as well," Mason said, handing Ward six bullets. "I unloaded your pistol."

"What'd you do that for?" Ward asked as he started to reload his pistol.

"No. Don't reload it until you get outside."

Ward nodded as he strapped on his pistol belt.

Pueblo—November 15

Luke Shardeen sat in the chair at the Model Barbershop, stroking his chin and examining his face in the mirror. It had been three years since he left the sea.

"Would you like a nice-smelling aftershave tonic?" Earl Cook the barber asked as he removed the cape from around Luke's neck. "Oh, the women all love it," he added with a smile.

"I have enough trouble keeping women away from me now," Luke teased. "Why would I want more coming around?"

For a moment the barber was surprised, then he realized Luke was teasing. "Yes, indeed, sir. I suppose a handsome fellow like you would have to put up with a lot of women. It must be quite a burden."

"Now, who is pulling whose leg here?" Luke asked, laughing as he paid the barber for his shave and haircut.

Cook laughed as well, then he looked around to make certain he wasn't overheard before he spoke quietly. "Have you seen the new young lady over at the Social Club?"

Luke chuckled. "I'm not one who visits such places. I'm not judgmental of those who do, you understand, but I'm not interested in a woman who will go to bed with anyone who meets her price."

The barber shook his head. "You don't understand. This new girl isn't like that. She used to be a schoolteacher, and they say she is very smart. She is also very pretty."

"So she is smarter and prettier than all the others. I still don't plan to pay her to let me take her to bed."

"Oh, I don't think you could pay this girl enough to get her in bed," Cook admonished.

"What are you talking about? Does she work at the Social Club or not?"

"Yes, she works there, but the only thing you can do is have a nice conversation with her. Oh, and maybe have a cup of coffee and some cookies. She's what they call a hostess. All she does is talk and smile."

"Do the people who go to the club know that?"

"Oh yes, they know that. And she is still the most popular girl there."

"How can that be, if she doesn't allow them to do anything?"

"It's because like I said. She is one of the prettiest women you'll ever see . . . and also the smartest. She has a way of talking with you that makes you feel like you are just as smart as she is."

"You talk like you know this first hand."

"I do know it first hand." Cook chuckled. "I'll tell you true, I never thought I would ever go to a place like the Social Club and not do anything but talk. But that's exactly what I've done, and I've done it more 'n once."

Leaving the barbershop, Luke thought about the conversation with Cook. He had to admit it had him intrigued. He walked by the Colorado Social Club three times before he finally got up the nerve to go inside.

He was met by a smiling, middle-aged, attractive woman.

"Why, Mr. Shardeen, how nice of you to visit us."

Luke was surprised to hear her call him by name. "You know me?"

"Oh, yes. You own Two Crowns Ranch and have

the reputation of being a real gentleman. I make it a point to know all of the . . . let us say *quality* . . . gentlemen of Pueblo. My name is Adele. What can I do for you?"

"I, uh, well, the truth is, this is all rather new for me. So I'm not sure exactly what to do."

Adele chuckled. "It's simple enough. I'll take you into our lounge, where you will see some of our young ladies. All you have to do is pick out one who interests you, and—"

"No. Not that."

Adele got a confused look on her face. "Then, I don't understand, Mr. Shardeen. What do you want?"

"I—uh, nothing, I guess. I'm sorry I wasted your time. Please forgive me."

"Oh, you didn't waste my time at all, Mr. Shardeen. It was a pleasure talking to you. Please come visit us again, sometime."

"Yes, uh, thank you. I'll just go now." Luke hurried out the front door, just as Jenny came into the foyer.

"Who was that?" she asked.

"That was Luke Shardeen," Adele said.

"What did he want?"

"I don't have the slightest idea. And what's more, I don't think he does, either."

Before returning to his ranch, Luke stopped by the post office to pick up his mail. He had a letter from Heckemeyer and Sons, a cattle brokerage company in the nearby town of Greenhorn. Anxiously, he opened the letter, hoping it was the answer he was looking for.

Mr. Shardeen,

Our company would be pleased to buy 500 head of cattle from you at the prevailing market price. Payment will be made upon delivery of the cattle.

Sincerely,
Anthony Heckemeyer
Broker

Greenhorn, Colorado—November 22

Luke shipped 500 head of Hereford cattle by rail to Greenhorn, paying five dollars per head to get them there. The railroad had off-loaded the cattle into a holding pen where they would keep them without charge for one day. If he made the sale, Heckemeyer and Sons would move the cattle from the pen.

"I tried to get you forty-two fifty, but the best offer I've been able to come up with, is forty dollars a head," Heckemeyer said. "That would be twenty thousand dollars for all five hundred head."

"Great," Luke said. "I was prepared to sell for thirty-five dollars a head. The five-dollar increase paid for shipping them over here."

"Well, then," Heckemeyer said with a broad smile. "We will both be happy, and you will be sure to tell others of the wonderful service provided you by Heckemeyer and Sons."

"Yes sir. I'll be glad to do that, Mr. Heckemeyer."

Luke signed the bill of sale, then left the office. Twenty thousand dollars was the most money he'd ever had, and he went on a short shopping spree, buying a new shirt, a pair of boots, and a rain slicker. After that he stopped by the saloon to have a celebratory drink before heading back to Two Crowns.

"Did you get your cows sold?" the bartender asked as he poured a shot of whiskey into Luke's glass.

"I did indeed. And a good price I got for them too," Luke replied. "Set the bar up for one round. This has been a most productive and profitable trip for me."

"One free drink to everyone," the bartender called. "Compliments of this gentleman."

With shouts of thanks, the other patrons in the saloon rushed to the bar as Luke saluted them with a raised glass.

In another part of the same saloon two men exchanged glances, then left the saloon.

"You think he'll have the money with him?"

"He just bought drinks all around, didn't he? Where else would the money be, if not on him?"

"Yeah, you're right. Where else would it be?"

"So, what do we do, now?"

"Let's get our horses. We'll watch the front of the saloon, and when he leaves, we'll follow."

* * *

Half an hour later, after exchanging good-byes with the new friends he had made, Luke left the saloon, mounted his horse, and started home.

"Tell me, Harry," he said, patting his horse on the neck. "How does it feel to be ridden by a rich man?"

Harry whickered and nodded his head.

Luke laughed. "All right, Harry, all right. I'm not really what you would call rich. But I'll have you know I am carrying more money than I have ever held in my hands in my entire life."

Chapter Six

"Here he comes," muttered one of the two men waiting for Luke.

"Let's go," the other instructed.

"Shouldn't we wait until he passes, then follow?"

"No, we'll ride ahead of him. That way he won't suspect anything, and we can set up and wait for him."

Shortly after leaving town, Luke noticed the two horsemen on the road ahead of him. Acutely aware of his environment because of the money he was carrying, he decided not to overtake them, but to keep them in sight. That worked well for the first fifteen minutes, and when he reached the top of the next rise he expected to see them still on the road just ahead.

They weren't there, and despite a very careful perusal, they were nowhere to be seen. Where did they go? There were no buildings to have entered nor crossroads to have taken, so what happened to them? He found it rather troubling that he could no longer see them.

Pulling his pistol, Luke checked the loads in the cylinder chambers, and satisfying himself that he was ready for any contingency, returned the gun to the holster. Shifting his eyes back and forth from one side of the trail to the other he rode ahead. Suddenly, through a break in the trees, he caught a glimpse of two mounted men waiting just off the side of the road. Drawing his pistol again, he cocked it and held it straight down by his side. Thus armed and alert, he continued forward.

When the two riders thrust themselves in the road in front of him, Luke was ready for them. Both men were wearing hoods over their faces, only their eyes visible through the eyeholes.

"Throw down your money!" one shouted.

"The hell I will!" Luke called back, bringing up his arm and firing in the same motion.

A little puff of dust flew up from the man where the bullet hit. A red spot appeared there as well, and the man who had challenged him fell from his horse.

The other rider, suddenly realizing he no longer had a two-to-one advantage, jerked his horse around and dug in the spurs.

Luke holstered his pistol and snaked his rifle from the saddle sheath. Jacking a round into the chamber, he raised the rifle to his shoulder and took very careful aim, but couldn't bring himself to shoot a man in the back. Carefully, he eased the hammer back down and lowered the rifle as he watched the rider flee.

Dismounting, Luke walked over to the man he had shot and saw that he was dead. The man's fate neither surprised nor bothered him. It had been a head-to-head confrontation, and the robber knew the chances he took when he set out. Luke pulled the hood off and tossed it to one side as he studied the man's face without recognition.

The road agent's horse had not run off, so, with some effort, Luke put the dead man belly down over the saddle. He thought about going back to Greenhorn, but he was almost as close to Pueblo, so he decided to take him there.

Riding up to the sheriff's office in Pueblo half an hour later, he was greeted by Deputy Sheriff Proxmire, who met him out in front of the office. "Who have you got there, Luke?"

"To tell you the truth, Deputy, I don't know who this man is," Luke answered. "But this fella and another man tried to rob me."

"Tried to rob you, you say?"

"Yes, I saw them ahead of me, saw them hiding behind some trees, so I got a little suspicious. I pulled my gun out and when they ordered me to give them my money, I shot one of them. This one." Luke nodded toward the body draped over the horse he was leading.

"What about the other man?"

"When I shot this fella, the other one turned and rode off. I could have shot him, too, but I don't have the stomach to shoot someone in the back. Anyway, I thought I may as well bring this one to you."

Proxmire turned toward the office and called, "Sheriff Ferrell, you want to come out now?"

The door to the sheriff's office opened behind Proxmire and another man stepped out. Luke was surprised. He believed it was the man who had gotten away. He was also surprised to see the man was wearing a star on his vest. There had been no star during the ambush.

"Deputy, I'm not sure, but I think this may have been the other man." Luke pointed toward the man behind Deputy Sheriff Proxmire.

"By other man, you mean he was with the man you shot?" Proxmire asked.

"Yes. He had his face covered with a hood, so I can't be positive, but he was about this size and was wearing the same kind of clothes. Only he wasn't packing a star when I saw him last."

"You say they were both wearing hoods?"

"Yes."

"What about the hood that was on this fella?" Deputy Proxmire asked. "Have you got it with you?"

"No, I just tossed it aside."

"What about you, Sheriff? Is this the man you encountered on the road?"

"It is, indeed. And you heard him, Sheriff. He just confessed to murdering Deputy Gates."

"What?" Luke replied loudly. "What are you talking about? I didn't murder anyone!"

"Did you, or did you not, shoot down my deputy?"

"Who are you?" Luke asked.

"I'm Sheriff Dewey Ferrell."

"Did you shoot his deputy, Luke?" Proxmire asked.

Luke pointed to the body that was still draped across the horse behind him. "If that man is this man's deputy, then yes, I shot him. But it was in self-defense. Whether this man is a sheriff or not, he and the man I shot tried to hold me up."

"We did no such thing," Sheriff Ferrell argued. "We were merely trying to stop him, so we could ask him a few questions. That's when he surprised the two of us by shooting."

"Deputy, I don't know what's going on here, but what happened is nothing like this man is saying. Both men were wearing hoods over their faces, and they demanded that I give them my money. You don't mask yourself with a hood if all you want to do is ask a few questions, do you?"

"You say we were wearing hoods, but you can't show the hood my deputy was wearing," Sheriff Ferrell pointed out.

"If the man you say tried to rob you was masked, how do you know this is the same man?" Proxmire pointed to the sheriff.

"He just said that he was."

"I'm going to have to take your gun and hold you in jail until this is all worked out," Proxmire said.

"Deputy, I'm telling you these two men tried to rob me."

"Why would they try to rob you, Luke? Do you carry so much money around all the time that someone would want to rob you?"

"I am now. I'm carrying almost twenty thousand dollars from the sale of my cattle. You can check with Heckemeyer and Sons over in Greenhorn. They will verify that I'm telling the truth."

"Oh, I don't doubt but that you sold some cows," Proxmire said. "But that's not the question. The question is, did the sheriff and his deputy stop you to ask a few questions as he says or did he and his deputy actually try to rob you?"

"They tried to rob me."

"Look at it this way, Luke. Right now it's just your word against Sheriff Ferrell's word, and seeing as he is an officer of the law, his word carries a bit more weight. But perhaps you can convince a jury to believe you."

"A jury? Look here, are you actually telling me this is going to court?"

"It is," Proxmire said.

Luke looked at Ferrell. "Will he be in court?"

"I'll be there," Ferrell answered. "I intend to see justice done for the killing of my deputy."

"All right," Luke said. "I won't argue with you, Proxmire. If you'll let me put this money in the bank, I'll come quietly and I'll stand trial."

"Good idea," Proxmire said.

* * *

Judge Amon Briggs sat back in the chair in his chambers and put his hands together, fingertip to fingertip. He was listening to Sheriff Ferrell.

"Luke can make a lot of trouble for us if we don't take care of this situation."

"What do you mean trouble for us?" Judge Briggs growled. "I didn't attempt to hold him up."

"Did you, or did you not, give Gates and me the information about him going to sell his cows? And were you, or were you not, going to be in for a third of the take? And that isn't the only deal we've been in. You got your share from the coach holdup two months ago, too, as I am sure you well remember."

Briggs held his hand out to quiet Ferrell. "All right, all right. There's no need to say anything else. The walls have ears. Don't worry. I'll take care of it."

"You'd better take care of it," Ferrell pressed. "Otherwise we'll both be in trouble."

Pueblo—December 5

Luke's trial was going to be held in the local courthouse with Judge Amon Briggs presiding. He was in his chambers meeting with the prosecutor. "I want him tried for first-degree murder."

"Your honor, I don't think I can make the case for first-degree murder," Lloyd Gilmore said. "I mean, even if what the sheriff says is true, if all he and his deputy were doing was confronting him for questioning, it still wouldn't be premeditated murder."

"It doesn't have to be premeditated," Briggs said. "He was resisting arrest, and that is a felony. Any death that occurs during the commission of a felony is automatically first-degree murder."

"According to Sheriff Ferrell's own testimony, he wasn't making an arrest, he merely wanted to question him. That's not resisting arrest. A good lawyer could say that Luke thought he was being held up, and Tom Murchison is a good lawyer."

"You're the prosecutor. It's your job to make hard cases against good lawyers," Judge Briggs answered.

"All right, I'll try. But I don't think I'll be able to convince the jury."

As Prosecutor Gilmore and Judge Briggs were discussing the case, Tom Murchison arrived at the jail to meet with Luke Shardeen.

"You've got ten minutes," Deputy Proxmire said, escorting the attorney to Luke's cell.

"You are wrong, Deputy," Murchison declared as he entered the cell. "Mr. Shardeen is my client, and I will visit with him for as long as it takes."

"Yes, well, uh . . ." Proxmire knew he had no response to that, so he shrugged his shoulders and shut the cell door. "Just call out when your visit is finished." He turned and walked back to the front of the jail.

Tom Murchison was the lawyer who had handled the estate of Luke's uncle Frank. Since Luke's arrival in Pueblo, he and Murchison had become good friends. Compared to Luke, Murchison was relatively short, standing five feet nine inches tall. He wore a red bow tie, and held an unlit cigar at a jaunty angle in his mouth.

He sat down on the other bunk in Luke's cell. "Tell me what happened."

Luke told of selling the cows in Greenhorn, then seeing the two men waiting in ambush for him on the trail back to Pueblo. He told how they braced him with drawn guns and demanded that he give them his money.

"I'll do what I can for you, Luke," Murchison said. "The truth is, we are playing against a stacked deck. Judge Briggs seems to have an unusual connection to Sheriff Ferrell. But you have never been in trouble since you have been here, you have made a lot of friends, and I have an affidavit showing where you sold your cattle for twenty thousand dollars.

"So, while our case will be difficult because the deck is stacked against us, theirs will be equally difficult because they have no motive."

Chapter Seven

Luke's trial was held the very next day. The prosecuting attorney presented his opening remarks.

"Your Honor, and gentlemen of the jury, Mr. Murchison will, no doubt, claim that Mr. Shardeen had no motive for killing Deputy Gates. And he will attempt to use that claim as proof that what happened wasn't murder.

"But Sheriff Ferrell and Deputy Gates were conducting an investigation, and all they wanted to do was ask a few questions. Mr. Shardeen shot and killed Gates, and Sheriff Ferrell barely escaped with his life. If an officer of the law cannot question a citizen without getting shot, then where does that leave the rest of us?"

Murchison had been making notes, and when Gilmore sat down, the defense attorney stood and walked over to the rail separating the jury from the rest of the courtroom. He took his unlit cigar from his mouth and held it in his hand, sometimes waving it around as he talked.

"I am glad that my learned colleague has already conceded that Luke Shardeen had no motive for killing Deputy Gates. Who is Luke Shardeen?

"He owns Two Crown Ranch, and he is an employer who is well respected by the men who work for him. He has done business in this town for the last three years and, during that time, has earned the respect and admiration of his fellow citizens. Before that he was a seaman, and not an ordinary seaman, but a ship's officer—one who, when his captain was swept overboard during a typhoon, assumed command of the vessel and brought his ship safely into port, saving twenty-eight lives.

"Now, let us look more closely at the prosecutor's contention that all Sheriff Ferrell and Deputy Gates wanted to do was question Mr. Shardeen. If that is true, what were Ferrell and Gates doing asking such questions in Pueblo County in the first place? They are from Bent County. They have no business questioning anyone in Pueblo County. If they had a suspect they needed to question who happened to be out of their jurisdiction, the correct procedure would have been to contact Sheriff John McKenzie and ask that a deputy go with them.

"That's the way it's supposed to be done. But they didn't do that, and Sheriff McKenzie is prepared to testify that he was never contacted. That means Sheriff Ferrell has no corroboration for his story."

There was very little cross-examination during

the trial. Ferrell reiterated that all he and Gates wanted to do was question Luke, and Luke repeated his claim that the two men attempted to rob him.

After their testimonies, Murchison and Gilmore made their summation.

"Prosecution says Ferrell and Gates were two law officers who wanted only to question Mr. Shardeen." Murchison stood, facing the jury. "But neither of them were wearing a badge, and both were wearing hoods over their faces."

He walked back over to the defense table and reached down into a sack, withdrawing a piece of cloth. He spread the cloth out, then held it up before the jury, showing a hood with two eyeholes.

Several in the gallery gasped.

"Specifically, one of them was wearing *this* hood, which I found exactly where Mr. Shardeen said it would be. Wearing a hood like this is hardly the way a couple lawmen would stop a suspect for questioning. I'm going to ask that you do the right thing, and find my client not guilty."

Murchison stuck the unlit cigar back in his mouth, then returned to the defense table to sit beside his client.

"Mr. Prosecutor, your summation?" Judge Briggs asked.

Gilmore stood, hitched up his trousers, then approached the jury box.

"What it all boils down to is Luke Shardeen's word against the word of Sheriff Dewey Ferrell. On the surface, one man's word against another would balance the scales. But there are two things that tip the scales. One is the fact that Dewey Ferrell isn't just another citizen; he is a sworn officer of the law. And the other issue is the fact that we have a dead body. Deputy Brad Gates is dead, and we have the defendant's own admission that he shot and killed him. As to the hood, I've no doubt but that Mr. Murchison found it where Mr. Shardeen said it would be. But that proves only that he put the hood there. It is my contention that he did that just to build his defense. Under the circumstances, I feel you can bring no verdict but guilty of murder in the first degree."

In the judge's charge to the jury he suggested strongly that the evidence pointed to first-degree murder, and that it was his belief that they must find in accordance with the evidence.

"I don't care what the rest of you say, I don't intend to find Luke Shardeen guilty of murder in the first degree. Why would he do it?" one of the jurors said when they were sequestered.

"If Ferrell and Gates were questioning him about a crime he committed somewhere, he might have shot them," another juror said.

"What crime? All the prosecution said was that Shardeen was being questioned, and didn't even say what he was being questioned about. If you ask me, this thing is fishy."

"Yeah? Well, he did kill the deputy. That's a fact

that he doesn't deny. And I can't see lettin' him get off scot-free."

The jury continued to argue for the better part of an hour, before they came to an agreement and signaled the bailiff they were ready to return to the courtroom.

"Has the jury reached a verdict?" Judge Briggs asked when they were all seated.

"We have, Your Honor," Lynn Thomas, the jury foreman, replied. Thomas owned a leather goods shop.

"Would you publish your verdict, please?"

"We find the defendant guilty of manslaughter in the second degree."

There was an immediate reaction from the gallery, who, based upon the judge's public charge of the jury, expected a verdict of murder in the first degree.

The judge slapped his gavel several times to get order, then looked back at Thomas. "You were not given the option of finding for second degree manslaughter. The charge was for murder."

Thomas stared back defiantly. "Your Honor, you can accept the verdict of guilty of manslaughter in the second degree or not guilty of murder in the first degree."

Briggs glared at Thomas for a long moment before he pulled his eyes away and spoke. "Will the defendant approach the bench?"

Luke moved up to stand before the judge.

"You have been found guilty of manslaughter in

the second degree. The maximum penalty for that charge is to be incarcerated for forty-eight months and you are hereby sentenced to the maximum allowed by law. Sheriff, take charge of the prisoner. This court is adjourned."

December 16

Jenny McCoy stood at the window of the private reception room of the Colorado Social Club and looked outside. It was cold and a light dusting of snow was beginning to fall. She watched as a rider passed by, the collar of his coat turned up and his hat pulled down. Behind her a cheery fire snapped and popped in the fireplace.

Her beauty, bearing, and education had quickly made her a favorite of the more affluent "gentlemen" who visited the club.

One such visitor was The Honorable Lorenzo Crounse, Governor of Nebraska. He stepped up to the window beside Jenny and put his arm around her. "Doesn't it make you feel good to be all warm and cozy inside, when it is so cold outside?"

"It certainly does," Jenny answered with a smile as she casually turned out of his arm and walked over to the table where sat a carafe of coffee. "And a good hot cup of coffee makes it even better. May I pour you a cup?"

Governor Crounse chuckled. "Indeed you may, my dear." He watched her as she poured. "I must say, you are the most beautiful woman I have ever laid my eyes on."

Jenny brought the cup of coffee to the governor and handed it to him with a smile. "My goodness, Governor, if you flatter everyone that way, it's no wonder you got elected."

"Oh, but I mean it, my dear. I mean every word. You are—"

The door to the private reception room was suddenly thrown open, interrupting the governor's statement. Four men rushed inside, three had pistols in their hands, and the fourth was carrying a camera.

"Here, what is the meaning of this?" the governor asked angrily. "Do you know who I am?"

"Oh, yes, Governor, we know exactly who you are. Now suppose you just go over there, have a seat on the sofa, and don't make any trouble."

"Who are you? What is all this about?"

"If both of you do exactly what we say, no one will be hurt. We just want a picture, that's all."

"A picture?" the governor asked, confused by the odd request.

"A picture, yes. Miss," the armed spokesman said to Jenny. "I want you to take off all your clothes and go sit with the governor. We want a picture of you, naked, beside him."

"No! That will ruin me!" the governor said.

"I will do no such thing," Jenny replied indignantly.

"Oh, you will be photographed naked with the governor," the spokesman said. "Whether you are dead or alive when we take the picture makes no difference to us. The effect will be the same. You can take your clothes off yourself, or I'll shoot you and we'll strip your dead body."

"You had better do what they say, Jenny," the governor said. "I have a feeling these men have been sent by my political enemies, and I've no doubt but that they will do just as they say."

"Well now, Governor, you are smarter than I thought you were." The armed intruder grinned.

Frightened, Jenny removed her clothes, then sat on the sofa beside the governor. The photographer took a picture, and a moment later, two of the sheriff's deputies were brought into the room. Seeing Jenny nude, with the governor, was all they needed to bring a charge of prostitution against her.

Luke was lying on his bunk with his hands laced behind his head, looking up at the ceiling, when Proxmire and another deputy came into the cell area with a young woman.

Proxmire opened the door to the cell next to Luke. "All right, Miss, in there."

Luke sat up with a start. "Wait a minute! What are you doing? You can't put a lady in this cell."

"She ain't no lady, she's a whore," the deputy with Proxmire growled.

"She is a female. And you can't put women in jail with men. They have to have their own facilities. That is the law."

"Hah! Since when did you become a lawyer?" Proxmire asked.

"You don't have to be a lawyer to know that."

"We ain't got no cell just for women, so she's goin' to have to stay here for a while." Proxmire closed the door on the cell, locked it, and he and the other deputy returned to the front of the jail.

The woman sat down on her bunk, leaned her elbows on her knees, and dropped her head in her hands.

"I'm sorry about this," Luke said. "It's not right, them bringing you in here."

She looked up at him. "Thank you for speaking up for me."

"I'm only doing what's right, Miss McCoy."

"Have we met?"

"No, we haven't. But I've wanted to meet you for some time now. I just wish it could have been under better circumstances, for both of us."

"I'm not a whore, by the way."

"No, ma'am. I know you aren't." Luke stuck his hand through the bars that separated their cells. "I'm Luke Shardeen. I own a ranch just north of town."

Jenny crossed her cell and shook his hand. "Luke Shardeen. Yes, I know who you are. You own Two Crowns. I read about your case in the paper. Everyone I know says that they don't believe you are guilty."

"I'm not. Oh, I killed Gates, all right, but he and Sheriff Ferrell were trying to hold me up."

* * *

"What are you doing putting this poor girl in jail?" a woman demanded. "You let her out this very instant, or I will go to the newspaper with the name of everyone who has visited the Social Club in the last six months. Do you understand what I'm saying, Deputy Proxmire? Everyone!"

"I can't let her out until the judge says I can," Proxmire replied.

"Really? Would that be the same Judge Briggs who was with," Adele took a piece of paper from her pocket and started reading from it, "Sandra, Sara Sue, Kate, and Ella Mae?"

"Uh, all right, I'll let her out. But she has to be present for her hearing tomorrow, and if she ain't, I'll hold you responsible."

"She'll be there."

Proxmire returned to the cell area and unlocked Jenny's cell.

"Looks like you're getting out," Luke said. "I'm glad."

"I hope everything goes well for you, Mr. Shardeen," Jenny said as Proxmire opened the door. "Good night."

"Good night."

Proxmire escorted Jenny to the front. "You just make sure you have her there for the hearing tomorrow," he demanded as Adele left with Jenny.

"I told you, you had no business bringing her here," Luke called out after hearing the door closed behind them.

"I don't need you tellin' me what is, and what

isn't my business," Proxmire replied with a low growling snarl.

"Your honor, Jenny McCoy is not a prostitute," Adele said at the closed hearing the next day.

"Does she, or does she not work for you?" Judge Briggs asked.

"Yes."

"And do you run a house of prostitution?"

"I run the Colorado Social Club."

"Which is a whorehouse."

"I don't like to think of it in quite those terms."

"Regardless of how you like to think about it, it is a whorehouse. And if you deny that, I will lock you up for perjury."

"All right I admit, Your Honor, that I do have, uh, ladies of that profession in my employment. But Mrs. McCoy certainly isn't one of them. Her only function is that of a hostess, not as a prostitute."

"But you do employ prostitutes?"

"You know that I do, Your Honor. I might even add that you have, let us say, personal knowledge of that fact."

Briggs cleared his throat and rapped his gavel on the bench. "I am not the one on trial, Miss Summers. Jenny McCoy is on trial. Unless you want me to extend the charges to you as well."

"No, Your Honor."

"Then we will continue the hearing, and you will add nothing except your responses to my questions."

"Very well, Your Honor."

"Would you say that Jenny McCoy is a hostess in your establishment?"

"Yes, that is exactly what she is. She is a hostess and nothing more. She is guilty of nothing."

"That's where you are wrong, Miss Summers. Mrs. McCoy was soliciting to provide sexual acts for money. Maybe she wasn't soliciting for herself, but she certainly was for others. And the penalty for solicitation for prostitution is the same as it is for prostitution itself."

"All right." Adele finally had enough. "If you are unable to see the difference, I won't argue with you. How much is her fine? I'll pay it."

"I'm afraid that won't work. This is far beyond having one of your women caught with a cowboy. You see, the gentleman she was with is the sitting governor of a neighboring state."

"I know that, Judge. Governors, congressmen, senators"—she paused—"and judges—have all visited the Colorado Social Club. And the more cultured of these gentlemen want to spend some time with Jenny, not as a sexual partner, but as a conversationalist.

"And why not? Jenny is the most educated and intelligent person I know, man or woman. And you can see with your own eyes how beautiful she is. It is no wonder that such people find her interesting."

"Nevertheless, if it gets out that the governor was with Jenny McCoy, it could have far-reaching consequences. Therefore, my sentence for you, Mrs. McCoy, is that you leave Pueblo."

"What?" Jenny asked with a gasp. "Where will I go? What will I do?"

"Like Miss Summers said, you are an uncommonly beautiful woman, Mrs. McCoy. I'm quite sure you will be able to find some means of supporting yourself. I just don't intend for you to do it here."

"I will not be a prostitute!" Jenny said resolutely.

The judge's only response was to bang his gavel. "This hearing is adjourned."

Adele walked back to the Colorado Social Club with Jenny, comforting her as best she could.

"I have never been so embarrassed and humiliated in my life," Jenny said.

"Nonsense, my dear. You have nothing to be humiliated for, or embarrassed about."

"But what will I do? Where will I go?"

"You can go to Red Cliff," Adele suggested. "I have a brother who owns a nice store there. I'll write to him, and ask him to give you a job."

"Would you? Oh, Adele, you have been such a wonderful friend."

Colorado Springs—December 17

Bob Ward was meeting Felix Parker, a man he had served time with in the Colorado State Prison in Cañon City. Also present at the meeting were three men Parker brought with him: Roy Compton, Gerald Kelly, and Melvin Morris.

"Michael is still in jail in Kiowa. From what I've

learned, he'll be transported on the Red Cliff Special, leaving Pueblo at nine o'clock at night on the nineteenth," Ward said.

"What day is that?" Parker asked.

"That will be Monday, day after tomorrow."

"How are we going to work this?" Morris asked.

Ward gave out the first set of instructions. "You four will board the train in Pueblo. The train will have to go through Trout Creek Pass. It is 9,000 feet high, so by the time the train gets to the top of the pass, it won't be goin' any faster than you can walk."

"That's when I'll go to work," Parker continued. "I'll go up front and stop the train."

"And while everyone is distracted by the train being stopped, Compton, you, Kelly, and Morris, will take care of the deputy escorting Michael, then come to the front with him."

"I'll disconnect the train from the engine, and we'll go on over the pass, leaving the rest of the train behind," Parker said.

"I'll meet you in Big Rock with horses," Ward continued. "After that, we'll go get the money."

"Are you sure the money is there?" Morris asked.

Ward smiled. "Let's put it this way. The money damn well better be there, because Michael knows what will happen if it ain't there."

"He's your brother."

"Yeah? So was Abel Cain's brother," Ward said.

Chapter Eight

Claro, Nevada

Matt Jensen opened his eyes and looked around his hotel room. The shade was pulled, but a small hole in the shade projected onto the wall a very detailed image, not a shadow but a photographic image of the winter-denuded cottonwood tree growing just outside the hotel.

He sat up in the bed and swung his legs over the side, remaining there for a long moment before padding barefoot across the plank floor toward the chest of drawers. He picked up the porcelain pitcher and poured water into a basin. The water was just short of freezing, but it had an invigorating effect as he washed his face and hands, then worked up a lather that enabled him to shave.

It was already mid-morning, but the heavy green shade covering the window kept out most of the light. Not until he was dressed did he open the shade to let the morning sunshine stream in.

He stood at the window for a moment, looking out onto the street below.

Across the street, an empty wagon with one of its wheels removed sat on blocks. Another freight wagon was just pulling away while a third was being loaded. That Claro was an industrious town was well demonstrated by the painted signs and symbols used to make the various mercantile establishments known to the citizens as well as the farmers and ranchers who came into town to buy their supplies. The apothecary featured a large cutout of a mortar and pestle. Next to that, a striped pole advertised the barber shop, and next to that a big tooth led patients to the dentist. Directly across the street, Matt could see the painted, golden mug of beer inviting customers in to the Red Dog Saloon.

Matt turned away from the window, pulled his suitcase from under the bed, and began packing. Nothing in particular had brought him to Claro, and nothing was keeping him there.

When his suitcase was packed, he took it to the depot and bought a ticket to Denver, figuring it was time he got back to Colorado. He decided to send a telegram to his friend and mentor, Smoke Jensen, informing him of his plans.

DEPARTING CLARO NEVADA 10 AM DEC 17 STOP ARRIVING DENVER 2 PM ON 19 STOP REPLY BY TELEGRAM TO CENTRAL PACIFIC DEPOT IN CLARO STOP MATT

Matt checked his suitcase in, then went over to the Red Dog Saloon to have his breakfast. He had made friends in the Red Dog and thought to tell them good-bye.

He took a seat at a table halfway between the piano and the potbellied woodstove that sat in a sandbox. Roaring as it snapped and popped, the fire put out too much heat if one was too close to it and not enough if one sat some distance away from it. Matt knew exactly where to sit to get just the right amount heat to feel comfortable.

Trebor von Nahguav was sitting at the next table, drinking coffee. An Austrian, he was a pianist who had studied under Chopin.

"Matthew, is it true you are actually leaving today?" Trebor asked.

"I am."

"I will not like to see you go. You have brought a bit of *bekanntheit* to the saloon, and to the town."

"Bekanntheit?"

"*Ja*. It means"—Trebor struggled for the word, then smiled as it came to him—"Fame. It is not every day that one gets to meet a character who has stepped from the pages of a book." He was referring to the Beadles Dime Novels, specifically those written by Prentiss Ingram and featuring Matt Jensen as the protagonist. Matt's friend Smoke had long been a character in the novels and, through him, Prentiss was made aware of Matt.

Matt chuckled. "Just remember, Trebor, the operative word there is *novel*. By definition, novels are fiction. I do not claim any of the accomplishments Colonel Ingram has written about."

"That is only because you are too modest," Trebor said. "I know about your exploits in Wyoming where you single-handedly eliminated the Yellow Kerchief gang and saved the young nephew of Moreton Frewen. What was his name? Winston?"

"Yes, Winston Churchill. He was quite an impressive young man."

Lucy Dare, a buxom blond with flashing blue eyes and an engaging smile, walked over to join the conversation. So far, the dissipation of her trade had not diminished her looks.

"Lucy, our friend is leaving us today," Trebor said.

Lucy leaned over Matt's table, displaying her cleavage. "Are you sure I can't talk you into staying with us?"

Matt laughed. "No, but you can sure make it damn tempting."

"I will play something for you before you leave," Trebor said. "I will play Tchaikovsky's Piano Concerto Number One. It is not something the average saloon patron would like but you, *mein freund,* I know, will enjoy it."

"Thank you," Matt said. "I am sure I will enjoy it."

Trebor moved over to the piano and played the piece, losing himself in the sweep and majesty of the concerto. Matt enjoyed it, but knew Trebor enjoyed it more. He used any excuse to play the classical music he loved, rather than the simple ballads he was forced to play night after night.

After his breakfast Matt told his friends good-bye and left the saloon. He'd walked about a block when a man suddenly stepped in front of him and pointed a gun.

"Give me all your money," the armed man demanded.

"Now why would I want to do that?"

"Why? Because if you don't, I'll blow a hole in your stomach big enough to let your guts fall out." To emphasize his threat, the man thrust the pistol forward until the barrel of the gun was jammed into Matt's stomach.

That was a mistake. Matt reached down and clamped his hand around the pistol, locking the cylinder tightly in his grip.

His assailant tried to pull the trigger, but it wasn't possible with the cylinder locked in place. He looked down in surprise, and Matt brought his left fist up in a wicked uppercut. The man relaxed his grip on the pistol as he went down, and it wound up in Matt's hand.

Bending down to check the robber's pulse, Matt saw the man was still breathing. He waited until the man came to, then walked him, at gunpoint, down the street to the office of the Claro City Marshal.

"Well, now, hello Percy," the marshal said when Matt turned his prisoner over to him. "It didn't take you long to get back in jail, did it? I just let you out this morning."

"What was I supposed to do?" Percy complained. "I didn't even have enough money to buy breakfast."

"If you had asked me for enough money to buy breakfast, I would have given it to you," Matt offered. "But pointing a gun at me doesn't put me in the sharing mood."

When Matt went to the depot later that day, he found there was, indeed, a telegram waiting for him.

DUFF MACALLISTER AT SUGARLOAF STOP COME SPEND CHRISTMAS WITH US STOP SMOKE

Matt had to pay for only two words in his return telegram.

WILL DO

He smiled at the thought of spending Christmas with Smoke, Sally, and Duff. Sally was a very good cook, particularly bear claws, an almond flavored, yeast-raised pastry that was the best Matt had ever tasted. He turned his thoughts to Christmas, which was supposed to be spent with family. But he had no family.

His parents and sister had been murdered when he was a boy. After spending some time in a brutal orphanage, he ran away in the dead of winter and would have frozen to death if Smoke Jensen hadn't found him and taken him in. Smoke was the nearest thing to a family Matt had, so much so that he had taken Smoke's last name as his own.

It would be good to spend Christmas with his old friend, and Sally's home-cooked meals would make it even nicer.

Matt extended his ticket from Denver to Pueblo, putting him in Pueblo at eight o'clock in the evening on the nineteenth, just in time to connect with the last train to Big Rock. That trip would require going through Trout Creek Pass over the Mosquito Range, a part of the Rocky Mountains.

He boarded the train at ten o'clock on the morning of the 17th of December for what the schedule said would be a two-and-a-half-day trip to Pueblo.

Pueblo—December 19

Jenny McCoy entered the train station at seven o'clock in the evening and bought a ticket on the Red Cliff Special, due to leave at nine. The judge had given her one week to settle her affairs and leave town, but it had taken her only three days.

That didn't leave time for Adele to write to her brother and receive a reply, so she wrote a personal and impassioned letter she gave to Jenny.

"Show my brother this letter. He's a good man with a good heart. When he reads this he and his wife will take you in, and if he can't find work for you in his own store, I've no doubt that he will help you find employment."

"Thank you, Adele. I don't know what I would have done in this town if it hadn't been for you. I don't know how I would have made a living."

"It is I who should thank you. You were a wonderful and classy addition to my business. I'm just sorry things turned out as they did. The judge had no right to order you out of town."

"I have made some good friends here, you especially, and I'm sorry to leave them."

"Someday you may come back, and when you do, remember that I will always count you as a dear friend." Adele hugged Jenny and left the station.

With Adele's letter secure in her purse, Jenny bought a newspaper, then settled in a seat near one of the roaring potbellied stoves and began to read the *Pueblo Chieftain.*

Another Cold Wave

MOUNTAIN TOWNS REPORT CONTINUAL SNOWFALL

Reports from the mountains show a snowstorm has been in progress several days, thus far without serious or unusual results. The storm is most severe in Eagle County, where snow is several feet deep and drifting. So far all passes are still open for trains.

At nine o'clock of the morning, the temperature was two below zero and growing colder. Those who watch the weather say Christmas Day will be very cold. That Christmas will be white is surely to be a joy to the children of the city, who will hope to see "Santa Claus" and his sleigh.

Michael Santelli to Pass Through Pueblo

OUTLAW IS ON HIS WAY TO BE HANGED

Michael Santelli, the notorious gunfighter who is said to have killed seventeen men, met his match when he was confronted by Deputy Sheriff Ben Mason and well-known Western figure Matt Jensen in the town of Kiowa. Santelli was tried for the murders of George and Elaine Rafferty while robbing Rafferty's Grocery in Red Cliff. Convicted of the crime, he is being transported to Red Cliff, where he will be hanged. He is expected to pass through Pueblo, where he will be put on the train to Red Cliff.

Deputy Sheriff Braxton Proxmire, who will escort the prisoner, says that he does not expect any trouble.

Senator Daniels to Visit Red Cliff

WILL SPEAK AT REPUBLICAN CHRISTMAS EVE DINNER

Senator Daniels has made no statement as to whether or not he will run for governor of Colorado in 1894. He has, however, been a frequent speaker at political gatherings such as the Republican Christmas-Eve dinner being held in Red Cliff on the 24th, thus giving rise to speculation of his future plans.

Senator Daniels is known to be a vocal opponent of the procedure of paying coal miners in "company script" that can only be redeemed in company stores. He has proposed a bill in the state legislature which would prohibit that practice. He has also proposed that mine owners be responsible for building shoring and other such means of ensuring miners' safety. As it now stands, all safety improvements are paid for by the miners themselves.

☞ ***For the Late Christmas Shopper***

Men, you can do NO BETTER *for your wives*

than to buy them a *new hat* for Christmas . . .

at FULLERS MILLINERY.

ဢ

All the *latest fashions* available!

She will be *pleased.*

CHAPTER NINE

As Jenny continued to read the paper she heard a few gasps and comments from others in the waiting room and, looking up, she saw Deputy Sheriff Proxmire coming into the depot with two men in handcuffs and shackles. One of them she recognized as Luke Shardeen, the man she had met during her brief time in jail. She had no idea who the other man was until she heard someone point him out.

"That's Michael Santelli!" The stranger's voice was filled with awe. "They say he's killed more 'n thirty men."

"He's only killed seventeen," another man corrected.

"Yeah, well, they're goin' to hang him, and he'll be just as dead whether he killed thirty or seventeen men."

The first man chuckled. "You got that right."

"That's Luke with him. What's he there for?"

"He's goin' to serve his four years in jail."

"He's goin' to Cañon City?"

"No, he's goin' to be put in the Eagle County Jail at Red Cliff."

The two prisoners were either unaware of the conversation about them or were ignoring it as they kept their eyes straight ahead. Deputy Proxmire prodded them toward the bench where Jenny was sitting. "You two men sit right there while I get the tickets," he ordered.

Jenny started to get up, but Proxmire looked at her. "No, you stay there. You are being run out of town, so you are as much under my authority as these two men are."

Jenny, with her cheeks flaming in embarrassment, sat back down.

"Hello, Miss McCoy," Luke said. "It's good to see you again."

Jenny appreciated the calm and respectful greeting, and it helped her overcome some of the embarrassment she had felt at Proxmire's harsh words to her. "Hello, Mr. Shardeen."

"You remember my name. I'm flattered."

"Of course I remember your name. I also remember that you are a rancher."

"I *was* a rancher. Now I'm a prisoner." Luke made the comment with a disarming smile.

"Oh, I'm so sorry."

"I am too. I have finally met you, a most attractive and very pleasant young lady, and now I must leave."

"Lady?" Santelli scoffed. "She ain't no lady. You heard what the deputy said, didn't you? This here woman's bein' run out of town. What did you do, girlie?"

Jenny didn't answer.

"Cat got your tongue?" Santelli laughed.

Several women came hustling into the depot, drawing his attention. They unfurled a big, hand-painted sign.

HARLOTS WILL FIND

NO WELCOME

IN PUEBLO

"Whoa!" Santelli said, holding his handcuffed hands out toward the women. "Did they bring that sign in here for you? Are you being run out of town because you're a whore?"

Still, Jenny didn't answer.

"That's it, ain't it? You're a whore. Well, I'll tell you what, darlin', I'm about to go get myself hung. And if you had any kindness in you, why, you'd let me enjoy this almost last night I'm goin' to have on earth. What do you say that me 'n you go over there in the corner and have us a little poke?"

"Please," Jenny said. "I'd rather not talk."

"I'd rather not get hung, too. But we don't always get what we want," Santelli said.

"Santelli, why don't you leave the lady alone?" Luke couldn't stay silent any longer.

"Lady? Ha! I told you, she ain't no lady. She's bein' run out of town because she's a whore, and you're calling her a lady?"

"Yes, I'm calling her a lady."

Santelli stared at Luke for a moment, then turned his attention back to Jenny. "Tell me, darlin', what if I—?"

Smack! With both hands cuffed together, Luke brought his fists around in a powerful stroke. The blow knocked Santelli out.

"I'm sorry, Miss McCoy," Luke said to Jenny. "I apologize for his rudeness."

"You have no need to apologize for him. You have nothing to do with him, and you have been most kind to me. I appreciate your coming to my aid."

At that moment Proxmire returned. "All right, I have the tickets here. We can board as soon as—" He stopped his comment in mid-sentence and frowned.

Santelli was sitting with his head thrown to one side, his mouth open and his tongue sticking out. He was totally unconscious.

"What happened to him?" Proxmire jerked his head toward Santelli.

"Oh, he went to sleep," Luke said.

The deputy stroked his chin. "He went to sleep, huh? Did you help him?"

"I might have sung a lullaby or something to him to get him in the mood," Luke suggested.

Jenny choked back a giggle over Luke's comment, and his smile showed that he appreciated her reaction.

"I don't know what's going on here, but it's not going to go any further. Luke, you sit on the other side of the girl, I'll sit on this side of her, and Santelli will be on the other side of me. That ought to keep the two of you apart.

Santelli came to a moment later and he stared straight ahead as if trying to orient himself. He reached up to touch his black eye and winced.

"What happened?"

"You fell out of your seat," Proxmire said. "You should sit up straighter."

It was obvious that Santelli didn't remember being hit by Luke, and when Jenny saw him adjusting his position in the seat so as "not to fall out again," she couldn't help chuckle a second time.

"Say," Luke said. "When I come back here four years from now, would you like to have dinner with me?"

"Oh, I"—Jenny started to say that she had no idea where she would be in four years, but found the idea of having dinner with Luke Shardeen a very pleasant one—"would be glad to have dinner with you." Besides, it would obviously make him feel better if he had something to look forward to, whether it ever happened or not.

"Good. Now, don't you be backing out on me. I plan to hold on to that thought for the next four years. That's what's going to get me through it."

State Senator Jarred Daniels stood before the checkout desk at the Victoria Hotel.

"We've been just real proud to have you as our guest, Senator," the desk clerk said. "Yes sir, being as you were one of the people most responsible for getting the Colorado Mining Museum here, why, it's an honor to have served you."

"Thank you. My wife and I sent our luggage down a while ago. Was it transported to the railroad depot?"

"Yes sir, it was, and it's all checked and ready to go onto the Red Cliff Special."

"Good man." Daniels paid the bill, then walked over to an upholstered sofa where his wife Millie and their daughter Becky were waiting for him. Millie was holding her hand to Becky's forehead.

"What is it?" Daniels asked.

"I don't know," Millie replied. "She feels as if she has a slight fever."

"It's probably from the heat here in the lobby. It's very cold outside, and I think they go overboard a little on the heat. How do you feel, Becky?"

"I don't feel good, Papa."

"Well, you'll feel better after we get out of this

lobby. A little cool air will do you good. Come on, the trolley will be here directly."

Millie made certain her daughter was well bundled up, then they stepped out into the frigid night air. It was so cold it nearly took Millie's breath away. She put her arms around her daughter and pulled her closer as they watched the approaching trolley, sparks flying from the wand connected to the overhead wires.

The trolley stopped and the motorman opened the doors. He smiled when he saw the statesman, who was easily recognizable because of his girth and his muttonchop beard. "Senator Daniels. Welcome aboard my car, sir."

"Thank you." Daniels turned to help his wife and daughter onto the car.

"Where are you going on this cold night?" the motorman asked. "I would think on a night like this, one would want to stay home before a warm fire."

"That might be true, young man. But, like you, I have work to do, work that calls me out on cold nights." Daniels sat next to Millie as the trolley started forward.

"I'm worried about her," Millie said. "She's being very quiet. You know she isn't normally like this."

"Naturally you are worried. You are her mother, and mothers tend to worry. But I'm sure there is nothing wrong with her. Once we get on the train she'll be warm, and she can sleep. Why, I'll bet she is fit as a fiddle come morning."

"I hope you are right."

"I know I'm right. You'll see." Daniels reached over to pat his wife on the knee.

Millie put her arm around her daughter and pulled her closer.

Just down the street from the depot, Parker, Compton, Kelly, and Morris were having a beer in the Lucky Strike Saloon.

"Are you sure he is going to be on this train?" Compton asked.

"That's what we were told," Parker answered.

"Besides which, it's in the newspaper today," Kelly added. "I seen the story myself."

"Yeah, but newspapers ain't always right."

"He'll be on the train," Parker said.

"Do you really think Santelli has enough money to give us five hundred dollars apiece?" Morris asked. "That's two thousand dollars."

"Ward says he does. And he prob'ly has a lot more 'n that," Parker insisted. "There's no tellin' how much money he has stole over the last three or four years. I would be surprised if he didn't have four or five thousand dollars hid away somewhere."

"Which ain't goin' to do him no good if he's hung," Kelly added.

"Exactly right," Parker replied. "So as soon as we get him away, he'll take us to where he's got the money hid."

"What if he don't do it?" Morris asked.

"You heard what Ward said. If he don't do it, we'll kill 'im." Parker snorted.

"Yeah, that's what he said, all right," Morris agreed. "But what if he just told us that to make sure we come in with him?"

"It's a little late to be thinkin' about all that now, ain't it?" Parker asked. "I mean we're already here. The train will be comin' tonight, and I say we go through with it. Unless five hundred dollars don't mean nothin' to you."

"No, no, I didn't say I wasn't goin' to go through with it." Morris quickly changed his tune. "I was sort of thinkin' out loud, is all."

"Well, don't think," Parker instructed. "There's no need to be thinkin'. Ever'thing's already been thought out for us."

"It's gettin' pretty close to time," Compton reckoned. "I expect we'd better get on down to the depot."

As soon as the four men left the saloon, they were hit by an icy blast of wind.

"Damn, that's cold!" Kelly shivered as they walked to the depot.

"Feels like it's goin' to snow," Morris surmised.

"What difference does it make how cold it is?" Parker asked. "We'll be on the train. They got heatin' stoves in all the cars, and they keep the cars nice and warm. Otherwise, they wouldn't have nobody ridin' the trains in the wintertime."

Once inside they moved to the stove for a moment, then stepped up to the ticket window.

"We want four tickets to Big Rock."

"Yes, sir, four tickets to Big Rock," the ticket agent said.

Parker pointed to Santelli. "What car is he going to be in?"

"Oh, sir, I don't know. Unless someone buys a ticket specifically for a Pullman car, I never have any idea where they will be. This is a narrow-gauge railroad, so there are no Pullman cars on this run. But I'm sure if you don't want to be in the same car as a murderer, you will be able to avoid him."

"We want to be—" Parker stopped mid-sentence. He'd started to say they wanted to be in the same car as Santelli, but thought that might make the ticket clerk suspicious. "That is, I really don't care what car we get put in."

"Well, I will say this, sir. Normally the Red Cliff Special is pretty much filled. But it being nearly Christmas, it seems there aren't as many passengers as normal, so you can probably sit just about anywhere you want."

After the four men received their tickets, three of them went over to the farthest side of the depot waiting room, but Parker went over to the prisoners. "Santelli, Bob Ward is an old friend of mine. He said if I saw you, I was to tell you hello."

"Really? You've met with him recently?"

"Just a couple of days ago."

"Well, thank you. And thank you for bringing the message," Santelli nodded indicating he understood.

"Here," Proxmire fussed. "Get away from my prisoner."

"I was just passing on a greeting from a mutual friend," Parker replied.

"You have no business with my prisoner. I'm going to ask you again, sir, to move away."

Parker held his hands out. "Whatever you say, Deputy. I'm not one to cause trouble." He turned away and went over to join his partners.

Jenny continued to watch the four men for the next few minutes. She was sure the man who'd spoken to Santelli had exchanged some sort of signal with him. She wondered if she should mention it to Deputy Proxmire. After a moment's consideration, she decided not to say anything about it. There was no law against exchanging glances, and though Jenny was of a suspicious nature, she convinced herself there was nothing significant about the way the men had looked at each other.

An overweight well-dressed man, a woman, and a child came into the depot then. The man pointed to one of the long wooden bench seats. "Millie, you and Becky wait there for me. I'll get the tickets."

"All right." The woman hustled the little girl to the bench.

"Mama, I still don't feel good."

"I know, dear. There's room on the seat, and you can lie down and put your head in my lap."

"What about when we get on the train?"

"I'm sure there will be room enough on the train, too, for you to lie down."

"Senator Daniels! Senator Daniels, I'm with the *Pueblo Chieftain.* Will you stand for an interview, sir?" a young man asked the girl's father as he started toward the ticket counter.

"Certainly, my good man, as soon as I secure the tickets for our travel."

So, Jenny thought, *that's Senator Daniels.* She looked over toward the senator, remembering the article she had just read about him. If he was going to give a speech in Red Cliff, they would be on the same train.

At that moment the depot began to shake and rumble as a train came into the station.

"Is that our train?" Santelli asked.

Proxmire shook his head. "No, that's the southbound. We'll be on the Red Cliff Special, going west."

CHAPTER TEN

Matt was on the train pulling into the Pueblo Station. He would leave that train and board the one going toward Red Cliff. Big Rock was on that line, being the first stop on the other side of the Mosquito Range of mountains. He was anxious to get to nearby Sugarloaf Ranch, where he planned to enjoy Christmas with his friends.

"Pueblo!" the conductor called, coming through the cars. "This stop is Pueblo. This is where you're getting off, isn't it, Mr. Jensen?"

"Yes, it is."

The conductor reached out to shake Matt's hand. "Well, sir, let me tell you it has been a real privilege having you aboard. I can't wait until I tell my son. He has read all about you. Oh, and I thank you for the autograph."

"It's quite all right," Matt said. "Tell your son I said hello."

"I'll do that, Mr. Jensen. Yes, sir, I will certainly

do that." He continued on through the cars calling out the stop. "Pueblo! This stop is Pueblo!"

Matt had been a little embarrassed at being asked for his autograph. He was always self-conscious about being connected with the literary work of Prentiss Ingram.

"It's hardly literature," Sally had said once, scoffing at the books Ingram had written, not only about Matt, but about Smoke and Falcon MacAllister, as well as books about and plays starring Buffalo Bill Cody.

Matt looked out the window as the train drew close to the Arkansas River, then passed several houses, the windows gleaming gold from the inside electric lights. Like Denver, Pueblo had been electrified. Maybe he was old-fashioned, but he preferred the soft, golden glow of gas lanterns to the harsh white of the electric lights.

Matt saw a buckboard, a young boy on the seat beside the driver. In the back of the buckboard was a freshly cut evergreen tree, no doubt soon to be sprouting tinsel and Christmas ornaments.

That turned his thoughts to Christmas with Smoke and Sally, and Matt realized it had been a long time since he had seen his friend. He was looking forward to seeing him again and renewing his acquaintance with Duff MacAllister. It was fitting they would be meeting at Christmas as he had first met him five years ago, during Christmas of 1888, when he helped Duff and Smoke deliver a herd of Abner cattle from Wyoming to Texas.

The train rolled into the station and rattled and rumbled to a halt. It was almost eight o'clock in the evening. Matt helped a young woman get her grip down from the overhead rack, then reached up for his suitcase. Carrying his coat, he followed the young woman through the car and down onto the depot platform. Immediately, he was hit by a blast of cold air. Shivering, he hurried across the brick platform and into the inviting warmth of the station as the train's overheated journals and bearings popped in the cold air.

Inside, he saw two men talking, or rather, one man talking while the other man was busy recording their conversation in a small notepad. Matt wondered what was so special about the man that everything he said had to be recorded. Then, he heard the man with the small, narrow notepad ask a question and he knew what it was.

"Senator Daniels, are you aware of the claim being made by the coal mine owners that paying in company script is the most efficient way to run their businesses?"

"I know it is what they say. But consider the miner, how he sweats and toils beneath the earth to mine coal, only to see that his remuneration is in paper that is worthless to spend anywhere except in a company store."

"Which provides all the necessities for living," another reporter said. "Food, furniture, clothing. What more does someone need?"

"In my opinion, that is nothing more than a form of slavery," Senator Daniels answered.

"But, according to the mine owners, this actually helps the miners' families as it prevents the miners from spending money on whiskey or gambling it away."

"Of course slave owners could justify their actions as being best for the Negro," Senator Daniels replied. "But we all know they weren't. Besides, who are the mine owners to make such decisions for someone else? No, sir, it is wrong. Wrong, I say, and I intend to fight against it, and I intend to fight with every ounce of my being."

"There are some who say you have no real interest in your bill, other than as a way to generate publicity for yourself," the reporter suggested.

"To what end, sir?" Daniels replied, obviously irritated by the question.

"Why, so you could run for governor during the next election. What about that, Senator? Do you have aspirations to run for governor? Or perhaps even a higher office?"

Senator Daniels reached up to stroke his mutton-chop whiskers before he responded. "Right now, I just want to be a very good state senator. But I have chosen politics as my profession, and anyone who enters into any profession would want to reach the top, would they not?"

"So you do want to be governor?"

"No, no, I didn't say that. And you can quote me on that."

The reporter looked at him in confusion. "I can quote you on what, Senator?"

"You can quote me on saying I didn't say that." With that rather convoluted comment, Senator Daniels left the reporter scratching his head as he walked over to join his wife and their nine-year-old daughter.

"How is Becky? Is she doing any better?"

"No, Jarred, I don't think she is doing well at all," Millie replied. "Maybe we should stay here and find a doctor for her."

"Nonsense. Do you really want to spend Christmas in Pueblo? You know how important it is that I be in Red Cliff for that dinner. Besides, I've no doubt the doctors there are just as skilled as the doctors here in Pueblo."

"Is the dinner more important than the health of our daughter?"

"Of course not," Senator Daniels replied. "But I don't think it is any more than a childhood malady of some sort, and I'm sure she will be over it soon enough."

Parker saw Matt come into the depot, and leaned over to speak to Compton. "Do you know who that fella is?"

"No, I can't say as I do."

"His name is Jensen. Matt Jensen."

"Damn! You sure?"

"Yeah, I'm sure. I've seen him before."

"You think he might be goin' on the same train we are?"

"It looks likely that he is."

"So, what do we do?"

"If he is in the same car as Santelli and the deputy, we ain't goin' to do nothin'."

"You mean we ain't goin' to get Santelli free?"

"That's exactly what I mean."

"If we don't get Santelli away from the deputy, we won't get paid."

"Is your life worth five hundred dollars? 'Cause if we go up against Jensen, we're likely to get ourselves kilt."

"Hell, there's just one of him."

"Yeah, but he's carryin' a gun with six bullets," Parker pointed out.

"So, what do we do now?" Compton asked.

"We wait and see. If he goes to a different car from Santelli, then we'll do just what we planned to do."

Matt checked the schedule board and saw that he had at least half an hour remaining until the westbound train was due. He hadn't eaten since lunch, but he didn't think he would have time to order a regular dinner. So, stepping up to the depot lunch counter, he ordered a piece of apple pie and a cup of coffee.

As he ate, he looked round the waiting room of

the depot, appraising as best he could the people who would be his fellow travelers.

The first ones he checked were the senator and his family. The little girl didn't look well and Matt was struck by the expression of concern on the mother's face. He saw considerably less concern reflected in the face of the young girl's father.

Matt noticed the two men in handcuffs and shackles, and was surprised to see one of them was Michael Santelli. He wondered why there was an attractive young woman sitting with them, then he saw the banner and could tell by her demeanor it was directed at her.

"Hey"—the reporter looked over toward Matt—"you're Matt Jensen, aren't you?"

Matt took a swallow of his coffee.

"Yes, you are. You are the one who took down Michael Santelli. He's here, you know, on his way to Red Cliff to be hanged. He's sitting right over there, right now." The reporter pointed toward the bench occupied by Santelli, Luke, Proxmire, and the young woman.

"Yes, I saw him."

"You know what would be good? If I could get a picture of you with Santelli. We use the half-tone method of reproducing photographs."

"No, thank you."

"Is Santelli the reason you are here in Pueblo?" The reporter kept hounding.

"No, I'm just passing through Pueblo. And by the

way, I didn't take him down. He was arrested by Deputy Sheriff Ben Mason. He is a fine officer."

"Yes, but everyone knows if you hadn't been there, Santelli would more than likely have killed Mason. You were the hero of that event."

"I don't agree," Matt said. "The fact that Mason took Santelli on, knowing that he could be killed, makes him the *real* hero."

"Yes, I guess you have a point there. But say, would you mind if I interviewed you for a story?"

At that moment a whistle sounded and a bright light illuminated the darkness outside as the beam from the great, mirrored headlamp announced the approach of another train. Everyone in the depot started getting ready to board the westbound train.

"Sorry," Matt said as he finished his coffee. "But that's my train."

As the others began gathering their belongings and getting ready to board, Matt walked over to the telegraph office and wrote out a quick telegram to Smoke.

IN PUEBLO BOARDING TRAIN NINE PM STOP ARRIVE BIG ROCK SIX AM TOMORROW STOP MATT

Matt paid the telegrapher, then, grabbing his small case, he hurried outside to join the others in boarding the train.

Just before they boarded, Proxmire looked over at Jenny. "Now look here, Mrs. McCoy. You ain't goin' to jump back off the train before we get started, are you?"

"Don't worry, Deputy. I have no intention of remaining in this town."

"Good. Because after I get these prisoners delivered, if I come back and find you are still here, it'll be more than just askin' you to leave town."

"Leave the lady alone, Deputy," Luke said.

"Mr. Shardeen, seein' as you're goin' off to jail yourself, it don't seem to me like you're in any position to be a' tellin' me anything. This here woman's bein' run out of town, and I'm charged to see to it that she leaves."

At Jenny's assurance she would stay on the train, Proxmire turned and steered his prisoners toward the train. Matt watched them shuffle to the next to last car. The four outlaws quickly followed.

From in the line behind them, Becky asked, "Mama, why are they telling that lady she has to leave town?"

"Hush, darling. I don't know, and it is none of our business," Millie replied.

Again, Matt saw the young woman's cheeks flame in embarrassment and watched as she climbed into the last car. He didn't recognize her, but at least knew he had seen her somewhere before. He just couldn't remember when or where. Without that information, he wasn't able to put a name to the face.

Matt and the Daniels family followed Jenny into the last car, illuminated by kerosene lanterns, three on each side, mounted on gimbals. Two coal-burning stoves—one at each end—were in the car, and the smoke was carried outside by chimneys, which passed through the roof. The stoves were well stoked and burning briskly so the car was comfortably warm, despite the brutal outside temperature.

Matt took the very last seat in the car, which was exactly where he wanted to be. From his position at the back, he could observe without being obvious. He looked at the woman the deputy had called Jenny McCoy. It was not a name he recognized, and if she was a prostitute as the sign had indicated, she was certainly unlike any prostitute he had ever seen before.

She was very attractive, but not garishly so as was the case with so many prostitutes. She was quiet and noncombative, and, even in her obvious embarrassment, there was a sense of bearing about her he would describe as regal.

Just as the train whistle blew, a man came flying out of the depot and ran up the steps of the last car. He sat down quickly in the front seat.

The train started forward then, jerking a few times until all the slack was taken from the couplings. It gradually and smoothly increased speed until it reached approximately twenty miles per hour, the speed at which it would run for as long as it was on flat ground. After a few hours, it would start on a long upgrade, and the speed would decrease sharply.

"I'm cold, Mama," Matt heard the little girl say.

"Don't be silly," Senator Daniels replied. "It's not cold in here. If anything, it is too warm."

"I'm cold," Becky repeated.

"Darling, she is ill," Millie objected. "She is probably having chills."

"Can I have a blanket?"

"I'm sorry, honey. We don't have a blanket," Millie explained.

Jenny, overhearing the conversation, got up and walked back to the seat where the senator and his family were sitting. She held out a long coat toward the little girl's mother. "Your little girl is certainly welcome to use my coat as a blanket," she offered with a smile.

"Madam, I saw the sign in the depot, and I heard the deputy address you, so I know who and what you are," Senator Daniels barked. "Just what makes you think I would want my daughter to use something from someone of your kind for a blanket?"

The smile left Jenny's face to be replaced by an expression of hurt.

"Jarred! Don't be rude!" Millie said sharply. Then, smiling at Jenny, she reached out for the coat. "How gracious of you to offer your coat. Yes, thank you. I think that would work quite nicely. But, I wouldn't want you to get cold."

"I'm close enough to the stove, I don't think I will get cold," Jenny answered, obviously grateful her offer had been accepted.

"It's a very pretty coat," Becky said.

"It will be even prettier when it's covering a pretty little girl like you." Turning, Jenny walked back to her seat.

"Did you hear what she said, Mama? She said I was pretty."

"Yes, darling, I heard it. And she was only telling the truth. You are a very pretty little girl."

"I think she is pretty," Becky said.

"Yes, I think so, too. Try and go to sleep now."

Matt saw Jenny McCoy smile at the little girl's words, and was glad.

Chapter Eleven

Sugarloaf Ranch

The Denver Pacific, the Denver and Rio Grande, the Kansas Pacific, the Colorado Central, the Burlington, Rock Island, and Missouri Pacific railroads had all laid tracks into Colorado. Those railroads linked the state with the rest of the nation's economy, bringing in the nation's manufactured goods and shipping out Colorado's minerals and cattle.

One of those taking advantage of the network of railroads was Kirby Jensen, known by everyone as Smoke Jensen. Since marrying his wife Sally and settling down, he had built one of the most successful ranches in Colorado. His ranch, Sugarloaf, was located near the town of Big Rock, just west of the south end of the Mosquito Range. Big Rock would be the first stop on the Denver and Pacific Railroad after the train had traversed Trout Creek Pass coming north and west, and the last stop before climbing the pass when going east and south. And, because that train could carry his cattle to the eastern markets, Smoke Jensen had become a very wealthy man.

At the moment, Smoke and his friend, Duff MacAllister, also a cattleman who owned a ranch in Wyoming, were in the parlor, decorating a Christmas tree. The tree was strung with red and green ribbons as well as brightly painted ornaments.

Underneath the tree was an exquisitely, hand-carved crèche. Duff picked up one of the sheep and examined it closely. "Whoever did this, did mighty fine job."

"That whole thing was carved by Preacher," Smoke said.

"An artist, was he?"

"Yes, he was an artist," Smoke agreed. "But he was much more than that."

"Aye? Well, I'll tell you lad, sure 'n if 'twas only for his art he was known, he would have a well-deserved reputation. I've never seen finer work done."

The smell of freshly baked pastries wafted into the parlor from the kitchen. "What is that wonderful aroma?" Duff asked, looking toward the kitchen.

"If I don't miss my guess, that would be Sally's bear claws. Come, let's go try out a couple."

"Aye, 'tis a good idea." Duff followed him willingly and eagerly into the kitchen.

Both of the men grabbed a bear claw from the table where several of the pastries lay.

"Smoke!" Sally scolded. "You aren't supposed to eat any of those now."

"Well, now, surely you'll want Duff and me to try them out, just to make certain they are good enough to serve at Christmas, won't you?" Smoke teased as he took a bite.

Sally smiled. "And how is it?"

"I'm not sure I can tell with just one. It'll take at least two, I think, before I'll know whether or not they are any good." Smoke finished the first one, then reached for a second. Duff followed suit.

"Uh-huh," Sally said with a condescending smile. "If you and Duff don't quit eating those bear claws, there won't be any left for Christmas."

"Sure there will be." Smoke he took a bite of the second pastry, then wiped his mouth with the back of his hand. "It's a few more days till Christmas. All you have to do is make a couple dozen more."

"I've already made two dozen. This isn't a bakery, you know."

"Just be glad Pearlie and Cal decided to spend Christmas in Denver. Otherwise you'd have to make about three dozen more. With them gone, you probably don't need more than another one or two dozen. Although, you could make three dozen more, just to be safe."

Sally laughed. "You're impossible."

"Of course I'm impossible. You wouldn't love me any other way. You know that," Smoke teased. Looking through the kitchen window, he saw a rider approaching. "Looks like we have another telegram. Here's Eddie again."

"Oh, Smoke, take a bear claw out to him," Sally said. "Bless his heart, having to ride out here in the middle of the night when it is this cold."

"It's only nine o'clock. It isn't the middle of the night. Besides, I thought you said we weren't going to have enough."

"You know I'm going to make some more."

Laughing, Smoke put on his coat, then grabbed one of the pastries and went outside to meet Eddie, the fifteen-year-old telegraph messenger.

"Another telegram?"

"Yes, sir."

"Hope there's no trouble with Matt getting here."

"No, sir. He's just tellin' you he's gettin' on the train, is all," Eddie said. "'Course, that don't mean there ain't goin' to be no trouble."

"Why, what do you mean?"

"We're gettin' reports from all over about snow. I know it ain't started snowin' here yet, but it's acomin' down just real heavy in the mountains, they say. I'm surprised they even let the train leave."

"Eddie, would you like to come inside and warm up a bit before you start back to town?" Smoke invited.

"No, sir. Thank you very much. If I come in and get warm, it'll be that much harder to come back outside again."

Smoke chuckled. "Young man, you are wise

beyond your years." He gave the boy a dollar and the pastry.

"Thank you!" the boy said with a broad grin. "There can't nobody make bear claws as good as Miz Sally can."

"Well, if you're going, you'd better get on back into town before you freeze to death," Smoke pushed. "It's really cold, and I have a feeling it's going to get a lot colder before this night is out."

"Yes, sir, I do believe it is goin' to do just that," Eddie agreed as he turned his horse and started back into the night.

Smoke looked toward the mountains, thinking of the train traveling through Trout Creek Pass. It had snowed quite a bit in the last several days, and he could see the white, almost luminescent, snow-capped mountain peaks against the dark sky.

Once back inside the house, he opened the yellow envelope and read the message aloud. "In Pueblo boarding train nine p.m. Arrive Big Rock six a.m. tomorrow."

"What time does that mean Sally will have to get up to go meet him?" Duff asked.

"I'd say about four-dark-thirty in the morning would get her there on time," Smoke teased.

"What? Not on your life, gentlemen. I'll have you know I will be warm in bed when you two go to town to meet him."

"Is that the way it's going to be? And here, I thought that being it is so close to Christmas, you'd have a little more compassion in your heart,"

Smoke teased some more. "All right, if that's the way it is, you can stay home. But there's no sense in Duff and me both going to pick him up. I'll go by myself."

"I'll be for goin' with you, lad," Duff offered. "I'd be glad to."

"Did you hear that, Sally? He's not only going to go with me, he'll be glad to go. That's what he said. He would be glad to go."

"I heard."

"Well, I think you should know it's good to see that I can count on some people," Smoke said pointedly.

"Try not to wake me when you leave," Sally taunted.

"What do you mean, don't wake you? Aren't you even going to get up to make coffee for us?"

"Nope."

"You are one cruel woman, do you know that?"

"So I've been told," Sally replied with a laugh.

"Eddie said there's been a lot of snow up in the mountains. I hope the train has no trouble getting through the pass," Smoke said.

"Don't they keep the tracks clear?" Duff asked.

"Well, yes, when they can."

Sally walked over to the window and looked up toward the mountains. "I don't know, Smoke, it looks like there might be a big storm brewing."

"Could be," Smoke agreed. "Sally, what was that poem about snow that Preacher liked so much? You remember, he was always asking you to say it to him. It was by . . . some poet. I can't remember."

"Ralph Waldo Emerson. 'The Snow-Storm.'"

"Yes, that's the one. Can you still say it?"

"Of course."

"Say it for us. Listen to this, Duff. I swear, you could hear this poem in the middle of the summer and start shivering."

Sally began to recite the poem, speaking with elegance, flair, and with all the proper emphasis.

"Announced by all the trumpets of the sky
Arrives the snow, and, driving o'er the fields
Seems nowhere to alight: the whited air
Hides hills and woods, the river, and the heaven,
And veils the farm-house at garden's end.
The sled and traveller stopped, the courier's feet
Delayed, all friends shut out, the housemates sit
Around the radiant fireplace, enclosed
In a tumultuous privacy of storm."

"That was beautiful, Sally. You have quite a way with words," Duff said.

"Thank you, but I only spoke the words. Emerson wrote them, and it was a loss to literature when he died."

Smoke chuckled. "Until I married Sally, I had never heard of him. One of the advantages of marrying a schoolteacher is that you get an education."

"I like to say I didn't educate him, I trained him." Sally grinned.

"Whoa, now. I wouldn't go that far," Smoke protested.

Sally and Duff laughed.

"I will say this, though. What Preacher didn't teach me, Sally did."

"Who is Preacher? You mentioned him before. He was the one who carved the crèche, I believe."

"Yes," Smoke said. "Preacher didn't exactly raise me, but he almost did."

"He gave you your name, too," Sally pointed out.

"That's right. I was called Kirby until Preacher changed it to Smoke. Did you know that he killed a bear with just a knife when he was only 14 years old?"

"Och, 'twould take quite a man to do such a thing."

"You've got that right. He was quite a man. You probably wouldn't like him, though. He fought against the English at the Battle of New Orleans. He was just a boy, then."

"I've no real love for the English, laddie, I can tell you that for sure," Duff declared.

"But you are English," Smoke argued.

"I'm a Scotsman, lad. We may be part of Great Britain, but there be no love lost between the Scots and the English, that I can tell you. 'Twill be another hundred years or more before the Scotts forgive the English for Flodden, and then forgiven it will be, but never will it be forgotten."

"Flodden? Yes," Sally said. "I think I once read a poem about Flodden."

Duff cleared his throat and began to speak.

"From Flodden ridge,
The Scots beheld the English host
Leave Barmoor Wood, their evening post
And headful watched them as they crossed
The Till by Twizell Bridge.
High sight it is, and haughty, while
They dive into the deep defile;
Beneath the cavern'd cliff they fall,
Beneath the castle's airy wall.
By rock, by oak, by Hawthorn tree,
Troop after troop are disappearing;
Troop after troop their banners rearing
Upon the eastern bank you see."

"Yes!" Sally said. "That is the poem."

"There's a song about the battle called 'The Flowers of the Forest'," Duff said. "If you'd like, I'll play a wee bit of it on m' pipes."

"I would love for you to," Sally said.

Duff went into his room then returned a moment later with his bagpipes. After filling the bag with air, he began playing the piece, the melody, with its poignant strains, re-creating the tragedy of the terrible event. When he finished, the last note lingered as a haunting echo.

"That was beautiful, Duff. Sad, but beautiful," Sally commented.

"Thank you," Duff acknowledged with a nod of his head.

"Uh-oh," Smoke remarked.

"What?" Sally asked.

"Look out the window."

Outside the snow was falling thick and fast. Huge, heavy snowflakes were quickly covering the ground.

"This can't be good," Sally said.

"Maybe, maybe not," Smoke said. "Just because it is snowing here, doesn't mean it is snowing in the pass."

"But it probably is, right?" Sally asked.

Smoke was silent for a moment, before he answered. He nodded. "Yeah, it probably is."

Chapter Twelve

Big Rock

Cephas Prouty had on woolen long johns under his clothes, and a wool-lined sheepskin over his clothes. He had a scarf around his neck, a stocking cap over his head, and heavy gloves on his hands. Thus attired, he set out in a handcar for the purpose of inspecting Trout Creek Pass. For the first eight miles the track was relatively flat and pushing the hand pump up and down was easy. But it got harder when he started up the long grade that would take him to the top of the pass.

Prouty was used to it, though, as he made the trip several times a week. And tonight, he didn't even mind the pumping. The extra exertion helped keep him warm in the subzero temperatures.

It took him an hour and a half to reach the summit. He set the brake on the car, then stepped down to have a look around. He checked the track, then examined the cut on either side. If he found any reason why the train couldn't make it through, he'd wire the station at Buena Vista, warn them the pass wasn't safe, and have them hold the train there.

Prouty walked along the track from its most elevated point to where it started back down on the west side. He turned around and walked up to the summit, continuing on to where it started back down on the east approach. Occasionally he would stick a ruler into the snow to measure its depth. Nowhere did he find the snow over two inches deep, and even then it wasn't accumulating on the rails. He didn't see any reason why the trains couldn't continue to come through the pass.

It wasn't only during the snow season that he would come up to check. He made frequent trips during other seasons as well, to ensure the rails were whole and unobstructed. On a clear night in the summer. he could look one way and see the lights of Buena Vista or look the other way and see the lights of Big Rock.

Tonight, though, the night was so overcast that when he looked out to either side of the pass he saw nothing but darkness.

His inspection done, Prouty got on his handcar and started back toward Big Rock. His trip up the grade to the top of the pass had been difficult, requiring hard pumping. Going back down was easy. No pumping was required until he reached the flat. In fact, he had to apply the brake to keep from going too fast. He was certain that he was doing at least forty miles per hour on the way down. He began pumping when he hit the flats, making his total trip down the mountain in less than an hour. He coasted into the station at about nine-thirty, moving the cart onto a side track before going inside.

"Well, Cephas, I see you made it back," the stationmaster said. "I figured you would be turned into an icicle by now."

"I damn near am one," Prouty replied as he stood shivering by the stove. "You got 'ny coffee, Phil?"

"Yes, stay there by the stove and warm yourself. I'll get it."

"Thanks."

"What about the pass?" Phil asked as he handed Prouty the cup.

Prouty took a welcome sip before answering. "I think it's all right."

"You *think*?" Phil chuckled. "That's not very reassuring. What do you mean you think? Don't you know? You were just up there, weren't you?"

"It's open now, but the next train isn't due through there until midnight. I believe that the pass will still be open, but I can't guarantee it."

"Should I stop the train at Buena Vista?"

"The next train through is a freight train, isn't it, Phil?"

"Yes."

"No, don't stop it. I think we should let the freight come on through. The Red Cliff Special isn't due through the pass until about five in the morning. When the freight pulls in here just after midnight, the engineer will have a more up-to-the-minute look at it, and a better idea as to the condition of the pass. We can get a report from him and make our decision about the passenger train then."

"Good idea," Phil agreed.

Prouty smiled. "You're a good station manager, Phil, offering a track inspector a hot cup of coffee after he's been out in the cold."

"Oh, I can do better than that. How about a cruller to go with your coffee?"

"Phil, you are indeed a gentleman," Prouty said gratefully.

On board the Red Cliff Special

On the other side of the Mosquito Range from where Phil and Prouty were having their discussion the Red Cliff Special was rumbling through the cold night. Matt kept repositioning himself, trying to get as comfortable as he could in the backseat. He had been on a train for over two days and was getting a little tired of the travel. The night before he had been in a Pullman car and had been able to sleep. But there were no Pullman cars on this run, so he had to make himself as comfortable as he could in the seat.

Fortunately, he had the seat to himself and was able to stretch out somewhat. He wadded up his coat and placed it against the cold window to use as a pillow. The kerosene lamps inside the car had been turned way down so that, while the car was illuminated just enough to allow someone to move about, it wasn't too bright to keep anyone from sleeping.

Falling into a fitful sleep, Matt dreamed.

An early snow moved in just before nightfall of the sixth day and the single blanket Matt had brought with him did little to push away the cold. It was also tiring to hold the blanket around him while walking. He considered cutting a hole in the middle but decided against it because he thought it would be less warm at night, that way.

As the snow continued to fall it got more and more difficult to walk. At first, it was just slick, and he slipped and fell a couple times, once barking his shin on a rock so hard the pain stayed with him for quite a while.

The snow got deeper and he quit worrying about it being slick, concerning himself only with the work it took just to get through it. His breathing came in heaving gasps, sending out clouds of vapor before him. Once he saw a wolf tracking him and wished he had his father's rifle.

He found a stout limb about as thick as three fingers and trimmed off the smaller branches with his knife. Using the limb as a cane helped him negotiate the deepening snowdrifts.

Just before dark he sensed, more than heard, something behind him. Turning quickly, he saw that the wolf, crouching low, had sneaked up right behind him. With a shout, and holding the club in both hands, he swung at the wolf and had the satisfaction of hearing a solid pop as he hit it in the head. The wolf yelped once, then turned and ran away, trailing little bits of blood behind it.

Matt felt a sense of power and elation over that little encounter. He was sure the wolf would give him no further trouble.

As the sun set he found an overhanging rock ledge and got under it, then wrapped up in the blanket. When night came, he looked up into the dark sky and watched huge, white flakes tumble down. If it weren't for the fact that he was probably going to die in these mountains, he would think the snowfall was beautiful.

"Here, try some of this."

Opening his eyes, Matt saw that he was no longer outside under a rock, but inside on a bed. How did I get here? *he wondered. A man was sitting on the bed beside him, holding a cup. Matt took the cup and raised it to his mouth, but jerked it away when it burned his lips.*

The man laughed. "Oh. Maybe I should have told you it was hot."

Matt tried again, this time sipping it through extended lips. It was hot and bracing and good. "What is it?"

"Broth, made from beaver," the man said.

"Don't know that I've ever tasted beaver, before," Matt said calmly.

The man laughed again.

"What's so funny?"

"I'll say this for you, boy, you do have sand. I found you damn near dead out on the trail, and now you are

telling me that you don't think you've ever eaten beaver before."

"I don't think I have," Matt answered as calmly as before. "Who are you?"

"The name is Jensen. Smoke Jensen."

Matt was awakened when the train ran over a rough section of track. He sat up and rubbed his eyes, bringing himself back from dreaming about the first time he ever met Smoke, or, more accurately, about the time Smoke had saved his life. Not surprised by the dream, he was sure the cold and snow had triggered an old memory. In addition, Smoke had been on his mind as he thought about spending Christmas with his friend and mentor.

It was dark in the passenger car, and pleasantly warm. According to the schedule he had read at the Pueblo depot, they weren't due into Buena Vista until two in the morning. That was a few hours away, so Matt repositioned himself in the seat and went back to sleep.

On board the Freight Number 7

Several miles ahead of the Red Cliff Special, a freight train was approaching the top of the pass.

"Better take it easy through here, Joe," the fireman said. "That snow is comin' down pretty good now."

"Yeah," the engineer said. "But it looks clear ahead. Look out your side. If you see anything, sing out."

The engine, which was pulling a string of ten freight cars, slowed until it was barely moving. Finally it reached the crest, topped it, then started down the other side.

"All right!" Joe cried. "Let's get out of here!" He opened the throttle, and aided by the fact that it was going downhill, the train reached fifty miles an hour. He started slowing it down three miles before they reached Big Rock, where they would have to take on water.

Big Rock station

Phil heard Freight Number 7 approaching, put on his heavy coat, and walked out to the water tank. He needed to talk to the engineer about the pass. He glanced up where a fire was kept burning in the large, cast-iron stove in the vertical shaft just below the tank to keep the water from freezing. When the train ground to a stop, the fireman climbed out to swing the huge water spout over to replenish the water in the tender.

The engineer leaned out the window of the cab and looked down toward the station manager. "What are you doing out here in the cold, Phil?"

"The Special will be coming through the pass about five in the morning. What do you think? Will they have any trouble?"

"We didn't have any trouble," Joe said. "The track and the pass are clear."

"There's a lot of snow higher up, though," the

fireman added. "If it don't come down, I don't see no trouble."

"What do you mean if it doesn't come down? Is that likely?"

"I don't think so," Joe answered. "I saw it too, and it looks like it's pretty solidly packed."

"All right, thanks," Phil said. "I'll send the word on back."

The fireman finished filling the tank, then swung the spout back. "Merry Christmas, Phil," he called out.

Phil smiled back at him. "Merry Christmas to you, Tony. And you, too, Joe." He started back toward the warmth of the depot, even as Joe opened the throttle and Freight Number 7, with ten cars of lumber, continued on its journey.

CHAPTER THIRTEEN

On board the Red Cliff Special

Matt awakened a second time when the train stopped. It was about two o'clock in the morning, which meant they had been under way for five hours. Looking through the window, he saw a small wooden building, painted red. A sign hung from the end of the building, but he couldn't see enough to read it.

"Folks," the conductor said when he stepped into the car. "This is Buena Vista and we'll more 'n likely be here for about half an hour. If any of you want to, you can get off the train and have a cup of coffee or maybe a bite to eat."

The porter went through the car, turning the lamps up brighter, and the other passengers started moving about, collecting coats, mittens, scarves, and caps.

"I don't want to go outside, Mama," Becky said. "I want to stay here and sleep."

"That's all right, darlin'. You won't have to go outside if you don't want to. You and I will stay here in the car, but we'll have to give the lady her coat back so she won't freeze when she goes outside."

"Your daughter can use this as a blanket," Matt said, handing his sheepskin coat to the girl's mother.

"Why, thank you, sir."

"And I thank you as well, Mr. Jensen." Jenny smiled as she retrieved her own coat.

"I was right," Matt said with a smile. "I knew that I had seen you before. I just can't remember where."

"It was a few years ago, on board a riverboat on the Mississippi. The boat was the *Delta Mist.*"

"Of course! You were the hostess for the Grand Salon. But, McCoy wasn't your name then. It was"—Matt hesitated for a moment, then he recalled the name—"Lee, wasn't it? Jenny Lee."

"Yes, I'm flattered you remember. I was married soon after that. Now I'm widowed."

"I'm sorry for your loss," Matt said automatically. Then, as they approached the door of the car he added, "I sure hope they have a warm fire going in the depot."

"I'm sure they will."

They stepped down from the train, and Matt figured the temperature was at least ten below zero. The wind was blowing so hard it cut through him, right to the marrow of his bones. By the time he crossed the platform and got inside, he felt half frozen to death. Moving immediately to the stove, he stood for a long moment with his arms out, circling the stove, as if embracing the fire. Finally, when the feeling gradually began to return to his extremities, he left the stove and stepped up to the counter to buy a cup of coffee, nodding to the man he'd seen board the train just before the train pulled out of the station. The man was leaning against the counter warming his hands around a cup of steaming coffee. Matt paid for his coffee and stepped aside. As he stood there drinking it, he looked around the room and saw that Deputy Proxmire had come into the depot with his two prisoners. The shackles had been removed from the prisoners' legs. Evidently, they were no longer a threat to run away, once on the train.

Santelli looked directly at him, the expression on his face registering surprise, as if seeing him for the first time. Evidently he had not noticed Matt back at the Pueblo Depot.

"Well if it isn't Matt Jensen. What are you doing here, Jensen?" Santelli called over to him. "Have you come to watch me hang? 'Cause if you have, you may have to wait around a while."

"I just happened to be on the same train with you, Santelli, that's all. You can damn well hang without me."

"Ha! Well, I got news for you, Jensen. I ain't goin' to hang. So what do you think about that?"

"I don't think anything about it one way or the other," Matt replied. "This may come as a surprise to you, Santelli, but you aren't important enough to even be on my mind."

"I told you one day that me 'n you would meet again, didn't I? Do you remember that?"

"I do remember that." Matt smiled. "And here we are, met again. I'm on my way to have Christmas with friends, and you are on your way to, what is it? Oh yes, to get your neck stretched."

"Yeah? Well don't you be counting on me gettin' hung, Jensen. No, sir, don't you be countin' on it, 'cause that ain't goin' to happen. And this here meetin' ain't the one I was talkin' about neither. There will be another time for the two of us to, let's just say, work out our differences."

"Santelli, why don't you shut up now?" Proxmire complained. "You've blabbered enough."

Santelli glared but said nothing more.

The man standing beside Matt at the counter had witnessed the exchange between the two men. Turning toward Matt, he stuck his hand out. "How do you do, sir? The name is Purvis, Abner Purvis."

"Matt Jensen." He shook Purvis's offered hand.

"I saw you talking with Santelli. Do you know him?"

"Not exactly, but I did run across him when he was arrested. Tell me, Mr. Purvis, do you know the other prisoner? Who is that with him?"

"I can't say that I actually know him, but I know who he is. His name is Luke Shardeen and I understand he used to be a sailor and has been all over the world. He's seen places the rest of us have just read about or heard about. Hawaii, China, India, Australia, but he gave all that up when he inherited some land from his uncle. He calls the ranch Two Crowns and he's been working it ever since, quite successfully, I'm told."

"Why is he a prisoner?"

"He killed the deputy sheriff from Bent County."

"He killed a deputy sheriff? That's pretty serious."

"I guess it would be if it was the way it sounds. But he claimed that the deputy and Sheriff Ferrell were trying to rob him. Of course, the sheriff said they were only stopping him to ask him a few questions."

"Evidently, the jury believed the sheriff," Matt said.

"Not entirely. It seems Shardeen had just sold a bunch of cows and had quite a bit of money with him. Naturally, he'd be worried if a couple armed men suddenly come up on him, wouldn't you think?"

"I could see that."

"You also have to wonder what a sheriff and a deputy sheriff from Bent County were doing stopping someone in Pueblo County. Why didn't they just go to Deputy Proxmire? Or to Sheriff McKenzie?"

"That's a good question. Evidently, though, it was answered to the satisfaction of the jury."

"The thing is, the jury pretty much had their hands tied."

"What do you mean, they had their hands tied?"

"If you ask me, Amon Briggs—he's the judge—sort of forced them into finding Shardeen guilty. Briggs is as crooked as they come, for all that he is a judge. He likes to do things his own way, and I'm not the only one that thinks this. Most of the folks think he browbeat the jury into finding Shardeen guilty." Purvis chuckled. "He didn't entirely get it his own way, though. He wanted Shardeen found guilty of first-degree murder, but the most he got was involuntary manslaughter and four years."

"Four years isn't all that bad."

"Ordinarily, I would agree with you, but I'm afraid in Shardeen's case it is. He won't have a ranch left when he gets out. He won't have anything left at all, so I don't have any idea what is going to happen to him."

Matt looked over toward Luke Shardeen and saw him sitting calmly beside the deputy sheriff and talking quietly to the girl.

"What about Miss Lee?"

"Who?"

"I mean Mrs. McCoy."

"Oh, yes, that's another example of the judge sticking his nose into everyone's business. Jenny McCoy worked for Adele Summers at the Colorado Social Club."

"Colorado Social Club? I take it the women there are . . . just real sociable?" Matt asked with a chuckle.

"Yes, they are. I'm not going to lie to you, Mr. Jensen, the Social Club is a whorehouse, pure and simple. But Jenny McCoy, now, she wasn't actually a whore. She was a hostess. I never heard of her going to bed with anyone, for all that they tried. But even if she wouldn't go to bed with anyone, she was very popular. Well, you can see how pretty she is. She's also very smart, and then she has a way of making people feel like they are someone important, no matter who they are. They also say that you could tell her anything you wanted, and know it wasn't going to get spread all over town. And if anyone was having troubles, why, she had a way about her of making them feel good. You know, making them think that everything was going to come out all right. But from all I've heard, she didn't whore with anybody."

Matt was glad to hear that. He remembered her from the *Delta Mist,* as well as her supportive testimony at his hearing in Memphis.

"I saw the sign back in the Pueblo depot. Someone thought she was a whore."

"Yes, well I guess she hasn't made friends with many of the women in town, that's true. But that isn't what got her run out of town. The thing that got her run out of town was having her picture taken when she was naked and sitting on the sofa with Governor Crounse."

"Naked?"

"She claims, and so does the governor, that some men broke in to the sitting room and forced her, at gunpoint, to take off her clothes so they could get a picture of them together like that. The governor thinks some of his political enemies were behind it. Nobody has said so, but I'd be willing to bet Judge Briggs was in on it from the beginning. Briggs is the kind of crooked no-good that can be bought off. Everyone knows that."

"If everyone knows that, why is Briggs still the judge? Isn't that an elective position?"

"Elections can be bought, and there's no doubt in my mind but that Briggs bought the election that got him there in the first place, and now just keeps on buying them. I wouldn't be surprised if Briggs doesn't find some way to take over Shardeen's ranch while he's gone."

Matt smiled. "You seem to have your fingers on the pulse of the town. Are you a newspaper reporter? Or are you just well connected?"

Purvis laughed. "Well connected? I wouldn't say that, exactly. But I do hear things."

"What do you do in Pueblo?" Matt asked. "Not that it's any of my business," he added quickly. "I'm just making conversation, here."

Purvis paused for a moment before he answered. "I suppose I'm what you might call a jack of all trades. I've done a bit of everything since I've been here, but I've seen the elephant now, and I'm going back to the ranch my family owns just outside Red Cliff."

One of the other passengers called out to Purvis, and he excused himself, leaving Matt standing alone. Matt continued to observe Luke Shardeen and Jenny McCoy, finding the study more interesting, now that he knew a little something about each of them.

CHAPTER FOURTEEN

At the far end of the depot, Matt saw the conductor and a man he assumed was the locomotive engineer talking to the depot agent. Their conversation was quite animated, so Matt moved closer to see if he could hear them. He gave a quick smile, thinking about using the trick Smoke had taught him, a trick Smoke had learned from Preacher, who had learned it from the Indians.

"In order to better hear what you want to hear, you have to systematically eliminate every other sound, so that nothing competes with what you want to hear," Smoke told him.

"How do you eliminate all the other sound?"

"You just sort of think about each sound for a moment, then, one sound at a time, put it out of your mind."

Outside the depot, the fireman was still on board the locomotive, still keeping the steam pressure up. As a result the water in the boiler was gurgling and hissing. But the real noise was coming from the pulsating relief tube, opening and closing rhythmically, making loud rushing noises as as if the train itself was breathing.

Matt quickly eliminated that sound and concentrated on the loudest remaining sound, which was the buzz and chatter of those conversationalists congregated in the waiting room. Their noise was punctuated by periodic outbreaks of laughter and the sound of small shoes on the floor as a couple young boys ran about in play.

After eliminating the many conversations and the children at play, Matt heard only the sound of the clacking telegraph and the ticking of the large clock on the wall nearby. He pushed those sounds aside as well, and could finally concentrate on the conversation between the engineer, the conductor, and the station agent.

"Look," the station agent was saying. "Last night a track inspector went up to the pass and checked it out. He said it was all right then, and a freight train went through after that, so the latest word we have, by telegraph, is that the pass is open."

"What if we get up there and we are blocked? What if we can't go ahead and we can't come back?" the engineer asked.

"I don't think that is likely to happen, at least not in the next twelve hours," the station agent said. "On the other hand, if you don't go now, and it does get blocked, you could be here for a month."

"I can tell you right now, Don, if that happens, we are going to have a lot of very upset people," the conductor said to the engineer. "Nearly everyone on this train wants to get somewhere for Christmas, and we don't have that much time left before Christmas is here."

"You're the conductor, Mr. Bailey," Don said. "So the decision as to whether to go on or stay here is up to you."

Bailey looked at the station agent. "Mr. Deckert, what is the latest time you received a report on the condition of the pass?"

"Well, like I said, a freight train went through no more 'n two hours ago, and the pass was open then. Do you want to hear the telegram?"

"Yes, read it to me," Bailey said.

Deckert pulled the telegram from his pocket. "Midnight. Trout Creek Pass open. No difficulty." He handed the telegram to the conductor who read it again.

"Hmm, 'no difficulty.' I find it interesting he says that specifically," Bailey commented. "That's a good sign, I would think."

"There has been no new snow since I received this telegram so my guess would be that the pass is still open."

"Your guess," Don quipped.

"It's not just a wild guess," Deckert reasoned. "It's based upon that telegram and the fact that there has been no new snow."

Bailey nodded, then stuck the telegram in his pocket. "All right, Don, I say we go."

"Like I said, you're the boss. How much longer before we leave?"

Bailey pulled out his pocket watch and examined it, even though he was standing right under the clock. "We shouldn't stay here too long. I would think the sooner we get to the pass, the better off we will be. I'll give 'em about fifteen more minutes, then I'll get them back aboard."

"All right, I'd better go tell my fireman." The engineer went outside to return to the locomotive and the station agent went back to his position behind the counter. Having heard what he wanted to hear, Matt let the other sounds start drifting back in, and turning toward the waiting room, he saw that Jenny and Luke were engaged in quiet conversation.

Their conversation looked to be private, so he made no effort to overhear them. Instead, he concentrated on the cup of coffee he was drinking.

Don Stevenson hurried across the brick platform and through the cold to the big 4-6-2 engine sitting on the track, wreathed in its own steam. Reaching up to grab the ladder, he climbed up and into the cabin.

His fireman, Beans Evans, reached down to give him a hand in. "So what's the story? Are we goin' on?"

"Yep."

"Then the pass is open?"

"They think so."

"They think so? You mean they don't know?"

"Nobody knows for sure," Don said. "But the last report they got was a telegram from Big Rock. Freight Number Seven passed through at midnight, and said that it was open."

"That was two hours ago, and it'll be another three hours before we get there," Beans pointed out.

"Yes. Well, if the pass isn't open, we can always back down the hill."

"Yeah, that is if there ain't another train comin' up behind us."

"Well, you know what they say, Beans. Ours not to reason why, ours but to do or die."

"Yeah? Well, who says that? Not the people who have to do or die, that's for damn sure," Beans replied.

"You've done a good job keeping the steam up."

Beans smiled. "I wasn't keeping the steam up, I was keeping myself warm."

Inside the depot, Jenny and Luke were still engaged in conversation.

"Nobody in town thinks you are guilty," Jenny said. "I've heard them talking."

Luke smiled. "Unfortunately, none of the people who thought I was innocent were on the jury. The men on the jury thought I was guilty."

"No, they were just too frightened of the sheriff and the judge to go against them, that's all. That's why they said it was involuntary manslaughter instead of murder."

"It wasn't even that. It was self-defense. The two men who accosted me were armed. Sheriff Ferrell and his deputy, Gates, tried to rob me."

"Ha!" Santelli had been listening in to their conversation. "People like you are never guilty. Why don't you own up to it? Take my advice. If you've done somethin', admit it."

"Santelli, the last thing I need is advice from you," Luke remarked.

"All right, don't pay me no never mind, I'm just tryin' to be helpful, is all."

"Would you like to move closer to the stove?" Luke asked Jenny.

"Yes, that would be nice."

Luke stood, then reached down with his handcuffed hands to help her up.

"Where do you think you're goin', Shardeen?" Deputy Proxmire asked.

"To get warm," Luke replied "You may have noticed, it's cold outside, and I left my coat on the train."

"Just don't try and run away."

"Where would I go without a coat on a night like this?"

Luke and Jenny found a place to sit near the stove that also afforded them a modicum of privacy.

"We have something in common," Jenny said with a smile.

"You mean because we are both under Proxmire's watchful eye?"

"Well, yes, I suppose there is that, but that's not what I'm talking about. I'm told that you used to be a sailor."

"Aye. That I was. I've crossed the Pacific eleven times. Wait, are you telling me you were a sailor?"

"Of sorts."

Luke laughed. "How can you be a sailor of sorts?"

"The difference is in the water we sailed. You were on the Pacific; I was on the Mississippi River. I worked for my uncle. I was a hostess on board the *Delta Mist* riverboat."

Luke nodded and smiled. "You're right. River, ocean, it makes no difference. We were both sailors."

"How long have you been in Pueblo?" Jenny asked.

"Three years. And you?"

"Not quite a year. I started teaching school, but when the school board learned I had been married to a gambler, they decided I was a bad influence on the children."

"Why, that's ridiculous," Luke said. "I can't think of anyone who would have a better influence on the children than you."

"Thank you," Jenny said with a small smile. "That is very nice of you to say."

"It takes no extra effort to tell the truth," Luke insisted.

"You are a very nice man. It makes me wonder

why we couldn't have—" Jenny interrupted her comment in mid-sentence.

"You mean why we couldn't have met before this?" Luke concluded.

"It doesn't seem fair." Jenny's eyes welled with tears. "I finally meet someone nice and where do I meet him?" She managed a weak laugh through the tears. "I meet him when we are both under the care of a deputy sheriff, you, going to jail, and I being run out of town."

Luke reached up with his manacled hands and, sticking a finger out, caught a tear as it slid down her cheek.

"It was almost different," Luke said.

"Oh? What do you mean?"

"I had heard about you. I went to the Colorado Social Club, just to meet you."

"Really?" Jenny had a questioning look on her face. "I don't remember meeting you. I'm sure I would remember."

Luke smiled. "You didn't meet me, because I didn't stay."

"Oh."

"I wish I had stayed."

"No, I'm . . . I'm glad you didn't stay. I don't think I would have wanted to meet you that way."

"I understand. I think that is probably why I left. But at least we have met now," Luke said. "And I'm thankful for that."

"Yes," Jenny agreed. "At least we have met."

"All right, folks!" the conductor called. "Let's get back aboard!"

Luke stood first, then helped Jenny up. They stood there for a moment, just looking at each other, then, with a smile, Jenny spontaneously gave Luke a kiss on the lips.

Luke raised his arms, then realized that, because his hands were cuffed together, he couldn't easily embrace her. "That's not fair. You took advantage of me when my hands are cuffed, and I can't put my arms around you."

"Under the circumstances, it is probably best," Jenny said.

Those passengers who had come into the depot house hurried through the brutal cold back onto the train. Fortunately, the cars had been kept warm.

Walking toward the back of the car, Matt shook off the chill. His coat was still drawn over the sleeping daughter of Senator Daniels. He stopped and asked Mrs. Daniels, "How is she?"

"I'm worried about her."

Matt reached down to feel her forehead. "It feels as if she has some fever."

"Yes. I wish we had stayed in Pueblo so she could see a doctor."

"There are some fine doctors in Red Cliff. At this point we are much closer to Red Cliff than we are to Pueblo."

"Yes, I was thinking that as well. Do you want your coat back?"

"No, I'm doing just fine. Let her keep it. She needs it more than I."

"Thank you. That is most kind."

During the entire conversation, Senator Daniels had been sitting in the seat facing his wife and daughter, staring out the window at the bleak and empty depot platform. He paid no attention to the conversation between Matt and his wife.

The train started forward with a jerk so severe Matt reached out and grabbed a seat back to keep his balance, then moved quickly to his seat and sat down. He had told Mrs. Daniels they were closer to Red Cliff than to Pueblo, and in terms of distance, that was true. But Trout Creek Pass was between them and Red Cliff, and though the consensus of the conversation he had overheard was that the pass was open, in the final analysis they had proceeded on toward the pass based upon the stationmaster's belief that the pass was open and the conductor's call to proceed.

Matt wasn't all that convinced.

Across the aisle from Matt's seat and in the very front, Jenny sat quietly, looking down at her hands folded on her lap. She was thinking of Luke Shardeen, and trying to analyze her feelings for him.

She wasn't feeling the same way she had felt about Nate McCoy when first she'd met him. At that time, she had thought Nate was the most handsome man she had ever seen. After spending eighteen months with him she realized what she had felt was little more than infatuation. And it was childish infatuation at that, for all that she was an adult at the time.

She wasn't feeling childish infatuation for Luke. In fact, she didn't think it was something she would even call infatuation, though she was certainly interested in him. What would have happened if he had come in to see her the night he visited the Social Club? Would she have felt the same interest? Or would she have put any such feeling aside as she did for all the other customers who had come to visit with her?

She shook her head a little. The best time to have met him would have been while she was still teaching school, before she got involved with the Social Club and before he got into trouble with the law. If she had met him then, they might have fallen in love and gotten married. She smiled.

Then suddenly, reality set in, and the smile left her face. What was she doing? She shook her head again. These thoughts were getting her nowhere. The best thing was to get such thoughts out of her mind. She settled back into her seat, let her head rest against the seat back, and drifted off to sleep.

Chapter Fifteen

In the car just ahead, Luke and Santelli were sharing a seat. Deputy Proxmire sat facing them so he could keep an eye on both at the same time. Luke sat closest to the window, looking outside. It had begun to snow again, the snow coming down in big, tumbling flakes, a swirl of white against the darkness.

"You know what I'm thinkin'?" Santelli said, his words interrupting Luke's contemplation.

"I don't really care what you were thinking," Luke said.

"I think you are fallin' for that whore."

Luke didn't answer.

"Yes, sir, that's what I think. You seen yourself a pretty woman and you fall for her. But here's the funny thing. You're goin' away to jail, and more 'n likely the girl is goin' to wind up in another whorehouse somewhere." Santelli laughed. "Tell me, how does that make you feel, knowin' your girl will be layin' with anyone who has the price?"

"You talk too much, Santelli," Luke muttered.

"Yeah? Well, talk is cheap. And right now, talk is all I've got. So I reckon I'll talk as much as I want."

"If you don't shut up talking about Jenny, I'll shut you up."

"Really? How are you going to do that?"

"I'll do it the same way I did it before."

"What do you—" Santelli stopped in mid-sentence, lifted his cuffed hands to touch his still-sore, black eye, and realized what had happened back in Pueblo. "Did you do this?"

Luke smiled, then turned to look back outside.

Parker, Kelly, Compton, and Morris were sitting across from each other in the front two facing seats, three rows ahead of the deputy and his prisoners.

"When do we make our move?" Kelly asked.

"Just before we reach the top of the pass," Parker said. "The train will be going slow enough that it will be easy to get it stopped."

"Who's going to go up on top?" Compton asked. "'Cause I'm tellin' you right now, you ain't goin' to get me on top of a movin' train. Most especially in weather like this when it's snowin' and the tops of the cars is likely to be slippery and all."

"Don't worry about it, I'll go. I've stole a lot of rides on freight trains, and I've run on top of a lot of cars in good weather and bad. It won't bother me none a' tall to run along the top of these cars." Parker went over the plan once again. "I'll get the engineer's attention, and as soon as I get the train stopped, you three take care of the deputy. Once we have Santelli, we'll cut the engine free, then go on down the other side of the mountain, and leave the rest of the train sitting up here on the track."

"I know you said you've stole rides on a lot of trains before," Morris said. "But are you sure you can drive this thing?"

"Drive it? Who said anything about drivin' the train? I don't have to drive it. All I have to do is stick a gun in the engineer's gut and he'll do all the drivin'. Yes, sir, he'll be more than glad to take us anywhere we want to go." Parker smiled. "At least, he'll take us anywhere we want to go as long as there is track to run on."

"I know Ward says Santelli has the money, but seein' as we're the ones that's actually takin' a risk here, I'm going to ask you again. What do you think? Do you really think he has the money to pay us?" Kelly asked.

"I wouldn't be doin' all this if I didn't think there was some payoff in it," Parker said. "I sure ain't doin' it 'cause me 'n Santelli is tight."

One hour after they left Buena Vista depot, Matt could feel by the angle of the car that they were starting up the long grade taking them to the top of the pass. The train also began to slow, going from a rapid twenty miles per hour down to no faster than a brisk walk.

The Denver, South Park and Pacific Railroad first laid tracks through Trout Creek Pass in 1879, and Matt had traversed the pass many times since then. He knew it well. The pass climbed to 9,300 feet at its highest elevation, and he knew they were coming very close to the top of the pass because he felt the train slow down even more.

Looking out through the window and into the darkness, he could see whirling white flakes and knew the snow had intensified since leaving Buena Vista. He shook his head, thinking the engineer and conductor were probably having second thoughts. If the track was closed ahead, they would have to back all the way down to Buena Vista, and backing at night, in a heavy snowstorm, down a steep grade, couldn't be a very good thing.

And still the snow came down.

In the engine of the train, Beans Evans was scooping up coal from the tender, then throwing it into the open door of the firebox. Inside the box, the flames leaped and curled around the added fuel, and even above the noise of the engine, Beans could hear the fire roaring. He closed the door and stood up. "That ought to keep us goin' till we reach the other side of the pass. Then we can damn near coast into Big Rock."

"Why don't you take a breather, Beans?" Don

said. "You've got enough fire to keep the pressure up for quite a while.

"Yes, sir, I think I will." Beans pulled a big red bandanna from the chest pocket of his overalls and wiped the sweat from his face. "You wouldn't think a body could get hot enough to sweat on a cold night like this."

"Why not?" Don answered. "We've got a fire going, and you've been working hard."

Beans chuckled. "I have to confess that I like standin' by the firebox a heap more in the wintertime than I do in the summertime."

"I agree," Don said. "Trouble is, I've got to keep my face in this window lookin' ahead all the time, and that lets the cold wind on me."

"It's funny, ain't it? I mean, what with both of us no more 'n five feet apart and here you are near 'bout freezin' to death, and I'm burnin' up, I'm so hot."

"Yeah," Don agreed. "Tell me, Beans, what did you get the missus for Christmas?"

"I bought her a cookstove."

"A cookstove?" Don laughed. "A cookstove? That's what you bought her for Christmas?"

"Yeah. She keeps tellin' me she don't have the right kind of stove to bake a cake, so I bought her one."

"Come on, Beans, what were you thinking? Women don't like things like that as Christmas presents. I mean, yeah, buy her a stove if you want, but women like pretty things."

"Oh, it's pretty all right. You should see it, Don. That stove is just real pretty."

Don laughed. "I don't think that's the kind of pretty women think of, when they think pretty."

"What about your kids?" Beans asked. "Are they excited about Christmas?"

"Oh, yes. They're wanting to see what Santa Claus will bring them." Don chuckled. "I know one thing he better not bring them. Not if I want to stay on the good side of Doreen."

"What's that?"

"Donnie wants a drum. Ha! Can you see him running around the house, banging on a drum? Well, it wouldn't bother me none. I mean when you stand here all day listenin' to all the noise this makes. But it would more 'n like drive Doreen crazy. Now Little Suzie, all she wants is a doll. Girls are a lot easier than boys. They don't seem to get into as much trouble. When you and your missus start havin' children, try 'n make 'em all girls."

"Ha!" Beans said. "Like you can choose."

"I know a witch that'll put a spell on your wife to make her have girls or boys. It only cost ten dollars."

"And it works?"

"Sure it works. Anyhow, you can't lose no money 'cause if she puts the hex on and it don't work, then she don't charge you nothin'."

"Ha. Sounds to me like she's got a real game goin' there."

"What do you mean? What kind of game?"

"If her hex works, she gets paid. If it doesn't work, she doesn't get paid. Is that what you said?"

"Yeah. So you can't go wrong, that way."

"Well, think about it, Don. All she's doin' is bettin' that you're goin' to have a boy or a girl. Only she ain't exactly bettin', 'cause she don't put up no money. She's just collectin' if she wins."

Don stroked his jaw for a second as he considered what Beans said. "I'll be damned." He smiled as he suddenly realized the truth of it. "You're right."

In the next to the last car of the train, Parker and the other three men were finalizing their plans.

"Remember"—Parker gave instructions once more—"make your move as soon as I get the train stopped."

"Yeah," Kelly said. "More 'n likely, Proxmire and ever'one else on the train will be tryin' to figure out why we're stopped."

"You can get the train stopped, can't you?" Morris asked.

"Yeah, don't you worry about that. I'll get the train stopped all right."

"All right," Compton said. "We're all ready, so let's do it."

With a final nod, Parker got up and left the car, passing through the front door and onto the vestibule. Crossing the vestibule, he went into the next car and then the next, proceeding through the cars until he walked through the dining car and started out the front door.

One of the dining car porters came up to him. "You can't go no farther, Mister. There ain't nothin' up there but the baggage and express car, and there ain't no passengers that's allowed in it."

Without a word in reply, Parker pulled his pistol and brought it down hard on the train crewman's head. The porter collapsed to the floor. Nobody else in the dining car saw it, and Parker went on without any more interference.

From the front vestibule of the dining car, he climbed up onto the top of the express car, ran across it, then jumped down onto the tender and moved toward the engine. He saw the engineer with his hand on the throttle and the fireman standing alongside, leaning on his shovel. Neither of them saw him because they were engaged in conversation.

"Hey! Engineer! Stop this train!" Parker shouted, but there was too much noise for him to be heard.

"Hey! Engineer!" Parker shouted again.

When neither the engineer nor the fireman heard him, Parker fired two shots into the air, which caught the attention of both the engineer and the fireman, and they looked around in surprise.

"I want you to—"

A deep and very loud roar interrupted what he'd intended to say.

Looking up, Parker saw an avalanche of snow cascading down the side of the mountain, set in motion by the sound of his gunshots. He barely had time to open his mouth in a scream before tons of snow swept him from the top of the tender, burying him, the engine, the tender, and most of the baggage car under hundreds of feet of snow.

The train to come to an immediate and jarring stop, causing many of the sleeping passengers to tumble out of their seats. A few shouted out in alarm.

"All right, boys, he's got it stopped. This is it!" Kelly shouted, and he and the other three advanced toward the rear of the car. Proxmire's back was to them as they approach, and he was sitting next to the window, trying to figure out what had caused their sudden stop.

"Hello, Santelli," Kelly said.

"Do not speak to the prisoners." Proxmire turned away from the window and was shocked to see a gun pointed directly at him.

"What are—"

Kelly pulled the trigger. The bullet hit Proxmire between the eyes, forming a fan-like spray of blood on the window behind him.

The other passengers in the car were either trying to recover from the sudden stop or staring out the window when they heard the shot fired. In alarm, they all looked around and saw Proxmire's bloody head leaning against the window. A woman screamed.

"Shut up!" Morris shouted, turning his pistol toward the other passengers. "I'll shoot the next person who makes a sound!"

Cowed by the threat, the others in the car grew quiet as they watched through wide, frightened eyes. A little girl started crying.

"Shut that brat up!" Morris shouted.

The father clamped his hand over the child's mouth.

Santelli held his hands up, showing his cuffed wrists. "The deputy has the keys in his jacket pocket."

Morris dug out the keys and opened Santelli's cuffs.

"What about him?" Morris indicated Luke Shardeen. "Should we take off his handcuffs?"

"No," Santelli said as he rubbed his wrists. "Just shoot him and be done with it. Better yet, give me a gun and let *me* shoot him."

Acting quickly, so quickly it caught the others by surprise, Luke stood up from his seat and shoved Santelli back into Morris, causing both men to struggle to maintain their balance. With them distracted, he dashed out the back door, then leaped off the vestibule into a pile of snow nearly as high as the railcar itself. He disappeared at once.

The three armed men rushed out the back of the car and onto the vestibule. Kelly fired into the snowbank where Luke had jumped. They heard a rumble up above the pass, and more snow came sliding down.

"Don't do that!" Compton shouted, reaching out to stay Kelly's hand. "Don't shoot again! You could bring the whole mountain down on us!"

Kelly swore. "Where did he go?"

"It don't really matter much. Hell, it's below zero and he ain't wearin' no coat," Morris noted. "Like as not he'll be froze to death in no more 'n ten minutes or so. What I'm wonderin' is, what happened to Parker?"

"I expect he's up in the engine, keepin' the engineer and the fireman covered till we get up there," Compton reckoned.

"So, what is the plan now?" Santelli asked.

"Soon as we get you free, we're goin' to go up to the front of the train," Compton answered.

"Yeah," Kelly added. "We're goin' to unhook the engine and go on down the pass, leavin' the rest of the train up here."

"Ha! Good plan," Santelli agreed. "By the time anyone figures out what has happened, we'll be long gone."

The four men started forward then, tracing the same route Parker had taken, earlier.

Passing through the cars they saw that the other passengers were in a state of confusion and worry as they gathered by the windows, looking out to see what had brought them to such a sudden and unexpected stop.

"Can you gentlemen tell us what has happened?" one of the passengers asked. "Why was there such a sudden stop?"

"Have we had a train wreck?" another asked.

"Just stay here in your seats and keep calm," Kelly said. "We're goin' up to the front of the train now

"Why would you pick on the conductor, dear? He
asn't driving the train," Millie said.

"No, but he is supposed to be in charge." Senator
Daniels fumed in anger.

"Senator, I'm quite sure this is not some childish
stunt," Matt said. "No doubt there is a perfectly
good reason for the sudden stop."

"There may be a reason for the stop, but I guaran
tee you, it isn't a good reason," Daniels complained
"I simply must get to Red Cliff in time to prepare for
my speech on Christmas Eve. Don't people realize
speech requires preparation?"

Luke sunk down several feet into the large bank
of snow. Snow got into his ears, his eyes, and hi
nose, and he realized he couldn't breathe. Fright
ened that he might suffocate, he began to flail hi
rms about until he was able to open up a littl
ocket of air in front of his face. Still unable t
reathe through his nose, he opened his mouth and
ok in a deep, gasping breath. The air that wen
to his lungs was so cold he felt a sharp pain in his
est, and for a moment he feared he might be
ving a heart attack.

Taking in the cold air with deep, painful gasps,
finally managed to work his way out of the snow-
nk and brush snow off his face. Opening his
, he saw a narrow gap right alongside the cars
pushed his way to it. Keeping his hand on the
to steady himself, he stayed on that band of

to find out what happened. We'll let the rest of you know as soon as we know."

"Thank you."

Nobody noticed that the man who had been a prisoner when the train left the depot was now as free as the others. And nobody noticed that all four had pistols in their hands, Santelli having taken Proxmire's weapon.

When the four men reached the dining car they saw the kitchen staff gathered around a man who had obviously been injured.

"What happened here?" Kelly asked.

"Some man came through and hit Pete over the head with his gun," a staff member answered.

Kelly smiled and looked at the others with him. "Looks like Parker left his calling card."

"The man who did this. Where did he go?" Santelli asked.

"As far as I know, he's dead, along with the engineer and fireman."

"He's dead? What do you mean he's dead? And what do you mean the fireman and the engineer are dead? What are you talking about?" Santelli exclaimed.

"Where you been, Mister? Didn't you notice the train come to a sudden stop?"

"Yes, of course I noticed it."

"Well, what do you think stopped it?"

"I would think the engineer."

"The engineer didn't have nothin' to do with it. The front end of this train is under about three hundred feet of snow. We been hit by an avalanche. We're stuck here."

Moving quickly to the front of the car, Santelli opened the door and discovered an impenetrable wall of white. "What the hell?" He slammed the door and turned around. "What happened?"

"What happened is the mountain collapsed on us. That's what happened. Like I told you, we're trapped here."

CHAPTER SIXTEEN

The sudden stop of the train jarred Matt, and he looked over toward Becky to see if she was all right. Fortunately, Becky's mother was sitting in the seat in a way that sufficiently braced her and the little girl, so the sudden stop caused no problem.

It had tumbled a sleeping Jenny out of her se though, and Matt hurried over to help her u you all right?"

"I'm fine," Jenny answered. "I wonder stopped so suddenly. You don't think we thing, do you?"

"No, I'm sure that the engineer must h something on the tracks ahead and br train to a stop. We weren't going very fa fairly easy to stop."

"What are they doing up there?" Sen asked, irritation in his voice clearly evi some puerile stunt? I intend to find th and give him a piece of my mind."

relatively clear path, hurried to the back of the train, and climbed up onto the vestibule.

Matt had just returned to his seat, when, unexpectedly, the rear door opened, and he felt a blast of frigid air. Looking toward the door he saw what appeared to be a snowman. He had to look a second time before he realized it was Luke Shardeen covered in snow and nearly frozen to death. His hands were still cuffed.

"Luke?" Matt asked, the tone of his voice mirroring his curiosity.

Luke moved away from the back door and stumbled into the car, his sudden and unexpected appearance startling all the other passengers. Without so much as a word to anyone, he moved quickly to the stove to warm himself.

Jenny was the next person to recognize the intruder under all the clinging snow. "Luke!" She hurried to him. As he shivered, she began brushing the snow away from him.

"What are you doing in this car?" Senator Daniels demanded. "You are getting snow over everything, and you are frightening the people."

"I'm . . . s-s-sorry," Luke stammered. He was shaking almost uncontrollably.

"Wait a minute! You are one of the prisoners, aren't you?" Daniels insisted when he saw the handcuffs. "What did you do, attempt to escape?"

Luke was still shaking too much to reply.

"Answer me!" Senator Daniels snapped sharply. "Did you attempt an escape?"

"Please, Senator, can't you see that he is nearly frozen to death?" Jenny asked.

"He's going to be worse than that when he is returned to custody. I'm going up to the next car, right now, and tell the deputy that his prisoner is back here." Daniels pointed to Luke. "I'll have you returned to his custody."

"You c-c-can't do that," Luke managed to say.

"And just what is going to keep me from doing it?"

Luke paused for a moment before he answered, this time managing to speak without stuttering. "You can't do it because Proxmire is dead."

"He's dead? Good heavens man, did you kill him?"

"No. Some men in the car were in league with Santelli. One of them, I expect, is responsible for getting the train stopped. The remaining three killed the deputy and set Santelli free."

"And you?"

"They were going to kill me as well," Luke answered. "But I jumped off the train into a deep snowbank and got away."

"I don't believe you," Senator Daniels uttered.

"I believe him," Jenny affirmed.

"Yes, I am sure someone like you would believe him," Daniels grumbled.

"I believe him, too," Matt agreed. "Hold your hands out, Luke. I'll get those cuffs off of you."

"You have a key?" Luke asked in surprise.

"Of sorts," Matt said with a smile as he held up his penknife.

"What?" Senator Daniels sputtered angrily. "What

are you doing? Don't you dare set this prisoner free! Why, I'll not allow you to do such thing!"

Ignoring the senator, Luke held his hands out. Opening the penknife Matt stuck it in where the handcuffs closed, wedging the ratchet down so he could pull the lock arm out. He did the same thing with the other side and within a moment, Luke was free.

"That's a good trick to know." Luke smiled as he rubbed his wrists. The severe shaking had stopped as the heat of the stove was beginning to take effect.

"What happened, Luke? Why did we stop, do you know?" Matt asked.

"Yes, I know. At least, I'm pretty sure I know. The entire front of the train is buried under snow."

"What do you mean *buried in snow*?" Senator Daniels snapped.

"I mean buried. You can't even see the engine or the tender."

"Will we be able to dig out?" Matt asked.

Luke shook his head. "I don't see how we can. It looks like the entire mountain came down on the engine; at least two hundred feet of snow. More than likely, the engineer and fireman are dead by now.

"Oh, my God! You mean we are trapped here?" Millie Daniels cried.

"Don't listen to a word this man says," Daniels prompted. "Can't you see he is merely trying to justify his escape? I don't believe we are trapped."

"Then why aren't we moving?" Purvis asked.

"I don't know. You'll have to ask the engineer why he stopped," Daniels answered.

Purvis stepped out of the car onto the vestibule, then leaned out so he could look toward the front. When he came back into the car, there was a look of shock on his face.

"It's too dark to tell, but I think Shardeen is right. It sort of looks like the whole front of the train is under snow."

"Oh! Then we *are* trapped!" Millie moaned.

"I wouldn't worry about it so much. I'm sure they will send another train up to get us," Senator Daniels informed her.

At that moment the porter came into the car, the expression on his face reflecting his concern.

"Porter, this man tells us that the front of the train is buried under an avalanche of snow," Daniels barked. "Is he correct?"

"Yes, sir, he is. And it's worse than that," the porter answered.

"What do you mean it is worse than that? How can it be worse?"

"This wasn't no accident," the porter said. "And the men that caused it are up in the dinin' car right now. They've taken it over."

"So they've taken over a car. What good is it going to do them if the train can't move?" Daniels asked pointedly.

"Well sir, that's where all the food is," the porter said.

"If they've got the dining car that means we are

likely to get awful hungry before this is over," Luke added.

"What's your name, porter?" Matt asked.

"My name is Julius, sir. Julius Kerry."

"Julius, do you know where the conductor is?"

"Yes, sir, he's in the car just ahead. His name is Mr. Bailey."

"Would you please tell Mr. Bailey to come back here?"

"I'm just the porter, sir," Julius replied. "I can't tell the conductor anything. I can ask, but that don't mean he'll come back here."

Daniels spoke quickly. "Tell him Senator Daniels has requested his presence. Do you understand that? Senator Daniels wants to speak with him."

"Yes, sir, I can do that." Julius left the car, then returned a moment later with the conductor.

Bailey approached Daniels. "Senator, Julius said that you wished to speak with me,"

"Mr. Bailey," Daniels jumped right in with his complaints. "I want you to know that I will hold the Denver and Pacific, and you, personally responsible should I be unable to fulfill my speaking engagement. Furthermore, I will also hold you responsible for any harm that may befall my family."

"I'm glad to see the welfare of your family is almost equal in concern to your speaking engagement," Matt said dryly.

"Of course it is," Senator Daniels answered, not perceiving the sarcasm.

"Is that why I was summoned back here?" Bailey questioned.

"It is indeed."

"Senator, I assure you, what happened here was entirely beyond our control, and certainly beyond my control."

"Really? Are you telling me you had no idea the pass could be blocked in with snow?"

"The latest telegraph information we had indicated the pass was clear," the conductor replied.

"Mr. Bailey, I'm glad you came back, because I would like to speak with you as well," Matt interrupted. "But I have no intention of making any accusations." He glared at Senator Daniels.

"Thank you, sir. What can I do for you?"

"It is our understanding that the engine is completely buried under a lot of snow. And that armed men have freed the prisoner Santelli and are now occupying the dining car."

"I'm afraid that is true, sir."

"How many are on this train?" Matt asked.

"When the train left Buena Vista we had forty people on board, counting the crew," the conductor said. "That is also counting the sheriff and his two prisoners. But the sheriff is dead, and I fear that the engineer and fireman are also dead. I don't know about Fred, Troy, and Pete."

"Who are they?"

"The three who work in the dining car. I haven't heard from any of them since the train stopped, and I am afraid they may be dead as well."

"That leaves thirty-seven people still aboard, but even if the dining car porters are still alive, no doubt they are being held by Santelli and the others so we may as well discount them. We must subtract the five bad guys, which leaves twenty-nine of us."

"That makes it twenty-nine to five," Daniels said, changing his tune. "We ought to prevail."

"Are you traveling with a gun, Senator?" Matt asked.

"A gun? No, of course not. What makes you think I would be traveling with a gun?" Daniels looked at Matt, perplexed.

"You can be sure all five of the men who took this train will have guns," Matt said. "That tilts the odds in their favor."

"Yes, if you put it like that, I suppose I can see what you mean." Once again, Daniels back-pedaled.

Matt took a count of the passengers in his car, all seven of them. In addition, the conductor and the porter Julius had come into the car. "There are nine in here, leaving twenty more in the other three cars. Mr. Bailey, do you know how many of the remaining passengers are men and how many are women?"

"We have three more woman passengers," Bailey said. "There are also six more children—four girls, the oldest about eleven and two boys, both about nine. The youngest child is about five."

Chapter Seventeen

Even as Matt and the others were discussing the situation, five of the remaining male passengers were huddled in the first passenger car, making plans of their own. Leading the discussion was Paul Clark, a deputy city marshal from Red Cliff. "I know these kind of men. I deal with them all the time. Basically they are cowards and get their way by bluffing. If we go into the dining car armed, like as not they won't even put up a fight. And if they do, we'll have the advantage of surprise."

"You can count on me," Dennis Dace said. "I was a sergeant in the army. I've fought Indians from Wyoming to the Dakotas."

"I'm in." Patterson was a teamster from Denver.

The other two men also agreed to be a part of the team. All five pulled their guns and checked the loads.

Clark looked back over the car at the other passengers, who were looking on with obvious anxiousness.

"You folks. I think you'd best go back to the next car. You'll be in less danger back there."

"What are you going to do?" one of the passengers asked.

"What's it look like we're goin' to do? We're going to take back the dining car. Unless you folks are ready to go hungry."

"There are at least four of them in there."

"And there are five of us," Clark replied. "Now, go on back into the next car. I wouldn't want any of you hurt when the shootin' starts."

Quickly, the passengers left the car.

Clark and Dace led the other three men out onto the vestibule between the passenger car and the dining car. Signaling them to stay low, Clark raised up to look in through the door window. The car was well lit inside, and he could see the four armed men sitting at one of the tables drinking coffee. The three dining car workers, easily identified because they were wearing white uniforms, were sitting at a table between the armed men and the front of the train, effectively being held prisoners. Because the front of the train was under snow, there was nowhere for them to go.

Inside the dining car, Santelli spoke quietly. "Boys, I think we are about to have a few visitors."

"What are you talking about?" Compton muttered.

"I just saw someone peek in through the window, then he ducked his head back down. I wouldn't be surprised if there weren't four or five men out there about to rush us. You'd better get ready."

Unaware he'd been seen, Clark turned to the other men with him. "All right. They are all sitting at a table at the other end of the car. None of them will be expecting us, so that gives us the advantage. Are you ready?"

"We're ready," Dace insisted. The other three men nodded, but said nothing.

"Let's go!" Clark shouted. Pushing the door open, he led the rush into the dining car.

"Here they come!" Santelli shouted, alerting the other three gunmen, and all four turned their guns toward the men coming through the doorway.

The attackers could only come through the door one at a time. Before they could even bring their guns to bear, Santelli and his men were shooting.

Clark went down first, then Patterson, then Dace. The last two men, who hadn't even made it into the car, withdrew quickly when they realized the attack had failed. One of them was nursing a wounded arm.

Compton and Morris started after them, but Santelli called them back. "Let 'em go! They can't do anything."

Outside they heard another rumbling sound.

"What's that?" Kelly called out in fright.

They felt the train shake as snow came down on

the dining car, but it stopped rather quickly, not covering the car completely.

"We'd better be careful about any more shooting," Santelli said. "I think that's what's causing all the snow to come down."

"Tell me, Santelli, how are we going to get out of here?" Kelly asked.

"What do you mean?"

"We was supposed to disconnect the engine from the rest of the train and take it on down the other side of the pass. We sure can't do that now, can we? I mean what with the engine under all that snow."

"We're all right here. We'll just wait it out."

"How are we goin' to do that?"

"Easy." Santelli made a waving motion with his hand, then smiled. "We've got food. They don't."

When Kelly realized what Santelli was saying, the expression on his face changed from one of concern to a broad smile. "Yeah. Yeah, that's right. We do have food, don't we?"

"But how long will it last?" Morris asked, a bit concerned.

"Quite a while, I expect. You know there is enough food to feed thirty or more people, and they always pack a bit extra. But there's only four of us that will be eatin' it. Yes, sir, we are in fine shape."

"What about the three men we just killed?" Kelly asked.

"What about them?" Santelli replied.

"I don't care to stay in this car with three dead men."

"That's no problem. Just push 'em off. The cold won't bother 'em none," Santelli added with an evil chuckle.

Matt learned of the aborted attack from one of the participants, a man named Turner. He had made his way to the last car.

"There was three of us that got killed." Turner had been shot in his left arm and was being attended to by Jenny, who had tied a bandage around the entry and exit wounds of the bullet. "Clark, he was the first one to go down. He was the one that talked the rest of us into doin' it. Then Dace went down, and after him, Patterson got kilt. Me 'n Simpson was still out on the vestibule, hadn't even made it into the dining car yet, but when them other three got shot, well, we turned and run off."

"Was Simpson hit?" Matt asked.

"No. He was just scared is all." Turner chuckled. "I was, too, to tell the truth."

"Well, there is certainly no need for shame," Senator Daniels said rather pompously. "To try and rescue the rest of us was a noble and brave thing."

"It might have been noble and brave, but it wasn't very smart." Matt let out a sigh.

"What do you mean it wasn't very smart?" Senator Daniels asked all in a huff. "What is your proposal? That we just sit here and do nothing while we starve to death?"

"I propose that, as much as possible, we do not shoot a gun nor incite them into shooting one. Any more shooting and the entire train could be buried under hundreds of feet of snow."

"Heavens!" Millie exclaimed. "We certainly don't want that!"

"Well, just what do you propose that we do?" Senator Daniels asked again.

"I think we should just sit tight. When the train doesn't reach the station in Big Rock, the station agent will telegraph back to Buena Vista, and they'll send another train after us."

"Yes"—Senator Daniels cheered up a bit—"I suppose that is true, isn't it? Unless . . ."

"Unless what?" Millie asked.

"Well, if the pass is buried under hundreds of feet of snow, the telegraph poles will be as well. They won't be able to get a telegram through. How will anyone know of our plight?"

"That's not a problem," the conductor said.

"What do you mean, it isn't a problem?" Once again Senator Daniels questioned what had just been said.

"We are used to lines being down for one reason or another," Bailey explained. "If they can't send a telegram directly through the pass to Buena Vista, they will send it where the wires are up. The telegram will be sent from station to station, going all the way around the pass, perhaps even as far as New York and back."

"To New York?" Millie repeated. "Oh, my, if it has to go that far it will take so long they'll never know about us."

Bailey chuckled. "How long do you think it takes to get a telegram signal to New York?"

"I don't know."

"As fast as you can blink an eye."

"He's right, Mrs. Douglas. It doesn't make any difference how far away it is, the telegraph signal gets there instantly. Why, a telegram can come all the way from London to New York, then by telegraph wire across the United States to San Francisco. It is so fast a message from London can reach San Francisco before it was even sent from London."

"What?" Millie gasped.

Luke smiled. "Well, maybe I am joking with you just a little. But you needn't worry if the telegraph has to go to other places before it reaches Buena Vista. Believe me, that won't slow it down."

Millie smiled. "Well then, we have nothing to worry about, do we?"

"Nothing at all, my dear," Senator Daniels said, putting on a brave front for his wife and daughter.

Up at the front of the train, the engine had withstood the avalanche. Don and Beans sat unharmed in the engine cab within what amounted to an air bubble. They'd been stuck there for several hours. Realizing they were beginning to run out of air, they were trying to decide their best course of action.

"You know what? I've got a shovel," Beans said. "There's no need to be trapped here like this. We can shovel our way out of here."

"Good idea," Don agreed.

Beans stepped to the edge of the steel plate between the tender and the engine and began shoveling. Within fifteen minutes his shovel hit something and he stopped. "I'll be damned."

"What is it?" Don stood and called out.

"It's a body. I think it's the fella that tried to stop us."

"He did more than try. He did stop us . . . but I don't think this was quite what he had in mind."

CHAPTER EIGHTEEN

Sugarloaf Ranch—December 20

When Smoke woke up he got out of bed and looked through the window. "Woowee."

"What is it?" Sally asked groggily.

"We had some kind of snow last night. I'll bet we had at least twelve inches."

"Um, I'll bet it's pretty."

Smoke raised the window then scooped up a little snow from the windowsill. "You want to see how pretty it is?" He dropped the snow onto Sally's head.

"Smoke! Have you gone crazy?" Sally shouted, though her shout was ameliorated with laughter.

"Poor Duff, he must think we are having a big fight in here," Smoke said.

"We are."

"Then I think the least you could do is get up and see us off this morning."

"Ahh. That was the whole idea of dropping the snow on my head, wasn't it?"

"You don't have to fix breakfast. We'll get something in town. Maybe just some coffee and warm up a couple of the bear claws."

Sally got out of bed and dressed, and soon the house was permeated by the rich aroma of coffee and warm pastries. Sally joined the men at the table. "How are you going into town? With this snow, I don't think a buckboard would be a good idea."

"I was thinking we might hook up the sleigh," Smoke said.

"Yes," Duff agreed. "That's a good idea."

Warmed and full of coffee and bear claws, it took only a few minutes to get the horses in harness and attached to the sleigh. Then, wrapped in buffalo robes, and taking an extra robe for Matt when they met him, the two men started into town.

The horses quickly found their footing, and the runners of the sleigh made a swishing sound as they slid quickly and easily through the snow. Reaching the depot a little before six o'clock, Smoke and Duff went inside to warm themselves as they waited for the train.

"Smoke, are you here to catch the train?" Phil Wilson, the station agent asked.

"Hi, Phil. No, I'm here to meet a friend who is going to spend Christmas with Sally and me." Smoke introduced Duff.

"I hope it gets through."

"Why do you say that? Have you heard something?"

"No, I haven't heard anything. It's just that, if it snowed so hard here, what must it have done in the pass?"

"Why don't you send a telegram to Buena Vista and see if they have anything to report?"

"I was going to wait until six-thirty, and if the train didn't arrive, contact them then. But there's really no sense in waiting, is there?"

Smoke and Duff followed Phil back to the corner where the telegrapher had his office.

"Johnny, contact Buena Vista for me, would you? See if they have any information on the train."

Johnny nodded, then reached out to the telegraph key. He clicked out the code for BV, or Buena Vista. He tried it several times, then looked up at the men gathered anxiously around his desk.

"I'm not getting a response. Their line must be out."

"Can you go around?"

"Yes. I can go south to Del Norte, and they can go through Pueblo. Pueblo should be able to reach Buena Vista."

Johnny keyed the instrument again, then it was answered with a series of clacks. Smiling, Johnny sent his message. "It'll take a moment for them to forward the message on," he said, looking up from the telegraph key. "I made some coffee if you fellas would like some."

They were drinking coffee and talking when, a

few minutes later, the telegraph instrument started clacking.

Johnny held up his finger, then hurried to the key to respond. After that, the instrument emitted a long series of clicks while Johnny listened and recorded. When it was finished, he read the message to the others. "The train left the station at Buena Vista on time last night. It has not returned to the station, and we have no further word."

"How do you interpret that, Phil?" Smoke asked.

"If it didn't return, then I think it is probably still en route. Even if the snow didn't close the pass, there is no doubt it would slow it down quite a bit. I suspect they are still on the way, just that it is coming very, very slow. I wouldn't be surprised if it didn't get here until sometime around noon, or maybe even later than that."

"All right. We'll wait for it," Smoke said.

"Where will you be if I get any further word?" Phil asked.

"We'll be in Longmont's Saloon." Smoke turned at the door. "Oh, Phil, is it all right if I leave the team and sleigh here for a while?"

"Certainly it's all right," Phil replied. "Tell Louis I said hello."

"Will do."

Smoke and Duff started toward Longmont's saloon, which was four blocks away. They passed several business establishments where the owners or employees were out front, shoveling snow off the boardwalk. As a result, less than half of their walk was actually through the snow. One large, lumbering wagon pulled by four mules was the only traffic on the street. The snow was so high it was an impediment to the wagon's forward progress.

Longmont's was on the opposite side of the road, so Smoke and Duff had to make their way through the knee-deep snow, too. Once they gained the walk in front of the saloon, they stomped their feet on the shoveled boardwalk to get rid of the snow clinging to their boots and the lower part of their trousers. When they had sufficiently divested themselves of the snow, Smoke pushed on the solid doors that had replaced the batwings to keep the cold out and they went inside.

Longmont's was one of the nicest establishments of its kind. The place would have been at home in San Francisco, St. Louis, or New York. It had a long, polished mahogany bar, with a brass foot rail that Louis kept shining brightly. A cut-glass mirror hung behind the bar, and the artwork was truly art, not the garish nudes so prominent in saloons throughout the West. Longmont's collection included originals by Winslow Homer, George Catlin, and Thomas Moran.

Louis Longmont was in the bar alone, sitting at his usual table in a corner. He was a lean, hawk-faced man, with strong, slender hands, long fingers, and carefully manicured nails. He had jet-black hair and a black pencil-thin mustache. He always wore fine suits, white shirts, and the ubiquitous ascot. He wore low-heeled boots, and a nickel-plated pistol with ivory handles hung low in a tied-down holster on his right side. If anyone thought the gun was an affectation, he would be foolish to call him on it. Louis was snake-quick and a feared, deadly gun hand when pushed.

He had bought the saloon with winnings at poker, and could make a deck of cards do almost anything, but had never cheated at cards. Possessing a phenomenal memory, he could tell you the odds of filling any type of poker hand, and was an expert at the technique of card counting.

"Smoke, good morning," Louis called. "Ah, I see you brought Duff with you. What are you doing here so early? Not that I'm not pleased to see you, just a little surprised, is all. Especially on a day like today."

"We're meeting the Red Cliff Special."

"Really? You mean even with all the snow we had last night, there will still be a morning train?"

"Yes, well, that is the question, isn't it? We were just over at the depot and as far as we know, it is still on the way."

"My cook's on duty, if you'd like some breakfast," Louis suggested.

"Well, yeah, that's why we came in here. You didn't think we were going to start drinking this early, did you?" Smoke teased.

"I thought you came in here out of genuine friendship, just to visit me," Louis said, feigning hurt feelings.

Smoke laughed. "Did the cook make any biscuits this morning?"

"Of course she did. Can you really have breakfast without biscuits?"

As Smoke and Duff waited for their breakfast, they carried on a conversation with Louis Longmont.

Four blocks down the street, Bob Ward went into the depot, approached the stove, and stood there for a moment, warming himself.

"Have you come to catch the train, sir?" Phil asked.

Ward stared at him, but didn't answer.

"Because the train hasn't arrived, and may not arrive."

"Why not?"

"The mountain pass is blocked with snow. It may be that the train can't get through."

"It *may be* that it can't? Or it can't?"

"I don't know. It might get here, but if it does, it will be very late."

Ward nodded, then walked back outside and mounted his horse. He rode down to the far end of the street, to an area known as the red light district, where the seedier saloons were, and where women were available for a price. He dismounted in front of Hannah's—a step above the cribs and the girls in the saloons, it made no secret of being a brothel—and went inside. "Where the hell are they?" he asked a middle-aged woman sitting behind a counter.

"I beg your pardon?"

"The women. Where are they? Isn't this a whore-house?"

"That's such a harsh word." The woman smiled. "I much prefer to say that we have ladies who will cater to your pleasure."

"Well?"

"Well, what?"

"The whores. Where are they?"

"Oh, I suspect most of them are sleeping. They do work nights, you know. And it is so cold and awful outside I'm quite sure nobody was expecting a client on a day like this."

"I'm a client. So, roust one of 'em up."

"Very well, sir. Which one?"

"Which one? How the hell do I know which one? I ain't never been here before. It don't make no never mind to me. Just choose one. Choose the one you like the best."

Hannah laughed a deep, throaty laugh. "Well, now, honey, I like men, not women . . . so I don't have a favorite. But they are all fine-looking ladies. I don't think you will be disappointed no matter who I select. Come to think of it, I think I saw Midge up a few minutes ago. Just a moment, and I'll find her for you."

On board the Red Cliff Special

Matt slept fitfully during the remainder of the cold night, but had fallen into a more sound sleep just before dawn. The sun streaming in through the window awakened him and he sat up, rubbed his eyes, and looked around the car.

Luke Shardeen and Jenny McCoy were on the front seat, asleep and cuddled together for warmth. Becky was asleep under Matt's coat, her head on her mother's lap. Mrs. Daniels was asleep with her head leaning against the window. Senator Daniels was snoring in the facing seat across from them.

Since stopping in the middle of the night, it was the first opportunity Matt had to actually see anything out the window. The snow had stopped, but it was piled up on the side of the train as high as the bottom of the windows.

He decided to see for himself how badly the front of the train was snowed in. Standing up, he stretched, then opened the back door, climbed up to the top, and looked forward. What he saw wasn't very reassuring. The front end of the train disappeared into a huge mountain of snow. They were fortunate the entire train had not been buried under the avalanche. Taking in everything around him, he realized they were totally locked in. Even if the engine had been clear, they could not go forward. And the snow was such that they could not go back down the track, either. That meant no rescue train would be able to come for them.

They were trapped at the top of the pass . . . under extraordinary circumstances.

It grew too cold for Matt to stay outside any longer. Once he was back inside the car, he saw that the coal supply for the heating stove was running low and realized that they would soon be facing a second danger. In addition to not having control of the food on board, they would soon run out of coal for the two stoves. When that happened, the temperature in the car would quickly drop below freezing.

That's just great, Matt thought. *It's not enough that we have no food; we are also facing a situation where we have no heat.* Matt picked up the half-full coal scuttle sitting beside the stove at the rear of the car and carried it up to the front where he set it beside the other scuttle.

"What are you doing?" Purvis asked.

"If we try and keep both stoves going, we are going to run out of coal in no time. I think it might be best if we just keep a fire going in one."

"Yeah," Purvis said. "I see what you mean."

The eight other people in the car moved to the front.

"Do you think they will send someone after us?" Millie Daniels asked after settling Becky back in her lap.

"I'm sure they will." Bailey took out his pocket watch, opened it, and examined it. "We were due in Big Rock over an hour ago. When they learn back in Pueblo that we haven't made it into Big Rock yet, why, they'll send a relief train after us."

Matt knew no train could get through, but didn't say anything, figuring it would be best if they thought help was coming.

CHAPTER NINETEEN

Big Rock

When Smoke and Duff returned to the depot, Phil was talking to a customer, so Smoke waited for the conversation to finish.

But seeing him, Phil called out. "Hello, Smoke. I'm afraid there is still no word from the train."

"No word means they haven't gone back to Buena Vista, doesn't it?"

"Yes. If the train had gone back, we would have been informed by now."

"So what you are saying is that the train is still up there, possibly trapped in the pass so it can go neither forward nor backward."

"That's a possibility." Phil nodded his head.

"That's not good. If they are up there too long, they'll run out of food, won't they?"

"I wouldn't worry too much about anything like that happening. A couple winters ago we had a train get snowed in up on top of the pass, and it was a week late getting here," Phil said.

"A week without food?"

"It wasn't anything all that significant. These trains carry enough food with them so that, by rationing, they could survive for two weeks or longer. I've no doubt, within two weeks enough snow will melt and the train will be able to proceed, or at worst be relieved by a rescue train."

"All right, Phil, you've been through this before," Smoke said. "I guess the best thing Duff and I can do now, is go back to the ranch and wait it out."

"You may as well," Phil agreed.

Smoke walked over to the telegraph office, where Eddie sat in the corner, reading. "Eddie, when the train comes in, I want you to meet a man named Matt Jensen. Tell him to wait here for me, and I'll come get him." Smoke gave the boy a five-dollar bill. "Then, I want you to come tell me that he is here."

"Yes, sir, Mr. Jensen!" Eddie smiled broadly as he took the equivalent of a week's pay.

Down the street, Hannah brought one of her girls into the parlor. The girl was in her early twenties, but looked younger. It was early in the day and she had not yet painted her face and lips, nor had she donned the garish costume of her profession. The dissipation of the trade had not yet worked its evils on her, and she looked like any young woman you might see on the street or in a shop.

Ironically, Ward found that much more appealing than if she was in full garb. It made her look innocent, and he was aroused by the idea of taking a young girl's innocence. "How much?"

"It will be three dollars, sir," Hannah said.

"Three dollars?" Ward replied. "What do you mean? There ain't a place in Colorado where you can't get a whore for two dollars."

"This isn't just anywhere in Colorado. This is Hannah's," the owner said proudly. "If you want one of my ladies, it is going to cost you three dollars. If you think I am charging you too much, you might try one of the saloons."

Ward ran his hand through his thin, blond hair and looked at the girl. She had dark hair and large, brown eyes.

"How long can I stay?"

"You can stay all day if you want. At least, until we get busy tonight."

"Yeah? Well if I leave to go get somethin' to eat, can I come back?"

Hannah smiled at him. "Why would you have to leave to get something to eat? We have a kitchen."

Ward chuckled. "So, I can stay here all day and eat here besides? All for three dollars?"

"I told you, there is no other place in Colorado like Hannah's."

Ward took out three dollars, handing the bills to Hannah. "You've got yourself a deal."

"This way," the girl said, turning and walking away from him.

Returning to the sleigh, Smoke and Duff drove back to the ranch house. When they arrived at the house they were met by a smiling Sally, though the smile faded when she saw that Matt wasn't with them.

"The train never made it to Big Rock," Smoke explained. "Or, perhaps I should say the train hasn't arrived *yet.*"

"What happened to it?"

"It's probably hung up in the pass somewhere, blocked by snow . . . from coming through and maybe even from going back."

"Oh, my, Smoke! Do you mean those people are trapped up there?"

"It's not as bad as all that. Phil says this has happened before, and the train probably has enough food for them to survive."

"Probably? That doesn't sound all that good."

"We may be imagining the worst. The train may yet get here today. If it does, Eddie will come tell us."

"Oh, I certainly hope it gets here before Christmas." Sally looked out the window at the depth of snow.

"We have a few days yet. We'll just wait and see."

On board the Red Cliff Special

By late afternoon everyone was beginning to get hungry. One of the dining car porters came hustling into the rear car with a message for the conductor.

"Troy!" Bailey called out. "I thought you were trapped in the dining car!"

"Yes, sir, I was. But the men with guns let me go so I could bring a message."

"What is the message?"

"Don't be mad if I say a bad word in front of the ladies, but it's the message they told me to say."

"Go ahead," Matt said. "We know it's not your words."

"Yes, sir." Troy nodded and took a deep breath. "Here is the message. The men with guns say, send them the whore, and they'll let the rest of the folks on the train have some food."

"What?" Luke shouted angrily.

Troy drew back. "I tol', you, sir, that's not my words. That's the words of the men with guns."

"And that's what they said?" Bailey asked. "Send them the whore and they'll give food to the rest of the passengers?"

"Yes, sir, that's what they said all right."

"Just who is the whore they would be talking about?" Bailey asked.

"I don' know, Mr. Bailey. All I know is what they said."

"We all know who the whore is." Daniels looked directly at Jenny.

"Jarred!" Millie scolded.

"I'm just saying what everyone else knows," the

senator insisted. "They're talking about you, miss." He pointed to Jenny.

She was sitting in a seat with Luke. He put his arm around her, drawing her close to him.

"It's up to you now," Senator Daniels continued. "You could do something good with your life. If you go to them, we'll all get to eat."

"No," Jenny said in a quiet, frightened voice.

"What do you mean, *no*?" Daniels shouted. "Good Lord, woman, it's what you do! It's who you are! Instead of doing it for money for yourself, do it for others. For my wife and my little girl. It can't have escaped your notice that my daughter is sick. Perhaps all she needs is a little food. And you can make that possible. Is that asking too much? It isn't as if you are the total innocent in such things."

"You don't understand." Once more, Jenny tried to explain. "You have the wrong idea about me. I'm *not* a prostitute and I've *never been* a prostitute."

"Don't lie to us, woman. We all saw that sign back at the depot," Senator Daniels said sharply. He pointed toward the front of the train. "I am a sitting state senator, which makes me an officer of the state government. And as an officer of the state government, I am ordering you to go to those men . . . for the good of everyone on the train."

"I won't do it."

"Oh, yes, you will." The senator moved toward her.

Luke stood up and stepped in between Daniels and Jenny. "If you so much as touch her, I'll throw you off this train," Luke said in a cold, intense voice.

"What?" Daniels barked. "You, a jailbird, are threatening a state senator?"

"It's not a threat, Senator," Luke said calmly. "It's a promise."

"You, conductor!" Daniels looked toward Bailey. "You are in charge of this train. What are you going to do about this?"

Bailey looked at Luke, then back at Daniels. "Senator, I clearly am not in charge of this train at the moment. It has been taken over by armed brigands."

"What?" Daniels sputtered. He pointed at Bailey. "The Denver and Pacific is going to hear about this. We should never have left the station in the first place. Now we are trapped in the mountains for who knows how long, and armed men, which you allowed to board this train, have taken us all hostage. And you stand by and let this man threaten me, but do nothing about it. Yes, sir, the Denver and Pacific will most assuredly hear about this."

"Jarred, you are frightening Becky." Millie tugged on the senator's arm. "Please, calm down."

"How can I calm down when our very lives are at stake? And this . . . *harlot* has the means to save us all."

Matt had heard enough. "Senator, even if the girl did go to the dining car, do you think they would let her live?"

"I don't know," Senator Daniels ranted. "But that's the chance you take when you become a prostitute."

"I told you, I am not a prostitute!" Jenny screamed.

"Then what are you doing on this train, can

you tell me that? You were run out of town, were you not?"

Jenny didn't answer.

"I thought so."

The senator made a move toward her, but Luke stepped between them again, and with a vicious backhand blow, sent the senator reeling back. The blow cut the senator's lip and it began to bleed.

Daniels pulled a handkerchief from his pocket and held it over his lip, glaring at Luke. "Young man, you have just made a huge mistake. Whatever your sentence is, you have just added fifteen years to it for striking a government official."

"Oh, Luke!" Jenny said anxiously.

Luke smiled. "Well, Senator, if I'm going to get fifteen years just for hitting you one time, I might as well make it worth my while. If you don't go back to your seat, sit down, and shut up, I'll beat you to within an inch of your life."

"What?" The word was filled with fear.

"Jarred, for heaven's sake, get back over here and sit down," Millie ordered.

Senator Daniels pulled his handkerchief away from his lip, looked at the blood, then glared once more at Luke. He neither made a move toward Luke and Jenny, nor did he speak again. Instead he acquiesced to his wife's demand and returned to his seat.

Matt watched the drama play out before him, but made no move to interject himself into the situation when it was obvious Luke had things well in hand. When he saw Senator Daniels return to his seat, and Luke and Jenny sit back down, he knew it was over.

"Troy," Bailey said, "you can go back and tell the gentlemen who have taken this train that the young lady will not be joining them."

"Yes, sir," Troy answered. "That's exactly what I would tell them if I was goin' back to the diner car." He shook his head. "But I ain't goin' back."

"What do you mean you aren't going back?" Bailey asked. "Good Lord, man, don't you understand the situation? We have no food here. All the food is in the diner. At least you would get to eat."

"No sir, it wouldn't do me no good to go back. The men with the guns, they had themselves a fine breakfast and a fine lunch, but me 'n Fred 'n Pete, we didn't have nothin' to eat at all. And if it's all the same to you, I won't be goin' back."

"All right, you can stay here in the car with us," Bailey conceded.

"Mr. Bailey, you may have noticed that he and the porter are colored," Senator Daniels felt the need to point out.

Bailey made an exaggerated point of looking at Julius and Troy. Then he hit his forehead with the palm of his hand. "By golly, Senator, now that I look at them, I believe you are right. They *are* colored."

Matt and Luke laughed out loud.

"Are you ridiculing me?" Daniels snapped.

"No, Senator, you are ridiculing yourself. Of

course I know they are colored. What is your point?" Bailey frowned.

"My point is, they can't stay here in the car with us."

"Just where do you think the porters stay when the train is under way?"

"I don't know. I never see them until I need something done, and then they just sort of appear. I'm just saying it doesn't seem right that they are in the same car with us. But I suppose, if they stay to the back of the car, it would be all right."

"The back of the car is getting pretty cold," Matt said. "With only one stove going, just the front half of the car will be heated. These two men will stay in the front of the car with us."

Senator Daniels glared at Matt, then he sat back down.

Julius stood up then. "Thank you, Mr. Bailey, and thank you, sir, for speakin' up for us."

"It's only common decency," Matt replied. "No thanks are needed."

Chapter Twenty

"We ain't gettin' nowhere," Beans said, sitting down on the floor of the engine, breathing heavily. His body gleamed gold from the single kerosene lamp illuminating the inside of the cab, as well as from the exertion of digging through the snow. "We've dug a tunnel forty feet long or longer, and all I see is snow and more snow. Besides, workin' this hard we're just breathin' harder and usin' up more air."

"We don't have any choice." Don frowned. "We have to keep digging, no matter how far we have to go. If we don't get from under all this snow, we will eventually run out of air."

"You're right there. But I tell you true, I don't see how we are going to do it."

Don took the shovel for his turn at digging. Then he turned back toward Beans with a smile on his face. "Whoa, I just thought of something. We're digging in the wrong direction!" He pointed down. "We need to dig down to the ground."

"Why? What good would that do us? That would just put us under more snow, wouldn't it?"

"Not if we get under the train. We'll dig down to the ground, then crawl under the train all the way to the back."

"What if the whole train is under snow?" Beans questioned.

"We'll just pray that it isn't."

For most of the day, one stove had kept the front part of the car bearable, if not comfortable. But by nightfall it became much colder in the car, so cold that sheets of ice covered the inside of the windows. The situation was made worse by having to use as little coal as possible, in order to save fuel.

"The irony," Bailey pointed out, "is that there is enough fuel in the tender to keep every stove on the train going until summer."

"You can't get to it," Troy said, shaking his head. "The engine, tender, and the baggage car are all under a pile of snow as high as a mountain."

"We've got to do something, or it's going to get very, very cold in here."

Suddenly the back door opened and two men blew in. As Luke had been earlier, they were covered with snow.

"Don! Beans!" Bailey shouted excitedly. He went to the two men and embraced them happily.

"Who are these people?" Senator Daniels demanded.

"The engineer and the fireman," Troy explained. "Praise be the Lord, they ain't dead!"

Moving quickly to the stove, Don told the others about the man who had attempted to stop the train and how shooting the gun had brought the avalanche down. Matt reported the current predicament, how four armed men were holding the entire train hostage by occupying the dining car and commandeering the only food.

"Who are these men anyway?" Don asked. "Why did they stop the train?"

Luke explained it had all been planned as a means to free Michael Santelli.

"But it backfired on them," Bailey added.

"Actually, it backfired on all of us." Luke muttered glumly.

Buena Vista

Deckert stroked his chin as he read the telegram from the station agent in Big Rock.

> TRAIN FROM BUENA VISTA NOT ARRIVED STOP
> FOURTEEN HOURS OVERDUE STOP PHIL WILSON
> STOP STATION AGENT BIG ROCK.

"Where do you think the train is?" Ticket Agent Garrison asked.

"Like as not it's stranded at the top of the pass."

"If they can't get through goin' forward, why don't they come back here and wait it out?"

"I don't know. Maybe they can't go either way." Deckert drummed his fingers on the desk.

"So, what are we going to do?"

"If we haven't heard anything by tomorrow morning, we'll send a relief train up after them."

"Good idea," Garrison said.

"I shouldn't have let them go."

"It's not your fault, Mr. Deckert. The conductor makes the decision as to whether or not to go . . . doesn't he?"

"Yes, and Mr. Bailey seemed hell-bent to go."

"Then it's not your fault."

"Yeah, that's what I keep telling myself."

"What about the people here in town? People who have relatives and such on the train?" Garrison asked. "When are you going to tell them?"

"I reckon I'll tell anyone who comes to ask about it. And no doubt it'll be in the newspaper soon enough."

"I'm sure glad I'm not up there." Garrison shook his head. "They might be there all the way through Christmas. I'd sure hate to spend Christmas stuck on the top of the pass."

"Ah, it won't be all that bad," Deckert pointed out. "They'll be warm enough, I reckon. I mean if they had to, there's enough coal in the tender to keep all the heating stoves going until next summer. And food enough for a week or two."

On board the train

Luke and Jenny were sitting together, as much for warmth as anything else. Suddenly, Luke stood up. "I'll be right back. I'm going into the next car for a moment."

"Luke, must you? What if those men are there? They tried to kill you, remember?"

"You heard the porter. They're in the diner. I'm sure they haven't come back into the train. When I jumped from the train, I left my coat up there. I'm going after it."

"All right, but please be careful."

"I will."

Luke glanced over toward Matt. He was sitting in a seat with his arms folded, staring at the stove as if by sheer willpower he could cause it to generate more heat. His coat was still spread over Becky.

Luke squatted down beside him. "I left my coat in the other car. I'm going after it. If Deputy Proxmire's coat is still there, I'll bring it back for you. I warn you, though, it may have some blood on it."

"A little blood won't matter," Matt said. "And thanks, I would appreciate that."

Luke left by the front door, crossed the vestibule, then stepped into the other car. He counted eight people in the car, and didn't see either coat. "Hey. Did any of you see the two coats that were left here?"

"That other fella, the one who was a prisoner with you?"

"You mean Santelli?"

"Yes. He come back and got both of them."

Luke noticed both stoves were still burning. "If I were you, I'd stop feeding this stove and just keep one of them going. That way your fuel will last longer."

"Good idea. What about food? Have you folks got any food back there?"

"None," Luke said.

"If them fellas don't let us have anything from the diner, we're goin' to get powerfully hungry," the passenger said.

Luke smiled and rubbed his stomach. "I'm already hungry."

"Yeah, I am, too."

"Ain't no need in worryin' about food," one of the others said. "We're likely to freeze to death before we starve to death."

Luke returned to the rear car and told Matt the coats were gone. "I'm sorry. It looks as if you and I are going to get pretty cold tonight."

Matt nodded. "I'm afraid so."

Luke returned to his seat beside Jenny, and Matt joined the engineer and the fireman close to the stove, fighting the urge to feed more coal into it.

"You know," Don said. "In a way, I'm almost glad this happened."

"What?" Beans asked, surprised by the comment. "What do you mean, you are glad this happened?"

Don chuckled. "I didn't say I was glad, I said I was *almost* glad."

"Why?"

"Tell me, Beans, when we are up there in the

engine, driving the train, do you ever think about the people we are hauling around the country?"

"Think about them?"

"Yeah, you know, wonder about them."

"I don't know as I have thought about them," Beans said. "Mostly the only thing I think about is keeping the steam up."

"Well, I think about things like that, too, but I'm always wondering about who is back here, and where they are going. Are we taking some soldier boy home to see his mama and daddy for the first time since he left home? Maybe some young woman is going to meet the man who's going to be her husband."

"Or maybe some folks goin' to see their grand-baby for the first time," Beans suggested.

Don smiled. "See, you do wonder about the people we carry."

"I reckon I do. It's just not somethin' I think about very much."

"So, here we are sittin' back here with 'em," Don said. "I've been drivin' a train for over twenty years, and this is the first time I've ever got to actually meet any of them."

"So, what do you think, Mr. Stevenson?" Matt asked. "I mean now that you have met some of the people."

"Some of 'em I like"—Don glanced over toward Senator Daniels—"and some of 'em, I don't like."

"But the little girl is sweet," Beans said. "Bless her heart, I hope she gets better."

"I'm surprised they haven't sent a rescue train after us," Don continued. "Come six o'clock tomorrow morning, we'll be twenty-four-hours overdue."

"Ha! What do you bet Doodle will be the engineer?" Beans asked.

"Oh, yeah, Doodle would love to be the one to come to the rescue. And to tell the truth, I'd love to see him pulling up behind us right now, for all that it'll give him a head bigger 'n a watermelon."

Abner Purvis couldn't sleep. He could hear the conversation going on by the stove, but that wasn't what was keeping him awake.

Purvis had told Matt he was going back home to the family farm just outside Red Cliff. What he hadn't told Matt was that his parents may not even let him back into the house. He had not written to his father to tell him he was coming back, because he was afraid his father would tell him he wasn't welcome.

Purvis had left home two years ago, to the great disappointment of his father, who had wanted and had planned for him to take a greater role in running the farm.

"Abner, someday, this will be yours, and your mother and I will live out the rest of our lives quietly and comfortably," his father had told him.

"If someday the farm is to be mine, how about just giving me enough money to get started on my own somewhere else? You can give my part of the farm to Aaron. He is more suited to it than I am, anyway."

Purvis's father had been very disappointed, but he borrowed a thousand dollars against the farm and gave it to Abner to go out into the world and make his mark.

Purvis invested the entire one thousand dollars in a gold mine claim, a claim that proved to be worthless. When all of his money was gone, he went through a series of jobs—mucking out stalls in a livery, emptying spittoons and mopping the floors of saloons, and tending pigs for a butcher.

Not once during the two years he was gone had Purvis ever written to his parents. They had no idea where he was, or if he was still alive. The longer he went without contacting them, the more difficult it became to reach out to them.

It was while he was tending pigs that he came to his senses. He had made a huge mistake in leaving the farm and the future his father had worked so hard to give him. He decided to go back home, confess to his father that he had been a fool, no longer worthy to be called his son, and beg to be allowed to return.

"I know that I have forfeited my right to any inheritance," he would say. "I ask only to be allowed to return and work as one of your hired hands."

Would his father take him back? That was the question keeping Purvis awake.

Chapter Twenty-one

December 21

The night had been long and cold, and Matt welcomed the sun. Bringing a little warmth with it had somewhat brightened his spirits. But it also ushered in another day without food. As Matt pondered the situation, he knew it was least ten more miles to the bottom of the pass and on in to Big Rock. Even if he could get through the mountain of snow, he couldn't attempt it without a coat. If he took his coat away from the little girl, she might die. His thoughts had come full circle, leaving him without a plan to improve the circumstances.

Troy had had a deck of cards in his pocket when he brought Santelli's message to Bailey. He'd started a card game the men, including Senator Daniels, had participated in at one time or another. The card game helped to pass the time. Facing another day with no food, another game was started while Jenny and Millie were engaged in conversation.

"My mother came to America from England. When the ship was halfway across the ocean it started taking on water. Fortunately, an empty cattle steamer was passing close by, and my mother's ship signaled they were in distress."

Jenny smiled. "And the captain of the cattle ship told the *Pomona* to launch the lifeboats and get as many women and children across as they could."

"The *Pomona*! Yes, that was the ship my mother was on! How do you know that?"

"My father was first officer on the *Western Trader*, the cattle ship that encountered the *Pomona* that day. I know the story, but only from my father's side. Please, do tell. I would like to hear the story from the other side."

Millie nodded and continued the story. "After all the women and children crossed, they sent across the older men, then finally the younger men and all the crew. All made it across safely, not one person was lost.

"The next day they could see the ship hanging at a list and within a few hours it went down. When my mother abandoned the *Pomona*, the only thing they let her take was a small handbag with thimble and scissors, a little money, and a few handkerchiefs. That was all she had when she first set foot in this country."

"What a wonderful story," Jenny said. "And what

a wonderful testimony to your mother's courage. You must be very proud of her."

"I am. And you should see her with Becky. Why, my mother thinks the sun rises and sets on this little girl. It would be awful if . . . if . . ." Millie's eyes pooled with tears.

Jenny reached out to take her hand. "I have a feeling Becky is going to be all right."

Wetmore, Colorado

Dewey Ferrell, Sheriff of Bent County, was in Custer County. He wasn't wearing a badge, and he was carrying a hood, ready to cover his face when necessary. Ferrell and Jeb Clayton were at the top of a long grade, waiting for the stagecoach. They could see the coach below them, still some distance away.

"He'll have to stop when he reaches the top of the grade, to give the horses a blow," Ferrell said. "That's when we'll hit them."

"How much money do you think he'll be carryin'?" Clayton asked.

"Judge Briggs said three thousand dollars would be in the strongbox."

Clayton smiled. "This is goin' to be a fine Christmas."

They could hear the driver's whistle and the occasional pop of his whip as the coach lumbered up the long grade.

"How much longer you plannin' on bein' the sheriff?" Clayton asked.

"What do you want to know for? You plannin' on runnin' against me?"

"No, I was just wonderin' is all."

"I got no plans on *not* bein' the sheriff. Things is workin' out just real good for me."

"Yeah." Clayton chuckled. "This has been real good for me, too. Only thing is, we got to be careful about how we spend our money, or folks is goin' to start wonderin' how we can do it on forty dollars a month. Well, forty for you. Thirty for me."

"No problem," Ferrell said. "We just need to go someplace like Denver, maybe even San Francisco, to spend it. That way, nobody will be the wiser."

On board the coach, Silas Cambridge took out a twist of tobacco and took a bite of it. He offered some to his shotgun guard, Jake Nugent.

"Thank you, no. I never took up the habit." Nugent broke down his double-barrel shotgun, checked the loads, then snapped it closed.

"You see somethin'?" Cambridge asked.

"Nothin' in particular. But the horses will be winded when we get to the top of this climb, and if someone is plannin' on hittin' us, that's more 'n likely where it'll be." Nugent set the shotgun down by his feet and pulled out his revolver to check it, too.

Dr. Grant, his wife, and three children were inside

the coach, wrapped up in buffalo robes against the bitter cold of the Colorado winter season. They were going to Yorkville, in Fremont County, to spend Christmas with Mrs. Grant's parents.

"Mama, will Grandma and Grandpa have Christmas presents for us?" Joey asked.

"I expect they will," Mrs. Grant said. "But don't you be asking for anything when we get there."

"I won't. But I wonder what it will be."

"Whatever it is, you will thank them for it."

"Yes, ma'am, I will."

The coach reached the top of the long grade, then it stopped. "Folks," Cambridge called down. "We're goin' to spend a few minutes here so the horses can rest up a bit. If you'd like, you can get out and walk around a bit."

"Mama, I want to go to the bathroom," Joey said.

"All right, as soon as we get out, you can go find a rock or a tree."

The entire family got out of the coach and the driver hopped down to check the harness on his team. Only Nugent stayed where he was, sitting up on the driver's box.

Joey hurried into the trees, then he saw two men tying off their horses. Forgetting the reason he was there, he started toward them to say hello.

"What about the passengers?" one of the men said. "Are we going to rob them, too?"

The other man chuckled. "Why not? As long as

we are robbin' the stage, we may as well get the whole hog."

Turning, Joey ran back to the coach, straight to his father. "Papa! Papa!" he said breathlessly. "There's two men in the woods, and they are going to rob us!"

"Whoa now, Joey," Dr. Grant caught him. "You aren't letting your imagination get away from you, are you?"

"No, Papa! I heard them. They said they were going to rob the stage and the passengers."

Nugent heard Joey and looked down toward the doctor and the others. "Dr. Grant, are you armed?"

"No, sir, I am not."

Nugent pulled his pistol, handed it down, and pointed to an outcropping of stones away from the trees. "Take your family over there behind those rocks and stay down. If anything goes wrong, use the gun."

"I'm not skilled with firearms," Dr. Grant advised.

"You don't have to be skilled. Just point it and pull the trigger. But let's hope you don't have to do that. Now, get over there fast before the robbers come up."

Dr. Grant nodded and shepherded his wife, whose face reflected her fear, and the three children to the relative safety of the rocks.

"Silas," Nugent called quietly from the box.

Cambridge looked up from the harness.

"Get over here on this side. Keep the team between you and the trees."

Cambridge, reading the seriousness in Nugent's voice, didn't waste time asking for clarification. He moved to the other side of the team as two men on horseback stepped out of the trees, their faces covered with hoods, their guns drawn.

"All right!" one called out as they approached the coach. "You know what this is. Put your hands up. Which one of you is the driver?"

"I am," Nugent answered before Cambridge could speak. Both men had their hands raised.

"Ha! Got your shotgun guard tending to your team, huh? Well, I reckon you're the boss and you can do that."

"I reckon so," Nugent replied.

"Call your passengers out."

"We ain't carryin' any passengers."

"What do you mean you aren't carrying any passengers? What kind of stagecoach makes a trip with no passengers?"

"A coach that carries only money and mail," Nugent disclosed.

"Good enough answer. All right. I want you to reach down and bring up the strongbox, then throw it down to us."

"I'll have to put my hands down to get to the box."

"Go ahead."

Nugent lowered his hands, then reached down toward his feet where the double-barrel shotgun lay. "Silas, where'd you put that box?"

"Don't you be giving them that box! Don't you dare give them that box!" Cambridge kept on shouting at the top of his voice, drawing the attention of both armed robbers.

That was exactly what Nugent wanted. The noise covered the cock of the shotgun and when he came up from the floor he fired off one barrel, then the other, and both would-be robbers were blasted out of their saddles.

Nugent jumped down from the driver's box and hurried over to them. "Doc! You'd better come take a look at these two."

"I want to see, too!" Joey shouted, running from behind the rocks.

"Joey! You get back here!" Mrs. Grant called.

The boy skidded to a stop and turned around. "Oh, Mama, why can't I see them? I've never seen anyone who was killed before."

"You just stay here," Mrs. Grant ordered.

Dr. Grant hurried over to the men and bent down to put his fingers on their necks to find the carotid pulse, though he could tell by looking at the massive wounds in their chests it wasn't necessary. When he didn't find a pulse in either, his suspicion was confirmed. "They're both dead."

Cambridge squatted down beside the two men and pulled their hoods off.

"I'll be damned! This is Sheriff Farrell from Bent County!"

"The sheriff? The sheriff was robbin' us?" Nugent sputtered in disbelief.

"Yes. That's sure some surprise, ain't it?"

"Maybe not as big a surprise as you might think," Dr. Grant replied.

"Why, what do you mean?"

"Back in Pueblo, a rancher there by the name of Luke Shardeen shot one of Ferrell's deputies. He made the claim the sheriff and his deputy had tried to rob him. Looks like he was telling the truth."

Chapter Twenty-two

On board the train

As the sun got lower that evening, the temperature in the car dropped again. Matt shivered, wondering how those who had no coat would get through the night. He looked down at the aisle for a second, and his eyes followed it all the way to the back of the car. He smiled. "Luke. I've got an idea."

Luke, who had been sitting with Jenny, came over to him. "I hope it's a good one."

Matt chuckled. "Yeah, so do I." He took out his penknife, opened it, then walked up to the front of the aisle and squatted down. He made a slice across the aisle carpet and pulled up the end.

"Help me pull up this carpet. We can make serapes out of it."

"Yes!" Luke said. "Yes, that *is* a good idea!

Bailey saw Matt and Luke pulling up the carpet. "Here! What are you doing? You can't do that! That carpet belongs to the Denver and Pacific!"

"We'll give it back when we are through with it," Matt said as he and Luke continued to pull up the carpet. When it was fully taken up, he cut it into long sections, then cut a hole in the middle of each section for a head to stick through.

The carpet made four serapes. He put his on first to demonstrate how to use it, then he gave one each to Luke, Julius and Troy. After a bit of good-natured teasing about how they looked, Matt walked over to the seat where the little girl was lying with her head on her mother's lap. "How is Becky doing?"

"Oh, Mr. Jensen," Millie apologized. "I'm so sorry you have to wear that."

"Don't worry about it. It's keeping me warm now. I just hope your daughter doesn't get too cold."

"I think that, with your coat, she is warm enough," Millie said. "In a way, I'm almost thankful she isn't feeling well. She has no appetite, so she isn't suffering from hunger the way the rest of us are."

"I'm sure it won't be too much longer before they send a relief train after us." Matt didn't believe that at all, but he thought it would be better to give her some hope.

"Yes. I'm sure you are right."

Conductor Bailey was also without an overcoat, so he maintained a position nearest the stove. With what heat the stove was putting out, Matt was reasonably sure he would be able to pass the night in relative comfort.

Chapter Twenty-Three

Sugarloaf Ranch

That evening, Smoke, Duff, and Sally sat in the keeping room, drinking coffee, looking out at the snow-covered ground, and basking in the warmth of the fireplace.

"Tell me, Duff, how did you fare during the great die-up?" Smoke asked. The question referred to the winter of 1887–88, when an enormous blizzard resulted in the death of almost half the cattle in the Northwest.

"I've got a natural shelter on my place, and I had enough hay stored, so for the most part I came through it without too much difficulty. But some of the English ranchers didn't fare so well. It completely broke Moreton Frewen. How did you do?"

"I had been through a few killing blizzards before, so I was ready for it as well." Smoke pointed toward the barn. "I've got enough hay laid by now that if this condition lasts, I'll be able to feed my stock."

"That's smart of you." Duff took a swallow of his coffee and was quiet for a moment as he recalled that winter.

"On the day after the storm, I rode out with a neighboring rancher to cut his fences so his cattle could drift on to shelter. We found hundreds of them frozen to death and others whose tails had cracked and broken off like icicles. Och, I don't think I'd ever seen a sadder sight, or heard a more heartrending sound than the moaning of cattle freezing to death. With the ice and snow so deep, they couldn't get to food, so many died of starvation. All we could do was to cut the fences and let any still alive drift, for if they stayed in place, they would have died, too. Later, when the snow was gone, you could ride for miles and not get away from the sickening sight of dead cows."

"Heavens," Sally said with a shiver. "It's nearly Christmas. Can't we talk about something more pleasant? Duff, tell us about Christmas in Scotland."

"Oh 'twas a fine time we had in Scotland. I remember that m' mither used to make a Black Bun cake."

"What is it? Maybe I could make one," Sally said.

"Na, for you have to prepare for it, gather a lot of fruit. The cake is filled with fruit of all kind, almonds, spices, and"—Duff smiled—"being as we are Scottish, it had to have plenty of whisky." He gathered the tips of his fingers, then opened them up. "Sure 'n 'twas quite a delight to eat."

"What other traditions did you have? Other than food," Sally asked.

"We had the *Oidche Choinnle,* which means the Night of Candles," Duff explained. "We put candles in every window to light the way for the Holy Family on Christmas Eve.

"Ah, but there was one custom that's for the rancher," he added.

"You have a Christmas custom just for the rancher?" Smoke asked.

"Aye. 'Tis called the Christmas Bull. A cloud in the shape of a bull crosses the sky early on Christmas morning. If the bull is going east, 'twill be a good year. If it is going west, 'twill be a bad year."

"Christmas morning, we'll have to remember to look for the bull in the sky," Smoke said.

"If we'll even be able to see the sky on Christmas morning," Sally mumbled.

"Aye, that's the question," Duff agreed. "For 'tis been an evil sky for some days now."

"Where will Matt be Christmas morning?" Sally wondered. "With us? Or will he still be on that train?"

"Either way, he will be all right," Smoke said. "He's on a train, after all, not stranded in the mountains. It may not be his most pleasant Christmas, but at least he will be warm, and well fed."

Big Rock

Inside Hannah's, Bob Ward stood at a window, looking out into the dark. He had been there for one night and two days, virtually the only customer because the weather had kept others away. So far his stay had cost him nine dollars, but he had been provided with food and a warm bed.

The bed had come with companionship, Midge the first day and Dora the first night. At the moment, he was in Annie's room.

"Honey, if you're goin' to be stayin' tonight, it's goin' to cost you another three dollars."

"All right. But bring me up something to eat, would you?"

Annie smiled. "I will, honey. You can count on me."

Ward had no intention of spending another night there, but he led Annie to believe that, so he could get another meal. As soon as he ate, he would tell her he was broke, and ask her if she could extend him credit. He knew she wouldn't, and would kick him out, which was what he wanted.

He drummed his fingers on the windowsill and wondered if the rescue of his brother had gone as planned. They weren't all that close, but Ward knew without Santelli, he would never be able to find the money.

On board the train

During the long, dark night, Luke and Jenny found a way to deal with the cold. Jenny took off her coat, and opening it up, spread it across the two of them like a blanket. Luke did the same thing with his "serape," and the two snuggled together. The arrangement kept them warm, but Jenny knew some of the warmth was coming from within, her reaction to feeling Luke's body pressed up so closely against her own.

Why was she feeling this way? She had just met him the night before. She knew he had a ranch outside Pueblo, and had heard about his trial from some of the "guests" who had visited the Colorado Social Club. For the most part, people had spoken well of him. And to a man, they said the verdict was a miscarriage of justice.

As she sat there, warm in his arms, she allowed herself the fantasy of thinking what it might have been like if she had met him earlier. Would he have courted her?

She expanded the fantasy, picturing them having dinner together in a fine restaurant, or going to a concert or show together in the Pueblo Theater. They would take walks together in the summertime, and—

Cold reality set in. She had been working at a whorehouse, and though it was the dream of every woman who was on the line to have a "prince" come to her rescue, marry her, and take her out of "the life," it rarely happened. Jenny wasn't naive enough to think it would have happened to her, even if she had met him earlier.

For his part, Luke was lost in his own reflections. He smiled as he recalled how he had gone to the Social Club for the purpose of meeting Jenny. At the last minute he had backed out. And then he was convicted of something he didn't do. Santelli made a break, the train got stranded by an avalanche, and in the middle of the night, he was sitting close to the most beautiful woman he had ever seen. He smiled as he realized he may be the only one on the train who was actually enjoying the current situation.

Luke put his arm around her, ostensibly for warmth, and he pulled her very close to him.

Jenny wasn't sure when it happened, but the embrace grew beyond one of warmth and comfort. She was aware of his muscular body against hers, and she leaned into him, enjoying the contact. They stayed that way for a long moment, then Luke turned toward her. She could see his eyes shining in the soft light of the dimmed lanterns.

Jenny wasn't surprised when he kissed her, but she was surprised by her reaction to it. She felt a tingling in her lips that spread throughout her body, warming her blood. When they parted, she reached up to touch her lips and held her fingers there for a long moment.

Luke backed away a bit. "I'm sorry. I had no right to do that."

"I'm not sorry," Jenny said, surprising herself

with her boldness in word and deed, for she leaned into him, lifting her head toward his.

Luke kissed her again, deepening the kiss as he pulled her more tightly against him. Then, gently, he tugged her head back to break the kiss. She stared up at him with eyes filled with wonder, and as deep as her soul. Her lips were still parted from the kiss, and her cheeks flushed.

"Jenny, this is doing you a great disservice. I'm going to jail. This isn't going anywhere. It can't possibly go anywhere."

Jenny felt a ragged disconnect, having allowed herself to come this far, only to be pulled back. *No,* she wanted to shout. *Not now, don't stop.* But she knew he was right. There could be no future between them.

She leaned her head against his shoulder, and he lowered his head so it rested on hers.

"Jenny," he said quietly. "Have you ever heard of the Samoans?"

"The Samoans? No, I don't think so. What are the Samoans?"

"They are natives to some South Pacific Islands. They are a very interesting and friendly people, wonderfully athletic."

"You have been to islands in the South Pacific?"

"Oh, yes, I've been there many times. And among the Samoan culture, there is a saying that applies to us right now, that is, to you and me. The Samoans say there is no difference in the heart of a flower that lives but a single day, and the heart of a tree that lives for a thousand years."

"That's a beautiful saying."

"Do you know what it means?"

"Yes," Jenny replied. "For us, it means we should live in the moment."

"Exactly." Luke kissed her again. Opening his lips on hers, he pushed his tongue into her mouth.

Involuntarily a moan of passion began in her throat. The kiss went on, longer than she had ever imagined such a thing could last, and her head grew so light she abandoned all thought save this pleasure. Realizing she was totally powerless before him, she made herself subservient to his will, totally surrendering to him.

Then the kiss ended, and he pulled away from her. Only then did Jenny's own willpower return, and she gave a silent prayer of thankfulness that Luke had been strong enough for both of them.

December 22

Santelli, Compton, Morris, and Kelly were enjoying a morning breakfast of bacon and eggs, still holed up in the dining car.

"What are we going to do, Santelli?" Compton asked.

"What do you mean, what are we goin' to do? We're sittin' fine here. We've got all the food we can eat, we're warm and cozy, and all we have to do is wait until some of the snow melts."

"This here is startin' our third day," Compton complained. "And we're still sittin' on this train. There's so much snow piled up on the engine and tender that it ain't likely to melt until August."

"It doesn't have to get all the way melted, just enough for us to get out of here," Santelli said. "In the meantime, we'll just enjoy our stay. Like I said, with just the four of us, we have enough food to last for a month, if need be."

"You know damn well the railroad people ain't goin' to leave us up here for a month," Morris put it. "I wouldn't be surprised if they come here tomorrow."

"How are they goin' to get here?" Santelli asked.

"Why, they'll come up in another train, I reckon."

Santelli shook his head. "No, they won't. I climbed up on top of the car to have a look around, remember? There's damn near as much snow behind us as there is in front of us. Certainly enough to keep any rescue train from making it here for quite a while."

"So we're trapped here." Compton voiced what the rest were thinking.

"No, we aren't," Santelli replied. "We"—he pointed to himself, then took in the others with a circle of his fingers—"are the trappers. The passengers are the trappees."

The others laughed at Santelli's comment.

"I wish that whore had come up here," Morris said, rubbing himself. "Hell, if we had her up here, we could have us a fine time just waiting it out."

"She'll come soon." Santelli smirked.

"How do you know?"

Santelli cut open a biscuit and slid a piece of bacon between the two halves. "Because"—he took a bite—"she's goin' to get damn hungry." He smiled as he chewed, and a few crumbs tumbled from his lips.

"Look at them," Fred whispered to Pete from the other side of the dining car. "Sittin' there, eatin' in front of us without so much as givin' us a crumb."

"There's no sense in ponderin' over it, Fred. There ain't nothin' we can do about it." Pete's stomach grumbled. He and Fred had been forced to cook for Santelli and the others, but had been denied anything to eat.

"Yeah, there is," Fred declared.

"What?"

"I aim to cut me off a piece of that bread. I'll get some for you, too."

"Fred, no. Don't do it."

"I'm goin' to do it," Fred said, picking up a knife, then getting a loaf of bread out of the breadbox.

Kelly saw Fred cutting off a piece of bread and shouted, "Hey!"

"What is it?" Santelli asked.

Kelly pointed to Fred. "That guy is stealing our food!"

"You, put that back!" Santelli ordered.

"It's only a bit of bread. Please, we ain't had nothin' to eat for two days," Fred begged.

"Throw him out of the car," Santelli said easily.

"No, sir! I don' have no coat!"

"You should have thought of that before you started stealin' food." Santelli nodded at the other three, and they grabbed the porter and dragged him toward the door. He put up a fight until Kelly hit him hard on the head with the butt of his gun.

"Fred!" Pete shouted as his friend went limp.

Morris nodded to Pete. "Get the door open. We'll drag him out."

"No, sir, don't take 'im out there now. He'll mos' like freeze to death out there without no coat, and him bein' knocked out an' all."

"He shouldn't have been stealin' bread," Compton justified.

"For the Lord's sake, mister, what kind of people would do somethin' like that?" Pete asked.

"If you're so worried about him, go join him," Santelli said.

"No, sir, I—"

Santelli pointed his pistol at Pete. "I said, go join him."

Compton and Morris walked over to Pete. "Are you going to go on your own? Or do we need to send you out the same way we did your friend?"

"No need to hit me. I'll go, I'll go," Pete conceded. He walked over to the door, looked back at the evil smiles on the gunmen's faces, opened the door, and stepped out into the snow.

Finding Fred, he grabbed him by the legs and

dragged him through the snow, far away from the dining car and the eyes of the four gunman. "Fred! Fred!"

Pete leaned down to examine his friend more closely. Fred's eyes were open and he wasn't reacting in any way to the snow on his eyeballs. Pete put his ear to Fred's chest, but couldn't hear a heartbeat. "Fred!" he called again.

But Fred couldn't hear him, because Fred was dead.

Chapter Twenty-four

Pueblo

City Undertaker Joe Ponder walked into the sheriff's office as John McKenzie was pouring himself a cup of coffee. "Sheriff, I just got a couple bodies in I think will interest you. You might want to come take a look at them before I get them ready to send back to Bent County."

"All right, Joe." McKenzie poured the coffee back into the blue metal coffeepot, put on his coat, and trudged through the cold to the mortuary.

"Murder victims?" McKenzie asked as they walked.

"No, sir, not exactly. Leastwise, I don't think so. According to Nugent, he killed both of them while they were trying to hold up the stage yesterday. The driver backs him up."

They entered the mortuary, where two bodies lay covered by shrouds.

McKenzie nodded to the bodies. "Who are they, do you know?"

"Yes, sir, I know both of them. That's why I come to get you. I think you're goin' to be mighty interested when you see who they are." Ponder pulled the shrouds back. The massive wounds in the chests were the first thing Sheriff McKenzie saw. Then he looked up at their faces. The faces were without color or any animation, but he recognized them at once.

"It's Sheriff Ferrell!"

"Yes, and the other fella is his new deputy. His last name is Clayton, but I don't know his first name."

"And you say Nugent killed them while they were holding up the stagecoach?"

"Yes, sir. That's what Jake Nugent and Silas Cambridge both say."

"Damn. You know what that means? It means Luke Shardeen was more 'n likely telling the truth. I'll tell Mr. Murchison. He'll for sure want to file an appeal. And I'll send a telegram to the Sheriff of Eagle County, telling him to have Proxmire bring Luke back for the new trial."

"After you see what I found, you may not be able to hold a new trial here."

"Why not?"

"Because it's likely we won't have a judge who can hold the trial."

"What are you talking about, Joe?"

"Well, sir, I found somethin' in Ferrell's pocket you might want to see."

"What is it?

"I slipped it back in his pocket so you could see where it came from. Seth Campbell was with me, and he'll back me up that it came from Ferrell's pocket."

"Are you going to tell me? Or are you just going to keep gabbing?"

"I don't have to tell you. I'll show you." Ponder reached into Ferrell's shirt pocket and pulled out a folded piece of paper. There was blood on the paper, but it didn't prevent the message from being read.

Stagecoach from Wetmore to Yorkville will be carrying three thousand dollars in cash. After you do the job, I shall expect one thousand as my cut.

Briggs

"Ha!" McKenzie slapped the note against his open palm. "We've got 'im! I've thought all along that damn so-and-so was crooked."

On board the Red Cliff Special

Julius was standing near the stove when he heard something at the back door of the car. Looking around he saw someone looking in through the window. "It's Pete!" Julius scurried to the back door and jerked it open.

Pete was covered with snow and shaking uncontrollably. Julius pulled him inside and he and Troy knocked the snow off him. Julius pulled his serape off and draped it over Pete.

"Come on up closer to the stove," Julius invited,

pulling him toward the front. "It's not puttin' out much heat, but it'll help some."

"Pete, where's Fred?" Troy asked.

"He's outside," Pete said, barely able to speak. "He's lyin' in the snow alongside the car."

"We can't leave him out there," Bailey said. "He'll freeze to death."

"He's already dead," Pete said bluntly. "Those men kilt him 'cause he tried to break off a piece of bread for me 'n him."

Julius, who had given up his serape, began to shiver. Troy took his off and gave it to him. "Here, Julius, you wear this for a while, then when I get too cold, give it back, and we'll swap it back and forth."

"You can do that, or we'll make another one," Matt suggested.

"How are we going to make another one? There ain't no carpet left," Troy said.

Matt smiled. "Not in this car."

Matt and Troy went into the next car. There were eight people in this car, a man, two woman, and five children. The body of Deputy Proxmire was slumped in a window seat.

"What do you want?" the man asked anxiously.

"We want to take up the carpet so we can make some more serapes, like this." Matt indicated the one he was wearing. "We have some people in our car without coats."

"All right," the man answered.

Matt looked at the firebox and saw there was

even less coal than remained in his car. "It looks like you don't have much coal left."

"No, sir, we don't."

"What's your name?"

"The name is Webb, Edward Webb. This is my wife Clara."

"My name is Timmy," said a boy about nine. Two younger girls sat next to him, but neither of them spoke.

"The two shy ones are Emma and Molly," Webb said.

"My name is Jensen—"

"Yes, sir. You are Matt Jensen," Timmy interrupted. "I've read about you."

"Have you now?" Matt asked with a smile. "Well, Timmy, I'm glad you are reading, but don't believe everything you read about me. Those are mostly made-up stories."

"I know," Timmy said. "But they wouldn't make them up about you if some of it wasn't true."

"Maybe," Matt granted.

He turned to the other woman. A girl and a boy sat in the facing seat. "And you, Mrs. . . . ?"

"My name is Anita Lewis. This is my daughter Barbara, she's eleven, and my son Steven."

"I'm nine, just like Timmy," Steven explained.

"Except I'm a month older," Timmy said quickly.

"Mr. Webb, Mrs. Lewis, I think you should take your families and the rest of the coal back into our car. We'll be able to consolidate the coal and make it last longer for all of us."

"That's a good idea," Webb said.

"All right," Anita agreed.

"Mr. Jensen, do you think we will be stuck here through Christmas?" Barbara asked.

"I don't know." Matt smiled, trying to put a good face on the situation. "But if we are, we'll just make the best of it. Why, we can have our own Christmas party."

"How can you have a party without food?" Steven asked.

"We'll just figure out a way," Matt said.

After the Webb and Lewis families left, with Mr. Webb carrying the scuttle of coal, Matt and Troy took up the carpet, then they returned to the rear car.

"That was a good idea, inviting them—and their coal—to our car," Luke said.

"Well, I would have just invited the coal, but I didn't think they would go along with that," Matt said. Webb stared at Matt for a moment, then when he realized Matt was only teasing, he laughed out loud.

It was good to hear laughter.

"Mr. Jensen, do you suppose there's more coal in the other car?" Troy asked.

"There may be," Matt said. "And good for you for thinking about it. We'll also cut up that carpet and make more serapes. We can't do anything about food, but at least we won't freeze to death."

Pueblo

Prosecutor Lloyd Gilmore was on the telephone in his office, talking to the governor. "Yes, Governor. Yes, I'm absolutely sure of it. Yes, sir, the sheriff and defense attorney are here with me now. Thank you, Governor. I will tell them. Yes sir. We will take care of it."

Gilmore listened for a moment, then looked over at Sheriff McKenzie.

"The governor wants to know if we have heard anything else about the stranded train."

"Nothing from the train itself, but I believe they are putting together a rescue train to go up and relieve them," McKenzie said.

Gilmore repeated the information to the governor, then hung up the phone. "There won't be any need for another trial for Luke Shardeen, Tom. I am dropping all charges."

"Thank you, Lloyd," Murchison said. "I've known Luke Shardeen ever since he came here, and I know he is a good man. You are doing the right thing."

"What are we going to do about Briggs?" Sheriff McKenzie asked.

"It has already been done," Gilmore said. "Governor Waite has just removed him from office. He wants you to inform him."

McKenzie agreed. "That is something I will do with great pleasure."

"May I come as well, Sheriff?" Murchison asked. "I very much want to see this."

"Sure, come along if you want to."

Accompanied by Gilmore and Murchison, Sheriff McKenzie walked to the courthouse. Inside, they climbed the stairs to the second floor, and stepped into the judge's outer office, where they were greeted by Arnold Rittenhouse, the judge's secretary.

"Gentlemen," Rittenhouse said. "Do you have an appointment with His Honor?"

"No appointment is necessary for what I'm about to do," Sheriff McKenzie declared. "And there is nothing honorable about him."

"I don't understand." The expression on the secretary's face reflected his confusion.

"Just stay out of the way and watch. You'll understand soon enough." McKenzie started toward the door to the judge's chambers.

"No, Sheriff, you can't go in there!" Rittenhouse shouted.

McKenzie jerked the door open and walked in.

"Here, what is the meaning of this?" Judge Briggs shouted, holding his pants up with one hand, while a young woman from the Colorado Social Club was busy trying to rearrange her clothes.

"You'd better leave, miss," Sheriff McKenzie said.

"What? Who are you to tell her to leave? If anyone is going to leave it will be you and this . . . this entourage you have with you." Briggs pointed at McKenzie with his free hand. "Get out! Get out of here at once, or by damn I will hold you in contempt of court!"

"I already hold you in contempt, you sorry excuse for a man," McKenzie said angrily. "Amon Briggs, you have been removed from the bench by order of the Governor of the state of Colorado. And you are also under arrest for stagecoach robbery."

"Stagecoach robbery! Are you out of your mind?"

"Tell him, Mr. Gilmore," Sheriff McKenzie said.

"Mr. Briggs—"

"You will address me as Your Honor or Judge Briggs," Briggs continued angrily.

"You are lucky I'm even addressing you as mister. You have been removed from the bench, Mr. Briggs, and I am filing charges with the Attorney General of the State, charging you with collusion with Dewey Ferrell and Jebediah Clayton for the attempted robbery of the Wetmore to Yorkville stagecoach."

"What do you mean attempted robbery?"

"It means they tried to rob it, but were killed," Sheriff McKenzie answered.

"What does that have to do with me?"

"We found a note in Ferrell's pocket—a note from you, Briggs—telling him the coach would be carrying three thousand dollars, and demanding one third of the money," McKenzie advised.

The expression of anger and defiance on Brigg's face faded, quickly changing to one of fear.

"Stick out your hands, Briggs," McKenzie said. "I'm going to cuff you.

"No, please," Briggs pleaded. "Don't parade me in handcuffs in front of the people! I'll lose all their respect."

"Tell me, Mr. Briggs," Gilmore said. "What makes you think anyone respects you now?"

CHAPTER TWENTY-FIVE

Buena Vista

Everyone in town had heard that the train was trapped at the top of the pass. About a hundred people were in the depot, most out of concern and curiosity. Those who had relatives and loved ones on the train had the greatest concern. Although they knew Deckert had no more information than they did, being at the depot made them feel closer to the people on the train.

The Chaffee County Times had put out a special edition extra, and they sold more copies than ever before.

Red Cliff Special Trapped in Pass

Word has reached this newspaper that the Red Cliff Special, which left the Buena Vista Depot at nine o'clock *post meridiem* two days previous, is now sitting at the top, or near the top of Trout Creek Pass. It is the normal procedure for a train unable to proceed farther through the pass to retrace its path and return to the station last departed. That the train in question has not done so is a disquieting indication it is probably entrapped.

There are forty people on board the train, not excepting the crew of engineer, fireman, four porters, and the conductor. State Senator Jarred Daniels, his wife, and daughter are said to be among the passengers. So too is Deputy Sheriff Braxton Proxmire with two prisoners, the infamous Michael Santelli and Luke Shardeen, a local rancher.

That Shardeen is aboard is an irony, for while he was found guilty of manslaughter and sentenced to four years confinement, the charges against him have been dropped. Though Shardeen did kill Deputy Gates, his defense was that Gates and Sheriff Ferrell attempted to rob him. Sheriff Ferrell was subsequently killed while he was in the act of robbing a stagecoach. That incident has provided sufficient veracity to Shardeen's defense claim to warrant the dropping of all charges.

Hodge Deckert, the Buena Vista stationmaster, says a rescue train has been assembled and will leave today.

* * *

An engine, a tender, and two passenger cars sat on the tracks ready to rescue the passengers stuck at the summit. The weather was fair, though it was exceptionally cold. By the time Deckert was ready to dispatch the rescue train, considerably over half those who had come to bear witness to the rescue effort had given up and returned home.

Although railroad personnel were confident the special had enough food, the rescue train was carrying food, anyway. In addition, they rightly figured fuel for the heating stoves would just about be exhausted, so they were also carrying a lot of blankets. Additional fuel for the heating stoves was not taken as the passengers would be returning on the rescue train.

The Buena Vista Fire Company band played as the rescue train got ready to leave. Finally, with salutes from the locomotive whistle and waves from the train crew, the throttle was opened and, amid chugs and great puffs of gleaming white steam, the engine got under way.

The departing whistle of the train was heard in every house and business establishment in the entire town. Those who had given up waiting breathed a prayer of petition that the train would get through and all on board would be returned safely.

Deckert watched the train leave, then he went back into the depot and walked over to the telegraph operator. "Send a telegram to Big Rock. Tell them the rescue train just got under way."

"I can't go directly to Big Rock. I have to go around."

"Send it however you have to do it, but just do it," Deckert ordered.

Big Rock

The telegraph instrument at the railroad depot began clacking. The telegrapher responded, then smiled as he began writing the message on his work pad. When he was finished, he signed off and took the message to the station agent. "Mr. Wilson, this just came in."

BV RESCUE TRAIN TO REACH STRANDED TRAIN NOON STOP WILL UPDATE STOP DECKERT AGENT BV

Phil read the article then nodded. "This is good to know. I'm not really worried about those people up there; they have enough food to have a comfortable wait until they are rescued. But they are bound to be more comfortable and less apprehensive if they are back in Buena Vista, even though that may not be where they want to spend Christmas."

"Mr. Wilson, do you think I should take word out to Mr. Jensen?" Eddie asked.

"Yes, I think that would be a very good idea. I'm sure he would like to know what's going on."

"All right, I'll saddle up and go right away." Eddie smiled. "I probably won't be back until after dinner."

Phil knew that, by dinner, Eddie was referring

to the noon meal, and he chuckled. "You're going to hit Miss Sally up for dinner, are you?"

"Why not? You know anybody that's a better cook?"

On board the stalled train

With the bright sun reflecting off the snow and pouring in through the windows of the car, the temperature in the car had risen so that, even with the smallest of flames, the stove was able to keep the car comfortably warm.

"Folks, I suggest that we put the fire out for now," Matt advised.

"Now, just why would we want to do a thing like that?" Senator Daniels protested. "We are all starving to death, but at least we are warm."

"Think about it, Senator," Matt said. "With the bright sun out, we're getting some heat in the car without the stove. But tonight, when the temperature drops several degrees below zero, we will need the heat the stove can provide. We have to save fuel to be certain that we will have it at night, when we need it."

"We've got extra coal now, and my daughter is ill," Daniels whined. "I'll not have you make it worse by putting out the fire in that stove."

"We've got some extra coal, yes, but I don't know how many more days we will be here. It's best to be as conservative as we can."

"Jarred, you know he is right." Millie laid her hand on her husband's arm. "You know how cold these last two nights have been. It will be worth being without heat in the daytime, if we can keep warm at night."

"We aren't going to be here much longer. Maybe not even tonight. I'm absolutely convinced a rescue train will reach us today," Senator Daniels said stubbornly.

"I certainly hope you are right, Senator. But I don't think we should take that chance."

"I don't, either," Luke put in.

"And you can count me in with Mr. Jensen," Bailey said.

"Mr. Purvis, what about you?" Senator Daniels asked.

"I'm sorry, Senator, but I'm going to have to go along with Mr. Jensen on this one."

"I'm not going to let my daughter get cold and get worse."

"I'm not so cold, Daddy," Becky said in a weak voice.

"All right, all right." Senator Daniels threw his hands up in frustration. "It is obvious I am the only sane one here. But I can't stand up to all of you. Put out the fire."

The fire was extinguished, and within fifteen minutes, the temperature began to drop.

"I told you it was going to get cold in here," Senator Daniels complained.

"It will be much colder tonight," Matt said.

During the discussion a man had come in through the front door.

Troy noticed him first and pointed. "It's one of them! It's one of the men who took over the dining car."

"Troy is right. This one's name is Morris," Pete said.

Morris reached out and grabbed Timmy, who was standing the closest to him.

"Mama!" Timmy called, trying to twist out of Morris's grip.

"Timmy!"

Morris tightened his grip and held his pistol to the boy's head. "You ain't goin' nowhere, boy."

"What do you want, Morris?"

"We want the whore. Give us the whore, and we'll give you somethin' to eat."

"If she didn't go before, what makes you think she is going to go today?" Luke asked.

"Because it's been two whole days since any of you have had anything to eat," Morris pointed out unnecessarily. "And if the whore will just come along with me, why, we'll feed the whole train."

"How you goin' to do that?" Pete asked. "There ain't no cooks left."

"Oh, we'll let one of you boys do the cookin'," Morris offered.

"She's not going," Luke insisted.

"Wait a minute," Abner Purvis interrupted. "The other day, I was on the woman's side. I figured she shouldn't have to go if she didn't want to. But now I'm thinkin', why not? I mean, we all know this is what she does anyway. So why not go ahead and do it again? Especially if it will get her and all the rest of us something to eat. There's no tellin' how long we're goin' to be sittin' here. You know if the rescue train coulda got through, it woulda come for us yesterday."

"She's *not* going," Luke repeated.

"Let me make it a bit easier for you to decide," Morris said. "If the whore comes with me, you all eat, and the boy lives. If she don't come with me, none of you eat, and I'll kill her, and the boy, and go back by myself."

"Morris, what makes you think you're going back with or without her?" Matt asked quietly.

"What do you mean?"

"I mean the young lady isn't going anywhere, and neither are you."

"Are you blind? You do see that I'm holding a gun to this boy's head, don't you? Now, I'm going to count to three. And if the whore don't say she's goin' back with me by the time I get to three, I'm goin' to kill this boy."

"I'm warning you, Morris, don't do that."

"Ha! You're warnin' me? One, two . . ."

Morris glanced over toward Jenny, and that was all the opening Matt needed. He drew and fired in one lightning-fast motion. The bullet hit Morris just above his right eye, and dropping the pistol, he was slammed back against the front door of the car.

The four women in the car screamed in shock and surprise.

"Wow!" Timmy cried. "Steven, did you see that?"

"Are you crazy?" Senator Daniels shouted. "You could have killed the boy!"

"No," Edward Webb said. "Morris could have killed my son, and I believe he would have, if it hadn't been for Mr. Jensen. Mr. Jensen saved Timmy's life."

"Wow!" Timmy said again. "Wait until I tell all my friends!"

"What difference does it make?" Purvis asked. "We're all going to starve to death anyway."

"Purvis," Matt said. "We may get hungry, but we aren't going to starve. I once went ten days without eating, and I've heard of people going for as long as a month without eating. In order to survive, first we need heat, so we won't freeze to death. Next, we need water, and with all the snow, we have plenty of that. The least important for our immediate survival is food."

"That might not be the most important, but my feelin' is we're goin' to get awful hungry before too long," Purvis complained.

"I'm hungry now," Troy said.

"Like I said, I've been through this before. We will get through it," Matt promised. "As long as Santelli and the others stay in the dining car, they are more trapped than we are. We are the ones who are going to be rescued, not them. When the rescue team comes, Santelli and the men with him will go to jail, and they will hang."

"Troy," Julius said, starting toward Morris's body. "Come help me take out the trash."

CHAPTER TWENTY-SIX

Sugarloaf

"It's been two days. Do you think the train will get in before Christmas?" Sally asked as she took two dried-apple pies from the oven. "Because, if it doesn't I'm going to have a lot of extra food to get rid of."

"Oh, I'm sure the train will get here before Christmas. But even if it doesn't, you don't have to worry about getting rid of the extra food. Duff and I can take care of that for you. And we may as well start by having a piece of pie." Smoke picked up a knife and started toward one of the pies.

"Absolutely not!" Sally said authoritatively. "The pies haven't even cooled yet."

There was a knock on the door, and Smoke smiled. "I'll bet that's Eddie telling me the train got there and Matt is waiting at the station."

Smoke hurried to the door and opened it. "So, Matt's here, is he? What time did the train get in?"

"No, sir, he ain't here and the train ain't got in," Eddie said. "And it ain't goin' to get in."

"What do you mean, it isn't going to get in?"

"They've done sent a rescue train for it. They'll be takin' ever'one back down the mountain to Buena Vista."

"Oh," Sally whispered. "That means Matt for sure won't be here for Christmas."

"No, it doesn't seem likely that he will," Smoke said, disappointment in his voice. "But at least, if the rescue train takes them back to Buena Vista, he won't have to spend Christmas Day trapped in the snow on the top of the mountain."

"Eddie, it is nearly lunchtime. Won't you stay and eat with us before you start back?" Sally invited.

"Yes, ma'am!" Eddie replied enthusiastically. "And thank you, ma'am."

The table was laden with food; roast beef and gravy, mashed potatoes, stewed carrots, and green beans Sally had canned. She had also made a loaf of bread, which disappeared quickly. For dessert they had hot apple pie, over which had been put a piece of melted cheese. Sally had prepared a much larger meal than normal, partly in anticipation of Matt's presence. The meal did not go to waste, though, as the two men and Eddie showed their appreciation by eating second helpings of everything.

"Well, I'd better be getting back," Eddie said after he finally pushed away from the table.

"I appreciate you coming out here to tell us about the train," Smoke said.

"Yes, sir, well I thought you might want to know."

"You will come tell us if you get any more word about the train, won't you?"

"Yes, sir, you can count on that."

"Eddie, would you like to take a bear claw along with you to eat on your ride back?" Sally asked.

"Oh, I don't know. I ate so much, I hate to take anything else."

"Well, I can understand if you are too full."

A broad smile spread across Eddie's face. "Only, I've near 'bout always got room for another bear claw."

"I swear, Sally, I'd hate to see this boy and Cal in an eating contest," Smoke said. "I don't know who would win, but they'd likely run us out of food trying to determine a winner."

Duff and Sally laughed, then Smoke walked outside to see Eddie off.

"It is cold out there." Smoke came back in, clapping his hands together. "And it is getting colder. No telling how cold it is up at the top of the pass."

"Oh, those poor people," Sally moaned. "I wonder how much longer they'll have to stay up there."

On board the rescue train

Doodle Reynolds, the engineer of the rescue train, moved the Johnson Bar and the train came to a stop.

"What is it, Doodle? What'd you stop for?" the fireman asked.

"Look up ahead of us, Greg, and tell me what you think."

The fireman leaned out the window and looked ahead. His gaze carried along the side of the engine, the brass work, the green paint of the boiler, then past the snowplow attached to the front. Fifty yards ahead of the train was a pile of snow across the tracks as high as the engine itself.

"Jehoshaphat, Doodle! I don't think we could even make a dent in that. How far up the track do you think it goes?"

"I don't know." Doodle put the train in reverse. "But I don't plan to get a second train stuck up here."

"I hate we can't get them out."

"They aren't in any trouble yet," Doodle said. "They probably have enough food to last a couple weeks, anyway. For sure by that time, they'll either be able to leave, or the snow will be melted enough that we'll be able to get through to them."

"The folks back in town are goin' to be mighty disappointed."

"No more disappointed than I am." Doodle laughed. "I would love to come to the rescue, just so I could lord it over my brother-in-law for a while."

"That's right. Don is your brother-in-law, isn't he?"

"Yeah, he didn't have any more sense than to marry my sister."

"She's going to be upset and some worried, I reckon," Greg said.

"I reckon so."

The train beat its way back down the track toward Buena Vista, leaving behind an impenetrable wall of snow and the Red Cliff Special.

On board the train

Every passenger on the train, plus the crew, were now gathered in the last car, making it very crowded, but Matt was convinced they had enough fuel to last for a while. He'd already decided wood pieces from the car would have to be the next fuel supply. Of course, he would dismantle the car ahead.

Again, some of the men were playing cards. Bailey was napping, the three porters were talking together, the five active children—Becky remained on her mother's lap—had found a game to play, Ed Webb and his wife were sitting quietly, while Senator Daniels sat in the seat facing his wife and daughter. The scowl had not left his face. Luke and Jenny were cuddled together in the front seat, and looking at them, Matt smiled. He could almost believe they were enjoying the situation.

Matt was still smiling as he looked out the window, then the smile left his face, replaced by an expression of surprise and hope. Alongside the car, in the area right by the track, was a coyote, probably looking for food and to get out of the snow.

He pulled his pistol and started to raise the window, thinking to shoot the coyote, but changed his mind. A gunshot outside the car might bring down more snow. He quickly devised a plan and looked back into the car. He was going to need help, and had to figure out which of his fellow passengers would most likely be able to help him.

Looking over everyone, he decided and called, "Julius. Julius, come here."

"Yes, sir?"

"Look out the window, right down there," Matt said, pointing.

"It's a coyote."

"No it's not. It's a small deer."

"Mr. Jensen, you done gone crazy from not eatin'? That ain't no deer. That's a coyote."

"Shh," Matt hushed. "Once when I was very hungry, I barbecued a coyote, and it tasted like deer meat. As far as these folks are concerned, it's a small deer, and by the time they see it, they won't be able to tell the difference."

"You goin' to shoot it?"

Matt shook his head. "I'm afraid if I shoot, it might bring down a lot more snow. I've got another idea, but I'm going to need your help."

"Yes, sir," Julius said enthusiastically. "I'll do whatever I can to help."

"I'm going out on the back vestibule. You go out on the front. Then I want you to chase the coyote toward me."

"Yes, sir, but what if the coyote runs under the car?"

"Let's just pray that he doesn't," Matt said.

"Yes, sir. I'm a prayin' man, sir."

"Good. We better get started."

"Yes, sir," Julius said again.

Matt went out onto the back vestibule, then leaned around just far enough to see the coyote. It was still there, sniffing around. He pulled out his pocketknife and flipped it open

Julius climbed down from the vestibule at the front end of the car and slowly walked toward the coyote. Matt watched and, as he had hoped and planned, the coyote started in his direction.

Matt moved to the edge of the vestibule, then, timing his jump, leaped off, landing in a belly flop into the snow. That he was successful was evidenced by the fact that he could feel the coyote under him. The coyote was moving rapidly, squirming around trying to get free, and Matt knew he had to be very careful that it not get away.

Carefully, Matt lifted his body just far enough to reach his hand under, grab the coyote by the back of the neck, and cut its throat. He lay on the creature until it stopped moving.

"Praise the Lord, Mr. Jensen! You got 'im!" Julius shouted.

Still holding the coyote, Matt rolled under the car to prevent anyone inside from seeing what he was doing, then he cut off the head and legs, and skinned it. When he rolled back out from under the car, he was holding an unidentifiable carcass.

Julius carried the carcass into the car and held it up. "Mr. Jensen kilt him a small deer!" he shouted, to the joy of the others in the car.

"How big is the small deer?" Don asked.

"He's about this big," Julius said, demonstrating with his hands.

"Oh, my, that is rather small, isn't it?" Clara asked.

"Yes, ma'am, I reckon it is. But we're goin' to cook him up and ever'one is goin' to get some of it."

"I hate to deflate everyone's joy," Senator Daniels said. "But there are thirty of us. How is a deer that small going to feed all of us?"

"We're going to make a soup," Matt said, coming into the car just in time to hear the Senator's question. "And we aren't going to waste any of it."

"It's going to be an awfully thin soup," Senator Daniels complained.

Matt smiled. "Trust me, it'll be the best thing you've ever eaten."

"It won't be all that good," Bailey said. "We don't have any vegetables. We don't even have any salt."

"Oh, yes, we have salt." Matt smiled. "I learned from an old mountain man friend of mine to never be without salt." He pulled a little cloth bag from his pocket.

"And I've got some pepper I brought from the diner," Pete offered.

"All we have to do now is gather up some snow, melt some water, and start cooking.

"What are we going to cook it in?" Purvis asked.

Bailey smiled. "I have the perfect stew pot for it. There is a brand-new chamber pot in the toilet that hasn't even been put out yet, so it hasn't been used. It'll be just right to cook this in."

"A chamber pot? We are going to make soup in a spittoon?" Barbara Lewis made a face.

"Trust me, it hasn't been used, not one time," Bailey said. "It'll make a fine pot for cooking."

"It'll be all right, honey," Anita said to her daughter. "Why, if it's never been used, what is the difference between it and a stew pot?"

"I guess nothing." Barbara looked at her brother and Timmy. "But don't either of you dare ever tell anyone we cooked soup in a chamber pot and actually ate it," she demanded.

"Why not?" Steven replied. "I think it's funny."

"Oooh!" Barbara thumped her thigh in frustration.

"They aren't going to tell anyone, are you, boys?" Matt looked the boys straight in the eyes.

"All right," Timmy agreed. "We won't ever tell anyone."

"All right, so we can cook," Purvis said. "But how are we going to eat it? We don't have bowls or spoons."

"I have a knife, a spoon, and a collapsible cup," Matt said. "We'll pass the cup around, and eat one at a time. The children will go first."

Using his penknife, Matt began to cut up the carcass.

Troy also had a knife, so he went to the back to help. He started to make a cut, then looked up at Matt with a questioning expression on his face. "Mr. Jensen, I have to tell you, this don't look like no deer I done ever seen before."

"You don't say."

"It looks more like a dog."

"In some cultures, dog is a delicacy."

"But this ain't no dog, is it?"

"No."

"What is it? A wolf? A fox? A coyote?"

"You've heard of mule deer, haven't you, Troy?"

"Yes, sir, but I know this ain't no mule deer."

"It's a coyote deer."

Troy laughed. "We ain't goin' be tellin' the others this, are we?"

"No."

Troy laughed again. "I expect this will be the best coyote deer I done ever ate."

While Troy was cutting up the rest of the carcass, Matt went back up to the front of the car. "You men, go outside and start gathering snow. Use your hats. Oh, and stay behind the train as much as you can, there's less chance Santelli and the others will see you that way."

"I want to help, too," Timmy declared.

"Me, too," Steven added.

"If it's all right with your parents, it's all right with me," Matt said.

"Are you sure they won't get in the way?" Ed Webb asked.

Luke smiled at the two boys. "I think they would be a great help, Why, I wasn't much older than these two boys when I went to sea for the first time."

"All right, Timmy, you can go with them."

"Mama?" Steven asked.

"Go ahead," Mrs. Lewis said.

"Miss McCoy, if you would, please get the fire going a little hotter, at least hot enough to boil water," Matt asked.

"All right," Jenny agreed.

"I'll help you," Mrs. Lewis offered.

An hour later, the entire car was permeated with the enticing aroma of the soup.

"When will it be ready?" Timmy asked. "I'm really hungry."

"Soon, I think," Matt said.

"Matt, I have a suggestion," Luke said. "It's something we did a few times on board ship when our rations were running low."

"I'm open to any suggestion," Matt said.

"For the first time, we'll just have the broth. It will be nourishing enough to maybe take some of the edge off. Then we can put more water in, cook it a second time, maybe even three times before we eat up all the meat."

"That's a good idea."

"You know somethin'? What is happenin' to us now, has all come right out of the Bible," Troy pointed out.

"What do you mean, it's all come out of the Bible?" Daniels asked. "I don't remember reading anything about a trapped train in the Bible."

"Well, 'cause there weren't no trains then. But the rest of it." Troy quoted, "'*For I was hungry, and you gave me food.*' Well, ain't that what Mr. Jensen has just done? Provide us with food? '*I was thirsty, and you gave me drink.*' That's what all the snow is, givin' us water to drink. '*I was a stranger, and you took me in.*' That's me 'n Pete and Mr. Stevenson and Mr. Evans. We was strangers, out in the cold, but you good folks took us in. '*I was naked, and you clothed me*'." Troy put his thumbs behind the serape and held it out. "That's what this here thing is. '*I was sick, and you visited me.*' That's the sweet little girl that's lyin' over there now. She is some awful sick, but we done ever' one of us took her into our hearts. '*I was in prison, and you came to me.*' Well, ain't we all sort of in prison now, I mean, what with bein' trapped in this car and all? So that last one, the part about bein' in prison, is for all of us. Yes, sir, ever'thing Jesus said in that parable just fits us."

"What parable is that, Troy?" Beans asked.

"That's from the twenty-fifth chapter of Matthew, Mr. Evans. It's the Parable of the Sheep and the Goats."

"Troy, how come you know that?" Julius asked.

"I thought I told you, Julius. My daddy is a preacher man."

"No, you ain't never done told me that. If you know all that stuff, how come you ain't never become a preacher man your own self?"

"My daddy is a godly man," Troy said. "I don't reckon I ever met a man who is finer 'n my daddy. But I ain't never been nowhere near as good a man as he is. I've done lots of things that ain't nowhere near godly. I just don't figure I'm fit to be a preacher man."

"Maybe being here like this is some kind of test for you," Don suggested.

"I don't mind Troy being tested," Pete said. "Only if he's the one bein' tested, how come the rest of us has to be with him?"

The others laughed, and it was the first good, deep laugh any of them had had since the ordeal began.

Chapter Twenty-seven

"If you ask me, Morris has done got hisself kilt, just as sure as a gun is iron." Kelly sat in the dining car with Santelli and Compton. "Otherwise, he'd be back here by now."

"More 'n likely," Santelli agreed.

"What if they come into this car after us?"

"They tried it once before, remember?" Santelli pointed out. "I don't think they're likely to try it again. The only way they can get into the car is through that door, and they can only come through the door one at a time.

"You know what?" Compton interjected. "We're goin' to run out of coal pretty soon. We won't have enough to cook our food or heat the car."

"No problem, just go into the next car and take whatever coal they have," Santelli suggested.

"Yeah, good idea." Compton stepped out onto the vestibule, pulled his pistol, then moved on into the car immediately behind the diner. Except for the bodies of the three men who had attempted to take back the diner, the car was completely empty.

Compton checked the stove and saw that the coal scuttle was empty. Walking through that car he looked into the next one, and it was empty as well, and was also missing a coal scuttle. As soon as he stepped onto the vestibule leading to the last car he heard laughter.

He frowned. Laughter? What did they have to laugh about?

Then he smelled the aroma of something being cooked. What could they be cooking?

Compton hurried back to the diner.

"Where's the coal?" Santelli growled out as soon as Compton entered.

"There ain't no coal in either of the next three cars," Compton answered. "There ain't no people there, either."

"What do you mean, there aren't any people? What happened to them?"

"They've all moved into the last car. And I figure they must've took their coal with them."

"Damn."

"And I'll tell you somethin' else. They're cookin' somethin'."

"What do you mean, they are cooking something? What have they got to cook?"

"I don't know, but I could smell it as soon as I got to the door. And the way they are laughing, you'd think they're having a party."

"Well, why don't we just go stop their party?" Kelly suggested.

"You really want to do that?" Santelli asked. "Morris ain't come back. Besides, Matt Jensen is with them."

"Are we not going to do anything?" Kelly asked in a huff.

"Why? Whatever food they have, it can't be much. And they have a lot of people to feed. We've got all the food we can eat for two weeks if necessary. As long as nobody does something foolish, things are fine just as they are."

Becky was the first person to be fed, and because it was a clear broth she was able to take it. She didn't take a full cup, but she took a little, and Matt was sure it would be good for her.

Timmy was offered the next cup. "I think my sisters and Barbara should get it before me and Steven. They're girls."

"Good for you, Timmy," Matt said with a smile. "And you are right, they should be next."

After the children took the cup, it went to the women, then to the men. When Troy started to drink it, Senator Daniels protested. "Are those colored men going to drink from the same cup as we?"

"Do you see any other cup?" Matt asked impatiently.

"That isn't right," Senator Daniels said adamantly. "I mean having a colored man drink from the same cup as whites." He shook his head. "No, sir, I won't share a cup with a colored person."

"All right, Senator Daniels, have it your way," Matt said.

Troy hadn't taken a swallow yet, and upon hearing Matt's comment, he looked up questioningly.

"What are you waiting on, Troy? Go ahead."

"Wait a minute!" Senator Daniels exclaimed. "I thought you said to have it my own way."

"I did say that," Matt replied calmly. "You said you won't share a cup with a colored person, so I'm not going to ask you take any of the soup. Which is fine, it'll just mean more for the rest of us."

"What? That's not what I meant."

"It's up to you, Daniels," Matt maintained, specifically omitting the title. "You can either share the cup with Troy, Julius, Pete, and the rest of us, or you can choose not to take the cup at all. Which will it be?"

"I'll, uh, I'll take the cup," Senator Daniels muttered.

"Yeah, I rather thought you might."

By the time they settled for the night, the coyote had been fully consumed. Nobody had a full stomach, but neither was hunger gnawing at them as much as it had the day before.

"Matt, I think we should post a watch tonight," Luke suggested as they sat in the darkened car. "Like we have onboard ship. There are enough of us that it won't require anyone to stay awake for too long."

Matt agreed. "Since we have all the coal now, I could see our friends in the dining car getting a little anxious, perhaps even anxious enough to try something. We'll post the watch."

Big Rock

Bob Ward had left Hannah's and started his evening in Longmont's, but he got loud and abusive and the owner had invited him to leave. Ward didn't want any trouble that might cause him to wind up in jail, so he'd moved on to the Brown Dirt Cowboy Saloon. He had to be in Big Rock when the train arrived, assuming it would arrive eventually.

He'd spent too much money at Hannah's. With barely enough to sustain himself over the next few days, he was trying to solve that problem by playing cards, but had not been successful in Longmont's, and was even less successful in the Brown Dirt Cowboy. "Well, you fellas have just about cleaned me out," he said jovially as he got up from the table.

"Don't feel like you are the only one, mister. This seems to have been Corey Calhoun's day." The player pointed to the winner, a cowboy who was temporarily out of work because of the season.

Smiling, Calhoun raked the pile of money toward him. "There must be near a hunnert dollars here. Why, this'll be enough to tide me over till spring roundup."

Ward tipped his hat. "Gentleman." He moved away from the table, but didn't go far.

"Some folks have it and some don't, Calhoun," one of the players griped.

"You got that right. I got the skill," Calhoun bragged.

"Ha! I was talking about luck," the player said. "I've never seen a worse player with better luck than you."

The others laughed.

"Oh yeah? Well, I'll tell you—" Calhoun paused in mid-sentence. "You're right. It was just dumb luck. But as my old pa used to say, it's better to be lucky than good. I probably should quit while I'm ahead. I'll put this money away, and when I come in here to play tomorrow, I'll bring no more 'n what I started with today."

"The way it's been snowing, what makes you think you'll even be able to make it to the saloon tomorrow?" one of the other players asked. "For that matter, we may all have a hard time gettin' home tonight."

"Yeah, well, at least we are down here," Calhoun said. "Think of all those poor folks trapped in a train up on top of the pass."

"Where are you sleeping tonight, Corey? You goin' to use some of your winnin's to get a hotel room?"

"No way am I goin' to waste this money on a hotel room. I'll sleep tonight the same place I sleep ever' night when I'm not out on the range," Calhoun replied.

"Yeah, that's sort of what I thought. You don't have a place, so you'll go over to the livery and bed down in an empty stall, won't you?"

"Mr. Vickery, he don't mind it. And there's plenty of clean straw to sort of burrow down into."

"How 'bout one more hand before you leave, Corey?" one of the other players asked.

"One more, but that's all," Calhoun agreed.

From his place near the wall, Ward heard every word and smiled. It was going to be just too easy.

He hurried through the cold, dark night, his feet making crunching sounds as he walked through the snow. Reaching the livery stable, he stood in the shadows outside for a long moment, making certain he hadn't been seen. Then he stepped into the barn.

It was almost as cold inside as it was outside. The only difference was the walls blocked the wind. The air reeked of horseflesh and horse apples. He moved into a dark corner and waited.

Calhoun was singing when he came into the stable.

"O bury me not on the lone prairie.
These words came low and mournfully
From the pallid lips of the youth who lay
On his dying bed at the close of day."

He moseyed over to one of the stalls. "Hey, Horse, what do you think?" I won a lot of money tonight and tomorrow, I'm goin' to buy you some oats to go along with the hay you been eatin'. What do you think of that?"

The horse whickered and stuck his head over the gate. Calhoun rubbed the horse behind his ears. "Yeah, I thought you'd like that."

Ward was sneaking up on Calhoun's back, walking as quietly as he could, but he stepped on a twig and it snapped.

"What?" Calhoun said, turning toward the sound.

Hiding a knife in his hand, low and by his side, Ward made an underhand jab toward Calhoun, holding the blade sideways so it would slip in easily between his ribs. The knife penetrated Calhoun's heart, and he went down without another sound.

Ward found the money in Calhoun's coat pocket, then quickly crossed the street and entered the Ace High Saloon, where he stayed just long enough to establish an alibi. After a couple drinks and a little flirtatious banter with the bar girls, he walked down to the Rocky Mountain Hotel, where he took a room.

CHAPTER TWENTY-EIGHT

On board the Red Cliff Special—December 23

They had selected the time of their duty by lot, and had decided whoever was on duty would stand, not sit, at the door, looking out through the door window. That way nobody would fall asleep while on watch, and since they were only doing one hour at a time, it didn't seem too harsh a duty.

Luke had the watch from one until two in the morning, but couldn't help taking frequent glances toward Jenny. Often, he caught her looking at him. For the first few times he caught her, she would smile in embarrassment at being caught. But after a few times, the embarrassment was gone, and they looked at each other openly and unashamedly.

He recalled a conversation he'd had with his sea captain.

"You aren't married, are you, Mr. Shardeen?" Captain Cutter asked once, when the Pacific Clipper *was anchored off Hong Kong.*

"No, sir."

"You are a smart man not to be married. No sailor should be married, for 'tis no life for a woman to always be waiting for her man to come home to her."

"But you are married, aren't you, Captain?"

"Aye, and 'twas the dumbest thing I've ever done."

Because of that conversation, and because he believed the captain was right, the thought of marriage had never before crossed Luke's mind.

But he wasn't a seaman any longer. He was a rancher with land and a house. What better could he offer a wife, than her own home? Working the land, there would be no long separations. He could get married. They could have children . . . a boy would be nice. He could start him in ranching when he was . . .

Shaking his head, Luke abruptly turned his thoughts in a different direction. He was going to jail for four years. There were very few voyages where a seaman would be absent for four long years. If he couldn't subject a woman to being married to a seaman, what made him think he could subject her to being married to someone who was in jail?

He clenched his jaw and turned away from Jenny. Thinking was getting him nowhere.

Jenny watched Luke turn away from her. *What is he thinking?* she wondered. *Does he think that because I worked at the social club I am a loose woman? Am I but a temporary diversion for him?*

Life had been a good teacher to Jenny, and she had learned well. She had developed an intuition that she trusted, and it was telling her Luke's feelings for her were genuine. She concluded the answer to those questions was no.

But what about her feelings for him? She had made a mistake once, succumbing to foolish infatuation. Was she experiencing the same thing? They had known each other for only three days. Love couldn't develop in three days . . . could it?

She knew Luke was going to jail, the result of an unjust verdict. She was certain his impending jail time was weighing heavily on his mind . . . so heavily it would undoubtedly cause him to put aside any feelings he might have for her.

Giving thought to the comment he had made about the Samoans, and how there is no difference in the heart of a flower that lives but a single day and the heart of a tree that lives for a thousand years, she decided that was exactly how she would look at their current situation. If but a few days, or even a few hours remained for them she would fill what was left with love for Luke Shardeen.

The morning dawned bright and sunny, heating the car inside. But there was little chance another opportunity for food would present itself as the coyote had done.

Abner Purvis went back to talk to Matt. "Me, Jones, Turner, and Simpson have come up with a plan."

"What is your plan?"

"We're goin' to walk out of here."

"Which way are you going?" Matt asked. "The snow in front is three hundred feet high."

"That's why we are going to go back to Buena Vista. If we can get through, we'll get a rescue train back up here."

"Mr. Purvis, there is absolutely no doubt in my mind but that there has already been a rescue attempt. If they could have gotten through, they would be here by now. That tells me that the way behind us is as blocked as the way before us."

"That may be, but we been talkin' about it, and we don't plan to stay here 'n starve to death. Besides which we had a little somethin' to eat yesterday, so we ain't goin' to be any stronger than we are right now."

"You might have a point there," Matt agreed. "But you aren't going to get anywhere without snow shoes."

"We can try," Purvis said.

"When do you plan to leave?"

"The sooner the better. If we leave now we might be over the worst part of it while there is still light."

It took Purvis and the other three men about five minutes to get ready, then everyone in the car wished them luck. With hopeful hearts they watched through the back window as the men attempted to go over the wall of snow piled up behind the train.

Their attempts to climb the snow met with utter failure. They got a few feet up the side, only to slide back down again, or the very act of climbing itself pulled down large slides of snow. They kept at it for half an hour without the slightest bit of success. Finally, breathing hard and tired of bringing frigid air into their lungs, they had no recourse but to give up and return to the train.

"I'm sorry," Purvis said as he and the other three men huddled around the stove. They were so cold and exhausted Matt had thrown in a few extra lumps of coal for more heat. He feared they might contract pneumonia.

"We tried, but we couldn't get over the snow," Jones explained, then sipped from the cup Matt was passing between the men. He had heated snow in the same chamber pot used to make the soup the day before, and though it was nothing but warm water, it made them feel better to drink it.

"What do we do now?" Bailey asked.

"We'll just have to wait and see what develops." Matt looked over toward Millie and Becky. "How is she doing this morning?"

"Not well," Millie said, choking back a sob. "Not well at all. She's not even conscious anymore. I'm—I'm afraid she might be dying."

Matt took some warm water over to them, making certain the water wasn't too hot. "Bathe her face in this," he offered. "It won't help with the illness, but if she can feel it, it might make her feel a little better.

"Bless you." Millie tore some of the hem off her skirt and using it as a washcloth, bathed Becky's face gently with the warm water.

Becky made no response.

"Mrs. Daniels, you have been sitting in that same position for ever so long," Jenny said. "Why don't you let me sit there and hold your little girl's head in my lap while you get a little rest?"

"Oh, thank you, dear. That would be wonderful . . . if you are sure you don't mind."

"No ma'am. I don't mind at all." Jenny changed places with Millie, and put Becky's head in her lap.

"I'm going to hold you for a while now, Becky, while your mama gets a little rest. I hope you don't mind." Jenny looked down and smiled at the girl but got no reaction. Concerned, she put her hand on the child's forehead and found her burning with a very high fever.

Dear Lord, Jenny prayed silently. *I haven't always led the life I should, and I know I have no right to ask you for anything. But maybe since I'm not asking for anything for myself you will hear this prayer. Please, Lord, don't let this innocent child die. It's nearly Christmas. Please send her the Christmas gift of life. Amen.*

"How many more days until Christmas?" Jenny heard Timmy ask.

"Christmas is in two days," Timmy's mother answered.

"I'll be glad when it's Christmas," Timmy's younger sister Molly said. "Won't you be glad when it's Christmas, Mama?"

"Yes, dear," Clara replied quietly. "I'll be glad when it's Christmas."

"Will we still be on this train at Christmas?" Timmy asked.

"I don't know," Clara answered.

"Can Santa Claus find us if we are still on the train?" Molly asked.

"If he can't find us on the train, he will find us as soon as we get home."

"This isn't like Christmas," Timmy declared. "We don't have a Christmas tree. We don't have any cookies. It's nothing like Christmas."

"Oh, but we have snow," Jenny said. "And every Christmas should have snow. Think of all the boys and girls who live way down south and have no snow at all."

Luke laughed. "You are quite a woman, Jenny, to find a bright side to the snow."

"Well, without snow, how would Santa Claus land his sleigh?" Jenny asked. "His reindeer, Dasher and Dancer, Prancer and Vixen, Comet and Cupid, Donner and Blitzen need snow."

"How do you know the names of Santa Claus's reindeer?" Steven asked.

"Why, from the poem 'A Visit From St. Nicholas,'" Jenny said. "Have you never heard that poem?"

"No, ma'am, I ain't never heard it," Steven said.

"I've never heard it either," Molly said.

"Why, that is such a wonderful poem for children. Would you like to hear it?"

"Yes, ma'am." Steven nodded.

"Me, too," Timmy said. "Do you know the poem?"

"Oh, yes, I know it. It was written by a man named Clement Moore for his children. Why don't all of you gather round, and I'll tell you the poem. And maybe Becky can hear it, too."

"Becky is very sick," Molly said somberly.

"Yes, dear, I know she is. But sometimes you can hear things, even when you are too sick to talk. I think Becky will be able to hear it. And I think she will feel better on Christmas Day."

Timmy and his two sisters, as well as Barbara and Steven, gathered around Jenny and Becky. Seeing all the eager young faces made Jenny feel good, and she could almost believe she was teaching a class again.

Smiling, Jenny began to recite the poem.

" 'Twas the night before Christmas, when all through the house
Not a creature was stirring, not even a mouse.
The stockings were hung by the chimney with care,
In hopes that St Nicholas soon would be there."

"St. Nicholas? Who is that?" Timmy asked.

"That's Santa Claus's real name," Barbara said. "Isn't it, Mrs. McCoy?"

"Indeed it is," Jenny said. Then she continued.

"The children were nestled all snug in their beds,
While visions of sugarplums danced in their heads.
And mamma in her 'kerchief, and I in my cap,

Had just settled our brains for a long winter's nap.
When out on the lawn there arose such a clatter,
I sprang from the bed to see what was the matter.
Away to the window I flew like a flash,
Tore open the shutters and threw up the sash.
The moon on the breast of the new-fallen snow
Gave the luster of mid-day to objects below.
When, what to my wondering eyes should appear,
But a miniature sleigh, and eight tiny reindeer.
With a little old driver, so lively and quick,
I knew in a moment it must be St Nick."

"St. Nick. That's Santa Claus!" Steven exclaimed.

"That's Santa Claus all right," Jenny said. She continued reciting the poem.

"More rapid than eagles his coursers they came,
And he whistled, and shouted, and called them by name!
'Now Dasher! now, Dancer! Now, Prancer and Vixen!
On, Comet! On, Cupid! On, Donner and Blitzen!
To the top of the porch! To the top of the wall!
Now dash away! Dash away! Dash away all!'
As dry leaves that before the wild hurricane fly,
When they meet with an obstacle, mount to the sky.
So up to the housetop the coursers they flew,
With the sleigh full of toys, and St Nicholas too.
And then, in a twinkling, I heard on the roof
The prancing and pawing of each little hoof.
As I drew in my head, and was turning around,
Down the chimney St Nicholas came with a bound."

Molly laughed. "That's funny—Santa Claus coming down through a chimney. Why, what keeps him from getting burned in the fire?"

"That's how Santa Claus gets into people's houses. And he doesn't get burned in the fire 'cause he's magic," Barbara said.

Jenny continued.

"He was dressed all in fur, from his head to his foot,
And his clothes were all tarnished with ashes and soot.
A bundle of toys he had flung on his back,
And he looked like a peddler, just opening his pack.
His eyes—how they twinkled! his dimples how merry!
His cheeks were like roses, his nose like a cherry!
His droll little mouth was drawn up like a bow,
And the beard of his chin was as white as the snow.
The stump of a pipe he held tight in his teeth,
And the smoke it encircled his head like a wreath.
He had a broad face and a little round belly,
That shook when he laughed, like a bowl full of jelly!
He was chubby and plump, a right jolly old elf,
And I laughed when I saw him, in spite of myself!
A wink of his eye and a twist of his head,
Soon gave me to know I had nothing to dread.
He spoke not a word, but went straight to his work,
And filled all the stockings, then turned with a jerk.
And laying his finger aside of his nose,
And giving a nod, up the chimney he rose!
He sprang to his sleigh, to his team gave a whistle,
And away they all flew like the down of a thistle.

But I heard him exclaim, ere he drove out of sight,
'Happy Christmas to all, and to all a good night!'"

"Oh, that was a wonderful poem, Jenny," Millie said. "And you spoke it so beautifully."

"Yes," Clara added. "And I think the children really enjoyed it, didn't you, children?"

"Yes, ma'am, I liked it a lot," Timmy said. "I just wish that Santa Claus could find us on the train."

"If he could find us, what would you have him bring?" Jenny asked.

"Something to eat for us." Timmy looked at Becky. "And some medicine for Becky, so she wouldn't be sick anymore."

"That is a wonderful gift to wish for," Jenny said.

"That won't happen, though," Steven said.

"Oh, I wouldn't be all that surprised if it happened." Jenny smiled. "Sometimes, wonderful things happen on Christmas. Christmas was the day Jesus was born, you know."

"I know," Timmy said. "He was borned in a barn."

"Why was the baby Jesus borned in a barn?" Molly asked.

"Because they didn't have hotels way back when Jesus was borned," Timmy said.

"Yes they did," Barbara said. "But they didn't call them hotels then. They called them inns. And Jesus was born in a stable and put in a manger, because there was no room at the inn."

"How do you know that?" Timmy asked.

"Because it's in the Bible," Barbara said.

"That's right. The whole Christmas story is in the Bible." Luke began to tell the story.

"'*And there were in the same country shepherds abiding in the field, keeping watch over their flock by night. And, lo, the angel of the Lord came upon them, and the glory of the Lord shone round about them: and they were sore afraid. And the angel said unto them, Fear not: for, behold, I bring you good tidings of great joy, which shall be to all people. For unto you is born this day in the city of David a Saviour, which is Christ the Lord. And this shall be a sign unto you; Ye shall find the babe wrapped in swaddling clothes, lying in a manger. And suddenly there was with the angel a multitude of the heavenly host praising God, and saying, Glory to God in the highest, and on earth peace, good will toward men.*'"

"Wow! I'm impressed!" Jenny said with a smile. "How were you able to do that?"

"I've spent many a Christmas at sea," Luke explained. "And I've often been called upon to read the Christmas story to the sailors. I've read it so many times that I finally memorized it."

"You know what?" Timmy said. "I think that, even if we are still on this train, it will be a good Christmas."

"Now why on earth would you say something like that?" Senator Daniels snarled. "We are stranded here, with no food."

"But we have friends," Timmy said with a broad smile. "And friends are about the best things you can have."

"Timmy, you are wise beyond your years," Luke said.

Chapter Twenty-nine

Big Rock

Again, Smoke and Duff took the sleigh into town. This time, though, Sally went with them. Smoke let Sally off in front of the Big Rock Mercantile, Duff got out in front of Longmont's, then Smoke drove on to the livery barn. Stopping just outside, he unhitched the team, then led them into the barn.

Liveryman Ike Shelby was just inside the barn talking to three other men—Sheriff Monte Carson, Dan Norton the prosecuting attorney, and Allen Blanton, editor and publisher of the *Big Rock Chronicle.*

"Gentleman," Smoke greeted. "Ike, I'd like to leave my team here for a while so they are somewhat out of the cold."

"Sure thing, Smoke. Billy, take Mr. Jensen's team," Ike called to one of his employees.

"What's going on?" Smoke asked.

"We had a murder here, last night," Sheriff Carson said.

"A murder? What happened?"

"When Billy came to open up this morning, he found Corey Calhoun's body lying over there." Ike pointed to a spot in front of a stall.

"Shot?" Smoke asked.

"He had been stabbed," Sheriff Carson answered.

"You knew him, didn't you, Smoke?" Blanton asked.

"Yes, I knew him."

"How well did you know him?" Norton asked.

"I knew him fairly well. He worked for me from time to time. He was a good man, and he, Pearlie, and Cal were friends. Stabbed, you say?"

"Through the heart," Ike said.

"Do you have any ideas on what happened?"

"According to some of the boys over at the Brown Dirt, Calhoun had a pretty good night at poker and won well over a hundred dollars."

"Let me guess. You didn't find any money on him," Smoke said.

"Not a cent," Sheriff Carson replied. "My guess is that someone saw him leave the table a winner, followed him over here, and killed him.

"What about footprints in the snow?" Smoke asked.

Sheriff Carson shook his head. "No help. There are hundreds of footprints everywhere, none that will do us any good."

"I hope you find him," Smoke said.

"We will."

Leaving his team with Ike, and his sleigh parked outside, Smoke walked down to the depot to see what he could find out.

"The rescue train tried to get through to them," Phil said, "but it failed because the tracks are blocked by snow."

"How do you know they failed?"

"These stories were wired to the *Big Rock Chronicle.*" Phil showed Matt the newspaper.

Special to the CHRONICLE *by wire, from the* BUENA VISTA NUGGET

RELIEF EFFORT UNSUCCESSFUL

TRAIN FORCED TO TURN BACK

The train that was to relieve the trapped Red Cliff Special was forced to return to Buena Vista when a wall of snow presented an insurmountable impediment. Doodle Reynolds, the engineer, stated that, not even with the plow affixed to the front of his engine could the snow be removed.

Hodge Deckert has assured those who have loved ones on board the train that the passengers are in no danger or great distress as the diner carries extra food for just such a contingency. It is expected the snow will be sufficiently melted within a few days to allow another rescue attempt to be made.

Amon Briggs Removed From Bench

MAY FACE PRISON TERM

Word has reached the Nugget that Amon Briggs, formerly a district judge located in Pueblo, has been removed from the bench by order of Governor Davis Hanson Waite.

According to Sheriff McKenzie, Briggs, who is now a guest of the Pueblo County Jail, was involved in a nefarious scheme with Sheriff Ferrell of Bent County. Briggs would inform Ferrell when money was being transferred, and Ferrell and his partner in crime, usually one of this deputies, would rob the victim so identified.

The latest attempt at robbery failed when Ferrell and his deputy were both killed by the heroic action of Mr. Nugent, who was riding shotgun guard.

Though Sheriff McKenzie has not yet disclosed the incriminating evidence discovered as a result of the failed robbery attempt, it is sufficient to result in the incarceration of Briggs until such time as a judge can be made available to try the case.

"Ha!" Smoke thumped his fingers on the paper. "That doesn't surprise me about Briggs. I never have trusted him. But what about the train, have you heard anything? Do you know if they are going to try again?"

"I'm sure they will when the some of the snow melts."

"I hate it that Matt and the others are trapped up there. But I figure they haven't run out of food yet."

Phil laughed. "They're probably having a good old time. I mean, what else can you do under a situation like that?"

"I guess you're right," Smoke agreed. "Listen, Phil, I'm probably going to be in town for the rest of the day, so if you get any further word about the train, you'll let me know, won't you?"

"Yes, of course I will. Where will I find you?"

"I don't know, at Longmont's I suppose. Sally came into town with us, and she'll want to have lunch, probably at Kathy's Kitchen. But if you don't find me, I'll be checking in with you from time to time.

"That's a good place for lunch, I often eat there myself."

Smoke stepped into Longmont's a few minutes later. Duff sat at a table, drinking coffee and reading the newspaper. Smoke joined him.

"The rescue train was turned back," Duff said, thumping the paper with his fingers.

"Yes, Phil told me that."

"There is an interesting story here. The deputy sheriff from Pueblo County is escorting two prisoners. One of the prisoners has had all the charges against him dropped but he doesn't know that, and there will be no way for him to know until they are freed."

"Who are the prisoners?" Smoke asked.

Duff referred back to the paper. "Michael Santelli and Luke Shardeen."

"I hope Santelli isn't the one who has been pardoned," Smoke said.

"Na, 'tis Luke Shardeen. Do you know Mr. Santelli?"

"I've never had the displeasure of a personal encounter with him, but I certainly know who he is. And he is a bad one. I don't like to think of him being on the same train, trapped in a snowslide, with a bunch of innocent people."

"Aye, the longer one has to hold him in custody, the greater the mischief he can create."

Louis Longmont brought Smoke a cup of coffee without being summoned. "Did you hear about the murder we had here in town last night?" Longmont asked.

"Murder is it?" Duff said looking up from his paper. "I've nae heard a thing about it."

"It happened over at the livery stable," Smoke informed him. "I was talking to Monte and a few others about it. Corey Calhoun got killed."

"Och, 'tis sorry I am to hear of it. Did you know him?"

"Yes, he worked for me from time to time. He was a good man, and a friend of Pearlie and Cal. They'll be upset to hear about it."

"I haven't talked to Monte since I heard about

it," Longmont said. "Does he have any ideas as to who might have done it?"

"Only indirect ideas," Smoke said. "It seems that Corey won quite a bit of money in a card game over at the Brown Dirt. Sheriff Carson thinks someone may have seen him win, then followed him from the saloon. He killed him in the livery stable."

"That means nobody saw it." Duff leaned back and crossed his arms.

"Yes, I'm afraid that is exactly what it means. And if nobody saw it happen, I think the chances of finding out who actually did it are rather slim," Smoke sipped the hot coffee.

"I'll keep an eye open," Longmont promised. "Oftentimes, when someone comes into an unexpected sum of money, they'll come in here and be big spenders all of a sudden."

A couple of Smoke's friends came in then and invited Smoke and Duff to join them in a friendly game of poker. They were still playing three hours later when Sally came into the saloon.

"Sally, ma belle, bienvenue à ma place," Longmont greeted effusively.

Sally smiled. "Thank you, Louis." She turned to the poker players. "Smoke, Duff, are you two getting a little hungry?"

"Hungry?" Smoke glanced over at the wall. "Oh, oh. It's one-thirty. Uh, we were supposed to meet you at Kathy's at noon, weren't we?"

"That was my understanding," Sally said, though her response was ameliorated by her smile.

"Sally, you should leave this man who so mistreats you," Longmont said. "If you had chosen me over him, never would you be disappointed by such forgetfulness."

"Louis, I would be impressed, but I know you say that to every married woman in town."

"Only to the pretty ones," Longmont assured.

"And only to the married ones," Sally replied.

Smoke laughed. "Louis, she has you pegged. You only carry on so with women you know are safe. You wouldn't dare say such things to a single woman for fear she would take you up on your offer."

"Ah, how well my friends know me," Longmont replied. "Enjoy your lunch at Kathy's. And tell her that I long for her."

"You never give up, do you, Louis?" Sally said with a laugh.

On board the Red Cliff Special—December 24

Bailey was looking through the window of the car, and called Matt over.

"Yes?"

"I'm sure they've tried to reach us, but gave up when they couldn't get through. They probably aren't that worried, figuring we have enough food to last. But if they knew our situation, I think they would make more of an effort." Bailey pointed toward the telegraph wire. "If I could reach that wire, I could send a message back to Buena Vista telling them of our serious condition."

"You could send a message? You mean you know telegraphy?"

"Yes, before I was a conductor, I was a telegrapher for Western Union."

"But, how would you send a message? We aren't connected."

"I am pretty sure the wire going forward is down. But it looks like the wire going back toward Buena Vista is still up. I can see it over the top of the snowbank behind us, and if it didn't go down here, I'm sure it is up for the rest of the way. All I have to do is connect to it."

"Connect what to it?"

"I have a telegraph key," Bailey said with a smile. "But I don't know how to get up there."

Luke had overheard the conversation and he went over to join in. "Did I hear you right? You can send a telegram?"

"If I could connect to that wire I could. But in order to do that, I would have to climb that pole, and it is covered with snow and ice. Climbing it would be impossible."

Luke looked at the pole for a moment, then he shook his head. "It will be difficult," he agreed. "But it isn't impossible."

"Wait a minute," Matt said. "Are you saying you think you can climb it?"

"Why not?" Luke replied. "I've climbed ice-slickened mainmasts before, and that's with the ship rolling in the sea. Yes, I think I can get up there."

"Oh, Luke, no," Jenny put in. She'd followed Luke. "That's much too dangerous."

"Ha! I laugh at danger," Luke said, thrusting his hand out in an exaggerated fashion.

"I'm serious," Jenny argued.

"Don't worry, Jenny. I've done this kind of thing before."

Matt and Bailey went outside with Luke to see how he would attack the pole. Worried about Luke, Jenny trailed behind. They studied the pole for a moment or two, rising as it did from the midst of a huge drift of snow.

"How are you going to even get to the pole?" Bailey asked.

"I don't know. That does seem to be a problem." Luke looked at the pole, then looked back at the train and smiled. "I'll climb up onto the top of the car, then leap over to the pole."

"Luke, no, you can't be serious!" Jenny cried.

"I don't have to leap onto the pole, just into the snowbank close enough to it to be able to grab hold," Luke explained.

Matt smiled. "You know, I think that might work. I wouldn't want to be the one to do it, but I think it might work."

Luke climbed to the top of the car, then stepped to the edge to examine the pole for a moment. Satisfied with what he saw, he moved to the opposite side. With a running start, he leaped across the opening and disappeared into the snowbank at the foot of the pole.

"Luke!" Jenny called in fear.

After a moment of anxious silence, Luke appeared out of the snowbank, his arms and legs wrapped around the pole. They watched as he climbed to the top, threw a leg over the crossbeam, and pulled himself into a secure sitting position. He looked down and threw his arms open with a big smile.

"Oh, Luke, hold on!" Jenny called.

"I'm all right. Why, this pole isn't even moving. Mr. Bailey, what do I do now?"

"Cut the wire," Bailey instructed. "And toss it over here so I can get to it."

"Will I get shocked?"

"No," Bailey explained. "Telegraph works by direct current. There's no danger."

"If I cut the wire, won't it mean you can't send a signal?"

"It'll be fine, as long as there isn't another break in the wire between here and Buena Vista."

Luke cut the wire as Bailey instructed, then tossed it down. Matt caught it and handed it to Bailey, who attached the cut end to his instrument.

Luke came back down the pole about halfway, then leaped into the snowbank. Again, he disappeared, but reappeared a moment later, covered in snow.

"I'm going to have to quit doing that," Luke teased as Jenny helped brush the snow away.

Bailey got the wire attached, then sent a BV signal.

"Is it working?" Matt asked.

"I don't know. I haven't gotten a reply." Bailey sent a BV signal again.

There was no reply.

He tried it a third time, then, with a sigh, looked up at Luke. "I'm sorry, Mr. Shardeen. It looks like I sent you up the post for nothing. We may as well get out of the cold. It was—"

Clackclackclackclackclack.

"We're through!" Bailey shouted excitedly. "We're through!" He listened to the clicks for a moment, then chuckled. "Bernie is apologizing because he was away from the key. He wants to know who is calling him."

Bailey began sending a message, his fingers moving rapidly as the clicks went out over the line.

CHAPTER THIRTY

Sugarloaf Ranch

Once breakfast was on the table, Sally joined Smoke and Duff. "I just hate to think of Matt being on that train. I was so looking forward to having him join us for Christmas."

"Matt's younger and resilient," Smoke said. "I imagine he can get through just about anything. But I would have enjoyed having him here for Christmas. Christmas should be with family, and we're the closest thing to family he has."

"We aren't just the closest thing to it," Sally said. "We *are* it. We are family."

"You're right. We are family."

Their breakfast was interrupted by a knock on the door. Sally started to get up, but Smoke held out his hand. "I'll get it."

He hurried to the front door and opened it to see Eddie standing on the porch.

"Eddie? Don't tell me the train is in?"

"No, sir, it ain't in. And it's worse 'n we thought."

"Worse how?"

"We got a telegram from the train. It's been sent out all over. Mr. Wilson thought you might want to read it."

SITUATION DIRE STOP PROXMIRE DEAD STOP
GUNMEN IN DINER STOP NO FOOD STOP
COME SOONEST STOP BAILEY CONDUCTOR

Smoke's expression was grim as he read it, then he looked up at the messenger. "Why don't you come on into the house, Eddie, have some breakfast?" Smoke invited.

"Thank you, sir!" Eddie said as a wide smile spread across his face.

Smoke led Eddie back into the dining room.

"Eddie," Sally said. "It's so nice to have your company. I'll get another plate. Smoke, you . . ." Sally stopped when she saw the expression on Smoke's face. "Smoke, what is it? What's wrong?"

Smoke showed the telegram to Sally, who read it quickly. "Oh, no."

Duff reached for the message and she gave it to him. He looked up after reading it. "What can we do?"

"I'm going up there," Smoke decided. "I'm going to load a sled with as much food as I can get on it and I'm going up there."

"Smoke, if a train can't get through, how are you going to get there?"

"I will get there because I must get there," Smoke said emphatically.

"I'll be going with you," Duff said.

"No need for you to go," Smoke protested. "This isn't going to be easy."

"Smoke, what kind of friend would I be if I didn't go with you? And what kind of friend would you be, if you didn't allow me to go?"

Smoke smiled, then nodded. "All right. Let's get ready. We need to get as much under our belt as we can while we've still got light. I've no doubt but that it'll be well dark before we get there."

"Aye," Duff said. "I'll find some warm clothes."

"Eddie?"

"Yes, sir?" Eddie replied, his mouth full of biscuit.

"I hate to interrupt your breakfast, so just grab yourself a couple bear claws. I want you to get back into town as quickly as you can and go by Ebersole's Bakery, and get as much bread as he has available. Then go to Dunnigan's store. Tell him to pack up as much jerky as he can get together. Tell him we're going to have to feed a lot of people. We'll be in to pick it up before we leave."

"Yes, sir," Eddie said, getting up quickly.

Sally handed him two bear claws and he left immediately.

Big Rock

Bob Ward was having lunch at Little Man Lambert's café and reading a special edition of the *Big*

Rock Chronicle. It had only two stories, and as it happened, both were of intense interest to him.

No Clues on Murder

Sheriff Monty Carson told the Chronicle he has no leads on the murder of Corey Calhoun. A well-known and well-liked young man, Calhoun worked as a cowboy during the season and was spoken highly of by all who knew him, employers and fellow workers alike.

Calhoun's body was found Friday morning by an employee of the livery stable.

Train Passengers in Peril

The conductor of the Red Cliff Special has sent a telegram in which he says Deputy Sheriff Proxmire is dead and gunmen occupy the dining car, denying food to the starving passengers.

That someone could be so evil in this Christmas season defies all understanding. We can but pray for the safe delivery of those unfortunate passengers, and the ultimate capture and execution of the evil men responsible for this reprehensible act.

With eight crates of bread loaded onto their sled, Smoke and Duff went to Dunnigan's for jerky.

"I don't have near enough jerky to do you any

good, Smoke," Ernest Dunnigan said. "But I tell what I do have. I have forty tins of sardines. And because they are in tins, it'll be pretty easy for you to carry them."

"All right," Smoke said. "Sardines it will be. Get them out here, and Duff and I will load them."

"Yes, sir," Dunnigan replied.

While Smoke and Duff were loading the sled, Ward left the restaurant and hurried to the livery where he was boarding six horses and tack to be used for the getaway.

"How much longer you plannin' on leavin' them horses here?" Ike asked. "Reason I ask is, they're takin' up a lot of room, and folks that's comin' into town are wantin' to board their horses to keep 'em out of the cold while they're here."

"I don't know how much longer," Ward said. "Until I need them."

"Here's the thing. You see them two horses there? They belong to Smoke Jensen and Duff MacAllister, and they're wantin' to leave them here while they go up to rescue them folks on the train. I reckon you heard about that, didn't you?"

"I heard about it," Ward said. "You mean they ain't goin' to go up on horseback?"

Ike shook his head. "There ain't no horse that can get up there now, and more 'n likely, no mountain goats either. The only way a body could get up there now is to climb the mountain. And that ain't goin' to be easy. Not with all this snow. But I reckon if anyone can do it, Smoke can."

"Yeah, that's what I heard someone say. They talk about Smoke Jensen like he is some kind of a hero or somethin'."

"Well, sir, you might say that he is," Ike said. "And that brings me back to them six horses you got boarded here. Would you mind if I sort of put some of 'em together? Like say, three stalls, with two horses in each stall. It would help me out, and you'd be savin' money."

"That'll be fine," Ward agreed. "But I need some of my tack, first."

"Sure, what do you want?"

"I want a poncho, blanket, and my rifle."

"Look here, mister, it sounds like you're goin' huntin'. If that's true, be awful careful 'bout where you shoot your rifle. You could cause an avalanche, and you for sure don't want to get caught in one of those."

"I'll be careful," Ward insisted.

"All right. You can come on back and get your tack." As they passed one of the stalls, Ike pointed. "I reckon you heard about the murder. Billy found 'im lyin' right there. He'd been stabbed."

"I read about it in the paper," Ward said.

"There's your tack, all there as you can see. Your stuff is safe here. Yes, sir, in all the years I been runnin' this livery, ain't never been nothin' stole from it."

"Just somebody murdered," Ward mumbled.

"What? Oh, yes, sir, I guess that's right. I sure ain't proud of it, but I guess it is right."

Ward pulled his rifle from the tack. Reaching down into his saddlebag, he opened a box of ammunition and scooped out a handful of extra rifle rounds, which he put in his pocket. The poncho and blanket were rolled together in a tight roll. He put the roll over one shoulder, let it fall diagonally across his body, and tied the two bottom ends together. This allowed him to carry the blanket and poncho while keeping his hands free.

"I appreciate you lettin' me put your horses together," Ike said. "That'll free up three more stalls."

Ward nodded, then stepped into the street in front of the livery. He looked toward the market, where, a few minutes earlier he had seen two men loading a sled. The men were gone, and he felt a moment of apprehension that he had lost them. Then, looking up the track, he saw them plodding along, pulling the sled behind them.

On board the train

The wire from the telegraph line had been run through the window of the car so Bailey could send and receive messages from the relative comfort of the car. Newspapers and pieces of carpet were stuffed into the open section of the window to keep as much cold air out as possible.

Some of the passengers had asked that he send messages back to let their family know that they were still alive. Senator Daniels asked if he could send a message to the Denver newspapers.

"All right," Bailey agreed.

Senator Daniels cleared his throat, then began to speak. "My fellow citizens. I am addressing you by the magic of harnessed lightning, to tell you that I am safe, though I, and the others with me, are being held hostage by a convicted criminal, Michael Santelli. He and other brigands with him have taken control of the dining car, wherein is stored all the food on this train. The result is four days of starvation and want.

"I want all my constituents to know that I, and the others herein exposed to such danger and privation, are doing all we can to fight against this evil, and it is my belief that we will prevail. But, I ask—no, I demand—the Denver and Pacific do whatever is necessary to come to our rescue.

"It is unthinkable that in this day of mighty steam engines and powerful, steam shovels, of telegraph and telephone, that a loud and resounding hue and cry has not gone out over all the land to cause a mighty mobilization of forces, sufficient to overcome any such barriers as may stand between us, and our eventual rescue.

"I further demand that—" Senator Daniels stopped in mid-sentence and looked down at Bailey. "You aren't sending this."

"Senator, I can't send all that. I can't send more than twenty-five words in each message."

"Why not?"

"Because this is not a regular Western Union station. We have what is called emergency access, which allows us but limited use of the line. If I attempted to send everything you just said, we would be cut off. And I feel that it is vital we keep this line open."

"Hrrumph," Senator Daniels grumped. "Very well, very well."

"If you have something you can send in twenty-five words or less, I would be happy to send it."

"All right, send this to the *Colorado Rocky News.*" Again, Senator Daniels cleared his throat as if about to deliver a speech. "Though we face starvation and privation, I have rallied the beleaguered passengers to show courage in the wake of hardship. We will prevail. Jarred Daniels, State Senator."

"That's twenty-seven words, Senator."

"Change 'we will prevail' to 'I will prevail' and sign it Senator Daniels."

Bailey sent the message, along with several other messages. Then, after a few minutes of quiet, the telegraph key began clacking. Bailey responded, then listened.

"Mr. Jensen," Bailey called. "There is a message coming in for you."

"For me?" Matt asked, surprised by the announcement.

"Yes, sir."

"What does he say?"

The machine clattered again, and Bailey recorded the message. Then he chuckled. "I'm sure this has some meaning for you."

"What?"

Bailey read aloud what he wrote. "Will pull your behind from snow again. Hang on. Rescue soon."

Matt smiled, broadly. "Yes, sir, it has a lot of meaning for me. It means Smoke is coming to get us. And it means that we will be out of here sometime within the next twenty-four hours."

"Smoke? Are you talking about Smoke Jensen?" Senator Daniels asked.

"Yes."

"I am well aware of the exploits of Smoke Jensen. However, he is but one man, and I don't see how one man can possibly come to our rescue. I mean, even if he gets here, what can he do? He can't free the train, and he is no more capable of taking the dining car back than we are."

"Never underestimate Smoke Jensen," Matt warned. "If he says he is going to rescue us, that is exactly what he is going to do."

"It must be refreshing to have such childish confidence in a person," Senator Daniels said sarcastically.

"Oh, there's nothing childish about it, Senator. As I am sure you will see soon enough."

The telegraph began clicking again, and once more, Bailey recorded the incoming message on a tablet. When finished, he reread the message. "Well, I'll be."

"What is it?" Matt asked.

Bailey showed him the message, and a big smile came across his face after he read it. "Luke, you might want to hear this message," Matt called.

Luke was sitting in the seat just across from Jenny, who was still holding Becky's head in her lap. He turned to Matt. "Yes?"

"This message pertains to you," Matt said.

Luke came over to Matt and Bailey, his face reflecting curiosity and a slight bit of anxiousness.

Matt read aloud from the paper. "Sheriff Ferrell killed robbing stagecoach. Judge Briggs indicted for collusion. Removed from the bench. Shardeen's charges dropped. Governor vacated sentence."

"Does that mean I'm free? Really free?" Luke asked.

"It does indeed," Matt congratulated. "When we are rescued from this train, you can go back to your ranch, a free man."

CHAPTER THIRTY-ONE

On the mountain

Smoke and Duff had been climbing for the better part of four hours, encountering one obstacle after another. On three separate occasions, they had come to an absolute halt. Each time, they had to backtrack, sometimes for two or three miles, until they found another route.

With each subsequent try the trail became more difficult. Walking in snowshoes made the trek more manageable, but it was still exhausting. They stopped, then sat down under a juniper tree, drawing in huge, heaving breaths that filled their lungs with cold air and caused their chests to hurt.

"It's hard enough just to get your breath at this altitude," Smoke pointed out. "It's even more difficult when you are exerting yourself as hard as we are."

"This trail seems somewhat more difficult than any of the others we have tried, so far," Duff said.

"It is. The other trails were much easier going, but as you saw, each of those trails reached a point to where we could go no farther. I would rather have the trail difficult, but with no insurmountable obstacle, than to have an easy trail that comes to a dead end."

"Aye, you have a point there," Duff agreed.

Ward was exhausted. He had not thought about bringing snowshoes, and struggled mightily with each step he took. Twice he lost trail of the two men he was following, only to see them coming back down the trail toward him. In those cases he was glad to be far enough away they didn't come across his tracks.

Panting hard, he pulled his feet up from the snow, feeling agony from the cold and the heavy breathing.

Grumbling about snowshoes, he continued on through the snow, step by agonizing step, when he noticed the men had stopped. Resting. Immediately, the solution came to him. He would kill them, take their snowshoes, then go on to the train carrying the extra pair of snowshoes. Once he reached the train he would give the other pair to his brother, abandon the men he had recruited to help him, and he and his brother would split the five thousand dollars between them. He gauged the distance between him and the two men to be no more than about fifty yards, an easy shot with the rifle. Raising the Winchester .30-06 to his shoulder, he aimed at the one farthest away, then pulled the trigger.

Smoke leaned forward to adjust his foot in the snowshoe, which proved to be a fortuitous move. He heard the pop of the bullet as it passed close to his ear, and knew what it was, even before he heard the sound of the rifle shot.

"What is it?" Duff called, looking around.

"Get down!" Smoke called.

As both men began clawing at their heavy coats, trying to get to their pistols, they heard another sound. Not that of a second gunshot, but the heavy thunder of cascading snow.

"Avalanche!" Smoke shouted, and he and Duff crouched behind the tree, looking up at the snow as it came barreling down the side of the mountain.

Smoke was certain he was going to die. He felt no fear, just a sense of wonder that he had survived so many gunfights and close calls only to be killed by an avalanche. His biggest concern was that he had failed Matt and the others on the train.

About three hundred feet above, the avalanche changed direction, and Smoke and Duff watched in fascination as more than a hundred feet of snow snapped trees and gathered rocks as it roared down the side of the mountain and right past them. Miraculously, the avalanche left them in the clear.

Following the moving mountain of snow with their eyes, they saw the shooter swept up into the massive slide. His head and shoulders protruding from the great slide, the man's face contorted in pain and terror just before he went under. A moment later, the snow appeared red with blood in spots, then the avalanche continued down the hill, breaking trees off at the trunk, the loud pops sounding like explosions. As the avalanche rolled on down the side of the mountain, the sound, in Doppler effect, decreased in volume until, way down at the bottom of the mountain, the crashing trees sounded more like snapping twigs.

"That was close." Smoke stood up in amazement.

"Aye, indeed it was. Who was that fellow, Smoke, and why was he shooting at us?"

Smoke shook his head. "I don't have the slightest idea." He let out a long, frustrated sigh. "After this, though, I don't see how we are ever going to make it up the rest of the way. I wouldn't be surprised if this didn't close every path there was. I'm not ready to give up yet, but—" Smoke stopped in mid-sentence and looked up the side of the mountain. "God in heaven! It can't be!"

"What is it? What are you talking about?" Duff craned his neck to see what Smoke was looking at.

"You don't see him?"

"See who?"

"How can you not see him? He's no more than fifty feet away!" Smoke said, pointing.

"The shooter? How can that be?" Duff asked in confusion.

"No, not the shooter. The mountain man! But it can't be who I think it is. It can't be!"

"Lad, have ye gone daft? There is no one in the direction you are pointing, be it fifty or a hundred feet away."

The man Smoke saw was an old mountain man dressed in buckskins and a bear coat. He was carrying a Hawkens .50 caliber muzzle-loading rifle, and he was smiling at Smoke. "It's good to see you again, boy."

Smoke shook his head. "This isn't possible."

"Smoke, what are you talking about? Who are you talking to?" Duff asked, puzzled by Smoke's strange actions.

"Are you going to tell me that you don't see anyone there?" Smoke asked.

Duff looked again in the direction Smoke was pointing, then looked back at Smoke with an expression of confusion on his face. "I see nothing."

"Never mind the Scotsman," the old mountain man said. "Follow me. I'll show you the way."

"How did you—?" Smoke asked, but the mountain man interrupted him.

"We've no time for palaverin' now, boy. We have to get a move on it. Ain't that right, honey?"

A little girl, who appeared to be about nine years old, stepped out from behind the old mountain man.

"We need you, Mr. Smoke," the little girl said. "Please come help us."

"What? God in Heaven, who are you?"

"My name is Becky."

"What are you doing here?"

"I came from the train."

"Where are your mama and daddy? Do they know you are here?"

"They think I'm asleep," Becky said.

"Yes, and well you should be. You've got no business being out in this weather. You'll freeze to death!"

"Please hurry," the little girl said. "We need you. Everyone on the train needs you."

"What is she doing here?" Smoke asked the old mountain man. "Did you bring her?"

"No, she came on her own, just to show you how much those folks on the train need you."

"Smoke, would you be wanting me to drag the sled now?" Duff asked.

Smoke looked at Duff, then back at the mountain man and the angelic little girl who was standing beside him. Both seemed to be glowing in some sort of ethereal light.

"Old man, can I ask you something?"

The old mountain man chuckled. "Now, Smoke, would you tell me when, for as long as I have known you, you have ever needed permission to ask me a question?"

"I've never seen you . . . uh . . . quite like this, before," Smoke said.

"All right, ask the question."

"Why hasn't Duff said anything about you or the little girl? Does he see you?"

"Duff has his own reality," the mountain man said. "And you have yours."

"Reality? Is that what you call this?"

"What do you call it?" the old mountain man asked.

"I don't know what to call it." Smoke looked at the little girl again, and thought that he had never seen a more beautiful child.

Smoke turned to Duff. "Do you see this old man and this young girl standing here before us?"

Duff was down on one knee, adjusting the cord to the sled. He gave no indication he had even heard Smoke.

"Why doesn't he answer me?"

"He doesn't hear you."

"How can he not hear me? He's right here."

"I told you. He has his own reality."

"Are you saying I'm not a part of his reality?

"Sometimes you are and sometimes you aren't."

"That doesn't make sense."

"Do you think that when a caterpillar is born, he knows someday he will be a butterfly?" the old mountain man asked.

"I don't know."

"Then let's leave it at that. Just because you don't know, doesn't mean that it isn't real."

"All right, let's accept this as my reality. How are we going to get up to the train? There's no way up the side of this mountain. It's for sure the avalanche has closed every passage."

"Not every passage," the old mountain man explained. "Come along and follow me. I know a way. Have I ever steered you wrong?"

"Are you sure the avalanche has closed every passage?" Duff asked Smoke. "Or would you like to go on and see if we can find something? If you want to go on, I'm willing to go with you."

"You heard that? You heard me say that the avalanche had closed all the passages?"

"Of course I heard it. I'm standing right here."

"But you didn't hear me talking to the little girl."

"What little girl?"

"Never mind. Are you game to keep going?"

"Aye. 'Tis for sure 'n certain we can't turn back now," Duff said. "You know this mountain, I don't. But I've got confidence you can find a way up for us."

"He's got faith in me, and he doesn't even see me." The old mountain man snickered.

"Ha. He said he has faith in *me*," Smoke boasted.

"It's the same thing, my boy."

"Where is the little girl? What happened to her?"

"What little girl?"

"She said her name is Becky."

The old mountain man chuckled. "Like I said, boy. You've got your own reality. Now, are you ready or not?"

"I'm ready," Smoke said.

"Good. Then I'm with you," Duff answered. "I'll draw the sled for a while."

The old mountain man led the way, trudging up the hill. He wasn't wearing snowshoes, but that didn't matter because he wasn't sinking into the snow. The trail became much easier as they went through areas that looked as if a channel had been dug just to clear the way.

"Smoke, have you noticed something curious?" Duff asked as they made their way up the mountain.

"Everything about this is curious," Smoke replied. "I'm glad to see that you have finally noticed."

"How can you not notice this trail?" Duff asked. "It's just seems too easy to be real, and I've got a feeling we're going come upon a sheer rock cliff, or something else just as impassable. I can't actually believe we've found a path that leads to the top."

"It's all a matter of reality," Smoke said. "Yours and mine."

"What?"

"Nothing. Apparently we have found a good trail, at least so far. But you may be right. We might wind up somewhere that is totally impassable."

CHAPTER THIRTY-TWO

Pueblo

Adele declared an open house on Christmas Eve. A huge, silver bowl was filled with eggnog, and cookies, fudge, pies, and cakes were laid out on the table beside it. Several of the town's leading businessmen were present, though she had put out the word earlier the night was to be social only. None of her girls would be available for anything more than friendly parlor conversation.

One of Adele's girls was playing the piano in the keeping room and a group of carolers, men and women, were gathered around it.

"God rest you merry gentlemen,
Let nothing you dismay,
Remember, Christ our Saviour
Was born on Christmas day,
To save as all from Satan's power
When we were gone astray.

O tidings of comfort and joy,
Comfort and joy,
O tidings of comfort and joy."

The Social Club was well decorated for Christmas, with staircase and fireplace mantel festooned with bunting and evergreen boughs. A large tree was decorated with ornaments and red and green rope, as well as candles. The candle flames were shielded by glass globes to prevent the flames from coming into contact with the pine needles.

"This is quite a party you are putting on, Adele." Charles Matthews was president of the largest bank in Pueblo.

"If you can't celebrate at Christmas, when can you celebrate?" Adele replied.

"You have certainly gone all out with the food. I don't believe I have ever eaten so well. So far I've had cookies and a piece of cake. I thought I might try a piece of cherry pie as well, if I can find room. But I'm stuffed."

"I feel a bit guilty," Adele said. "Here we are surrounded by food, while up at the pass, an entire trainload of people are starving. And that includes Jenny McCoy, bless her heart."

"Jenny McCoy? She's on that train? Well, no wonder I haven't seen her tonight. I figured she would be sitting on a sofa somewhere, holding court with her many admirers."

"No, she's been gone for the better part of a week now."

"Gone to visit someone for Christmas, has she?"

Adele shook her head. "No. Mr. Matthews, are you not aware that she was run out of town by Judge Briggs?"

"Ha! You mean former Judge Briggs, don't you? He's in jail now, which is exactly where he should be. And no, I wasn't aware. What do you mean she was run out of town? Why would that be? From what I know of Jenny McCoy, she has done nothing that would cause her to be run out of town. Why, she wasn't even one of your girls. Not in the traditional sense. Unless there were certain, uh, special people who could enjoy her favors, of whom I'm not aware. At least, I was never able to do more than have a conversation with her."

"There were no special people who could enjoy her favors," Adele said. "For all the time she was here, she remained chaste."

"Then what happened to cause Briggs to run her out of town?"

"She was hosting the Honorable Lorenzo Crounse, Governor of Nebraska, in the tearoom, when some armed brigands broke in on them. They forced poor Jenny to disrobe, then took a picture of her, sitting nude beside the governor."

"Uh-oh. That sounds like political chicanery," Matthews said.

"Yes, I'm sure it was," Adele said. "And I wouldn't be surprised if Briggs was behind it."

"I don't doubt that for a moment. Well, he won't be doing things like that anymore. I expect he is going to spend a long time in jail." Matthews chuckled. "And here is the interesting thing. A lot of his fellow inmates will be people that he put there."

"What poor timing. If Briggs had gone to jail a week or so ago, Jenny would be right here, enjoying the party along with the rest of us." Adele was quiet for a long moment. "Instead she is trapped on that train, starving to death."

"Well, it's too late to do anything about her being on that train, but we can certainly make it so she can come back to Pueblo," Matthews said. "That is, if she wants to. After the shabby way she was treated, she may not even want to come back."

"You are right about that. Jenny is a young woman with a lot of personal pride and self-confidence. Coming back to Pueblo might be about the last thing she has on her mind. But I think she ought to have to option to come back if she wants to."

"Yes, well, I don't know what made Briggs think he could run her off in the first place. But with him no longer on the bench, his order that she be run out of town is certainly without authority now. I tell you what, the mayor is over there. I'm sure he has the authority to vacate Briggs's order. Especially since Briggs has been removed from the bench."

"Oh, do you think so?" A smile of hope crossed Adele's face.

"I not only think so, I'm so sure of it I'll go ask him right now."

"I'll go with you."

His Honor Mayor C. E. "Daddy" Felker, a man of

rather imposing girth, was sitting on the sofa, squeezed between two of Adele's girls. It was obvious he didn't mind the closeness, as he had a big smile on his face when Matthews and Adele approached him.

"Merry Christmas, Mr. Mayor," Adele greeted.

"Yes, yes indeed, Merry Christmas," Felker replied. "What a wonderful party you are throwing tonight."

"It would be more wonderful if Jenny were here."

"Oh, that's right. She was forced to leave town, wasn't she? Such a shame. She would have been a wonderful addition to the party."

"She was run out of town by Amon Briggs," Matthews informed.

"Amon Briggs. What a disreputable character he turned out to be," Felker said. "I expect we will find that he was involved in a lot more chicanery than we even know about."

"Mr. Mayor, you could undo some of the evil Briggs did," Matthews suggested.

"Oh? And how is that?"

"You could vacate his order that Jenny McCoy be banished."

"Do I have the authority to do that?"

"Who is going to tell you that you don't? You are the mayor."

"Yes." Felker pounded his knee. "Yes, by golly, I am the mayor, aren't I? You know, I believe I do have the authority to do that."

"And will you do it?" Adele asked.

"Consider it done, my dear."

* * *

Fifteen minutes later, Adele was at the telegraph office in the Denver and Pacific Depot. "I understand that we have been getting telegrams from the trapped train."

"Yes, that is true. Mr. Bailey, the conductor, used to be a telegrapher and they have tapped into the wire."

"Is it possible to send a telegraph to someone on the train?"

"Yes, we have already sent a few. Do you wish to send one?"

"Yes."

"Who will be the recipient?"

"Jenny McCoy."

"Jenny McCoy? You mean the young woman who was run out of town?"

"Yes, that is the Jenny McCoy I'm talking about," Adele said pointedly.

"All right." The telegrapher picked up a pencil and a pad. "What is the message?"

"Judge Briggs is gone. Mayor Felker says you can come back. I hope that you are willing to do so. And sign it Adele."

"Very well. I'll send it," the telegrapher said.

As Adele left the telegrapher, she heard some carolers singing, and she stopped, just long enough to listen.

"Silent night, holy night
All is calm all is bright
'Round yon virgin Mother and Child
Holy infant so tender and mild
Sleep in heavenly peace
Sleep in heavenly peace."

Adele stepped into the narthex of St. Paul's Episcopal Church. Despite her profession, she was a very religious woman. Dipping her fingers into the baptismal font, she made the sign of the cross and thought back to when she had asked Father Pyron, the Episcopal priest, if he would accept her in his parish, and if she would be allowed to take the Eucharist.

"And why wouldn't I allow it?" Father Pyron replied.

"Because I am a prostitute," Adele said. "Well, I'm not really a prostitute, at least, not any longer. But I'm sure you know that I run a house of prostitution."

"Have you considered closing it?"

"I have considered closing it. But if I did, where would my girls go? What would they do? They would wind up in cribs somewhere, barely eking out a living. And without my protection, some might even be killed."

Father Pyron smiled. "You do have a powerful argument for your sin. But it has been suggested that Mary Magdalene was a prostitute. 'She whom Luke calls the sinful woman, whom John calls Mary, previously used the unguent to perfume her flesh in forbidden acts.' And of course, we know that Mary Magdalene was present at the crucifixion, the burial, and the resurrection. So if Jesus could accept Mary, then who am I to deny you the rite of communion?"

That conversation had taken place two years ago, and Adele had been a regular parishioner ever since.

She walked down to the chancel, genuflected before the cross, then knelt at the rail, crossed herself again, and prayed aloud. "Please, Lord, be with Jenny and all the other poor people trapped on that train. And let her find it in her heart to forgive the town, and return."

She crossed herself again, stood and genuflected one more time, then left the church. She walked back to the depot, on the chance that Jenny might answer the telegram.

On board the train

When the telegraph began to clatter again, Bailey hurried over to it to write down the message. "Mrs. McCoy. This message is for you."

"For me?"

"Yes, ma'am."

"Who would be sending me a message?"

"It's signed by the person who sent it," Bailey said.

Jenny read the message, then felt tears welling up in her eyes."

"Jenny!" Luke said. He hurried to her. "What is it? Is something wrong?"

"No. Something is right." She smiled through her tears and showed the message to Luke. "It's from Adele, and it looks like we might be able to have that dinner together after all."

Luke read the message, then embraced Jenny.

"Mr. Bailey, can I send a message back to Adele?"

"Yes, ma'am," Bailey said. "What do you want to send?"

"I want to say, Thank you, Adele, so much for this welcome news. I am sure you had a lot to do with it, and I'm very grateful. And sign it Jenny."

Bailey translated the message into telegraph speak and sent it on its way.

CHAPTER THIRTY-THREE

On the mountain

Smoke and Duff took turns pulling the sled. Unlike the first part of the journey where pulling the sled had been laborious, it trailed behind Smoke as easily as if it weren't loaded. They followed the wide, flat path set out in front of them, amazed at how much easier it was to climb and how clearly it could be seen. The snow shimmered so brightly it looked as if it were being illuminated by lanterns.

Duff had never seen anything quite like it and he stared at it in curiosity. "'Tis a miracle of sorts, don't you think?"

"What do you mean?"

"I mean, here it is, so dark you can't see your hand in front of your face, and yet the path before us is glowing in the moonlight, almost as if it had lights of its own."

"Yes. You could say it is a miracle." Smoke looked

at the old mountain man who was leading them. He was about twenty feet ahead of them, moving as easily if he were walking across a parlor floor. As before, there was an aura around him, an enveloping silver glow that looked, not as if it were shining on him, but as if it were coming from him. That same light spread out along the path they were following.

Smoke knew, of course, it wasn't possible the light was coming from the old man. A full moon could be really bright, especially when reflected by the snow. No doubt what he was seeing was, as Duff had said, a reflection of the moonlight.

Smoke had climbed, hunted, and trapped on this mountain, many, many times in the past. He knew every inch of it as well as he knew his own backyard. But he had never seen a path like that, and had no idea how it had gotten there. He wasn't one to turn his back on opportunity, though, so he kept putting one foot in front of the other, following the path that was making their climb incredibly easy.

"How much farther do you think it is to top of the pass?" Duff asked.

"Do you smell that?" Smoke called back to Duff.

Duff took a deep sniff, then smiled. "Yes. I do smell it. It's smoke."

"And not just any smoke. It's coal smoke. That means we are very close now. I would say we are within a mile, maybe even closer."

"I don't know how you found this trail," Duff said. "But it has certainly made our effort much easier."

"I didn't find it. Preacher did."

"You have mentioned Preacher before. Tell me about him."

"Preacher is as fine a man as I've ever known. One of the original settlers of Colorado, he came out here to live in the mountains when there weren't more than two or three hundred white men within a thousand miles. He trapped beaver, lived off the game he took—bear, deer, elk, mountain goat."

"Why do call him Preacher? Was he an ordained minister? A man of God?"

"He wasn't an ordained minister, but he was, and I have to say is, definitely a man of God."

"Aye, 'tis a pleasure when one can find such a man, and a treasure when you can call him your friend. You are truly blessed, Smoke."

"Yes, I am." Smoke looked back to the path in front of him, but the old mountain man was gone. "Where did he go?"

"Who, Preacher? What do you mean where did he go? I thought you said he had died."

"Yes. Yes, that's true. Preacher is no longer with us."

They continued their trek up, following the path to the top of the mountain.

"What now? We're at the top of the mountain, and there's no train," Duff said.

Smoke realized then that the path had taken them all the way to the summit of the mountain, to the very top of the cut, above the pass. Approaching the edge very carefully, he looked down and saw the train, or rather, what could be seen of the train, well below them. It was sticking out from a high wall of snow, almost like an arrow protruding from a target. Lights could be seen in the windows of the last car and the coal smoke they had smelled earlier was drifting up from the chimney.

"Come over here, but be careful," Smoke said. "This is the top of the cut and there's a sheer drop here."

Duff approached, and Smoke pointed. "There's the train."

"Aye. 'Tis easy to see why they are trapped. There's a mountain of snow in front of them."

"And behind them as well. It looks to me like this train could be stuck here for a month."

"How are we ever going to get them out?" Duff asked.

"Let's feed them first, then we'll worry about getting them out," Smoke proposed.

"My word," Duff marveled.

"What is it?"

"Look at the moon. I thought it must be full, but it's only in its last quarter. Now, would you be for tellin' me, how a moon like that could produce enough light to make our path glow as it did?"

"I don't know," Smoke admitted. "Maybe it was the way the snow was spread out, just right to reflect what light there was."

"That can't be it. I mean it was almost like the snow itself was lighting our way for us. I know that sounds strange, but if you will look back at the path you'll see what I'm talking about. It—" Duff paused in mid-sentence. "Smoke? The path!"

"What about the path? Is it still glowing?"

"There is no path!" Duff's voice was laced with awe. "Look behind us, Smoke. There is nothing there but rocks and trees and snow. There is no path, lit or unlit. How did we get here? We could not possibly have come up that way."

"You aren't making sense, Duff. We're here, aren't we?"

"Yes, but—"

"But nothing. We are here, which means there had to be a path. We just aren't standing where we can see it clearly, that's all. Anyway, what is behind us doesn't matter. We still have to get down to the train."

"Aye. 'Twould be a shame to have come this far, and not be able to go the rest of the way. There's nothing now but the sheer wall of the cut. And even if we could climb down it, how would we get the sled down? If we show up without any food, we've just made the situation worse. We have to go on, or our trip has been nothing but a waste of time."

"I am determined that it not be a waste of time," Smoke declared. "We will get there, and we will deliver the food."

"Aye, 'tis my belief as well that we will succeed. I *dinnae* think the Good Lord would be for bringin' us this far if we *cannae* go on."

"Let's wait until sunup. I'm sure we'll find a way.

If nothing else, we'll just push the sled over, then find a way to climb down."

"I'm putting my trust in you, my friend. You haven't failed us yet," Duff avowed.

"I thank you for your vote of confidence, Duff," Smoke replied. "I just hope I can live up to it. What do you say we take a breather for a while?"

"Good idea," Duff replied.

The two men sat down in the snow and leaned back against the sled.

"Duff, do you believe in ghosts?"

Duff chuckled. "How can I not believe? I'm from Scotland. Do you not know the story of the Scottish King MacBeth and Banquo's ghost?"

"I've never heard of it."

"'Tis a story told by Shakespeare. I'll quote a bit for you." Duff extended his arm.

"What are you holding your hand out like that for?"

"Have you never been to a Shakespearian play? "Sure m'lad and 'tis necessary for me to establish the mood, tone, and tint."

Duff began reciting, as if on stage.

"Avaunt! and quit my sight!
let the earth hide thee!
Thy bones are marrowless, thy blood is cold;
Thou hast no speculation in those eyes
Which thou dost glare with!"

"Very good," Smoke said.

"So, why did you ask me about a ghost? Have you seen one?"

"I don't know exactly what I've seen," Smoke replied. "Let's nap until daylight."

"Yes, we seem to have lost our mysterious light, so it probably is smart to wait until daylight before we look for a way down," Duff agreed.

After a few more minutes, both men had drifted off to sleep.

On board the train

As they had on previous nights, Luke and Jenny were sitting side by side in the very front seat of the car. They were protected against the cold by her coat and the serape, and by their body heat.

She could hear Luke's deep, measured breathing, and knew he was asleep beside her. She knew also it was more than just the wraps and the shared body heat that warmed her. It was something else, some visceral reaction she was having to his closeness.

As she thought about it, she found the situation a little frightening. When she knew that he was going to be gone for four years, and that she was being forced to leave Pueblo, there was a certain degree of detachment between them. They were like that passage from one of Longfellow's poems:

Ships that pass in the night, and speak each other
in passing,

Only a signal shown and a distant voice in the darkness.

That very detachment protected her. She could enjoy his company and lose herself in fantasy. As long as she realized that it was but fantasy, she wouldn't be hurt when it didn't come to pass.

But everything had changed. Luke wasn't going to jail, and she wasn't being banished from Pueblo. What did that mean? Would Luke return to Two Crowns, and she to the Social Club? If they met on the street, would they acknowledge each other's presence? Or would they look away, and pass each other with no outward sign that they had ever even met?

It wasn't fair. It just wasn't fair to have met someone she could truly love, only to have that love denied her. And she was certain that once they returned, that love would be denied.

Jenny wept quietly.

On the other side of the car, Herbert Bailey drummed his fingers on the cold window and looked out into the night. It was his fault everyone was stuck on the mountain pass. He was the one who'd insisted the train move on ahead—because he knew the railroad would lose money if the trip wasn't completed—even though Don had been hesitant about it. And by that foolish insistence, he had put every soul on the train in danger.

He had believed the railroad would recognize his

boldness, and as a result, his position and authority, to say nothing of his salary, would be increased, even though he had only been a conductor for a couple months.

Bailey had been a telegrapher, but though the job was interesting and provided a much-needed service to others, he'd wanted the money and prestige that came with being a railroad conductor. Looking into the dark night he remembered his father's attempt to change his mind.

"You are being foolish, Herbert," his father said when Bailey told him of his intention. "You are the only telegrapher in this town. If you leave it may be a long time before we can get another to take your place. What if there is an emergency, a need for a message to go forth, and there is no one to send it? It could be a matter of life and death, with no one to turn to, because you are gone."

"But, Father, don't I have to think of myself, first?" Bailey had replied. "I will make much more money as a railroad conductor, and people will respect my position."

"You put money and importance ahead of all else. The mark of a good man is his service to others. Don't you know that when you die, the only thing you can take with you are the good deeds you have done? When you answer to the Almighty, will He be more pleased that you made money and had prestige by your position? Or would it please Him more if you could bring Him a lifetime of service to others?"

"I must do what I must do," Bailey said.

Bailey's father handed him a Bible. "I know you have made your decision, so I will not try to change it. But I ask, only that you read Luke twelve, verses sixteen to twenty-one."

To satisfy his father, Bailey read the recommended text.

> *"And he spake a parable unto them, saying, The ground of a certain rich man brought forth plentifully:*
>
> *"And he thought within himself, saying, What shall I do, because I have no room where to bestow my fruits?*
>
> *"And he said, This will I do: I will pull down my barns, and build greater; and there will I bestow all my fruits and my goods.*
>
> *"And I will say to my soul, Soul, thou hast much goods laid up for many years; take thine ease, eat, drink, and be merry.*
>
> *"But God said unto him, Thou fool, this night thy soul shall be required of thee: then whose shall those things be, which thou hast provided?*
>
> *"So is he that layeth up treasure for himself, and is not rich toward God."*

His father's attempt to change his mind had had no effect, and Bailey had eventually become a conductor. Ironically, it wasn't his position as conductor making a difference during the Red Cliff Special ordeal. It was through his ability as a telegrapher. His father had been right. If he died during this ordeal, what good would the increased salary and position be?

He knew the small town of Higbee had been

unable to locate a replacement telegrapher. Making a fist, he tapped the window once as if confirming his decision. When he got out of this situation, if he got out, he intended to go back to his old job as telegrapher for the town of Higbee.

Chapter Thirty-four

On the mountain—Christmas morning, December 25

Wrapped tightly in several blankets, Smoke was the first to awaken, and when he opened his eyes, he saw the old mountain man standing in front of him. The butt of his Hawkens was on the ground before him, and his hands were crossed and resting on the muzzle. His head, covered with a coonskin cap, was tilted to one side, and he was smiling down at Smoke. "I wondered when you were going to wake up."

"I thought you were gone," Smoke mumbled as he stretched.

"You didn't think I would bring you this far, then not let you finish the job, did you?"

"You've brought us to the train, now what? There's no way down to it."

"I'll show you the way."

"There *is* no way," Smoke said emphatically. "I've

been here dozens of times. I know this pass like I know my own ranch."

"Wake up Duff, and follow me," the old mountain man said.

"Duff, wake up." Smoke gave his friend a poke, then threw off his blankets to start the morning.

Duff opened his eyes, but didn't move a muscle, staying snug in his blankets.

"Come on, we're going down to the train."

"How?"

"Just trust me."

"I'm with you." Duff stretched, then climbed out of the blankets and stomped his feet. "Whew. Didn't get any warmer overnight, did it?" He made a few quick jumps to get the blood flowing and picked up the leader to the sled. "Where are we going?"

"That's a good question," Smoke said. "Where are we going?"

"Don't worry about where we are going. In all the years you have known me, have I ever steered you wrong?" the mountain man replied.

"What do you mean, where are we going?" Duff asked. "Don't you know? You're in front of me. Sure, lad, and I'll be going where you go."

"I wasn't asking you," Smoke muttered.

"Well, who were you asking? There's nobody else here, but the two of us."

"I . . . I guess was just talking to myself."

Duff chuckled. "Don't talk to yourself like that. It makes me nervous to think I'm wandering around out here in the mountains with a man who has suddenly gone mad."

Smoke laughed as well. "What makes you think I suddenly went mad? If you ask Sally, she'll tell you I've been crazy from the moment she first met me."

"Ha!" the old mountain man put in. "You were crazy long before you ever met Sally."

"You haven't changed, have you?" Smoke said. "You are as cantankerous now as you ever were."

"Cantankerous am I?" Duff questioned.

"No, not you. I'm not talking about you."

"Oh, I see. You're talking to your invisible friend, are you?"

Smoke chuckled. "I guess I am."

On board the train

"Oh, Jarred," Millie said, her voice choked by sobs. "I can't wake Becky up."

"Becky! Becky! Wake up, child! Wake up!" Senator Daniels called.

"Oh! Jarred! Is she . . . Is she . . . ?" Millie couldn't finish the question.

"I . . . I don't know." Senator Daniels pinched his nose. "Oh, Millie, it's my fault, it's all my fault. I'm sorry. You were right. We should have stayed in Pueblo and taken her to a doctor. It's all my fault, I got us into this mess."

"It's not your fault," Millie said. "You had no way of knowing anything like this was going to happen. If it had been a normal train trip, we would have been to Red Cliff long before now, and a doctor would have seen her."

Senator Daniels knelt on the floor beside Becky, then leaned over to kiss her on her forehead. "I'm sorry, I'm so sorry."

Senator Daniels stood up. It was morning, and the sun was streaming into the car. Those who had slept fitfully through the night were awakening. Some had overheard Daniels and his wife and were looking toward them with concern.

"Could I have your attention, please?" Jarred called. "I want to make a public confession and a public apology. I have been, well, there is no other way to say it, but to just come out and say it. I have been a jerk on this trip. No, not just on this trip. I have been a self-centered, arrogant jerk for some time." He looked down at his daughter for a moment, trying to compose himself. "And now my daughter is dying . . . if she hasn't already . . ." He couldn't force himself to say the word *died.* "If we had stayed in Pueblo, a doctor might have been able to help her. Or maybe not. The point is, against my wife's instincts, I insisted we make this trip because I had a very important speech to make tonight.

"But as it turns out, it wasn't really all that important after all. It was important only as far as my political career is concerned. The fact that I missed the speech is of no consequence to anyone.

"I want to apologize to everyone in this car." Senator Daniels looked over toward the porters. "And I especially want to apologize to you three gentlemen.

My actions and comments toward you have been bigoted and small-minded, and I am heartily sorry. I ask your forgiveness, and from all of you, I ask your prayers for my daughter."

"Senator, I been prayin' for your little girl from the first I learned she was sick," Troy said.

"Thank you, Troy." Senator Daniels lowered his head and pinched the bridge of his nose. "And I thank the rest of you for giving me a moment of your time to let me make this public apology."

"Senator, I would say the speech you just made is a hundred times more important than any speech you would have given at that dinner in Red Cliff," Matt said.

"Hear, hear," Luke said, and when he began to applaud, the others joined in.

After Senator Daniels's apology, the passengers settled back into the routine they had established during the long ordeal. Luke and Jenny sat together, warmed by her coat, his serape, and the closeness of their bodies.

"Luke, when you asked if I would have dinner with you when you came back in four years, I said yes, because I didn't know what else to say. The truth is, I had no idea where I would be four years from now, and I still don't. But I do know where I will be if we ever get off this train. I'll be back in Pueblo, and if you were serious, if you really want to see me again, I would be happy to have dinner with you."

"Why wouldn't I want to see you again?"

"You know who I am. You know where I work."

"I'd rather you not go back to work at the social club, though," Luke said.

"I . . . I don't really want to go back there, either. But Adele has been a wonderful friend. And I don't know where else I would be able to work."

"What about raising our children?" Luke asked. "Wouldn't that be work enough for you?"

"Raising our children?"

"Yes, I would like to have children, wouldn't you?"

"Luke, let me get this straight. Are you asking me to marry you?"

"Well, yes. I mean, we really should get married before we start having children, don't you think?"

Jenny laughed. "But . . . that's insane! We've only known each other for four days!"

"Remember the Samoans."

"There is no difference in the heart of a flower that lives but a single day, and the heart of a tree that lives for a thousand years," Jenny repeated what Luke had told her earlier.

"We've known each other for a thousand years, Jenny. Will you marry me?"

"Yes! Yes, Luke, I will marry you!"

They sealed the decision with a kiss.

Suddenly, Timmy shouted, "It's Christmas morning! Hey, everybody, Merry Christmas!"

Bailey chuckled. "Oh for the spirit of a youngster. At a time like this, he can still be excited by the fact that it is Christmas."

"He's right, though. It is Christmas," Luke said, getting to his feet. "And it is the most wonderful Christmas of my life. I've an announcement to make, folks. Jenny McCoy has agreed to be my wife. Merry Christmas "

"Merry Christmas to you as well, young man, and congratulations," Purvis said.

For a few moments after the announcement, and despite the fact that they were stranded and without food, a bit of good nature prevailed among the passengers. Anita and Clara came to talk excitedly to Jenny about her upcoming marriage.

Matt went over to Becky, who was lying on the seat, either asleep, or unconscious, or perhaps even dead. It was difficult to tell. "When was the last time she was awake? Do you know?"

"I don't know," Millie said. "I think she may have been awake for a bit, yesterday. But I don't think she was awake at all during the night. I . . . I don't even know if she is still alive. She is so . . . so unresponsive."

Matt opened his knife, then took one of her fingers and pricked it with the point of the knife, studying the little girl's face as he did so. She gave no reaction to the stimulus.

"Do you have small mirror in your handbag?"

"No, I'm afraid I don't."

"I do," Jenny said, having overheard the conversation. She opened her handbag and took out a small compact, opening it to expose the mirror.

Matt held the mirror under Becky's nose. A small cloud of condensation appeared on the mirror, and he smiled, then showed it to Millie. "She's still breathing, Mrs. Daniels, so she's alive. Don't lose hope. She may be in what they call a coma. I've known people to be in them before and come out of them. All the people in this car are praying for her. And like Timmy said, this is Christmas. I've seen things happen on Christmas, wonderful things that defy understanding. One Christmas I saw a baby born in a barn when all the odds were against it.* That birth reminded us all of that first Christmas."

"If you folks don't mind, I'd like to say a Christmas prayer," Troy offered.

"I don't think we would mind at all, Troy," Senator Daniels said. "In fact, I think we would appreciate it. I know that I would."

Troy nodded and bowed his head. "*Lord, we thank you for the sweet baby Jesus that was born so many years ago. Thank you that He paid for our sins by dying on the cross. We are in a dark time now, and we pray that you guide us through it, and Lord, we pray for this sweet child, Becky, who is so sick. Put your healin' hand on her Lord. In Christ's name we pray. Amen.*"

"Thank you, Troy. That was a wonderful prayer." Senator Daniels turned to the conductor. "Oh, and Mr. Bailey?"

"Yes?"

**A Lonestar Christmas.*

"Forget about what I said about holding the Denver and Pacific responsible. I am going to make a report to the Denver and Pacific, but it will be to praise you and all the rest of the train crew for your exemplary service under extraordinary conditions."

"I deserve no praise, Senator. It was my insistence that we continue on that put you, your family, and everyone else on this train in danger."

CHAPTER THIRTY-FIVE

On the mountain

"I dinnae believe my eyes," Duff said. "There is a path down the sheer side of this cut, and 'tis no ordinary path, but one that is wide and flat and hard packed with snow for the sled."

"I told you we should wait until sunrise." Smoke grinned.

"You mean you knew about this path? Of course you did. You live here. How could you not know?"

Smoke was silent for a long moment. Taking a deep breath, he said honestly, "I've never seen this path before in my life."

"How could you nae see it? 'Tis almost like a ramp."

"It wasn't here before."

"Then how did it get here?"

"I don't know," Smoke admitted. "Maybe it was created by the storm. Weather does such things, you know."

It took less than ten minutes to reach the bottom of the cut, where they found themselves at the back of the train. A black man lay on the ground just off the track, a dark shadow against the brilliant white of the snow.

Duff knelt on one knee and put his hand to the man's neck, though the fact that he was lying there, unmoving, and with both eyes open, made any further investigation unnecessary. "Och, the poor man is dead."

Smoke and Duff climbed up onto the rear platform and tapped on the door to the car.

Nobody inside the car had seen the approach of the two men and the sled, so the tapping on the door was unexpected.

"It must be Santelli!" Purvis shouted.

"Everyone down, behind the seats!" Matt called, pulling his pistol and pointing it toward the back.

The passengers scurried to follow his directions.

The door opened and two men bundled in winter coats came in.

"Hello?" Smoke called out tentatively.

"Smoke!" Matt shouted happily. Holstering his pistol, he rushed to him. "You made it!" Matt grabbed Smoke's hand and pumped it vigorously."

"Why is it I always find you bottom-lip deep in snow?" Smoke teased.

Matt grinned and turned to Smoke's friend. "Duff!"

"Aye. Happy to be able to help."

Matt called the others from their hiding places and introduced Smoke and Duff. "I told you he would come." Matt couldn't stop grinning.

The passengers expressed their happy gratitude.

"Oh, by the way, is anyone hungry? I've got food on the sled outside," Smoke said.

Several people made a mad rush for the door.

"Wait, wait!" Smoke held up his hand. "We'll bring it in to you. It's only bread and sardines, but that should hold you until we get you out of here."

"Praise the Lord, he's done delivered us loaves and fishes!" Troy called out.

"By golly, Troy, you are right!" Bailey acknowledged. "But I hope it's more than five loaves and two fishes."

Smoke stood on the rear platform as Duff took the food from the sled and passed it up to him. Smoke passed it to Matt, who handed it to Luke. Luke and Bailey opened the tins of sardines and passed them out, one each to everyone in the car. There was no crowding or feeling of fear that they wouldn't get their share. On the contrary, everyone was solicitous for others.

"Mama, this is the best Christmas dinner I've ever et," Timmy said.

Clara laughed. "You mean the best that you have ever eaten, and I agree with you. It is delicious."

"I wish Becky could enjoy it," Barbara said.

"So do I, Sweetheart," Anita said. "So do I."

"Becky?" Smoke asked, the name piquing his interest. "You have someone here named Becky?"

"Yes. She is Senator Daniels's daughter, and she has been ill from the time we left Pueblo. Over the last twenty-four hours she has been unconscious." Matt looked around to make certain he wasn't overheard, then he added, "I've been trying to keep their spirits up, but to tell you the truth, I'm not sure she is going to make it."

"And her name is Becky? You are sure that it's Becky?"

"Yes. Why are you so curious about that particular name?"

"Because I—" Smoke stopped in mid-sentence. Duff already thought he had gone mad. If he told Matt he'd seen Becky out on the trail, that she had come to him, Matt would also think he was crazy. "Nothing. I would like to see her."

"She's over here." Matt led Smoke over to the seat where Becky lay, still covered by Matt's coat. Senator Daniels and his wife were sitting together in the seat across from Becky, eating their sardines and bread.

"This is my friend, Smoke Jensen," Matt said.

Senator Daniels started to get up, but Smoke held out his hand. "No, don't get up."

"Mr. Jensen, I know I speak for all of us when I tell you how thankful we are for your courage in tackling this mountain to bring us food and hope. I didn't think you could do it, but here you are."

"I heard about your daughter," Smoke said. "I just thought I'd like to take a look at her."

"Of course you can," Millie agreed.

Smoke pulled the coat down slightly, so he could get a better look at her. He wasn't at all surprised she was the same little girl he had seen on the mountain. He didn't understand it, but he wasn't surprised. He reached down to place the back of his hand against her cheek. "I have come, Becky," he said quietly. "Can you hear me? I have come."

"We are so worried about her." Millie's voice shook a little.

"She will be all right," Smoke declared.

"I pray that you are right."

"I know that she will be all right," Smoke said emphatically. "I can't tell you how I know, but I know."

Tears welled in Millie's eyes, and she took Smoke's hand in hers, the same hand that had touched Becky's cheek, and she raised it to her lips to kiss. "I believe you."

Smoke nodded a confirmation to the Danielses and he and Matt walked back to the rear of the car. Matt tore off a piece of bread and picked up an open tin of sardines. "How in the world did you two get up here? I know this mountain, if you don't come up through the pass, it is practically impossible to climb."

"It was easier than you think. We just followed a path up to the top, then down here. Look, you can see the path coming down the—" Duff stopped in mid-sentence. There was no path. There was nothing but mountains of snow all around them. There weren't even any tracks in the snow left by Smoke, Duff, and the sled.

"What happened to the path? It's just like when we were coming up the mountain. That path was gone, too. I don't understand."

"The path left when Preacher left," Smoke said quietly. "He is the one who led us here."

"Preacher?" Matt exclaimed. "Who are you talking about?"

"You know who I mean by Preacher. You met him," Smoke pointed out.

Matt shook his head. "Excuse me, but you aren't making any sense. Preacher is dead. At least the one I know. But you're saying Preacher led you here. Unless you are talking about someone else."

"No, I'm talking about the same one. He's the one that guided us here."

"Smoke, sure 'n did the cold freeze your brain?" Duff asked. "There was no one that guided us here. You led and I followed, every step of the way. I heard you mumbling and talking to yourself, but you were in the lead. There wasn't anyone else."

"Then how do you explain there is no path, and that we left no tracks?" Smoke asked.

"I don't know. I can't explain it."

"I can. The path was there when Preacher was there. And when Preacher left, the path left. And I'll tell you something else. Becky?"

"What about Becky?" Matt asked.

"She was there, too. I saw her on the mountain. The same little girl that's lying over there on that seat." Smoke pointed toward the Daniels.

"That's impossible," Matt argued. "She hasn't left

this train. She's barely been conscious. So how do you explain that you saw her?"

"I can't explain it. Just like I can't explain how I saw Preacher. But I saw Preacher, and I saw Becky." Smoke was absolutely positive what he saw.

"Smoke, Matt, sure 'n let's not be for tellin' this tale to anyone else," Duff suggested. "They'll think we've all gone daft. And I don't know but that they would be right."

"Look!" Bailey suddenly shouted, pointing to the track behind them. "The track behind us is clear! We can get out now."

"I'm not walking back down this track," Senator Daniels fussed. "I'm not leaving Becky."

"There's no need to leave anyone," Don the engineer advised. "And there's no need for anyone to walk. I've made this run so many times I know every inch of this track. All we have to do is disconnect this car . . . and we can roll all the way back to Buena Vista."

"I believe he is right," Bailey said.

"Let's try it," Smoke suggested.

Matt, Smoke, Duff, Bailey, Don the engineer, and Beans the fireman worked on the coupler until they got it free. Then they strained against the car, pushing to get it started.

Suddenly, a bullet careened off the side of the car, raising sparks where it hit the metal frame, then ricocheting off with a loud, echoing whine.

They turned to see Santelli, Kelly, and Compton

coming toward them, all three with pistols in their hands. Santelli fired again, and again he missed.

Smoke and Matt drew their pistols, but Don called out. "No! Don't shoot! You might start an avalanche!"

Even as he shouted the warning, they heard a roaring thunder high up in the mountains. And, though they could hear it, as yet, they saw nothing.

"Get the car moving! We have to get out of here!" Matt shouted, and the men turned to the task at hand, starting the car to roll, slowly at first, then more rapidly, then faster still, until gravity took over and the car started rolling on its own.

Don and Beans jumped on first, then Smoke and Duff. Bailey and Matt were the last two aboard, barely catching up to the car, so fast was it rolling.

"Don't you leave us!" Santelli shouted. "Don't you dare leave us! *Don't . . . you . . . leave . . .*"

Beyond that, Matt couldn't hear him. Santelli's words faded as the distance increased, and were quickly silenced by the growing roar coming from the mountaintop.

"Look!" Bailey shouted in awe, pointing to the top of the mountain.

A fifty-foot-high wall of snow, half a mile wide, came sliding down the side of the mountain, its churning white wave filled with rocks and broken tree trunks.

Santelli, Compton, and Kelly stood looking up at it, their mouths and eyes wide open in horror. Matt was sure they were crying out a death scream of terror, though from his position on the car, he couldn't hear anything but the roar of the avalanche.

The gunmen disappeared under the huge wave of snow, rocks, and broken tree trunks as the avalanche smashed against the train cars, crushing them as if they were naught but children's toys.

As the men watched from the free-rolling car, the avalanche was increasing in width as more and more of the mountain began coming down. It moved fast, racing down the track behind them, easily matching the car in speed.

Fortunately, it wasn't going *faster* than the car, and therefore, not overtaking it, though Matt feared it might, so close was it behind them. He literally willed the car to go faster until, finally, the distance between the cascading snow and the rapidly moving car was increasing. After a full minute, he was satisfied the car was no longer in danger and went back into the car.

The engineer had gone to the other end of the car and was standing out on the platform, looking ahead as the car swept rapidly down the track. Matt joined him, and felt the cold air knifing through him as the car rushed ahead.

"We are really going fast," Don said. "I'm pretty sure I've never gone this fast."

"I don't know how fast we are going, but we

needed every bit of it. The avalanche was coming down the track toward us, and we barely escaped."

"Count off twenty seconds. I'll count the number of rail joint clicks. The number of clicks we hear in twenty seconds will tell us how fast we are going in miles per hour."

Matt counted off the seconds, but when he got to twenty, Don shook his head. "We're going too fast for me to get an accurate count, but my guess would be that we are doing at least sixty miles per hour."

"Wow! Sixty miles per hour? Is there any danger of us running off the track?"

"I don't think so. Most of the turns are long and gentle. Though, certainly none of them have ever been taken at this speed."

"What do you say we go back inside the car and get out of this cold wind?" Matt suggested.

"Yes," Don replied. "That's a good idea."

Duff was standing just inside the car, and he had a question. It was a question Matt had already considered, but hadn't yet asked.

"How do we stop this thing when we get there?" Duff asked.

"That won't be a problem," Don said. "The track flattens out for the last half mile before we get into the station. By the time we get to the depot, we won't be going any faster than a walk."

Senator Daniels came over to join them. "Well, all I can say is this. Gentlemen, this has certainly been an adventure."

"You can say that again," Don replied.

"We sure are going fast," Becky said. The little girl's words stunned everyone into shocked silence. She was standing just behind her father.

"Becky!" Senator Daniels shouted.

"Oh, Becky, Sweetheart! You are up!" Millie said, hurrying over to her, and sweeping her up into a big hug.

"Jarred! The fever! I don't feel it! It's gone!" Millie said excitedly.

Everyone else in the car reacted in amazement at seeing the little girl who, but a short time ago, had been in an unresponsive state of unconsciousness. Now she was up and talking. All called out in excitement, and Barbara ran over to her, spontaneously giving her a hug.

"Daddy, I'm hungry," Becky said.

Half a dozen passengers offered her food, and she accepted a piece of bread from Anita.

"How do you feel, honey?" Millie asked.

"I feel good, Mama. I feel real good. Just like Mr. Preacher said I would."

"*Who* said that?" Smoke asked curiously.

"An old man. He was dressed in funny clothes, with a furry coat and a little furry cap that looked sort of like a squirrel." Becky laughed. "You know who he is. You were with him out there in the cold. I saw you. You were with him, weren't you?"

Smoke glanced over at Duff and smiled at the

expression of shock on his face. "Yes, honey. I was with him."

When the car finally rolled in to the depot at Buena Vista the news was spread far and wide. A Christmas celebration was held at the depot, and the entire town participated. People brought roast turkey, duck, chicken, beef, and ham, as well as vegetables of every hue and description, along with pies, cakes, and candy.

"Hey!" one of the railroad employees shouted, coming into the depot. He was holding up a Hawkens .50 caliber buffalo rifle. "Somebody left this back in the car. Anybody know who it belongs to?"

Chapter Thirty-six

Pueblo—January 15, 1894

An article appeared in the *Pueblo Chieftain*:

> ***Track Cleared, Ten Bodies Recovered***
>
> The Denver and Pacific Railroad has cleared the track through Trout Creek Pass of the terrible wreckage left by the avalanche, which has, for these last three weeks, rendered traffic through the pass impossible.
>
> Our readers are well aware of the ordeal the passengers who took the Red Cliff Special five days before Christmas, with the intention and full expectation of spending Christmas with their loved ones have endured.
>
> The nefarious scheme of Michael Santelli and the four brigands he had

enlisted to aid him ruined Christmas for the innocent passengers. They suffered great hardships during the time they were trapped in the train, with no food and little fuel for warmth.

The train was subsequently reached by Smoke Jensen and Duff MacAllister, their bravery supplying a happy ending to the unhappy adventure. It may also be said that poetic justice was served, as the perpetrators of the crime: Michael Santelli, Felix Parker, Roy Compton, Gerald Kelly, and Melvin Morris, were all killed by avalanche. Their mangled bodies were found in the wreckage.

Also found were the bodies of five innocent men: Deputy Braxton Proxmire, Dennis Dace, and Andrew Patterson of this city, Paul Clark, Deputy City Marshal of Red Cliff, and Fred Jones, a colored porter.

Red Cliff—January 16

Abner Purvis was a passenger on the first train to make the trip to Red Cliff after the pass was reopened. He walked the seven miles from the Red Cliff train station to his father's farm.

His brother was out feeding the pigs, and was the first to see him. He reacted in great surprise at seeing his older brother coming down the road toward him. "Abner? Is that you?"

Abner held his hand out toward Aaron. "Don't

disturb yourself. I know that I walked away from my inheritance. I know the farm is yours. I want only to be treated as a hired hand."

Aaron smiled. "Come with me to see Pop."

Abner followed his brother into the machine shed, where their father was working on a plow shear.

"Pop, look who is here," Aaron said.

Arnold Purvis looked up to see who Aaron had brought to him. There was only a second's hesitation before his face was wreathed by a huge smile.

"Abner? Abner, my boy! You have come home!" Arnold cried excitedly, getting up from the workbench and hurrying over to embrace his son.

"Aaron, run quickly to tell your mother. Tell her I will kill a hen, so she can make chicken and dumplings." The elder Purvis looked back at Abner. "I know that is your favorite meal."

"Pop, I've already told Aaron. I've no wish to deprive him of the inheritance. The farm shall rightly be his."

The elder Purvis looked at Aaron with a confused expression on his face. "You haven't told him?"

"No, Pop. I haven't told him."

"Told me what?" Purvis asked.

"Abner, I have an appointment to West Point. I'll be leaving soon. I don't want the farm. It's all yours."

"Welcome back, son," Arnold said with a wide grin.

Pueblo—January 18

Luke had suggested they get married in the Colorado Social Club. Jenny was hesitant at first, but then she thought, *why not?* Adele Summers had been a very good friend to her, as had all the other girls who worked there. It was a bit unconventional, but Jenny didn't care. For those who declared themselves her friends, no explanation was necessary. For those who were openly hostile toward her, no explanation would be understood.

Adele had gone all out to decorate the club, and insisted the girls dress demurely as if they were going to church.

Father Pyron of St. Paul's Episcopal Church had never been in Adele's establishment before. While he was drinking a cup of coffee before the ceremony, he admitted he was looking forward to it. "I always wanted to know what this place looked like inside. This way I can come here without compromising myself."

Father Pyron wasn't the only one whose appearance in the club had caused no small degree of curiosity. Troy, Julius, and Pete were also there, the first time anyone of their color had ever set foot through the doors.

Senator Daniels and Millie were there. Becky was very proud to serve as Jenny's flower girl. Also in attendance was Herbert Bailey, who was no longer a railroad conductor, having been rehired as a telegrapher for the town of Higbee.

Smoke, Matt, and Duff were present for the wedding, and Duff had volunteered to play Pachelbel's "Canon in D" on his pipes. It was the first time anyone had heard the traditional wedding song played on the pipes, and so beautifully was it played there wasn't a single dry eye among the girls of the Colorado Social Club.

After the wedding, everyone went down to the train depot to wish the happy couple well as they left by train on the first leg of their wedding trip.

"Where in the world is Samoa?" Adele asked. "And why do they want to go there?"

Nobody had an answer.

As Smoke turned to leave the depot, he thought he saw an old man dressed in buckskin, carrying a long-barreled, Hawkens .50 caliber buffalo rifle and wearing a coonskin cap.

When he blinked, the man was gone.

Epilogue

Lambert Field, St. Louis—December 20, 1961

"Attention, passengers, the runways have been cleared, and the airport is now open. Please check with the schedule board to learn the status of your flight." The announcement came over the speaker.

"I fully recovered from my illness, whatever it was, and never had another recurrence," Rebecca said, completing the story of that Christmas, sixty-eight years ago.

"And your father went on to become governor," Margaret pointed out.

"That's right, he served two terms as governor, then in 1912, he was very nearly selected as the Vice Presidential candidate for Mr. Roosevelt. After that, he gave up politics and became a successful businessman in Denver."

"Speaking of successful, your life has been a steady string of successes. You have been a schoolteacher, a college professor, an accomplished author, and finally the United States Ambassador to Greece."

"Yes, my life has been blessed," Rebecca agreed.

"Mrs. Robison, in the story you just told, you met Mr. Jensen and Mr. MacAllister out on the mountain as they were coming to rescue the passengers."

"Yes."

"But that's not possible, is it? I mean, particularly when Matt Jensen said that you were in a coma, and that you never left the train."

"You would think so, wouldn't you?" Rebecca replied. "But I clearly remembered seeing Mr. Jensen and Mr. MacAllister out on the trail. It was probably a dream, but if it was, Mr. Jensen had the same dream, because he remembered seeing me out on the trail, as well."

"You also said someone named Preacher came to see you while you were in a coma and told you that you would be all right. Was that just a dream?"

An enigmatic smile spread across Rebecca's face. "I don't know. Was it? I'm still here, nearly seventy years later."

A uniformed airport attendant walked over to where Rebecca and Margaret were having their discussion. "Mrs. Robison, we are now loading first-class passengers for your flight to Denver."

"Thank you, young man."

"Will you need help in boarding?"

"No, thank you, I'm still quite mobile." Rebecca got up then, but before she left the lounge, she looked back. "Margaret, your young man is going to propose to you over dinner tonight. Say yes. You will have a wonderful marriage."

"What?" Margaret gasped.

"Merry Christmas, dear," the old lady said as she turned and walked toward the boarding gate.

Keep reading for a special preview of the next Smoke Jensen adventure!

VENOM OF THE MOUNTAIN MAN

When Smoke Jensen sees a gang of outlaws holding up a stagecoach, his gunfighter instincts take over and he storms in with guns blazing. He kills one of the gunmen, and the rest scatter like the rats they are. But the dead man is the brother of the notorious outlaw Gabe Briggs, and Briggs will want revenge . . .

Tired of the savagery of the lawless countryside, Smoke's wife, Sally, heads back East for a spell, only to find the big city choking in filth, violence, and corruption. Before Sally can return home, though, she's snatched right off the street.

When Smoke gets word that Sally's been kidnapped, he hops the first eastbound train. But Gabe Briggs and his ruthless band of badmen are along for the ride. Unless Smoke can punch their ticket to hell first, they'll blow this train sky high . . .

THE JENSEN FAMILY
FIRST FAMILY OF THE AMERICAN FRONTIER

Smoke Jensen—*The Mountain Man*
The youngest of three children and orphaned as a young boy, Smoke Jensen is considered one of the fastest draws in the West. His quest to tame the lawless West has become the stuff of legend. Smoke owns the Sugarloaf Ranch in Colorado. Married to Sally Jensen, father to Denise ("Denny") and Louis.

Preacher—*The First Mountain Man*
Though not a blood relative, grizzled frontiersman Preacher became a father figure to the young Smoke Jensen, teaching him how to survive in the brutal, often deadly Rocky Mountains. Fought the battles that forged his destiny. Armed with a long gun, Preacher is as fierce as the land itself.

Matt Jensen—*The Last Mountain Man*
Orphaned but taken in by Smoke Jensen, Matt Jensen has become like a younger brother to Smoke and even took the Jensen name. And like Smoke,

Matt has carved out his destiny on the American frontier. He lives by the gun and surrenders to no man.

Luke Jensen—*Bounty Hunter*
Mountain Man Smoke Jensen's long-lost brother Luke Jensen is scarred by war and a dead shot—the right qualities to be a bounty hunter. And he's cunning, and fierce enough, to bring down the deadliest outlaws of his day.

Ace Jensen and Chance Jensen—*Those Jensen Boys!*
Smoke Jensen's long-lost nephews, Ace and Chance, are a pair of young-gun twins as reckless and wild as the frontier itself . . . Their father is Luke Jensen, thought killed in the Civil War. Their uncle Smoke Jensen is one of the fiercest gunfighters the West has ever known. It's no surprise that the inseparable Ace and Chance Jensen have a knack for taking risks—even if they have to blast their way out of them.

Chapter One

Salcedo, Wyoming Territory

The hooves of Smoke Jensen's horse Seven made a dry clatter on the rocks as Smoke made a rather steep descent down from a seldom-used trail. Seeing the road below, he felt a sense of relief. "There it is, Seven, there's the road. Taking the cutoff wasn't all that good an idea. I was beginning to think we never would see that road again."

Seven whickered.

"No, I wasn't lost. You know I don't get lost. I just get a little disoriented every now and then."

Seven whickered again.

"Ah, so now you're making fun of me, are you?"

On long rides, Smoke often talked to his horse because he wanted to hear a voice, even if it was his own. Talking to his horse seemed a step above talking to himself.

Smoke dismounted and reached up to squeeze

Seven's ear. Seven dipped his head in appreciation of the gesture.

"Yeah, I know you like this. Tell you what. Why don't I walk the rest of the way down this hill? That way you won't have to be working as hard. And when we get on the road, we'll have a little breather."

Before they reached the road, Seven suddenly let out an anxious whinny, and using his head, pushed Smoke aside so violently that he fell painfully onto the rocks.

"What was that all about?" Smoke said angrily.

Seven whinnied again and began backing away, lifting his forelegs high and bobbing his head up and down.

Smoke saw the rattler, coiled and bobbing its head, ready to strike. He drew his pistol and fired. There was a mist of blood where the snake's head had been, the head now at least five feet away from the reptile's still coiled and decapitated body.

"Are you all right?" Smoke asked anxiously as he began examining Seven's forelegs and feet. He found no indication that the snake had bitten him. He wrapped his arms around Seven's neck. "Good boy. Oh, wait. I know what you really want."

Again, he began squeezing Seven's ear. "Well, as much as you like this, we can't hang around here all day. We need to get going."

Smoke led Seven on down the rocky incline, then just before he reached the road, his foot slipped off a rock, and he felt the heel of his boot break off.

"Damn," he said, picking up the heel. "Don't worry. I'm not going to remount right away, but probably a little earlier than I previously intended."

He limped along for at least two more miles. When he was certain Seven was well rested, he swung back into the saddle. "All right, boy. Let's go." He started Seven forward at a trot that was comfortable for both of them.

"We'll be coming into Salcedo soon. Tell me, Seven, do you think this bustling community will have a shoe store?"

Seven dipped his head.

"Oh, yeah, you would say that. You always are the optimist."

Salcedo was the result of what had once been a trading post, then a saloon, then a couple houses and a general store until, gradually, it became a town along the banks of the Platte River. The river was not navigable for steamboats, and even flatboats had a difficult time because of the shallowness of the water and the many sandbars and rocks along the route.

A sign at the town limits, exaggerting somewhat, stated

SALCEDO
POP 210

Smoke had been to Rawlins and was on his way back to his Sugarloaf ranch when he broke the heel. He found a boot and shoe store on Main Street, and the cobbler said that he could fix the boot. As Smoke stood at the window of the shoe repair shop, his attention was drawn to a stagecoach parked at the depot just across the street.

"Swan, Mule Gap, and Douglas!" the driver shouted. "If you're goin' to Swan, Mule Gap, or Douglas, get aboard now!"

Five passengers responded to the driver's call—two men, and a woman with two children. The coach had a shotgun guard, and as soon as he was in position, the driver popped his whip, the six horses strained in their harness, and the coach pulled away.

"Your boot is ready," George Friegh, the shoemaker, said as he stepped up beside Smoke watching the coach leave. "It's carryin' five thousand dollars in cash money."

"You mean that's common knowledge?" Smoke replied. "I thought stagecoach companies didn't want it known when they were carrying a sizeable cash shipment."

"Yeah, most of the time they do try 'n keep it quiet. But you can't do that with Emile Taylor."

"Who is Emile Taylor?" Smoke asked.

"Taylor's the shotgun guard. He's an old soldier, and like a lot of old soldiers, he's a drinkin' man. I heard him carryin' on last night while he was getting' hisself snockered at the Trail's End."

The Trail's End was the only saloon in Salcedo.

"He started talkin' about the money shipment they're takin' down to Douglas. Five thousand dollars he said it was."

"He told you that?"

"Not just me. Hell, mister, he was talkin' loud enough that ever'one in the saloon heard him."

Smoke examined the boot, then paid for the work. "You did a good job," he said, slipping the boot back on. "I'd better be getting back on the road."

Five miles south of Salcedo on the Douglas Pike

Four men were waiting on the side of the road, their horses ground hobbled behind them.

"You're sure it's carryin' five thousand dollars?" one of them asked.

"Yeah, I'm sure. I heard the shotgun guard braggin' about it."

"The reason I ask if you're sure is the last time we held up a stage we didn't get nothin' but thirty-seven dollars, 'n that's what we got from the passengers. Hell, you could get shot holdin' up a stage, and thirty-seven dollars ain't worth it."

"This here stagecoach has five thousand dollars. You can trust me on this."

"Here it comes," one of the other men said as the coach crested the hill and came into view.

"All right. You three get mounted and get your

guns out. Gabe, you hold my horse. I'll have 'em throw the money bag down to me. Get your hoods on," he added as he pulled a hood down over his own head.

Smoke heard the unmistakable sound of a gunshot in the distance before him. There was only one shot, and it could have been a hunter, but he didn't think so. There was a sharp flatness to the sound—more like that of a pistol rather than a rifle. He wondered about it, but there was only one shot, and it could have been anything, so he didn't give it that much of a thought.

When he reached the top of the hill he saw the stagecoach stopped on the road in front of him. It was the same stagecoach he had watched leave Salcedo, and the passengers, including the woman and children, were standing outside the coach with their hands up. The driver had his hands up as well. For just a second he wondered about the shotgun guard, then he saw a body lying in the road beside the front wheel of the coach.

Four armed men, all but one mounted, were all wearing hoods that covered their faces. There was no doubt that Smoke had come upon a robbery.

Pulling his pistol, he urged Seven into a gallop and quickly closed the distance between himself and the stagecoach robbers. "Drop your guns!" he shouted.

"What the hell?" one of the robbers yelled, and all four of them shot at Smoke.

Smoke shot back, and the dismounted robber went down. There was another exchange of gunfire, and one of the mounted robbers went down as well.

"Let's get out of here!" one of the two remaining robbers shouted, and they galloped off.

Smoke reached the coach then dismounted to check on the two fallen robbers to make certain they presented no further danger to the coach. They didn't. Both were dead.

A quick examination of the shotgun guard determined that he, too, was dead.

"Mister, I don't know who you are," the driver said, "but you sure come along in time to save our bacon."

"The name is Jensen. Smoke Jensen. Are all of you all right? Was anyone hurt?"

"We're fine, Mr. Jensen, thanks to you," the woman passenger said.

From the *Douglas Budget:*

> Smoke Jensen is best known as the owner of Sugarloaf, a successful ranch near Big Rock, Colorado. He is also well-known as a paladin, a man whose skillful employment of a pistol has, on many occasions, defended the endangered from harm being visited upon them by evil-doers.
>
> Such was the case a few days ago when fate, in the form of the fortuitous arrival of

Mr. Jensen, foiled an attempted stagecoach robbery, and perhaps saved the lives of the driver and passengers. The incident occurred on Douglas Pike Road, some five miles south of Salcedo, and five miles north of Mule Gap.

Although Mr. Jensen called out to the road agents, offering them the opportunity to drop their guns, the four outlaws refused to do so, choosing instead to engage Jensen in a gunfight. This was a fatal decision for Lucas Monroe and Asa Briggs, both of whom were killed in the ensuing gunplay. Two of the men, already mounted, were able to escape.

Although the bandits were wearing hoods during the entire exchange, it is widely believed that one of the men who got away was Gabe Briggs, as he and his brother, Asa, like the James and Dalton brothers, rode the outlaw trail together.

Wiregrass Ranch, adjacent to Sugarloaf

Wiregrass Ranch had once belonged to Ned and Molly Condon. When they were murdered, Sam Condon, Ned's brother, came west from St. Louis. Sam had been a successful lawyer in that city, and everyone had thought he was coming to arrange for the sale of the ranch. Instead, he'd decided to stay, and he brought his wife, Sara Sue, and their then twelve-year-old son Thad with him. Both adjusted to their new surroundings quickly and easily. Thad not only adjusted, he thrived in the new environment.

Sam had made the conscious decision to sell off all the cattle Ned had owned and replaced them with two highly regarded registered Hereford bulls and ten registered Hereford cows. Within two years he had a herd of fifty, composed of ten bulls and forty cows.

Keeping his herd small, he was able to keep down expenses by having no permanent cowboys. Although not yet fourteen, Thad had become a very good hand.

Sam Condon's approach to ranching paid off well, and he earned a rather substantial income by selling registered cattle, both bulls and cows, to ranchers who wanted to improve their stock.

Sam and Sara Sue were celebrating their seventeenth wedding anniversary, and they had invited Smoke and Sally, their neighbors from the adjacent ranch, to have a celebratory dinner with them.

"Chicken and dumplin's, Missouri style," Sara Sue said.

"Oh, you don't have to educate me, Sara Sue," Smoke said as his hostess spooned the pastry onto his plate. "It's been a while, but I'm a Missouri boy, too."

"Well, I'm from the Northeast, but I've learned to enjoy chicken and dumplings as well," Sally said.

"Smoke loves them so, that I had to learn how to make the flat dumplings."

"She learned how to make them all right," Smoke said. "She just hasn't learned how to say *dumplin's,* without adding that last *g,*" he teased.

The others laughed.

"Mr. Jensen, I read about you in the paper," Thad said.

"Oh?"

"Yes, sir. I read how you stopped a stagecoach holdup, 'n how you kilt two men."

"Thad," Sam said. "That's hardly a subject fit for discussion over the dinner table."

"But that is what you done, ain't it? You kilt two men?"

"That's what you did, isn't it?" Sara Sue said, correcting Thad's grammar.

"See, Pa, even Ma is talking about it," Thad said.

The others at the table laughed.

"I'll tell you what," Sam said. "We'll talk about it after dinner. That is, if Smoke is amenable to it."

"*Amenable.* Oh, a good lawyer's word," Sally said with a smile.

After dinner, Smoke, Sam, and Thad sat out on the front porch while Sally helped Sara Sue clean up from the meal. In the west, Red Table Mountain was living up to its name by glowing red in the setting sun.

"The newspaper said that one of the men who got away was Gabe Briggs," Sam said.

"He probably was, but they never removed their masks, so there is no way of knowing," Smoke replied.

"Would you have recognized him if he hadn't been wearing a mask?"

Smoke shook his head. "No, I don't think I would have. I've heard of the Briggs Brothers, but then, who in this part of the country hasn't? But I've never seen either of them before that little fracas on the road."

"But he did see you," Sam said.

"Yes."

"Doesn't that worry you a little? I mean, he knows what you look like, but you don't know what he looks like. If he is bent upon revenging his brother you could be in serious danger."

"I appreciate your concern," Smoke said, "but my life has been such that I have made as many enemies as I have friends. I never know when some unknown enemy is going to call me out or, even worse, try and shoot me from ambush. I've lived with that for many years. Gabe Briggs will be just one more."

"How many men have you kilt, Mr. Jensen?" Thad asked.

"Thad! That's not a question you should ever ask anyone!" Sam scolded.

"I'm sorry," Thad said contritely. "I didn't mean it in a bad way. I think Mr. Jensen is a hero."

Smoke chuckled softly. "I'm not a hero, Thad,

but I have always tried to do the right thing. I'm not proud of the number of men I've killed. No one should ever kill someone as a matter of pride. But I will tell you this. I've never killed anyone who wasn't trying to kill me."

Chapter Two

New York, New York

In operations such as gambling, prostitution, protection, and robbery, the Irish Assembly and the Five Points Gang had been competitors for the last three years. For a while they had been able to establish individual territories, and thus avoid any direct confrontation, but over the last couple months, the Irish Assembly had been expanding the area of their franchise and they and the Five Points Gang had renewed their hostilities.

It had come to a head two days ago when a member of the Five Points Gang was killed by the Irish Assembly.

Both gangs were currently gathered under the Second Street El. They had started their confrontation by shouting insults at each other, but the insults had grown sharper until a shot was fired.

For fifteen minutes guns blazed and bullets flew

as merchants and citizens along Second Street stayed inside to avoid being shot. When it was over, the Five Points gang hauled away their dead and wounded, and the Irish Assembly did the same.

"Three killed," Gallagher said. "We lost three good men!"

"So did the Five Points Gang," Kelly said.

"Aye, well, they can afford it, for 'tis a lot more people they have than we do. Would someone be for tellin' me what good did it do?"

"Here now, Ian, you wouldn't be for lettin' them be runnin' over us, would you?" Kelly asked.

"Gallagher's right. I think the time has come for us to change," one of the others said.

"And give up ever'thing we've built up?" Ian asked.

"We've built nothing 'n if we don't change, we'll be for losin' it all."

"In what way would you be for changing? I'm asking that," Gallagher said.

"I'd say come to an accommodation with the Five Points gang," Kelly said.

"You'd be for givin' up to 'em?"

"Aye. Let's face facts. 'Tis time to realize that we can't beat them. The only thing we can do is find some way to work with them."

Sugarloaf Ranch

"You're sure you want to do this now?" Pearlie asked.

"Yes," Thad said.

"Maybe we ought to ask your mama before you do something like this."

"No, Pearlie, don't do that. She would just say no."

Smoke had recently bought five new, unbroken horses. Pearlie and Cal always broke the new horses, and so far Cal had broken two, and Pearlie two. There was one horse remaining, and Thad, who had come over to Sugarloaf Ranch with his parents, had left them visiting with Smoke and Sally while he went out to watch. It was just before Pearlie was about to mount the horse that Thad had asked to be allowed to do it.

"I'm thirteen years old. I'm not a baby."

"All right," Pearlie said. "I guess this is as good a time as any to learn."

"What do I do?"

"Keep a hard seat and keep your heels down. Watch his ears. That'll help tell you when it's coming. Keep his head up. As long as his head is up, he can't do all that much."

Pearlie pointed to a loop. "Put your right hand in here and grab a fistful of mane with your left hand. And don't be afraid to haul back on the mane. That'll let 'im know who is in control."

"All right," Thad said somewhat tentatively.

"You gettin' a little nervous? You want to back out? Nobody is goin' to say anything to you if you do back out. Ridin' a buckin' horse is not an easy thing to do." Pearlie chuckled. "And there's most that'll tell you, it's not exactly a smart thing to do, either."

"I'm a little scared," Thad said. "But I want to do it anyway."

A broad smile spread across Pearlie's mouth. "Good for you. If you weren't scared, I would say that you are too dumb to ride. If you admit that you are scared, but you are still willing to do it, then you may have just enough sense and courage to have what it takes to do this. Climb up here, and let's get it done."

Thad climbed up onto the side of the stall where, a few minutes earlier, Cal had brought the already-saddled horse. Thad paused for a moment, then he dropped down into the saddle just as Cal opened the gate.

The horse exploded out of the stall, leaping up, then coming down on four stiffened legs. The first leap almost threw Thad from the saddle.

"Pull back on his mane!" Pearlie shouted.

"Hang on tight!" Cal added.

The horse kicked its hind legs into the air, but Thad hung on. It tried to lower its head, but following Pearlie's instructions, Thad pulled back on the mane and prevented the horse from doing so. It began whirling around, but it was unable to throw its rider.

"Yahoo!" Cal shouted.

"Thata boy, Thad! Hang on!" Pearlie called.

"THAD!" Sara Sue screamed, coming out with the others to see what was going on.

"Watch, Ma! Watch!" Thad shouted excitedly.

The horse tried for another several seconds then, unable to rid itself of its rider, began trotting around the corral under Thad's complete control.

"What are you doing?"

"Well, Sara Sue, it looks to me like he's just broken a horse," Sam said with a big smile.

"And you approve of that? He could have broken his neck."

"He didn't break his neck, but he did break the horse. I not only approve of it, I'm proud of him. In fact, Smoke, if you would be willing to sell him, I would like to buy that horse from you. Seems to me that any boy who can break a horse ought to own the horse that he broke."

"I'm sorry, Sam, but that horse isn't for sale," Smoke said.

"Oh? Well, I'm disappointed, but I understand."

"He isn't for sale because I'm giving him to Thad," Smoke said with a big smile.

"Really? This horse is mine?" Thad said while still in the saddle of the now docile horse.

"He's yours."

"Oh, thank you!" Thad shouted.

"Yes, Smoke, thank you very much. That's very nice of you," Sam said.

"What are you going to name him?" Pearlie asked.

Thad bent forward to pat the horse on his neck. "I'm going to name him Fire, because I got him from Mr. Smoke Jensen. Smoke and fire. Do you get it?"

"I get it. And I think it's a great name," Pearlie said, "because this horse also has fire in his belly."

"Open the gate to the corral so I can ride him around," Thad said.

"Cal, open the gate," Pearlie called.

Cal opened the gate.

"Now, watch us run!" Thad slapped his legs against Fire's sides, and the horse burst forth like a cannonball. Thad leaned forward but an inch above Fire's neck. He galloped to the far end of the lane, about a quarter of a mile away, then turning on a dime, raced back before he dismounted.

"Ma, when we go home, can I sleep in the stable with Fire tonight?"

"You most certainly cannot."

Sam laughed. "I guess we're lucky he doesn't want to bring Fire in to sleep in bed with him tonight."

Sara Sue laughed as well, then ran her hand through her son's hair. "Come on in. Mrs. Jensen has supper on the table."

"What are we havin'?" Thad asked.

"Thad! We are guests! A guest never asks the hostess what is being served," Sara Sue scolded.

"I just wanted to make sure she wasn't serving cauliflower. I hate cauliflower."

Smoke laughed. "Then you are safe, young man. Sally never serves cauliflower, because I don't like it, either."

New York City

"Mule Gap? And is it serious that you be, Warren Kennedy, that you would be going to a place called Mule Gap?"

"Aye, Clooney, 'tis serious I am," Kennedy replied.

The two men were in Grand Central Depot, awaiting the departure of the next transcontinental train. Clooney had come to see Kennedy off.

"And would you be for tellin' me, why you would pick a place with the name of Mule Fart, Wyoming?"

Kennedy laughed. "Mule Gap, not Mule Fart. And the why of it is because there is nothing left for me here in New York. Our last adventure was too costly. I have studied Mule Gap, 'n 'tis my thinking that such a wee place can provide opportunity for someone with an adventurous spirit 'n a willingness to apply himself to the possibilities offered."

"I've read about the West," Clooney said. "There are crazy men who walk around out there with guns strapped around their waists. They say that such men would as soon shoot you as look at you."

"'N are you for tellin' me, Ryan Clooney, that in this very city the people who lived along Second Street weren't dodging the bullets that were flying through the street? Aye, 'n we as well."

"That was different. There was a war bein' fought between the Five Points Gang and the Irish Assembly, 'n we just happened to be caught up in it," Clooney insisted.

"Aye, that may be true. But I'd just as soon not be

caught up in such a thing again. 'N before someone decides to start another war, 'tis my intention to be well out of here."

"I can't believe you would leave New York 'n all your friends 'n family behind."

"I have no family but m' father, 'n he has said he wants nothing to do with me. I can make new friends."

"Still, it'll be strange havin' you gone."

"All aboard for the Western Flyer!" someone shouted through a megaphone. "Track number nine. All aboard."

"That's my train," Kennedy said, starting to the door that led to the tracks. "If you think you'd like to come out, let me know, and I'll find a place for you."

"Find a place for me? Find a place doin' what?"

"Same as before. Doin' whatever I tell you to do," Kennedy said with a little chuckle.

He boarded the train, then settled back into his seat. Born in Ireland, he had lived in New York from the time he was four years old. He knew nothing but New York, yet he was leaving it all behind him.

And he didn't feel so much as one twinge of regret.

Walcott, Wyoming

Seven days later, after just under two thousand miles of cities and small towns, farmland and ranches, rich cropland and bare plains, desert and mountain, the train pulled into the small town of Walcott, Wyoming. When the train rolled away, continuing its journey on to the coast, Kennedy had a moment of indecision. He was used to big buildings, sidewalks crowded with people, all of whom were in a hurry, streets filled with carriages, trolley cars, and elevated trains. The entire town of Walcott could be fitted into one city block.

He went into the depot to claim his luggage.

"This here luggage says it was checked in at New York City," the baggage master said. "Are you from New York?"

"Aye, that I am," Kennedy replied.

"I've never been to New York, but I've read about it. Is it true what they say as to how big it is?"

"Two million people."

"Two million people? I can hardly think about such a number. Tell me, are you just visitin' or are you plannin' on settlin' down here?"

"Neither. I'm headed for Mule Gap. I plan to make that my residence."

To Kennedy's surprise, the baggage master laughed.

"What is it? What's so funny?"

"I can't imagine a New York feller like you wantin' to live in a little ol' place like Mule Gap. Walcott, maybe, I mean, bein' as we're a pretty big town our ownselves, but a little ol' place like Mule Gap? Now that, I've got to see."

Kennedy was beginning to have even more reservations about the wisdom of moving to Mule Gap. If a resident of Walcott thought it was small, it must be miniscule indeed.

"In for a penny, in for a pound," he said.

"Now, mister, I don't have the slightest idea what it is you just said, but here's your luggage."

Carrying his luggage with him, Kennedy walked to the stagecoach depot, which was just next door. There, he bought a ticket for Mule Gap.

Warm Springs, Wyoming

"These are good-looking horses," Dooley Lewis said. "They'll make a fine addition to my string. But I thought you said you had five horses you were going to sell me."

"One of them got waylaid by a thirteen-year-old boy," Smoke replied with a smile.

"Well, never let it be said that I would step in between a boy and his horse. I'll take these and be proud to have 'em." Lewis owned DL Ranch, just outside Warm Springs.

"How'd you fare the winter?" Lewis asked.

"We got through it just fine," Smoke said. "You?"

"We had a pretty severe storm, but we was fortunate. None of the ranchers lost many cows. I did lose a couple horses, though, which is why I'm grateful to you for selling me these four. By the way, you wouldn't want to sell that horse you're ridin', would you?"

With a chuckle, Smoke reached up and grabbed one of Seven's ears and began squeezing it gently. "Don't you listen to him, Seven. You know I would never sell you."

Seven dipped his head, then pressed his forehead against Smoke's chest.

"Set much a store by that horse, do you?" Lewis asked.

"He's more than just a horse," Smoke said. "He's same as flesh and blood."

Lewis nodded. "I reckon I can see that. I've had a few critters I've felt about like that, myself.

"Glad you understand. I'll be getting on, then." Smoke swung into the saddle and started the long ride back to Sugarloaf Ranch.

His Uptown Girl

Gail Sattler

Published by Steeple Hill Books™

STEEPLE HILL BOOKS

ISBN 0-373-81223-X

HIS UPTOWN GIRL

This edition published by arrangement with Steeple Hill Books.

www.SteepleHill.com

Printed in U.S.A.

"Are you only helping me because you feel sorry for me?"

Bob gazed into Georgette's blue eyes. Of course he felt badly about the way her father had rejected her, because she wanted to build a life of her own. Actually, he felt proud of her, too.

And yet, he didn't feel at peace with what was happening between them.

Until now, Georgette hadn't had to work. She could have lived a life of leisure, and it wouldn't have been wrong.

But now, all that was gone.

That a working-class guy like him could be her employer was one of life's cruel jokes. For now, having to work and save money to get what she wanted, and even the necessities of daily life, was a novelty. Very soon, that thrill would wear off....

Falling in love with someone from the other side of the tracks only worked in romance novels and fairy tales.

GAIL SATTLER

lives in Vancouver, British Columbia (where you don't have to shovel rain), with her husband of twenty-six years, three sons, two dogs, five lizards, one toad and a Degu named Bess. Gail loves to read stories with a happy ending, which is why she writes them. Visit Gail's Web site at www.gailsattler.com.

He gives strength to the weary
and increases the power of the weak.
—*Isaiah* 40:29

Dedicated to my husband, Tim.
Just because I love you.

Chapter One

The electronic tone of the door chime echoed through the shop.

Bob Delanio laid his wrench down on the tool caddy, wiped his hands on his coveralls, then walked into the reception area of his auto-repair shop.

"Need some help?" he asked his newest customer, trying not to sound as tired as he felt.

The phone rang. Both lines lit up at the same time.

"Oops, 'scuse me," Bob mumbled as he picked up the receiver. "Bob And Bart's, can you hold?" He pushed the button and answered the second line. "Bob And Bart's. Yeah. Hold on." Bob hit the hold button, walked a few steps, and poked his head around the corner.

"Bart!" he yelled. "Get line two. It's Josh McTavish."

Bob nodded at the man still waiting at the counter. The chime sounded again. Just as Bob picked up the phone to talk to the first caller, a man who a week ago had ignored Bob's warning that he needed a new head gasket stomped in. Bob glanced through the door to see a tow truck outside, the driver waiting to be told what bay to back the man's car into.

Bob gritted his teeth. It appeared he was going to spend yet another Friday night working until midnight.

He handled the latest influx, then did his best to juggle his time between the door, the phone, and actually getting some work done.

At seven o'clock, an hour past their posted closing, Bart finally had the time to flip the switch on the sign on the door to Closed. Despite that positive turn, neither of them would be leaving just yet.

"This is nuts," Bart grumbled as he dropped some change into the pop machine for a cold drink. "We can't keep this up."

Falling backwards onto the worn couch, Bob stretched out his aching feet. "I know. It's great that business is picking up, but I'm exhausted." He extended one arm toward the unfinished work orders lined up on the board. "No matter what time we get out of here, we'll have to be back at five in the morning."

"My wife isn't very pleased about these long hours. At least you're still single," Bart retorted.

"Maybe this is why I'm still single."

Bart turned to look outside at the row of cars they had promised their customers they could pick up sometime within the next twenty-four hours. "We have to hire some help."

The growing pile of invoices and purchase orders on the counter, spurred Bob's reply. "I was just thinking the same thing."

Bart turned and walked behind the counter. He grabbed a blank piece of paper and pulled a pen out of his pocket. "The newspaper charges by the word, don't they? What should I say? Wanted. Light-duty mechanic?"

Without leaving the couch, Bob scanned the boxes of orders, requisitions, receipts and charge bills to be submitted, as well as deposit slips from the bank. "We're busy, but we're not busy enough to add another full-time mechanic. If we hire a bookkeeper, then that frees us up to get more done in the shop."

Bart scratched his head, pen in hand. "But there are decisions a bookkeeper can't make, stuff one of us would have to decide. Besides, we don't have enough paperwork to keep someone busy full-time. When all this stuff is caught up, we can't afford to pay someone just to sit here and answer the phone."

"We're nearly a week behind even on the small jobs," Bob said, gesturing at the work orders piled under pushpins on their work board. "I've got an overhaul that's been waiting three days. I guess you're right. We need a mechanic."

Bart stuck his hand in the closest box and lifted out a handful of papers. "It's almost our fiscal year-end, time for our corporate taxes. Your friend Adrian always needs everything balanced, reconciled and printed out so he can file for us. You're right. We need a bookkeeper."

The two men stared at each other in silence.

"We need both," Bob mumbled, "But it would be too hard to hire two part-timers. I don't want to invest all our time and money to train someone, then have them quit for a better job elsewhere that can give them more hours when they get enough experience. Maybe we should forget about it."

Bart shook his head. "The baby is three weeks old. I never see her except when she's up in the middle of the night crying. And that's when I should be sleeping, too. I can't keep this up."

Bob felt his whole body sag. Neither of them could continue working eighteen-hour days, six days a week. Lately, the only time Bob wasn't working was when he took off a few hours Wednesday evening to practice the songs he would be playing on Sunday with his church's worship team. Up until recently, he refused to work Sundays, but they were so far behind, he'd started to work a few hours on Sunday, too.

He didn't know when control had first eluded them, but they'd reached their breaking point. Soon they were going to start making mistakes, which, where cars and people were concerned, could not happen.

It had to stop.

"You're right. We both need to slow down. Let's hire two part-timers, a mechanic and a bookkeeper, and we'll see what happens." The stack of work orders lined up for Saturday, was well beyond what they could accomplish, even if both he and Bart worked twenty-four hours nonstop.

Dropping his pen suddenly as if at a thought, Bart turned to the computer. "I just remembered something. I don't have to write out that ad. I heard that you can do it online. I can even put it on my charge card."

Bob stood. "You've probably missed the deadline for tomorrow's paper."

Bart found the right Website, and started typing in his usual hunt-and-peck, two-finger mode. "Maybe I haven't."

Suddenly Bob's head swam as the magnitude of the process hit him. "I just thought of something. What about all the phone calls, and the time it's going to take to set up and do interviews?"

Bart's fingers stilled. "What are you trying to say?"

"We don't have that kind of time. People are going to start taking their business elsewhere."

"Have you got a better idea?"

Bob walked to the counter, and reached for one of the boxes containing incomplete purchase orders. He tore off the flap to the box, picked up the black felt pen, and began to write.

HELP WANTED—APPLY WITHIN
Part-time light-duty mechanic
Part-time office assistant
Hours and wages negotiable.

He dug a roll of black electrical tape out of the drawer while Bart watched, and taped the cardboard to the window.

"What are you doing?"

Bob turned around. "Saturday is our busiest day, and lots of people come in. If any of them are interested, we can take care of interviewing right there. We should forget about the ad."

"You're kidding, right?"

Bob raised his hand toward the sign, which was slightly crooked. "Do I look like I'm kidding?"

"I guess you're really not kidding," Bart mumbled.

Bob sighed. The business had supported both him and Bart for years, and now there was also Bart's family. They couldn't fail now. There was too much at stake. "God will provide," Bob said softly. I've always believed in God's timing, and I still do."

Bart resumed his typing. "You're crazy. Certifiably crazy."

Bob spun around. "Don't you believe God can send us the right people?"

"I doubt God will have the right people simply fall from the sky. But I do know one thing. If we don't get McTavish's 4X4 finished, we'll be in trouble when he comes to get it at 7:00 a.m. I'm putting this ad in the paper. I'm sure God will have the right people fax in their résumés."

"I still think we'll do better with the sign in the window. We don't have the time or the energy for millions of faxes and phone calls. Besides, there's more to hiring than just looking at résumés."

"But that's where we have to start, and the only way we're going to get qualified people to send us those résumés is through the paper." Bart hit Enter. "Done. The ad's in."

Bob crossed his arms over his chest and turned his head to look at his sign. "And the sign is up. It looks like the battle is on."

Bart killed the browser. "Yeah. May the best man win. Now let's get back to work."

"Daddy! This dress is horrible!"

Georgette Ecklington's father flashed her a condescending smile. "The girl at the store told me you would look great in it."

Georgette gritted her teeth and pressed her lips together so hard they hurt. The "girl" in question was thirty-five years old. Because her father was one of their best customers and always paid full price, the woman happily told him anything he wanted to hear.

Still, the woman was probably right. Georgette knew she would look "good" in yet another overly frilly, fussy, pink dress with enough lace to choke a horse. If that was the way she wanted to look.

Which she didn't.

"Don't disappoint me, Georgie-Pie." Her father's stern gaze belied the familiarity of the nickname.

Georgette stifled a scream. She hadn't been five years old for twenty years, but whenever her father wanted something, he called her the childish nickname to remind her of something she could never forget.

She was William Ecklington's daughter.

And William Ecklington was in control. Always.

He'd picked that particular moment to give her

another dress she hated because the household staff were in earshot. She couldn't disobey his orders in front of the staff or any of his peers. He would never forgive her for any act of defiance, or anything that might diminish his public image.

Tonight, at yet another Who's Who function, Georgette was expected to stand at her father's side and smile nicely, showing her support of everything he did. Besides his financial empire, the next most important thing to her father was the respect of his peers. After her mother had left him, he'd refused to marry again. He never dated because he was certain that women were only after his money. So, his younger daughter became second-best.

Georgette's only escape from her father's tyranny would be to do what her sister had done—to get married. But God said that marriage was forever. Georgette didn't want to be under the thumb of a man who was a younger version of her father—a man so critical and demanding he had driven their mother away. Her influential father also sabotaged every attempt she made to find a job, completely nullifying all her attempts to become independent. Not that she needed to worry about money, he gave her a generous allowance in exchange for her work on his charity projects. But Georgette wasn't happy.

"Be ready at five-fifteen. Karl will be driving."

With that lofty pronouncement, her father turned and left.

Georgette crumpled the dress in her closed fists, and raised her head to the ceiling in a silent prayer. She needed to escape, and she had only one place to go, the only place her father left her alone.

The garage. The garage was her haven. Some women made crafts or baked when they needed something to do. Rebuilding an engine was Georgette's respite from "society." She detested being involved with the social climbing of her father's shallow world.

Working on the car, she didn't have to be Georgette Ecklington, socialite. She could simply be, as her friends at the pit crew of the local racetrack circuit called her, George. Today it would help her prepare herself for the ordeal of another taxing night.

She walked out of the room and handed the dress to Josephine, the housekeeper. "This needs pressing. I have some shopping to do, and then I need to be left alone until it's time to get dressed."

Josephine smiled and nodded. Josephine often covered for Georgette when her father was looking for her.

Soon Georgette was on her way to an out-of-the-way, but spectacular, auto shop she'd discovered, where the owners frequently found salvaged items from auto wreckers for her. She needed parts for her current project—restoring an old pickup truck she'd bought from one of the families in her church. The man had lost his job and the family needed money. They wouldn't accept charity, so instead, Georgette had bought the family's derelict pickup truck for many times more than it was worth, a sum that would keep their mortgage at bay for at least six months. She was now working to restore the truck. Perhaps someday the thing would even run again.

As she pulled into the shop, Georgette formulated her priorities. In three hours she had to be showered and ready, so she needed to make good use of her time.

Her thoughts cut off abruptly when she approached the store and saw a cardboard sign in the window.

HELP WANTED.

Georgette's breath caught. She quickened her pace, able to read the smaller print when she stood beside the door.

Light-duty mechanic.

She could do that. Fixing and rebuilding engines might just be a hobby, but she did it well.

The pros at the race track confirmed it again and again. She'd never tackled a project she couldn't complete. And unlike the other times her father had ruined her job chances with a phone call, her references could be her friends at the race track. Her father didn't even know about this place, not that he'd deign to go to an auto shop any way. Georgette said a short prayer that they wouldn't ask for more, and pushed the door open.

The phone was ringing, and two customers waited impatiently ahead of her. Bob was behind the counter, taking notes as a woman listed the problems with her car. The voice of Bart, the other proprietor, echoed from the shop, over the noise of the hydraulic hoist, as he called for another customer to come out. Help certainly was wanted at Bob And Bart's Auto Repair.

While she waited for her turn, Georgette watched Bob a little more closely. Even though she'd been there before, she'd paid more attention to the spectacular finds he'd made for her than what either of the men looked like.

He carried himself with confidence as he dealt with his customers. Considering his job, he was relatively tidy in appearance, although his dark hair could use a cut. His olive-green eyes and Roman nose made her suspect an Italian heritage, though, the poster on the wall advertising a discount at Bob's brother's Italian restaurant, was a pretty solid hint, too.

As she stepped ahead in the line, she continued to study Bob.

He was a good-looking man. When he smiled, the hint of crow's feet at the corners of those amazing eyes put him at thirtyish.

After a short conversation, the man ahead of her followed Bob to the opening between the lobby and the shop. Bob called out to Bart, left the man where he was, then returned to his place behind the counter. "Can I help you?" Bob asked as he reached for a blank work order. As he turned to her, his frown turned to a small smile. "Right. I left a message on your cell phone. Your parts are in. I'll go get them. What's your name again?"

Georgette's stomach quivered. "Ecklington. George Ecklington."

His smile widened. "Of course. George. How could I forget? I'll be right back."

"No! Bob! Wait!" Georgette called as he took his first step away.

When he turned back to her, she cleared her throat. "Yes, I'm here for my parts, but I see you're hiring. I'd like to apply for the job."

His smile widened even more. He pulled an application from beneath the counter and slid it toward her. "I didn't have time to make our own applications, so I borrowed a few from my brother. It says Antonio's Ristorante at the top, but just cross it out, and write Bookkeeper in the corner so I'll put it in the right pile."

Georgette tried not to let her annoyance show. She didn't want the bookkeeper's job. Usually she could understand when people in her father's circle treated her like a frail little tulip, but to Bob, she was a customer—a customer who frequently bought parts, and installed them. Herself. She didn't like his assumption, but she'd had to prove herself at the raceway, too.

However, it wasn't as if she couldn't do the bookkeeping. Having been confined to her father's charities, she'd picked up the skill, including receivables, purchasing and handling the disbursements. She could imagine her father's blood boiling at the thought of his daughter doing work that paid by the hour. But not a dime of the allowance he'd given her was truly hers.

This job and its salary, independent of her father, or of anyone who had any association with her father, would be.

Georgette looked up at Bob, trying to show more confidence than she felt. "Actually, I'd like to apply for both jobs."

"Pardon me?"

"I can do bookkeeping, but I'm also a light-duty

mechanic. Your sign said the hours were negotiable. Could two part-time jobs add up to one full-time job?"

Bob's smile dropped. "I'm sorry, but we need a real mechanic, not just someone to change oil and check spark plugs."

"But I *am* a real mechanic. I usually do rebuilds, but there's no reason I couldn't work on current models."

"Well, maybe you could, but I don't think—"

As she pictured herself actually working there, the things she knew she could do bubbled in her mind. "When people come in and they don't know what's wrong, if you just hired a bookkeeper, you'd have to stop what you were doing and listen to them. If you hired me, I would get a pretty good idea of what was wrong right off the bat, even if I wasn't the one to do the actual work."

Bob raised one finger in the air. "But—"

Her words tumbled over his protest. "Then you'd have the option of being able to use me in the shop or the office, wherever I was more needed at the time. Or I could—"

Bob put up his hands. "That really wasn't what we had in mind."

She narrowed her eyes. "Are you saying a woman couldn't do this job?"

"No! That's not what I'm saying at all..."

"I might be a woman, but I'm a good mechanic, and that's what you're hiring. I would do a good job for you. For *both* positions. I could even start Monday."

"Monday? Really...?" Bob's voice trailed off. He closed his eyes, and pinched the bridge of his nose. "Bart and I never discussed this possibility. We have to think about it. Why don't you fill out the application, and when you're done I'll call him in here so we can talk about it?"

Georgette tried to calm her racing heart. It was a possibility. Thoughts of her father's vehement disapproval slammed into her, but she pushed them aside. If Bob offered her the job, she would come up with a way to deal with her father. She couldn't think of anything she wanted more than this job.

The chime sounded behind her as another customer walked in. Georgette slid to the end of the counter to fill out the application, using her race track friends as references, though she had to list her father's holding company as current employer.

When she finished writing, she waited for Bob to complete the work order for his current customer whom she could hear describing the problem he was having with his car.

After the man left, Georgette spoke up. "It's the coil," she said. "Sounds faulty."

"You think so? I was just thinking the same thing."

Before she could respond, Bart walked into the lobby, wiping his hands on the back of his coveralls. "You here for the office job?" he asked.

Bob glanced at Bart, then back to Georgette. "You may not believe this, but she's here for both jobs." He handed Bart her application along with the newest work order. "Pull this one into bay four. If it's the coil that's causing the problem, we just might have found ourselves a new mechanic. And bookkeeper. Bart, this is George."

One of Bart's eyebrows raised. "George?"

She stiffened. "It's short for Georgette. My friends call me George."

He scanned the application, and gave a slight nod when he saw her racetrack references. "This is good. I know Jason from the track. I'll talk to him. But I know I've seen you somewhere before. Do you go to Faith Community Fellowship?"

Georgette shook her head. "No. I attend a church nearer to my house. I don't live nearby. But I buy most of my parts here."

"Must be it." Bart walked back to bay four with Bob.

Her heart pounded as she watched them check her assessment, nodding as they discussed the faulty coil.

When they returned to the lobby, she couldn't hold back any more. "Was I right?"

"Looks like it. As soon as Bart puts a new coil in and test drives it, he's going to watch the front desk so you and I can go into the office and discuss the details. You said Monday is good?"

"Monday is great." She marveled at her calm tone. "But I want to do my first official duty right now."

One eyebrow quirked.

Without waiting for him to respond, Georgette turned, walked to the cardboard sign in the window, and flipped it into the garbage can.

She had a job. A real job. And she'd done it without her father.

Chapter Two

The early-morning spring breeze drifted into the shop, doing its best to combat the smells of gas, oil and lubricants.

Bob had just reached down to check the power-steering belt of the car he was working on when an expensive sports car with tinted windows stopped in front of the bay next to him and began to back in.

Bob straightened, wiped his hands on the rag from his pocket, and watched the door to the car open.

A sleek, spike-heeled shoe poked out, followed by a slender, shapely leg. A swish of soft fabric brought the flow of a skirt, followed by the rest of the beautiful blond driver.

"Hi, Bob. I brought my tools. Where should I put them?"

Bob's heart pounded. He stared openly at his

new mechanic. If she hadn't spoken, he wouldn't have recognized her, she was always so casually dressed the other times she'd come into the shop with her blond hair tied up in a ponytail, probably an attempt to make herself appear taller. Today, George wore makeup and a hairstyle fit for a magazine cover. Her outfit was nicer than most women he knew wore for special occasions. It was probably more expensive as well.

He didn't want or need a fashion model. He needed someone who could change a head gasket.

Bob wondered if he'd made his decision to hire her too impulsively. He tried to think of how to tell her that maybe he would have to reconsider, when George reached into the car, pulled out a duffel bag, and slung it over her shoulder. "I'll be right back. I have to change into something more suitable before I start working."

Before he could think of a response, she dashed off, the click of her high heels echoing against the concrete as she ran.

Bob checked his watch. It was fifteen minutes before her agreed start time. If he told her he'd changed his mind before she actually started, that might not count as actually firing her. It would probably be less painful that way.

She reappeared in minutes in comfortably worn jeans, a T-shirt proclaiming the tour of a popular

Christian musician, and appropriate steel-toed safety boots. Turning as she spoke, she tossed the duffel into the back seat of her car. "I didn't know if you had coveralls that would fit me, so I brought my own. I hope that's okay."

"Uh...yeah..."

Bob shook his head to clear it. At least he would see what she could do. "Ready?"

"Soon as I unpack my tools. They're in the trunk."

Bob turned to stare at her car, which was probably worth at least triple the sticker price of his. "Nice," he said, positive she'd been driving something else when she'd applied for the job. He couldn't see why someone who could afford such a car would apply at his simple shop, she was obviously used to living on more money than he could pay.

"This car does tend to turn heads. It's my father's."

Bob's father had never owned such a car. And if he had, Bob knew he would never get to borrow it.

She pushed the remote button on her keychain. The trunk popped open to display a neat array of good-quality tools packed neatly in two boxes.

"I wasn't sure what to bring, so I brought just the basics."

Bart chose that moment to appear. He immediately walked to the car and picked up George's power wrench testing the heft with visible appreciation.

"Do you have a tool caddy for me?"

"We've got four bays," Bob answered. "Since you're the one who's going to be answering the phone most of the time, you take Bay One, which is closest to the lobby. Put your tools in the shelving unit on the wall over there."

In only minutes they had George's tools packed away in the appropriate place.

Bart stood beside Bob as George moved her car away. "I hope we're not taking this 'trusting God' thing a little too far."

"I don't know. All day yesterday at church, I kept thinking that God was sending us someone who really needed the job, but obviously she doesn't. I wonder if this is some kind of test."

Bart shook his head. "Let's not ask for more trouble. If nothing else, she'll look good when customers come in. Too bad she took her hair down and wiped off her makeup. Yowsa."

Bob stiffened. "I won't resort to the trick of hiring only pretty girls, like some of the places that deliver parts. I hired her because she immediately identified that coil problem."

"Okay, she knows something about mechanics.

But can she balance a spreadsheet? Did you notice that she only had those track references? It probably would have been a good idea to check out her former employer, but that would have made things difficult for her if they hadn't known she was interviewing. Anyway, now it's too late."

"There's only one way to find out what she's like. Let's get her started."

Bart shook his head. "I don't have time to show her anything. They're coming to get that red sedan in an hour, and I'm not sure I'll be finished. You hired her, so you train her."

Bart walked off before Bob could respond.

Bob entered the lobby at the same time as George.

"Where do I start?" she asked.

"I guess the first step is to enter all the purchase orders into the computer," Bob said as he led her to the shop's computer. "We've kind of been letting it slip. When we're so busy, the paperwork is the last thing to be done. It drives our accountant nuts. Fortunately he's a friend."

He showed her how to enter a few transactions. "Write the journal entry number on everything as you enter it, and then put them in that box. I take the box home once a month just so everything will be in a separate location if anything happens."

She nodded as she entered a new purchase order. "This is a good program. I've used it before."

Bob stood back and watched her work. She entered everything quickly and with obvious proficiency, and her skill got him to thinking.

On Saturday, she'd appeared more the tomboy type, especially since she claimed to be a competent mechanic. But today, after seeing her grace and refinement when she came in, and now her bookkeeping skills, he was riveted to her every movement.

He watched as she paused in figuring out how to handle a difficult transaction. When she found the correct category for the particular part, she smiled to herself, and kept typing.

As she started to reach for another piece of paper out of the box, the phone rang.

Her hand froze in midair. "Should I get that?"

"Yep, that's another reason you're here."

She grinned and picked up the phone. "Good morning, thank you for calling Bob And Bart's Auto Repair. How may I direct your call?"

Bob dragged his hand down his face.

"One moment, please," she chirped, then pressed the hold button. "Larry Holt wants to know if his car is ready, and how much it will be."

"This isn't an executive office. You can say 'good morning' if you want, but we just say 'Bob 'n' Bart's' without having to make a speech about it. Things are pretty simple here. Tell Larry his car will be ready at two, and we're not sure how much yet until we know if we have to replace the ignition switch. And try to be less formal."

Her face reddened. She finished the call, then returned to the entry on the computer.

At the sight of that attractive blush, Bob decided to linger a bit, just in case she had questions. He had wondered what it would be like to have another person around, especially a woman. He'd never had an employee before. Bart and he had been friends long before they became business partners, and it was only their friendship and their shared faith in God that sustained them through the hard times.

This was different. George was an attractive woman and Bart was, well, Bart. But George was also his employee, and no more. He'd often heard not to mix business with pleasure, and this was definitely one of those times. It was his decision to hire her, and conversely, if she messed up, it would be his responsibility to fire her.

He didn't want to think of firing her when she'd been there less than an hour. He wanted to give her a chance to prove what she could do.

He cleared his throat. "I'm going to get back to work now. If you need help, just call and one of us will come."

George frowned at the computer and looked up

at him. "There's an awful lot of stuff not entered. I'm okay for now, but the true test will be when I have to do the monthly reconciliations. You do reconcile monthly, don't you?"

"Uh… We try, but not always. Anyway, we'd like you to do the paperwork in the morning, then after lunch you'll work in the shop. We need you to get right into routine today."

She smiled. "Of course. While I don't mind the paperwork, remember, it's the mechanic's job I applied for first."

Bob stared at her face, which held nothing but sincerity, trying to make sense of her. While he'd met a few women who could tell an alternator from a fuel pump, he didn't know many who were willing to touch them, much less actually change them.

"I'll leave you alone, then. Call me if you need anything."

She nodded, and Bob walked into the shop to finish his own work.

The morning moved more slowly for him than any other morning in the history of their business. It didn't help that he kept looking through the glass partition between the shop and the office to see how George was doing.

Just as she had when he was beside her, George appeared to be doing fine without him.

The real test would be when lunch break was over, and the second phase of her duties began.

Georgette looked up at the clock. Right on time, Bob walked into the lobby.

"I'm back. It's time for your lunch break, and then I'll get you started on a few tune-ups and things."

Georgette folded her hands on the countertop. "Actually, I ate my lunch as I worked. I hope that's okay." Her father would have died to think that she'd eaten while standing at the counter, as people came in and out. However, with all the excitement of doing something new, and running back and forth between the shop and the phone all morning, she'd been hungry an hour before it was technically lunchtime.

It was actually kind of fun, breaking the rules.

"I hope you don't think we mean for you to work through your lunch break, because we don't. If you've already eaten, would you like to go for a walk or something? There's a place down the block that has great ice cream cones. It's opened early because of our great May weather." The second the words were out of his mouth, he paused as if to gauge her response.

Georgette broke into a smile. She couldn't remember the last time she'd had the simple pleasure of eating an ice cream cone, or any kind of ice cream that wasn't a part of a fancy dessert, meant to impress. Her father didn't think ice cream cones were very dignified.

She reached under the counter for her purse. "I'd love an ice cream. How long will we be gone?"

"We? I… Uh…" Bob looked up at the clock, then shrugged his shoulders. "I hadn't intended for any of us to take our breaks at the same time, but we can probably make an exception for your first day. Just a sec." He turned and walked the three steps to the door leading to the shop, and opened it. "Bart!" he hollered. "I'm taking George for an ice cream down the street! We'll be back in twenty!"

Bob didn't wait for a reply. "Let's go while things are quiet. This doesn't happen often."

He shucked his coveralls off, pressed a few crinkles out of his jeans and T-shirt with his hands, and met her at the door.

"What about the phone?"

"Bart will do the same thing we've always done. He'll keep working, and when the phone rings, he'll go answer it."

"It's really nice that you don't ignore your calls and let them go to voice mail."

Bob nodded. "When we've got someone's car, they don't want to talk to a machine. They want an answer from a person, even if it's an 'I don't know.' I feel the same way when I'm calling for status."

Georgette thought of her father's charity. Only people who wanted to ingratiate themselves with him called. They found leaving a message more efficient.

She hated dealing with the machine because she missed the personal contact. On the other hand, the way everything was handled now suited her well. She'd told her father that she could handle the organization's details in the evening, since it only took an hour each day, and she never talked to anyone, anyway. This left her free to seek out something else to do during the daytime. He wasn't pleased she had found something now, but didn't press her for details probably figuring it wouldn't last.

As they crossed the intersection, Bob pointed to the north. "There's a small mall down that way, if you ever need anything. Next door to the mall are a couple of fast-food places." He jerked his head in the opposite direction, toward the residential area. "But if you want one of the best corned beef on rye sandwich in the world, there's a neighborhood market down that way."

"It sounds like you know the area really well."

Bob smiled. Little crinkles appeared in the corners of his eyes. His whole face softened, confirming her earlier opinion that her boss was quite a good-looking man.

"I grew up here. The reason Bart and I chose the location is because most of our initial customers were people we knew. It's worked well, so we're still here."

As they walked, they passed a number of specialty stores and small office buildings in the small commercial district. Not a single building was over two stories tall, and there were actually open metered parking spots on the street. The ambience of the district was nothing like the hustle and bustle of downtown. Georgette liked it.

By the time they arrived at the ice cream shop, Georgette could feel effect of the unaccustomed weight of the steel-toed safety boots on her lower back, far different from too-high high heels. Thinking of her closet-full of spike heels, and the shoes she'd worn earlier, she inwardly shuddered at the thought of forcing her feet back into such things to go home.

"What flavor do you want?"

Georgette stared up in awe at the board listing the flavors.

She probably could have picked an old standard, but today was a day of new experiences. Today was her first day of independence. Therefore, she wanted to pick the wildest flavor she could.

She tipped her head toward Bob and whispered, "What's Tiger Tiger?"

He pointed to a bin containing swirls of black and orange stripes. "I've had that before. It's a little strange. Orange and licorice. My favorite is the Chocolate Chip Cookie Dough."

She didn't care if it was strange. She wanted to have an ice cream flavor she'd never had before, to celebrate her first day of doing a job she'd never done before.

She turned to the kid behind the counter. "I'll have the Tiger Tiger, please."

When the clerk began scooping the bright colors into a huge waffle cone Georgette reached to open her purse, but Bob stopped her.

"No, this is my treat. In honor of your first day."

"Really?"

Bob smiled and turned to the clerk. "And the usual for me. Thanks." He paid the teenager.

Georgette didn't know how to respond. Of course it was only a simple ice cream cone, an inexpensive treat, but no one had ever given her anything when her father hadn't been either watching, or would be informed later.

"Thank you," she muttered, thinking that she didn't know enough nice people. Of course the people at her new church were nice, but she didn't know any of them that well, since she'd only been attending church for a few months.

When the clerk handed her the cone, Georgette gave it an experimental lick, confirming that Bob was right about the exotic flavor—it wasn't bad, but it was a strange combination.

On their way back to work they walked faster than she would have liked, but they didn't have time to dawdle.

"The phone hasn't stopped ringing, Bob." She paused to stifle her smile. Apparently there had been an ad in the help-wanted section of the newspaper. It had given her great pleasure to tell everyone that both positions had been filled. "Is it always like this? It hasn't been when I've shopped before."

"It never used to be this busy, but lately it has been. We hope with you here, it won't be so hectic, and we can all go home at a decent time."

She would gladly have worked as many hours as they needed, but she never would be able to explain longer hours to her father, who was not exactly pleased that she'd found a job on her own.

By the time they arrived back at the shop, both cones were finished.

"Let's get you started in the shop. Unfortunately, you'll still have run into the lobby to answer the phone, but it doesn't ring as often in the afternoon."

"Why don't you have a cordless phone?"

Bob smiled. "Sorry, but that doesn't work here. When the phone rings, we've got power tools going or we're banging on something. It's impossible to hear the caller speak. So you really do have to leave the room."

"I didn't think of that. I understand."

"I'm going to give you all the tune-ups to do," Bob continued.

She opened her mouth to protest that she was capable of much more, but stopped herself. The terms under which she'd been hired stated light-duty. "Sure," she mumbled, trying to smile graciously.

Bob walked behind the counter and stacked a few work orders into a pile. "Do these, and when you're finished, come see me."

Georgette picked up the pile and moved the first car into Bay One, anxious to begin the job she couldn't have foreseen in her wildest dreams.

As she worked on her tune-ups and waited for the oil to drain, she watched her bosses as they worked. They both worked hard and appeared to share all tasks and decisions equally, yet they still remained friends.

Of all the people Georgette knew, she couldn't call a single woman a real friend. She seldom saw them outside formal events, and even then those events were mainly venues to make or strengthen contacts. Even at the gym, Georgette felt as if her life was a competition.

She liked to think of the guys at the track as her friends, but she never saw them anyplace else. She suspected much of that had to do with their wives and girlfriends being suspicious that she was there for more than automechanical work.

Everyone at church was friendly, but three months wasn't enough time to nurture any real friendships, especially when she only saw them once a week, and then rushed home directly after the service, since her father didn't want her going in the first place.

At four twenty-five, Bart appeared beside her. She hadn't finished the pile, but it was time to go home in five minutes.

"Didn't get as much done as you thought you would, did you?"

"No, I didn't," she said quietly.

"Before you go, Bob wants to see you. He's in the office. Okay?"

Georgette stepped out of her coveralls, hung them on the hook, picked up the pile of work orders she hadn't completed, and made her way to the lobby. Her stomach clenched with the thought that she wasn't good enough, or fast enough, and that her first day was also going to be her last.

Chapter Three

Bob paused at his customer's question, halfway through typing the invoice. "It was just a tune-up, Don," Bob responded. "I guarantee all the work we do, and I guarantee this, too." Bob hadn't hovered, but he had watched George when she couldn't tell he was there.

She knew what she was doing.

"If you tell me what you think she did wrong, I'll fix it."

"Well, maybe I spoke too quickl tomer said. "It seems to be running smo n't see any oil on the ground. A

"You won't see any, ei job."

"Do I get a disco

Bob gritted h happy when n

your car last year. You didn't ask for a discount then. What makes the difference now? Is it because a woman did the tune-up?"

Don's voice deepened. "No. Of course not."

Bob typed the last code for the computer to add the tax, and hit Print. "Good. Will that be on your charge card?"

A flicker of movement in the doorway to the shop caught his eye.

George was standing in the doorway, stiff as a board, holding the orders he knew she hadn't had time to do. She cleared her throat. "You wanted to see me?" she asked in a raspy squeak.

"Yes. Can you meet me in the office?"

He swiped the card, completed the transaction, closed the program, and waited until Don was out the door before he joined George. He sat behind the desk. "Bart and I had a little talk today about you."

He slid an envelope across the desk. She stiffened in the chair.

"Unfortunately, as a mechanic, you really stick out being a, um…uh…a woman. Our customers have this corporate image of us, as a business, even though there's only been the two of us. We [illegible] you'd fit in better if you didn't use those blue [illegible] bought gray ones, like ours. Bart's [illegible]ing on the weekends, so buy [illegible]'s a few crests with our logo. Sew them on right here." He patted the logo on his own coveralls. "Of course we'll reimburse you. This is something I should have thought of sooner. Sorry about that."

She picked up the envelope, and pulled out one of the crests. "This is what you wanted to see me about? My coveralls?" Her blue eyes, big and wide, and very, very pretty took him in.

Her voice lowered to barely above a whisper. "I thought you would be angry because I didn't finish everything you gave me."

"That's nothing to get angry about. We knew you wouldn't be able to finish everything in that pile in one day, especially with the way the phones have been ringing. But we would like you to get those coveralls as soon you can. I could probably phone the place I usually go. They size them by height. How tall are you?"

Her cheeks darkened. "I'm five foot three. I hope you're not going to ask me what I weigh."

"I have three sisters and one of m... ...ers is married." A smile tugged at his lip... ...r."

"You have brothers and sis...

"Yes. I have three sister... a large family. What ab...

"I only have one si... see her much any...

"I don't se...

since I switched churches." He shrugged his shoulders. "But that's okay. I still see them at family functions and stuff."

"You can't see your family because of church? I don't understand."

"Well, every Sunday I play on my church's worship team with three of my friends. Actually, four friends, now. You remember me mentioning the accountant? His name is Adrian. He's one of them."

Her eyes widened as she stared at him in open astonishment. "My church has a lady who plays the piano, which my father tried to get me to learn as a child, but I just couldn't get it. What do you play?"

"Drums."

Her eyes flitted to his arms, before returning to his face. "I've never seen drums in church. But then I've only ever been to one."

The words were out of his mouth before he had the chance to think. "You're more than welcome to come and worship with us one Sunday. It's a very contemporary service, and the crowd is very informal. Sunday evenings we have coffee and donuts after the service."

Her eyes widened even more than they had be- "Coffee and donuts? At church?"

ah..." He let his voice trail off, not eply. Her surprise told him that ian very long.

"I'd love to go. Thank you so much for inviting me. Can you write down the address?"

Warnings about not mixing business with pleasure clanged through his head. George had done well today, but today was only one day. If her skills and abilities didn't mesh with what they needed, and if he became too friendly with her, it would cloud his ability to make a rational judgment when her probationary period was over. That clashed with his duty toward her fledgling Christianity, which included widening her Christian circles. He couldn't very well take back his invitation.

He scribbled down the address for Faith Community Fellowship. "Would you like directions? It's actually not far from here."

She scooped the paper up quickly. "That's okay. I'm sure I can find it. I can hardly wait."

He pictured the way most people dressed for church, compared to the way George h d been dressed when she first arrived that m

A newcomer was always notic ly during the evening service. A n with him, dressed to the *nir* newsworthy enough to wouldn't hear the end

"Just one thing. I there. Please, w

* * *

"It's Sunday night. Where are you going?"

Georgette smiled at her father. "I'm meeting a friend from work. Then we'll be having coffee and donuts. Don't wait up for me! Bye, Daddy!"

She closed the door behind her before her father could question her further. Every day, he became increasingly irritated at the lack of details she provided him about her job, but she didn't know what to tell him. Her clothes on the first day, suitable for work in an office, let him initially believe what he wanted to believe. But the questions became more and more insistent, and she'd finally told her father she was working as an assistant for two gentleman entrepreneurs in a limited partnership. She had told him her primary job was working in the accounting department, but part of her duties involved customer service.

He watched her leave daily, openly showing displeasure that she was going to work. However, at the same time, he seemed proud that she dressed well. He'd even noticed her new bright-red nail polish, and asked if it was because she ...as trying to attract a man.

...ette detested wearing nail polish. She did ...rease she couldn't get out from ...he took the nail polish off on the way to work, while sitting in traffic, then put it back on, on the way home.

She knew Bob wondered why she arrived at work every day dressed to impress and then changed clothes, but she found herself caught in a cycle she couldn't break. In order to make the long drive across town and be on time, she had to leave before her father. She couldn't let him see her leaving the house wearing anything other than what his preconceived ideas told him she should be wearing.

So the household staff wouldn't have to lie for her, Georgette changed back into her good clothes in the gas station washroom on the way home. But, once at home, she changed in order to work on the old truck in the garage, so her father wouldn't wonder why she smelled like oil at supper time.

Instead of confronting her father, she was acting like a coward.

She pushed that thought aside as she [illegible] into the parking lot of a well-cared-for [illegible] at looked as if it had once housed so[illegible] business. Inside, everything [illegible] and decorated in neutral [illegible] browns, giving the pl[illegible] sphere. Signs indic[illegible] gymnasium were[illegible] ward, soft music from the worship team echoed in the background.

A couple welcomed her as they gave her a bulletin.

"Welcome to Faith Community Fellowship. My name is Kaitlyn," the woman said, smiling. "Are you new to the area?"

Georgette smiled back. "No, I actually don't live near here. I'm here with Bob Delanio, except he had to come early."

The woman's eyebrows arched. She quickly glanced at the man she was with, then turned back to Georgette. "Then you'll want to go in right now, so you can find a seat close to the front. Would you like me to show you where to go?"

Georgette shook her head. "I'll just follow the music. Thanks."

As she'd said, Georgette followed the music until she was in the sanctuary where Bob, two other men and a woman were at the front.

Georgette slid into a chair, and surreptitiously she checked the place out. It was nothing like the church she'd been attending.

Even though she felt strange, she had worn jeans because Bob had told her to do so. Now she was glad [illegible]tened to him. Everyone was wearing either [illegible]lothes. Not a single man wore a tie, [illegible]ught might be the pastor.

Instead of a stately sanctuary with stained-glass windows and wooden benches, this sanctuary was a large rectangular room. A large opening in the wall showed a kitchen, which indicated that the sanctuary also doubled as a banquet hall. But for now, a single, plain wooden cross at the front, and banners on the walls clearly defined it as a church setting.

Most of the people in attendance were her age, except for a large group of teens, who took up at least a quarter of the seats in the back.

At the church she'd been going to, everyone was solemn, and once inside the sanctuary, silent.

Here, all around her, people talked and even laughed. Out loud.

"Hello, everyone!" a voice boomed from the speakers mounted on the walls. "Welcome to Faith Community Fellowship. Please stand and let's worship God together."

Georgette hustled to her feet. To her surprise, the first song was from one of her praise CDs that her father hadn't managed to find and throw out.

She forced herself not to watch Bob, and to pay attention to the words.

Until now, the only time she'd actually sung God's praises out loud was in the closed car, but here things were different. The enthusiasm of the crowd around her encouraged her to ignore her father's warnings not to make a spectacle of herself. Here, she joined in with the rest of the congregation to praise God in song. Being able to express herself out loud among other people opened a rush of emotion she hadn't experienced before.

By the time they had sung the fifth song in praise and wonderment of God's glory, tears streamed from her eyes, and she didn't care if her mascara ran.

When the songs were over, she quickly reached down and started digging through her purse for a tissue.

Bob sat beside her just as she was blowing her nose.

"Hi, George. I'm glad you found us."

She nodded and stuffed the used tissue into her purse to hide it, taking her notepad out to record the sermon. "I've never been to a place like this." She stopped as the pastor began speaking.

Bob whispered, "If you want, we can get a tape. Randy records everything for the church's tape library."

She stopped writing. "Really? I can have one?"

"Of course."

At the end of the pastor's message, Bob rose quietly and returned to the front. The worship team closed the service with one more song, one that she knew she would hear in her head all week long, encouraging her to think about God more over the days to come.

The congregation quickly left their seats and flocked to the back of the room, where coffee and trays of donuts sat on a large table. Georgette was in the process of reaching for a donut when a man with dark hair and vivid blue eyes shuffled in beside her.

"You must be George, the mechanic."

Immediately, she backed up. The man grabbed a Boston cream donut, and smiled at her. "I'm Randy. Bob told us you'd be here tonight and I saw you together. You'd better grab that donut fast. The Boston creams go quickly."

Before she could think of something to say, Bob's voice sounded from behind her. "You don't waste any time, do you?"

Randy shrugged his shoulders. "If you snooze, you lose."

Bob stiffened. "I gather you've met my friend, Randy?"

She smiled. "Briefly."

As they spoke, the other members of the worship team joined them.

"Everyone, this is George, the new mechanic and bookkeeper I told you about. George, this is Paul, Celeste, and Adrian."

Adrian, the only one of the four men who wore

glasses, smiled. "Welcome, we hope to see you back here."

Georgette nodded. "Yes, I think you will." She doubted she would be able to attend the morning services at Bob's church because of her obligations to her father, but she was free to attend Bob's church on Sunday evenings, especially since her father thought she was going out on a social visit, not to church.

She looked up at Bob, who was now standing beside her.

She couldn't help but like him, even though she told herself what she was feeling was simply a schoolgirl's crush, a few years too late. For the first time she was happy with her life, and everything centered around Bob.

However, it was neither practical nor wise to become personally involved with one's boss, regardless of his strength of character. She enjoyed her job too much to jeopardize it in any way.

Bob spoke up, "We have to go put our stuff away. I'll be right back."

Celeste shook her head. "I can pack up the drums for you. Why don't you two visit? We can all go out for coffee together after. You're not in a rush to get home, are you, George?"

The opposite. Since her father thought she was going out to visit friends, he wouldn't expect her back for a long time. "No. That sounds like fun."

Bob's friends all returned to the front, leaving her alone with him, or as alone as they could be in the crowd.

"What did you think? You were saying this is quite different from where you're going."

"Yes. Where I've been is quite formal. Your church doesn't even have pews."

Bob nodded. "Yes. We also use this room for banquets and things like the women's auxiliary functions."

Her heart ached, thinking of just sitting around with a group of women, talking about nothing in particular—not about who was cheating on whom or the other backstabbing theatrics that passed for conversation in her current social circle.

Bob told her about how his parents and most of the rest of his family attended the main church, of which this one was a plant. While they talked, a bunch of the teens cleared and stacked the chairs to make the place ready for the next group using the room.

Just as the last of the chairs were stacked away, Randy joined them.

"Sorry, I can't go with you, after all. I have to go to Pastor Ron's place to fix his computer."

Bob nodded. "I guess I'll see you Wednesday,

then." Bob turned to Georgette. "We practice at Adrian's house every Wednesday night for the coming Sunday."

She knew Bob worked every evening except Wednesday. Now she knew why. "You mean even when you're this far behind, you stop working and go do church stuff?"

"Yup. Every Wednesday."

Georgette studied Bob's face, which held nothing except honesty. Taking time off meant a loss of income. She couldn't imagine what her father would have thought of someone willingly taking a financial loss on a regular basis to do something for church. "That's pretty dedicated," she muttered.

Bob smiled. "God's done a lot for me. This is only one small thing I can do for Him. Besides, it's something I enjoy."

She could imagine that after a frustrating day, or week, there might be significant release in being able to whack a drum set.

Paul was coming down the steps of the stage as they were starting to go up. "I just remembered that I have a super early staff meeting tomorrow morning I need to prep for. I'll have to take a rain check. Sorry."

Bob blinked and looked at Paul. "Must be a very early meeting. See you Wednesday, then."

They passed Paul and got up on the stage just as Adrian closed the zipper on the electric piano case. Celeste stood off to the side, talking on her cell phone.

"Celeste's mother needs some help moving some furniture. I'm sorry, we can't go after all."

Bob's eyes narrowed. "On Sunday night? This just came up *now?*"

Adrian shrugged his shoulders. "Sorry. See you Wednesday."

Bob rested his fists on his hips as Adrian carried off the electric piano. Celeste tucked her phone into her purse, picked up Adrian's guitar case, waved, and also walked off the stage.

"If I didn't know better..." Bob muttered. He turned to Georgette. "I guess that means it's just you and me. Still want to go out for coffee and a donut?"

Georgette's foolish heart fluttered. While she'd certainly enjoyed working with him, she had also learned in casual conversation that Bob was single. Very single. Besides, she would have been stupid if she couldn't recognize the way people in the church did a double-take at seeing Bob at church with a woman.

She also had her suspicions about why Bob's friends had suddenly changed their minds about joining them for coffee.

Going out with Bob away from a work setting wasn't smart.

Georgette looked up into his eyes and cleared her throat.

"Yes."

Chapter Four

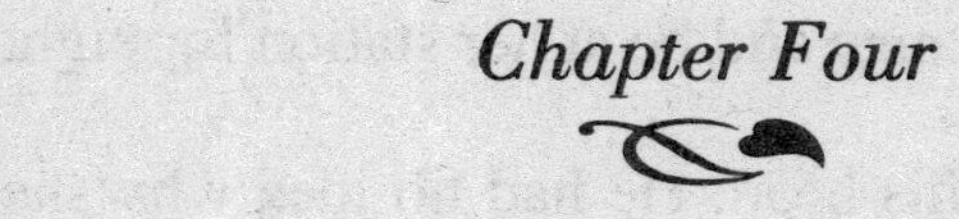

Bob unlocked the door to the lobby promptly at 7:00 am, punched in the alarm code, then headed straight for the coffee machine.

He couldn't remember the last time he'd needed coffee so badly.

At first he'd been a little nervous about going to the twenty-four-hour donut shop with George alone, but today he had no regrets. They'd talked, they'd laughed and they'd talked some more. It was well after midnight by the time they'd realized they both should have been home asleep. Bob couldn't remember the last time he'd been so tired after a weekend, but he also couldn't remember the last time he'd enjoyed himself so much.

It told him it had been too long since he'd set the worries of the business aside, and gone out to do something just because it was fun. Now that he had help in the shop, he could look forward to trying some new things.

People started coming in before the coffee was ready, dropping off their cars on the way to work.

Bart arrived as usual at seven-thirty and George arrived with enough time to run into the washroom, change and be at her station for eight o'clock.

Bob shook his head. He had no idea why she did such a thing, but he had to admit he enjoyed watching her run by before she re-emerged in the shapeless coveralls.

When the washroom door opened, Bob had her coffee poured, complete with double cream and no sugar.

"Thanks, Bob," she mumbled as she closed her eyes to take her first slow, luxurious sip, then sighed. "What's lined up for today?"

"About the same, nothing critical. We'll get the morning rush caught up, then you can get back to the bookkeeping."

"Okay." She nodded, then took a bigger sip of the hot coffee. "The way you've got me splitting my duties is working really well. I'm making good progress."

Bob smiled. He was pleased with how fast she was getting everything organized, and Adrian would be even more pleased. "Great. We've got the usual tune-ups lined up for the morning, but after lunch I've got some bigger jobs for you."

He started to go over the row of work orders pinned to the board with George when the electronic chime for the door sounded.

They both turned simultaneously as a tall, good-looking man in an expensive suit walked in.

George fumbled her coffee mug, spilling a little over the edge. A splash of coffee dribbled onto one boot.

Bob stared at this new potential customer, one better dressed than the majority of people who walked in off the street. He'd probably had a breakdown mid-trip, as the neighborhood wasn't exactly the center of the high-rise financial district.

Instead of looking at Bob, as most potential customers did when they needed help, the newcomer only had eyes…and raised eyebrows, for George. He surveyed her from head to safety-workboot covered toes.

"Hello, Georgette."

Her voice came out barely above a whisper. "Hello, Tyler."

Tyler gazed around the room, taking in everything from the work board to the coffee machine to the old couch, and treating Bob as just another furnishing. Bob tried not to take it personally.

"I need some work done on my car." Tyler focused on the crest on George's coveralls, blinked, then looked back up to her face. "Can you help me?"

George cleared her throat. "What seems to be the problem? With your car."

"It, uh… It makes this noise every once in a while, and I thought I should have it looked at."

It was Bob's gut feeling that there wasn't really anything wrong with Tyler's car, and that Tyler was there only to see George.

To give them some privacy, he walked into the shop.

"Hey, Bob, did you see what just pulled in?"

He turned toward Bart. *I don't want to know what Tyler drives,* Bob thought. "What?" he asked.

Bart jerked his head in the direction of Bay Four's open door.

He could see a shiny new Porsche through the large opening.

A Porsche so new that any alleged noise would be covered by the warranty, and could be fixed at the dealership.

Bob resolutely ignored the car, fixing his attention instead on the large window between the office and the shop. George was standing at the counter, writing something down. Tyler was leaning forward, resting his elbows on the counter.

"Looks like you've got competition," Bart's voice drifted from behind him.

Bob spun around.

"No one is competing," he mumbled, then began searching through his tool caddy for just the right wrench.

"If you say so." Bart shrugged, then turned around to continue his current project.

As soon as Bart was busy, Bob turned to watch Georgette.

She didn't seem very excited to see her acquaintance, and Bob didn't know why he found that comforting. Her behavior reinforced it—she shook her head a few times, then glanced through the window, straight at him.

Bob quickly turned his head down and continued his search for the wrench. When he found his spare, he picked it up and turned to continue the job he was supposed to be doing when the movement of the door of Tyler's Porsche opening caught his eye. Slowly and carefully, the Porsche was backed out of the parking spot and driven away, purring like the well-tuned machine it was, not a suspicious noise to be heard.

Bob pulled the rag out of his pocket, wiped his hands, and returned to the lobby, where George was busily typing purchase orders into the computer.

"I see your friend left."

He waited for her to deny that Tyler was her friend, but she didn't.

"I told him that if he thought there was a problem, he should take it back to the dealership where he got it, because anything wrong would still be under warranty."

He again waited for her to say something more, *anything,* but silence hung between them.

He cleared his throat and stepped behind the counter. "Let's go over today's lineup together."

She nodded silently as he paged through the orders. When he'd divided up the work for the day, she logged off the computer, picked up her pile, and made her way quietly into the shop.

Bob couldn't remember the last time a day had dragged this way. Even though the three of them didn't talk any more or any less than they had in the past week, a heavy silence seemed to hang in the building, despite the constant noise of their repair work.

His earlier thoughts about shaking up his social life continued to echo through his head during the rest of the day. He was thirty years old and ready to settle down. Yet, he couldn't remember the last time he'd had a steady girlfriend.

Only days ago, Adrian and Celeste had announced to the worship team that they were getting married. That, along with Bart's endless baby pictures, reminded Bob how boring and predictable his life had become.

Of course, to start something with George would be unwise. She was his employee. However, that didn't mean they couldn't hang out as friends. Her reaction to Tyler indicated that although she had some sort of history with him, it didn't appear to be romantic.

When it was time for George to go home, she disappeared into the washroom to clean up and Bob moved to the large window in preparation. When the washroom door opened again and she'd cleared it by a few steps, Bob entered the lobby, hoping she would think the timing was coincidental.

George started in surprise at seeing him in the lobby at that hour of the day, without the phone ringing. "Goodnight, Bob," she said on her way to the door. "See you tomorrow."

"Wait," he said, and she stopped.

"Before you go, I wanted to ask you something. I haven't been able to go as often as I used to, but every Monday night my church has a Bible study. It's at the home of one of the deacon couples, and it's really informal. I was wondering if you'd like to go with me tonight."

She blinked a few times, then glanced toward the door. "Sorry, I can't," she mumbled, then kept walking. She opened the door, stepped outside, then just before the door closed, she said, "I'm going out with Tyler."

Georgette stepped back to look at herself in the mirror.

The housekeeper had helped to style her hair into perfect order.

It was stiff and felt artificial.

Her makeup was flawless, her shadow just the right color to accent her eyes. Her nail polish matched her lipstick. The artifice brought back a memory of posing for promotional photographs meant to encourage people to help the starving children of the world. It had raised only marginal funding, but it brought phenomenal publicity for her father. The experience was a good reminder of how shallow people could be.

Just like at that session, her outfit was the height of fashion, and emphasized her figure to perfection while binding it uncomfortably.

Her shoes were darling, and the perfect accent to her legs. They also pinched her toes, and she didn't know if she could stand more than twenty minutes in them. If she took them off under the table to wiggle her toes, she knew she would never get them back on.

Georgette looked perfect.

She felt like a fake.

"Georgie-Pie, honey, you look magnificent!"

Georgette inhaled deeply, pasted on a smile that was as phony as the rest of her appearance, and turned to face her father, who was standing in her bedroom doorway. "Thank you, Daddy. Tyler should be here in a few minutes, and I want to be ready."

"Always a stickler for punctuality." He grinned and playfully wagged one finger in the air at her. "It wouldn't hurt to be fashionably late."

"We have reservations for dinner." Besides, Georgette considered being fashionably late incredibly rude and self-centered. It was only one of many ways to draw attention to oneself. She hated that, too. "Now, if you'll excuse me, I need a few more minutes to finish getting ready." She didn't bother to watch him leave.

It was at times like this she thought of her mother, and wondered if the endless social charade was one of the things that had driven her mother away. Georgette had been very young when her mother had left. Her father had told her it was because her mother didn't want to be part of their family anymore. It had hurt terribly at the time, and still did. As an adult, though, Georgette could see how her father's tyranny made her family dysfunctional. She could only guess at the difficulty of being married to him. She often thought about how bad it must have been to make her mother run away and abandon her two children.

On the way to the closet, Georgette's step faltered. She had one picture of her mother left that her father hadn't found and destroyed. She kept it hidden in the lining of her purse, and whenever she switched purses, she made sure the picture went with her. It would never do to have her father find it now. She turned in time to see her father close the door behind him.

When the door was closed, Georgette dumped the contents of her purse haphazardly onto the bed, but she carefully removed the laminated and carefully preserved picture from where she'd hidden it in the seam of the lining.

She paused to sit on the bed to study the picture, and to remember.

As an adult, the resemblance between her and her mother was strong. They had the same light-blond hair color, the same blue eyes, and, sadly, the same lack of height. The picture had been taken only days before her mother had left. Georgette had been ten years old, and the two of them had been together, laughing and making rabbit ears behind each other's heads with their fingers.

Josephine had taken the picture in the afternoon, while her father was at work. He never would have permitted such nonsense if he'd been there. Georgette had sneaked the picture out of the package and taken it to school to show a friend. When she'd arrived back home, not only was her mother gone, but so was everything her mother owned, and every reminder of her. It was a clean sweep. All she had left of her mother was one candid photograph and a small gold cross on a delicate gold chain that she never took off, not even at night.

"Georgie-Pie, honey. He's here!"

She gently tucked the photograph into its new secret hiding spot in the new purse lining, then rammed everything else in as quickly as she could. "I'll be right there!" she called, taking one last look at herself in the mirror. She stuck out her tongue at her reflection, stiffened and walked slowly, in a dignified manner, out of the bedroom, and down the stairs.

Tyler smiled, but he didn't leave her father's side. "You look lovely, Georgette."

"Thank you, Tyler," she said gracefully. She batted her eyelashes coyly, positive that Tyler wouldn't catch her sarcasm.

Bob would have caught it if she did such a thing to him. In fact, Bob would have laughed.

She should have been with Bob right now. She'd been thrilled that he'd invited her to a Bible study meeting. But instead, she was with Tyler because she couldn't take the chance he would tell her father he'd seen her. She needed to talk to Tyler immediately.

Tyler held the car door open for her and whisked her away to an intimate and very expensive restaurant.

She was almost surprised he hadn't taken her somewhere splashy, somewhere people they knew would see them, but she guessed Tyler wanted the privacy rather than the notoriety, at least for the moment.

They made polite chitchat until their meals came and the waiter made the obligatory last visit to make sure everything was satisfactory before leaving them alone.

Georgette had been dreading the moment they would be assured of privacy.

"So, tell me, Georgette, what in the world were you doing at that place?"

"I think it should be obvious. I work there. What were *you* doing there?" She still didn't know if she'd ever overcome the shock of seeing someone she knew on that side of town.

"I told you what I was doing there. I was on my way downtown when I heard a noise. I must have just run over something, because the noise didn't happen again."

Georgette poked at her salmon with her fork. "I suppose," she said. It was possible, but unlikely. Bob And Bart's was nowhere near the route between Tyler's home and his office downtown. The only way Tyler, or anyone, for that matter, would have run into her was if they already knew she was there, because it wasn't the type of neighborhood any of her acquaintances would normally ever go to.

She cleared her throat. "I meant, what were you doing there in the first place? It's kind of out of your way, isn't it?"

Tyler flashed her his most charming smile—a smile clearly meant to distract her from their conversation. "It might be a little out of my way, but I felt like taking an indirect route that day."

Indirect, nothing. His little side trip doubled his commute.

Unless he had been following her...

"Was there any particular reason you felt like going out of your way? Did you see my car when I was on the way to work or anything?"

"Yes, actually, I did see your car. That's why I stopped in. When I walked in the door, I was certainly surprised to see you. And what a getup!"

She noted that he avoided any mention of when he'd seen her car. She was positive it wasn't in the parking lot. It was long before that. A long, long time before that. Possibly when she was backing out of the garage at home. He could have been behind her the whole time, following her, and she wouldn't have noticed. Of course, if she accused him of following her, he would never admit it.

She narrowed her eyes. "Lots of people wear uniforms and the like, you know."

Tyler choked on his mouthful, swallowed, coughed and cleared his throat. "But not like that. I could see you doing accounting, but why are you delivering parts?"

Georgette's heart skipped a beat. She wasn't ready for anyone she knew, especially someone so close to her father, to know what she was doing. But she'd been caught and now it was time to defend her choices.

"I don't deliver parts. I work in the shop, fixing things. Getting my hands dirty." Georgette laid her knife and fork down, and clasped those hands in front of her. "And that's exactly the job I wanted. I'm only doing the accounting because I couldn't get one without the other."

Tyler shook his head. "You should be working for your father."

Been there, done that. She hated her father manipulating her like a puppet on a string. This was her first chance at independence, and nothing was going to take it away from her. Nothing. "Maybe. But for now, this is what I want to do."

"What could that two-bit outfit possibly be paying you to make it worth your while?"

Georgette sighed. She wasn't there for the money. The allowance her father gave her for the hour a day she spent managing his charities was more than double her full-time salary. It was one more thing her father used to control her, paying her for her loyalty. It made her feel as if she was being bought, and she hated herself for it.

"Auto mechanics is a hobby for me, so I consider this a hobby that pays."

"You know what your father would say if he found out, don't you?"

She shuddered at the thought. He would consider what she was doing pure defiance, and in a way, it was. But it was also the only place where she was out from under her father's thumb. Even though she'd told Tyler she considered it a hobby, she worked hard at her job and when the day was done, she was at peace with herself and with God, and she could sleep well at night.

She raised one hand up, pressing into the tiny cross, something else her father didn't approve of. "I don't think I'm ready to tell Daddy the specifics yet." In fact, she didn't know if she would ever be ready to tell him. But at the same time, she knew that one day she would have to. To think otherwise was unrealistic.

"Tell me, Georgette, does anyone else know? Besides me?"

Her breath caught in her throat. "I don't know," she muttered, at least she hoped and prayed no one knew. That Tyler knew was not in her favor.

He leaned forward toward her, over the table. "I could help you keep your secret."

Her heart began to pound. She didn't trust Tyler, but he had her between a rock and a hard place. Perhaps graciousness on her part would evoke a similar response. "Could you? I'd really appreciate that." She wondered nervously what he would ask for in return. She had nothing to offer. To offer money would be an insult. Any work he would ever need done to his car was best done by the dealership where he bought it.

"But in return, there's something you can do for me."

Here it was. She leaned closer to Tyler. "What do you have in mind?"

Tyler sat back and crossed his arms over his chest. "I need to attend a number of functions, and it doesn't look good for me to go alone. I need you there as my companion. Your father would be pleased to see us together, you know, in the past, he's encouraged me to spend time with you."

Georgette forced herself to breathe. Tyler came from old money, but that wasn't enough for Tyler. He was ambitious, which shouldn't have been bad, except that like her father, Tyler didn't care who he stepped on.

"I don't know..." she let her voice trail off, trying to give herself more time to think.

Tyler tipped his head to one side. "You scratch my back, I'll scratch yours."

Maybe to him, it was back-scratching. To Georgette, it sounded an awful lot like extortion.

But until she could figure out a way to approach her father, she didn't have any choice. By not dealing with the problem sooner, she had set herself up to become an easy victim.

"I can't believe that you, of all people, would be unable to find a date. I'm sure there are any number of women who want to go out with you."

"Maybe. But it looks better if I go to these things with the same person. It gives me a reputation for stability and maturity."

Georgette's blood boiled. What Tyler looked like on the outside to strangers was more important to him than anything.

Bob would never have behaved in such a manner. Even though Bob wasn't in the upper echelons of the corporate world, he was still a successful business owner. He was a good Christian man, and he made an income he was comfortable with. His entire business was built on one thing. Doing honest work in order to satisfy his customers.

The only one Tyler wanted to satisfy was himself, no matter what the cost.

"How many times? Does today count?"

"Today we're negotiating. Does this mean you agree?"

For now, Georgette didn't have a choice. Soon she would find an appropriate time to tell her father, on her own terms, but until the time was right, she would have to put up with Tyler.

"I agree," she muttered, then pushed the plate containing her half-eaten meal slightly forward on the tabletop. "Do you mind if we leave? I'm not as hungry as I thought I was."

Tyler signaled the waiter for the bill, but continued eating. "Great. Today is Monday. I've got to go to a wildlife fund-raiser on Wednesday. I'll pick you up at five-thirty. It's a dinner engagement. Dress appropriately."

Chapter Five

Georgette pushed a little more sawdust over the spill with the toe of her workboot. "It should be absorbed by tomorrow," she mumbled to Bart, who reached out to run his finger along the seal of the leaky oil filter of the car on the hoist above them.

Bob appeared beside her. "Did you find out what's wrong?"

Georgette nodded. "I don't know where she went to change the oil, and I don't know how they could have done it, but the O-ring was twisted and it wrecked the seal. That's what's been causing the leak."

Bart looked up and watched as another drop leaked out. "Mrs. Jablonski is going to be happy. She was so afraid of what it would cost to fix, she's just been adding more oil instead of bringing it in. The only reason she finally came was because her neighbors were complaining about the growing puddle on the street." All we have to charge her for is changing the filter."

"You mean you're not even going to charge her for the full oil-change package?" Her father's mechanic charged a service fee just to look at any vehicle, then took the money off the cost of the repair later. However, if nothing was done, they kept the money for their time, which was only fair.

"Naw. It took under a minute to see what the problem was. Besides, we never charge for estimates."

"But how are you going to make money on this, then?"

"Mrs. Jablonski is living on a pension. We'll get back our time in the markup on the new filter we're going to give her, so it's not like we're losing anything. The only reason she brought it here is because my mother told her I would look at it and fix it for a fair price. I'm not doing it for free. I'm just being reasonable."

"But..." She let her voice trail off. An oil filter wasn't free, but it was still an inexpensive item. She couldn't imagine there was much markup on it. It might pay for one minute worth of their time, when calculating all the expenses that went with running a business. Georgette turned to Bart. "And you agree with this decision?"

Bart shrugged his shoulders. "I don't do anything to contradict a promise made by Bob's mama. This, you too, will learn." He turned to Bob. "Don't forget to give Mrs. Jablonski the seniors' discount."

In response, Bob nodded.

All Georgette could do was stare.

Her father had always drilled into her head to get top dollar, no matter what. Charity work, when plainly labeled *charity,* was different. Her father received his rewards in publicity, product placement and good will. But in business, her father refused to open any doors where people might take advantage, and that meant no favors. The point of being in business wasn't merely to survive. He risked money to make money, and he protected his investments. The first thing her father had taught her was that nice guys always finished last.

Georgette looked around her. The building that housed the auto repair shop was old—showing both wear and age. The lobby and the washrooms had been renovated at least once, and the walls needed another couple of coats of paint. And that was just for starters. For their modest requirements, the building was adequate, but not much more.

She couldn't see that either Bart or Bob were doing much better personally.

Bart had just purchased a new vehicle, but it was

only a mid-priced minivan. Yet, he was proud of his family-man vehicle. Bob's car was also mid-priced, mid-sized and three years old, a year older than any car her father ever owned. For two men who were risking everything they had to keep their business going, they weren't very far ahead.

Because they were nice guys.

But as far as she could tell, even though Bob worked hard, he was happy. And Georgette was happy working for him.

That was why she was taking the risk she was now taking, and why she had accepted Tyler's terms for his silence in keeping her secret from her father. For the first time in her life, she was happy. She was doing something she wanted to do, dealing with people who had nothing to gain by knowing her.

Besides, it didn't seem like her father's world held anything Bob would want. He was conscientious and honest, and lived his life the way God wanted him to. The more she came to know Bob as she worked with him, the more she liked him both personally and professionally. She couldn't say the same about Tyler.

Georgette sighed. For now, she was simply *George the Mechanic*. But tonight, she would again have to become *Georgette the Fake* to help Tyler rub elbows to further himself and his business ventures. She'd much rather help Bob with his business ventures, but he didn't need a pretty showpiece. He needed a good mechanic and a proficient bookkeeper, not to mention some extra money for renovations.

She had the money, but she couldn't give it to him without revealing her background. She also knew he'd find the gift insulting. For now, all she could do to help him was be the best mechanic and best employee she could be.

"I should be finished this in twenty minutes. What have you got for me next?"

"Every large job we have right now is waiting for parts. I've got the orders lined up on the board. Just take the next up, Bart and I will do the same, and by tomorrow we should be all caught up and ready for when the backlog of parts comes in."

She kept busy all day, but when the day was done, she felt satisfied about her contribution.

She unzipped her coveralls, stepped out of them, made a quick inspection to see if they were still acceptable for one more day without a trip through the washing machine, then hung them on the hook at her station.

As she squatted and reached into the bottom of her tool caddy to retrieve her purse, footsteps echoed on the concrete floor behind her. She turned to see Bob towering above her.

"I'm sorry I didn't catch you sooner. I was wondering if you wouldn't mind staying an hour later tonight to finish up the last order on the board. Tonight is Wednesday, practice night for the worship team. I've got be out of here at six-thirty, and I had really wanted to get everything done so we'll be ready for tomorrow morning. I'll pay you overtime. I don't expect you to do it for nothing."

Georgette's heart sank. "I'm so sorry. Any other day, I'd love to stay. But tonight I have to be somewhere at five-thirty, and I can't." She checked her watch. It was four-thirty on the dot, and even leaving on time, she was pressing her luck. By the time she made the trip across town in rush-hour traffic, including her quick change back into her skirt and blouse in the washroom at the gas station, which left only fifteen minutes to shower, wash, dry her hair and run the curling iron through it, and scramble into the dress, hose and accessories that she'd already set aside.

"Oh. Sorry. Don't worry about it. I'll just come back after the practice is over and finish up."

"You'd do that?"

"They just called and said they needed the car tomorrow morning, so I said I would do it. I try not to make promises I can't keep."

Georgette stepped closer, "You put in such long hours. I know you're often here at six-thirty in the morning to take people's cars in before they go to work when you're not scheduled to be in until seven." Frequently he even stayed very late to get a job done, which it appeared would happen again tonight. "How about if I come in early tomorrow?"

Bob shook his head. "No. You're going on a date tonight, and I don't want you to ruin your evening by cutting your night short so you can come in early."

Georgette bit back a smile. Needing to go home early would work in her favor. "I really didn't plan to be out late, anyway. I'm sure Tyler will understand."

He stiffened. "Tyler seems very understanding. I know a lot of guys who wouldn't want their wives or girlfriends doing a job like this."

Not to mention daughters. Her father immediately came to mind, as both an understatement and a confirmation of Bob's statement.

She looked up at Bob. "Actually, I really hate going out to the kind of places Tyler and I are going tonight. It's a big animal shelter fund-raiser and even though I know it's a worthy cause, I'd still rather just make a donation than get all dressed up and go to a banquet with people I don't care about seeing. They're only there to see who's currently with whom, and to try to make an impression. Even if we didn't have this project at work, I have something in my garage at home I'd be doing. It's something I've been working on for a long time." Strangely, she found that her new job hadn't lessened her joy in fixing up the old pickup truck. If she kept it up, the old beast would be running very soon.

Bob smiled, and his eyes became unfocused. "Yeah. I have a project like that." He smiled and looked off into the distance for a few seconds. Suddenly, he recollected himself. "I'm keeping you. You're going to be late."

Once again, she checked her watch. It was getting later by the minute, yet she wasn't motivated to hurry. "I guess," she replied.

"I'll take you up on that offer another day. Goodnight, George."

She nodded. "Sure. Goodnight, Bob."

Randy Reynolds did the same thing he always did at the end of a good practice. He headed right into Adrian's kitchen, grabbed first choice of the donuts, poured a fresh cup of coffee, then sauntered back into Adrian's den while everyone tidied up their music and put their instruments away.

"Hey, Randy, you could always help, you know," Bob called out.

Randy turned toward his best friend, took a bite out of the donut, then waved it at Bob as he spoke.

"You're only saying that because taking down the drum set takes the longest."

"Which means you should help me every week instead of stuffing your face."

Randy pressed his hand onto his stomach, being careful not to smear any of the icing from the donut onto his shirt. "I'm a growing boy."

Celeste shook her head while she wound up one of the patch cords. "I don't know how you stay so slim; you eat so much junk food."

Randy grinned. "It's a gift. Besides, this might be my only chance to get my favorite donuts for a whole week, at least for free. Did you see Bob's new girlfriend at church Sunday night? She likes the same kind of donuts I do."

"She's not my girlfriend," Bob muttered as he started disassembling the stool. "She's my new light-duty mechanic."

Randy snorted. "And that's why you took her to church? My boss never takes me to church."

"That's different."

"Yeah, right."

"It's true. She's my employee. She works for me and that's all."

Randy tried not to laugh, but failed. "Methinks thou doth protest too much," he chortled.

Bob sighed as he tucked the seat into the case. "I'm not protesting. I'm stating a fact. Besides, she's got a boyfriend, and tonight he's taking her to a fund-raising banquet downtown."

Randy froze. "Don't you think that's a little strange?"

"No. Lots of people go to those kind of things. It's how they raise money for worthy causes."

Randy noticed that both Adrian and Paul had suddenly become silent, and were watching his conversation with Bob. So they wouldn't listen in, Randy shoveled the rest of the donut into his mouth, set his coffee mug on Paul's amp, and shuffled in closer to Bob.

"When I asked if you thought it was strange that she was going to something like that, I didn't mean that it's a bad thing to give money to help the animals. I meant, it's not your average mechanic-type person who goes to things like that. I saw mention of that event in the community pages in the paper, and it's pretty pricey. When's the last time you went to a fund-raising banquet like that?"

Bob opened his mouth to reply, but Randy quickly raised one hand to silence him.

"You don't have to tell me. I know the answer. The answer is never. When you make a donation, you just make a donation. Not only that, but those things usually run hundreds of dollars a plate. I'm not saying that it's not a good thing to do, but you see a lot of people who are there for the same reason as the Pharisee on the street showing how wonderful he was to everyone who cared to look."

Bob's eyebrows knotted.

"What?" Randy asked.

"Funny you should say that. George said something very similar, only she didn't spell it out quite like you did. She's only going because her boyfriend wants to go."

Randy whistled between his teeth. "Your low-paid new mechanic must have a very rich boyfriend to go to stuff like that."

Bob squirmed. "She's not that low-paid. I'm paying her what we can afford, until we see if this works out. It's also an entry-level position."

"I think you know what I meant."

Bob's voice dropped to a gravelly mumble. "Who she goes out with is not my concern."

Randy moved even closer and lowered the volume of his voice even more. "Are you sure about this boyfriend? I saw the way she looked at you Sunday night. She likes you."

Bob stiffened. "She looks up to me as her boss and as someone who shares her love of mechanics. I have to admit it's kind of flattering, but that's it. You're taking it wrong."

"I don't know. I think—"

Paul's voice boomed behind him. "Will you two quit whispering and get finished? Randy, you're parked behind me in the driveway. I want to go home sometime tonight."

Randy stood. "Sorry." He tucked the pieces of the stand into the case, and turned around. "I'll be right back," he said to Bob. "Don't go away."

Randy followed Paul outside, and put his hand on the door of Paul's car, preventing Paul from opening it. "Before you leave, I want to talk to you about last Sunday night."

Paul turned around. "Sunday night? You mean when Bob brought that girl to church? He said she was his new mechanic."

Randy nodded. "That's right. Did you see the way she was looking at him? He's not exactly a hermit, but when was the last time Bob had a steady girlfriend?"

Paul smirked. "More recently than you."

"You know what I mean. What do you think?"

Paul shrugged his shoulders. "I think you should mind your own business and leave Bob alone."

"I just found out that she's got a rich boyfriend," Randy continued. "But I saw how she looked at Bob Sunday night. Trouble's brewing especially if she tries to hook Bob. Bob won't spend his money foolishly, not on some spoiled princess. It'll break his heart when she dumps him."

"Dumps him? Princess? She's a mechanic! They're not even going out! You are insane!" Paul rolled his eyes. "Bob can handle himself just fine. And speaking of Bob, there he is." Paul raised one hand and waved at Bob, who was walking toward his car, which was parked on the street.

Randy turned around. "Hey! Where are you going? I thought we were going to talk."

Bob opened his car door. "Sorry. I don't have time. I've got to get back to work. I promised a customer I'd have his car ready by tomorrow morning, and that transmission isn't fixing itself while I'm here talking."

"Work?" Randy checked his watch. "At this hour? I thought after you hired someone, you would be cutting back your own hours."

"That day will come, but not yet. We were further behind than we thought. I hate to think of the shape we'd be in if it wasn't for George." He smiled, and his eyes became unfocused for a few seconds. He blinked, shook his head, and opened the car door. "See you on the weekend, I guess."

Before Randy could respond, the door closed, Bob started the engine, and drove off.

He turned back to Paul. "See?"

"I don't see anything except that Bob's working too much, as usual. Which means he doesn't have time for a girlfriend, even if she is right under his nose all day. Now if you'll please move your car, I have to go, too."

Chapter Six

"George? What are you doing here?" Bob clearly had not expected company at the shop.

"I wasn't having a very good time at the banquet, so I left early. Need some help?" Georgette tried to appear casual, but her stomach was completely tied up in knots. All during the banquet, all she could think of was Bob. As soon as she could, she made an excuse to leave, although she knew he could do the work himself.

"Well..." Bob's voice trailed off, and he ran his fingers through his hair. "Now that you're here, I could use a hand. But only if you're sure. You work a forty-hour week, and I don't want you to think you need to do more."

Georgette looked down at her feet, still in her best shoes. "I'm not here to put in overtime. I'm here because I'd prefer to help you with the transmission than sit at the banquet and smile for strangers."

Bob shook his head. "Fine. Two people will make the job go faster. To tell the truth, it's not so bad working such long hours when it's daylight. But when it's dark and everything outside is quiet, it feels worse because it's obvious the rest of the world is at home with their families, and I'm working late again. Once you're caught up with the bookkeeping, you'll be spending more time in the shop, and when that happens, I think we'll be able to keep up with what comes in on a daily basis without anyone having to put in much extra time."

"If it helps, I can see a difference already, even in the short time I've been working here."

"You're right about that." Bob smiled, and Georgette's heart rate suddenly accelerated.

Since the first day she'd seen Bob she'd thought he was good-looking, and the faint crow's feet which appeared at the corners of his eyes when he smiled made him more attractive. Now that she was starting to get to know him, she knew those little lines weren't from age; they were because of the kind heart behind his easy smiles.

She adjusted the strap on the duffle bag on her shoulder. "You should know I'm here on my own time; you don't have to pay me overtime."

"But—"

Georgette held up one palm to silence him. Bob needed the money far more than she did. "I mean it. If you insist on paying me overtime for this, I'm going to go back home." Not that she wanted to go home. If she did, she would have to explain to her father why she wasn't at the banquet with Tyler.

Bob sighed. "This isn't normally something I would allow, but you're not giving me a choice. Okay. On your own time. Thanks."

Just as she did every morning, Georgette hurried into the washroom to slip on her jeans and a T-shirt, then pulled her coveralls off the hook and stepped into them. Bob had already removed the transmission and was starting to replace the first clutch plate, which was burnt.

"So you and Tyler weren't having a good time at the banquet?" he muttered as he yanked out the old piece.

Georgette leaned to the side to check the alignment on the rest. "Tyler was doing fine, but he likes those kind of things. After a while I couldn't take it anymore."

"Was Tyler okay with you leaving the banquet?"

Georgette eased up on her motions, thinking of Tyler's comments.

He hadn't been pleased, but she'd reminded him that she had fulfilled her obligations for the night, and she'd been a part of the appropriate conversations. Tyler begrudgingly conceded and took her home. Fortunately her father wasn't home yet, and Josephine was too busy vacuuming to notice her. She'd quickly grabbed her duffel and hurried out to her car, which she'd left parked on the street, and had driven away before anyone noticed that she'd been home at all.

During the drive to Bob's shop, she'd experienced a feeling of freedom such as she'd never felt before. The only thing that could have made it better was if she had been riding on a big, noisy motorcycle, the wind blowing through her hair. Still, despite her silly fantasy, she *was* free, at least for the balance of the evening.

"Tyler wasn't happy, but I didn't care. I did what I had to do."

Bob laid his wrench down on the bench. "Pardon me?"

"I only went with Tyler because I owed him a favor." The trouble was, what Tyler called a favor was better known as blackmail. Tyler had her trapped, and they both knew it.

Bob's brow knotted. "I don't understand. When I take a date somewhere, it's somewhere we both want to go. I wouldn't enjoy myself if I knew my date didn't want to be there."

While Georgette couldn't divulge the details of her personal life, she needed Bob to think she had better sense than to go out with the likes of Tyler. She took a deep breath.

"I'm not actually dating him. He just needs to have someone with him when he goes to certain functions, and he's calling in a favor to have me go with him." Every minute she spent with Tyler made her pray even more that she could find a painless way to tell her father the nature of the job she went to every day.

"Oh..." Bob's voice trailed off. He quickly picked up the torque wrench and began tightening one of the belts on the transmission. He didn't look at her as he spoke. "I probably shouldn't stick my nose where it doesn't belong, but it sounds like you only went under protest. Please take care of yourself—you wouldn't want to end up compromising your faith."

Georgette stiffened. So far, Tyler hadn't asked her to do anything that wasn't proper, but she really didn't know how far he would push things. She knew she shouldn't have been trying to cover up her new life, but she was trapped by circumstances beyond her control.

She smiled weakly at Bob. "It's okay. I'm fine."

"Good. Let's get this back where it belongs, and we'll be done"

Bob resealed the casing, and together, they carried it back to the car and fastened it in place. He started the engine, and they watched to make sure there were no leaks.

While they waited, Bob pulled the rag out of his pocket, and wiped his hands. "I think everything's finished." He pushed at his sleeve and checked his watch. "We made good time, between the two of us. I know it's not exactly early, but can I take you out for coffee or something? Especially if you won't accept any pay for doing this."

Georgette felt a tremor of excitement. "Not tonight. I really should go home. It's getting late." Her father knew what time the banquet ended, and he would be expecting her back. "But if you'll take a rain check, I accept."

Bob smiled back, and those adorable crinkles appeared again at the corners of his beautiful green eyes. "A rain check it is, then."

She felt like skipping out of the building after she'd changed back into her finery, but she forced herself to maintain her dignity.

When she arrived at home her father was in the living room, waiting for her.

"Hi, Daddy. I'm back."

He smiled politely. "I see that. Did you have a good time?"

She shrugged her shoulders. It wouldn't do to say something bad.

"I noticed that you had your car. I thought Tyler came earlier to pick you up."

She held up the bag with the gas station's logo. Every time she used their washroom to change, she bought something as an excuse to go inside. "I had to go to the gas station."

Her father's expression tightened. "You didn't buy oil for the car, again, did you? We can have a mechanic do that. Or is this something for that ridiculous project of yours in the garage?"

"It's a snack, Daddy."

His eyes narrowed. "I hope you're watching your figure. You've been eating a lot of snacks lately."

"It's okay, Daddy. I've been exercising. I've actually lost weight in the last week."

Immediately, he softened. "That's my girl. This job must be good for you to start thinking of such things."

She couldn't help but smile back. "Yes, Daddy, this job has been very good for me. Now if you don't mind, I've had a long and busy day, and I'm tired. I'm going to bed."

Bob stopped what he was doing once again to watch George run from her car to the washroom in order to change. Every day for three months, she'd done the same thing. He could only assume that she had another part-time job, although it would have to be a very early job. He didn't like to think she needed a second job, after all, he was paying her a fair salary, considering her experience and duties.

It was none of his business, though, so today, as on every other day, Bob remained silent when the washroom door opened. George re-emerged wearing jeans, a T-shirt and the required steel-toed safety footwear.

"Hi, Bob!" she called out as she waved, then tucked her duffel under the counter, and logged in to the computer.

He waved back, then quickly turned around and resumed his task.

George was his employee, and nothing more. Yet, at the same time, he didn't want to see her working herself to death. She worked hard for him, and she did a good job. A couple of regular customers had specifically asked for her to do the work on their cars.

Not long after she'd shown up to help him on the blown transmission that evening, he'd taken her out for dinner as a thank-you. They had had so much fun that night that they'd agreed to make dinner on Thursday evenings a standard routine. Even so, he still didn't know much about what she did away from work, and he still didn't know why she arrived every morning looking as if she was coming from another job.

Georgette Ecklington was both an asset and a mystery. He couldn't help but like her. She was feisty, spoke her mind, and wasn't afraid to get dirty. He was glad that she joined him at Faith Community Fellowship for their evening service every week. Her enthusiasm and honest questions as a new Christian were both refreshing and a reminder that he wasn't setting aside enough time for God in his own life.

As soon as they got more caught up and didn't have to work so much, that would change, and it was because of George.

"Hey, Bob! What are you doing?" Bart's voice echoed from behind him. "Why are you staring at the wall?"

"What?" Bob felt his face heat up. "Never mind," he mumbled. "I was just thinking about something."

"Yeah. Thinking about George."

Bob turned around, about to contradict his friend, but the second he opened his mouth, Bart started laughing.

"Give it up, Bob. Nothing you say can change the truth. I can tell. You've got George on the brain."

Bob gritted his teeth and tromped back to the

car he was working on. *"Ma fatti affari tuoi,"* he muttered.

Bart laughed louder. "Have I touched a nerve, Roberto?" he asked, rolling his *R*s as he spoke, just as Bob's Italian-born mother did, because Bart knew it annoyed him. "Would you like to repeat that? In English?"

Bob spun around. "I said, I wish you would mind your own business."

Bart chuckled again. "I hope I haven't pushed my luck, but speaking of business, I need a favor."

"What?" Bob snapped as he crossed his arms over his chest.

"I can't go to the Chamber of Commerce dinner. Anna didn't realize it was tonight, and she bought tickets for a play. She got dinner reservations, a babysitter and everything. Can you go for me?"

Bob tapped the socket wrench repeatedly into his palm as he contemplated Bart's request. It was part of their agreement as partners that Bart would attend the few social functions related to their business, and Bob would meet with their suppliers. Occasionally they reversed the roles, but it hadn't taken long to see that Bart did better in group situations, and Bob did better working one-on-one.

But he couldn't turn down his friend's request. "Yeah. I can go for you."

One corner of Bart's mouth turned up. "Actually, I was thinking.... Why don't you ask George? You know you hate handling this stuff alone."

Bob glanced at George, who was haggling with a customer over the price of an overhaul. She was good with people, of that there was no doubt. Bob thought he would enjoy going to the Chamber banquet with George, those Thursday-evening dinners were fun and a chance to talk about what was happening at work. It may have been a bit odd, but they both found they needed—and wanted—the break from the shop.

But there were times they didn't talk strictly business, and it was those times that gave Bob pause about asking her to accompany him. Every time Tyler took her to another "event," she spent a large part of the next Thursday evening complaining bitterly to Bob, both about Tyler and about the evenings. She always thanked Bob profusely for letting her vent her frustration, making him feel as if he'd been at least helpful.

It would have been nice not to go to the Chamber banquet by himself, but Bob knew George didn't enjoy such things.

He turned back to Bart. "It's okay. It's only a couple of hours. I'll go alone."

Chapter Seven

Georgette walked into the boutique with the bag containing her father's latest purchase tucked under her arm. She sucked in a deep breath and made her way to the counter.

"I'd like to exchange this dress," she said to the clerk, who frowned making it very clear that the store didn't approve of returns.

"Of course. What seems to be the problem?"

"I really don't like it. I want to exchange it for something more suitable. I need something classic and more understated." In other words, Georgette wanted something that would help her fade into the woodwork.

The clerk pulled the dress out of the bag. Her frown deepened. "This is odd. A gentleman bought this dress yesterday..." her voice trailed off. "Wait. William Ecklington bought this. You must be Georgette." She extended one hand. "It's a pleasure to meet you finally."

Georgette smiled politely. They had met once before, but in the shadow of her father, the woman had barely acknowledged her presence. "It's a pleasure to meet you, too. I have no idea how much my father paid for this dress, so please show me which things would constitute a straight exchange."

The woman directed her to an alcove at the back of the store, bearing a sign reading Designer Fashions, New Arrivals. Georgette couldn't see any prices from where she stood, but the security guard lurking at the entrance to the alcove made it obvious they were the most expensive in the store.

"Anything from this area can be a straight exchange."

She quickly sorted through the racks, and selected a dark-green sheath with no adornments other than a single black button at the throat. It was a simple dress, but she didn't care how she looked in it. She wanted it only for the color.

The dress was the same green as Bob's eyes.

"I'll take this one."

"Don't you want to try it on?"

That's not necessary, I love it and I know it will fit."

The woman entered the exchange in the computer, put Georgette's selection in a bag and wished her a pleasant evening.

"Thank you," Georgette said as she turned around and returned to her car. She doubted she would have a pleasant evening. Not only was she again forced to spend another evening with Tyler, but her father would also be there.

Bob straightened his tie, and walked into the banquet hall. He hated formal functions, but today's dinner was a buffet rather than sit-down meal, which allowed the guests to mingle more freely. It also meant he could leave early.

He chatted with a few people he knew, as he filled his plate, when a face he hadn't expected to see caught his attention.

Almost as if she felt his eyes on her, George turned around. The second they made eye contact, her mouth opened slightly in visible surprise. She spoke to a man to her right and left the group of people to join Bob.

Bob smiled at the sight of her. Normally, George dressed well, at least first thing in the morning. But tonight, she was positively striking.

"Hey, George. Nice dress," he said softly, meaning only to compliment, and not to make it look as though he was ogling her. "That color really suits you."

A slight blush highlighted her cheeks. "Thanks." Her voice lowered. "What are you doing here?"

Bob glanced at the group she'd just left, recognizing Tyler. "Bart couldn't make it, so I agreed to come for him. Are you enjoying yourself?"

She looked down at her plate, picked up a canapé, popped it into her mouth and grinned. "I didn't think I would have a good time, but I discovered a trick. I can put a polite amount of food on my plate, eat it all, then go back for seconds. I just have to make sure I join up with a different group of people each time, which isn't hard with a crowd like this." She pointed to her plate. "This is my fifth round of 'seconds.' Not bad, don't you think?"

His smile dropped. "So you're here with Tyler?"

"Uh...yes." She turned and searched the room, then quickly turned back to him. "But my father is here, too. My father knows Tyler's family quite well."

Part of him wanted to ask her to introduce him to her father, but part him wanted to run and hide, even though he knew the impulse was foolish. He wasn't dating George, and even if he were, he was well past the age of it being rational to fear a girlfriend's father. Once again, he glanced to the group of people she'd been with. "I guess I should let you get back to Tyler, and I'll go find—"

A tall man with graying hair appeared beside George, cutting off Bob's words. "Georgette, honey. I've been looking for you." The man turned to Bob. "I'm William Ecklington. Have we met before?" William shuffled his plate to his left hand, and extended his right.

Bob did the same, returning George's father's handshake.

"No. I don't believe we've met. I'm Bob Delanio."

"Pleased to meet you, Mr. Delanio." William's eyes flitted to Bob's off-the-rack suit, a sharp contrast to his tailor-made one. "I'm curious. How do you know my daughter?"

"I'm—"

"Daddy, why don't we sit down at one of the tables to talk? It's almost time for the speaker, and we should get good seats."

William frowned at her interruption, then turned back to Bob. "I suppose."

As they walked toward a free table, George turned quickly to him, and mouthed a word that looked like "help," which made no sense to Bob.

The second they were seated, George leaned toward her father. "Mr. Delanio is my boss, Daddy. He's the co-owner, with his partner."

William picked up a canapé and inspected it, replacing it on his plate before addressing Bob. "I haven't had much of a chance to talk to my daughter since she started working for your corporation. What is it exactly she does for you?"

"Uh..." While he and Bart had decided a few years ago to incorporate, they'd never thought of the tiny repair shop as a "corporation." "Well, your daughter is my..." Under the table, Bob felt a sharp tapping on his ankle, halting his words. He raised one hand to his mouth and pretended to cough to give himself some time to figure out why George was kicking him.

"Administrative assistant, Daddy. I'm positive I told you that before. Please, let's not talk so much business tonight. I hear these shrimp canapés are simply divine. You should go get more, before they run out."

Instead of leaving, William pushed his plate away. "That's okay, I've had enough. Tell me, has my daughter been doing a good job for you?"

Bob picked up a shrimp canapé and popped it into his mouth, hoping that chewing would buy him some time to assimilate the image she wanted him to project. He'd never had an administrative assistant. He didn't even know what one did. George did the bookkeeping, which was the only office-type function needed.

"She handles all our accounting."

William frowned. "Accounting?"

Again, Bob felt a sharp tap on his ankle.

"Yes, but that's only a small part of her duties. George..." His words cut off at another sharp tap at his ankle.

"...ette," he continued, noting an almost inaudible sigh from George, "has been instrumental in expanding our customer base." He rubbed the spot with the top of his other foot. He wasn't wearing his safety boots. If the kicking didn't stop, he was going to have a very sore left foot.

William smiled, and when William smiled, George smiled, telling Bob that he was saying what they both wanted to hear.

He wasn't lying. Upon completion of all work orders, they routinely asked new customers how they'd found out about the shop. Lately, a number of people said a friend had been impressed by the new mechanic, and had recommended them. Reading between the lines, he knew a number of the younger, single men had simply come to check out the hot chick. Still, it was new business, and he had to give George the credit for it.

William leaned back in his chair. "I was very surprised she had taken a job. I'm glad she's doing well."

"Yes. She's been very good for the company."

"So, Mr. Delanio, what is it your company does?"

George's eyes opened farther than Bob had ever seen, and he could see the beginning of panic as her whole body went stiff.

Bob couldn't bear to watch her; he cleared his throat. "We deal mostly with the automotive industry. Because of your daughter, we're now in a position to expand." By adding another phone line.

"Ah." William nodded. "So it's a small company. My company began that way, of course, but it has never been small in *my* lifetime. The chain was founded by my grandfather, passed on through two generations. I'm chairman of the board now, but I insist on overseeing the area managers, who oversee the individual stores coast to coast. A smart businessman pays attention to details."

Bob's stomach lurched, and all the good food he'd eaten so far turned to a lump in his stomach. He recognized the name. He'd read in the financial section of the paper recently that William Ecklington's chain of department stores had topped sales from previous years, and the value of the stocks had taken an unprecedented jump.

Bob tried not to feel intimidated and failed. Of course he'd noticed her last name, but he'd never connected her with *those* Ecklingtons. He didn't understand why George was working for his pitiful little local garage when she came from such a wealthy family.

William stood. "If you'll excuse me, there are a number of other people I have to talk to. It's been a pleasure meeting you, Mr. Delanio. I hope to see you again at the next Chamber function."

Bob stood. "Usually it's my partner who attends these functions, but it's been a pleasure meeting you, too."

Bob shook William's hand and they parted company. He immediately turned to George, his plate of food forgotten.

George's lower lip trembled as her eyes widened. Her voice cracked as she spoke. "I suppose I owe you an explanation, don't I?"

Bob's voice lowered. "Yes, and I think we'd best go outside."

Chapter Eight

Georgette hadn't been looking forward to attending another function with Tyler, but never in her worst nightmares could she have foreseen what had just happened. She nodded, and followed Bob outside to the patio, to a bench at the edge of the deck, away from the other people who were also outside.

She sucked in a deep breath, held it for a few seconds, then exhaled deeply. "I don't know what to say."

Bob didn't respond.

Georgette didn't think that was a good sign.

"Am I fired?" she asked, trying to hold her voice steady.

"I don't know what to say either. I can't fire you when you're doing a good job. But I don't understand why in the world you're working at my little garage when you're an heiress. Don't you have something better to do with your time?"

"I need this job, but not for the reason you think." She paused, and lowered her voice. "My father is smothering me. I couldn't take it anymore."

Bob remained silent.

"I'm so sorry, Bob. I was afraid to tell you." She turned her head away, so he couldn't see her face. "But by waiting, I've only made it worse." Georgette stared off into the darkening night sky, and sighed. "I don't know if this is going to come out right. I know it makes me sound very ungrateful. I get all the financial benefits of being my father's daughter, but I'm so unhappy. My father refuses to give me a chance to prove myself or do anything worthwhile."

"Certainly there's a place for you somewhere in his corporation," Bob said wryly.

Georgette shook her head. "You'd think so, but he won't give me a chance. I even told him I'd go to university, but my father wouldn't pay for anything business or finance related. He said if I want to go to university, I have to take something in arts and sciences."

Bob stiffened. "When Bart and I first started the shop, I couldn't afford to go to university. My family helped me pay for a few business courses at the local community college. The rest I learned by experience, mostly the hard way."

Georgette hunched her shoulders and lowered her head. "My father has made it very clear he that he doesn't think either my sister or I are capable of running the business. He said once I get married, he'll make my husband a junior partner, or give him some kind of management job, like he did for my sister's husband, but other than that, he doesn't believe in husbands and wives working together. Or fathers and daughters. The only way I'll ever be a part of the business is to marry someone my father finds suitable, and hope he can convince my father to let me do something even as insignificant as filing. But I can't see that happening. Otherwise, the only other way is to wait until my father dies, and I inherit part of the business. I don't want either one to happen. I want to control my own future."

"And you think working as a junior mechanic is a bright future?"

She stared down at her shoes. "Maybe not. But at least I'm happy. I really feel God pointed me in the direction of your shop that day. At the end of the day I go home feeling as though I've done something to deserve my paycheck." Her voice dropped to a scratchy whisper. "The allowance my father gives me is a pay-off to be seen at his side like the family dog. I like to think I'm worth more than that."

"But he seemed happy that you're my administrative assistant, though it's a pretty lofty title within a three-person operation."

Georgette still couldn't look at Bob and began to absently play with a leaf hanging near the armrest of the bench. "At first, he was angry that I even found a job, so I stretched the part about my function as your bookkeeper, and omitted the mechanic part. I meant to tell him, but for the first time in so long, he seemed really proud of me, watching me leave all dressed up to go to work in the morning. I later found out that it was because he thought I had taken a job in order to find a husband. By then it to was too late to tell him everything."

"So that's why you come to work all dressed up."

All she could do was nod.

He remained silent for a few minutes. "We should go back inside so we don't miss the speaker. I guess you're sitting with Tyler."

"Yes."

"What's up with Tyler, anyway? I can't figure out how he fits into this picture. He obviously knows you're working for me in a not-so-glamorous position."

"That's the point. He knows about my job, and he said he'll do me a favor and not tell my father if I help him make contacts to further his position."

"That's not a favor. That's blackmail."

"I know. But I don't have any other choice."

"But now your father has met me."

Georgette shook her head. "Nothing has changed. From what he sees, you're an executive, and I'm your administrative assistant. Now it seems I've only dug myself in deeper. I don't know what to do."

"There's a proverb from the Bible about that. I forget exactly how it goes, but it says that if you trap yourself by what you've said, then humble yourself and talk about it with that person, and don't wait. God gives us good advice. You tell me every Thursday how Tyler forces you to go places you don't want to be, and now I understand. So you didn't want to be here either, huh?"

Georgette looked at Bob. Her father thought the world of Tyler, even knowing Tyler often manipulated and coerced people and situations to get what he wanted. But Bob would never do that. Bob was ten times the man Tyler could ever be.

"You're right of course. I can't take much more of this. It's driving me crazy."

He stood, as did Georgette.

"Things like this drive me crazy, too. And on that note, we should take our seats." he said. "I probably won't see you until church Sunday night."

"Thanks, Bob. For everything."

He nodded, then walked away.

Georgette made it back to the table to sit with Tyler just as the master of ceremonies stepped up to the podium to make a few announcements and introduce the speaker.

Tyler leaned toward her. "Where have you been? I was beginning to think you'd left."

"Of course I didn't leave. My boss is here. I introduced him to Daddy, and then we had a few things to talk about."

"You're kidding, right?" Tyler made a snide laugh. "You introduced your father to that grease monkey?"

Georgette gritted her teeth. "Bob isn't a grease monkey. He's co-owner of a registered, incorporated business."

Tyler snorted. "Okay. He's a grease monkey with credentials. Come on, Georgette. Get serious."

"He's worked very hard to get where he is. Give him some credit."

"I don't extend credit to people like him."

"I don't need to listen to this. You've dragged me to enough of these things, more than I even originally agreed to. Our arrangement is over. And I think you—"

Her words were drowned out by the applause as the guest speaker approached the podium.

Throughout the entire presentation, Georgette's mind churned. All she could think about was how fast she could get out, and away from Tyler.

It was a relief when the audience applauded the close of the speaker's comments. Just as she reached under her chair for her purse, another voice sounded behind her.

"Georgette, honey. There you are."

"Daddy! You startled me."

"I was looking for your boss, Mr. Delanio, but I couldn't find him. I thought maybe he was with you."

"I think he went home."

"After we met, I made a few inquiries. No one seems to know who he is."

Georgette froze, then forced herself to smile graciously. "His company is very small."

"Exactly how small? Does he employ under fifty people?"

"Yes, it's well under fifty people. But it has good potential." She moved to get away, but her father blocked her path.

"I didn't recognize the family name, and no one I knew recognized the name, either."

"It's a first-generation company."

Georgette cringed as her father contemplated the implications. All his business associates were "old money." Even their new ventures weren't really "new," because they were financed with that "old" money.

Bob's parents were Italian immigrants, having come to the country shortly before he was born. His father worked in a blue-collar factory job, and still had many years before he could retire. Bob expected to do the same, a lifetime of long hours and hard work.

"It's okay, Daddy. The company is stable and has an established client base."

Tyler's laughter made Georgette flinch. "She's right on that issue, William. As long as there are middle class people with low class cars, Bob Delanio will always have an established client base."

"I don't understand."

"He's the Bob of Bob And Bart's Auto Repair."

"I've never heard of it."

"And you likely never will, either. It's not exactly a multi-national corporation."

"Tyler!" Georgette hissed. "What are you doing?"

Tyler made a self-satisfied snort. "You don't think that I just happened to appear in a neighborhood like that by accident, do you?"

"I don't understand."

"When your father said you got a job, I thought I'd find out what it was. No one seemed to know anything about it."

Georgette's heart turned cold. What she had suspected was now confirmed.

Tyler smirked. "I also did a little background check on your Bob and Bart. One look at their business history tells me that they only hired you for the potential financial backing you carry with your name."

"That's not true."

"Why else do you think they hired you? For your mechanical skills?"

"Yes!"

Beside her, her father gasped. "Mechanical skills?"

Tyler continued. "Didn't you think a background check would turn up who you were?"

"They don't have the money for a background check. They hired me because Bart knew the person I used as a reference on my résumé."

"Then they're fools."

"They're not fools. They're honest working men. And they trust people they associate with." Georgette bit her tongue. She knew her argument would go nowhere with Tyler. Tyler trusted no one. For that matter, neither did her father.

Her father held up his hand for silence. "What do you mean, mechanical skills? I spoke to Mr. Delanio. He said that Georgette was his administrative assistant."

Tyler spun around. "I don't know what Mr. Delanio calls an administrative assistant. All she does that's administrative is type up invoices for the repair work Mr. Delanio and his partner do. They're mechanics. Nothing more."

"That's not true. I do more than that."

All the color drained from her father's face. "You work for a couple of mechanics?"

Tyler's smirk returned. "She's right there. She does do more than type up invoices. She's also their spare mechanic."

"Spare mechanic?" her father sputtered, and then his face turned to stone. "Do you know what this looks like, my daughter accepting a job like that?" He buried his face in his hands. "My daughter is a *mechanic.* I'll be a laughingstock." He dropped his hands and glared at her. "How could you do this to me?"

"I didn't do anything *to* you. I did something *for* me for the first time in my life. No one has to know."

Her father waved one hand in the air, something he only did when he was very, very angry. "What were you thinking? Of course people will find out. Tyler found out."

Only because Tyler had been following her that day he first showed up at her job. His intent had been solely to curry favor with her father by relaying information about her. However, Tyler had discovered a better way to take advantage of his ill-found knowledge, much to her dismay. What she didn't understand was why Tyler had suddenly decided to divulge what he knew.

"Tyler has asked for your hand in marriage, who knows why. Even after what he knows, he'll still have you."

Her stomach sank like a rock. "Have me? That's not what marriage is all about! I can't marry Tyler."

"Yes, you can. And you will. You have disgraced our family name and my reputation. If he'll still have you, this is the only way to maintain my dignity."

"*Your* dignity?" She pressed her palms over her heart. "What about me?"

"You have shamed me. This is no longer about you."

"It's very much about me. This isn't the fifteenth century."

"Reputation is more important than anything, particularly in business. You will do as I say. Fortunately people have seen you together often lately, so you can set a date quickly."

Georgette's head spun. "I'm not marrying Tyler. I don't love him." She gritted her teeth. "I don't even like him." She turned and glared at Tyler. "We had a deal. You weren't going to tell my father what you knew, and in exchange I did what you wanted me to do. I can't believe I fell for it. People thought we were actually dating! I played right into your hands, didn't I?"

Tyler shrugged his shoulders. "This is really for your own good, Georgette. You can't believe that you have a future being a mechanic. Your rightful place is in society. You should be able to see that."

"All I see is that you're good at double-dealing. Now I trust you less than ever."

Her father stepped closer and crossed his arms. "I had a deal with Tyler first. He said he would find out exactly where you were working, and why you were being so evasive with me. He did exactly what he was supposed to do and what I would have done in his place. The ability to know when to turn the tables will take him far in business. And speaking of business, now I've met your 'boss,'" her father spat out the word with the utmost disdain, "you can't seriously believe his pathetic business has a future for you, or for our family. The only place you have a future is with Tyler. You will marry him, or...or...or I'll disown you."

Georgette grasped the edge of the table to steady herself. "You don't mean that."

"I've put up with your foolishness until now, but

this job is the final straw. I've given you everything you wanted, and more, and now I find out that you're spending your time with some backwoods grease monkey! It's time for you to put your ridiculous ideas aside, and start doing things my way. You've forced my hand on this."

Georgette's entire life flashed before her eyes. It was true, she knew she'd been spoiled, but, except for the job, she'd always done everything her father desired.

"And from now on, I want you to attend Sunday-morning brunches either with me or with Tyler."

"But I go to church on Sunday mornings."

"Church is a crutch for people who are weak. You won't be going back there. Or to your job. Is this clear?"

Her voice trembled. "No, Daddy, it's not clear. Why are you doing this to me?"

His voice deepened. "You are an Ecklington. You don't need church. And you certainly don't need a job."

Perhaps she didn't need the job, but she did need church—and God—more than she ever had in her entire life. She knew God wouldn't turn His back on her if she didn't go to church on Sunday, but she had so much to learn, and she needed to be with other believers. Even though she could be close to God anywhere, she found it difficult when surrounded by decadence. Church was where she truly felt God's presence. God's presence wasn't exactly welcomed in her home.

Her father's voice broke into her thoughts. "I'm sending you home in the limo to give yourself time to think. I'll follow with Tyler. When we get there, I will hear your decision."

"My decision won't change," Georgette snapped. She scooped up her purse and stomped outside to the limo. The driver opened the door, she slid inside and the door closed, cutting her off from her father and the rest of the outside world. In the past, she'd always considered the limo a safe haven. Tonight, it suffocated her.

She turned around and watched through the rear window as Tyler and her father walked into the parking lot together.

They were a matched set. Tyler would do anything her father said, and anticipate his every need for the possibility of gaining his favor. Her father reveled in Tyler's adoration, which made Tyler expect even more from the relationship. Everyone knew where things were heading. Tyler would rise up quickly in the ranks of her father's empire.

Knowing Tyler, Georgette should have expected his duplicity. Not to see that he'd initially been acting on her father's instruction made her ten times the fool. But then, it was her own fault. It had been easier to believe what she wanted to believe and that had b been her downfall. She knew what Tyler was capable of doing. He acknowledged no guilt in taking advantage of her or forcing her hand in marriage.

It didn't matter what her father said or what threats he made. She would never marry Tyler. For any reason. Ever.

If she was going to marry someone, she would marry a man like Bob—a man who was honest and hard-working, and a wonderful example of how to lead a good life, with God in the middle of it.

The car stopped in front of the house instead of pulling into the garage.

She wondered if she could tell the driver to keep going, but the door opened, sending in a draught of cold air. Her father must have taken a short cut.

He released the door handle and stepped back. "What do you have to say for yourself?" he ground out between his teeth.

"Certainly you can't expect that I'm going to marry him," she pointed at Tyler as she scrambled out, "just because you don't approve of my job or the people I've been seeing lately."

"I most certainly do. For a long time, I've hoped that you would marry Tyler. He would fit well into the business, and our family. In fact, I'm considering a plum position for him right now, based on his dedication."

Tyler might have been a good match for the business and for their dysfunctional family, but not for Georgette's heart. After attending dozens of events since their "arrangement," she liked him even less than she had before. Now, after what he'd done today, he downright disgusted her. She certainly couldn't marry him. The only reason she would ever marry was for love.

She turned to her father. "Why did you marry Momma?"

"I married your mother because she was pregnant. Getting married was the right thing to do."

"Did you love her?" she choked out. They'd always been told Terri had been premature.

He cocked his head to the side. "Not really. But she loved me." He arched one eyebrow and turned to Tyler who smiled in response. "I was young and our parents saw to it that that we did what was expected. Everything was fine until your mother got all those ridiculous ideas in her head."

Georgette pressed her hand over the gold cross beneath her dress. She had a feeling she knew what he meant by "those ridiculous ideas," and wondered for the first time if her mother had really left, or if she'd been "disowned," to use her father's term, for her beliefs. It didn't matter.

Even if the reward was the smallest corner of her father's corporate world, she couldn't marry for any reason other than the love of a good man.

Like Bob. Not that she was in love with her boss, of course, she corrected herself.

She cleared her throat. "I already told you. I won't marry Tyler. Ever."

Her father extended one arm, drawing her attention to a stack of boxes stacked haphazardly on the grass. Clothing and some of her personal items from her bedroom stuck out at odd angles, telling her that the boxes had been packed in a hurry by his staff. A cold numbness started to overtake her. Georgette stepped forward, reached into one of the boxes, and pulled out the stuffed teddy bear that she kept on top of her bed.

"I'm giving you ten seconds to change your mind."

When her father had said he'd disown her, she hadn't thought he'd meant that he would kick her out immediately. This must be the same way her mother had disappeared in one afternoon.

Tyler's voice sounded behind her, every word echoing into her brain. "I'll be a good husband to you."

Her mouth opened, but no sound came out. Her

father called himself a good husband, too, claiming the failure of the marriage was her mother's fault and nothing could be blamed on him. He'd kicked his wife out, and now he was kicking out his daughter.

"Your time is up. What's your decision?"

"I haven't changed my mind. I'm not going to marry Tyler, I'm not going to quit my job and I'm not going to quit going to church."

"You're no better than your mother." He pointed into the center of his chest. "I'm the one who brings in all the money. I'm the one who provides a home and all the perks that go with the fortune I bring into this house. I gave her anything she wanted. She had no right to refuse to do things my way. And neither do you!"

After experiencing a sample of what he considered publicly acceptable in order to get ahead, Georgette could only guess at his less public methods. "But what if what you're doing is wrong?"

His face turned red. "How dare you criticize me, after all I've done for you! Is this what that church does to you? Teach you to question my judgment and my success? Your mother was exactly the same. Get off my property. I no longer consider you an Ecklington."

Georgette stared at the pile of the boxes, not

many, really, considering all the material items she considered hers, even though most of it had been paid for by her father. Her father had obviously instructed the staff to be very selective in order to keep what was "his" by purchase.

"And get that monstrosity you call a truck off my property, as well. If it's not gone by morning, I'm having it towed to the junkyard."

She turned to see that her truck was in the driveway, not in the garage, where she had been storing it while she continued to work on it. In all the excitement, she hadn't noticed it. "But..." her voice trailed off.

"Don't try using any of your credit cards. They're all in my name, and I've cancelled them. Soon I will be removing all the money I have deposited in your account since that account has my name on it too. All that will remain is the money you've put in from your pathetic job. Less what you've spent in the past month, of course, if that leaves anything at all. I'm giving you one last chance to get some sense into your head and change your mind."

Georgette stiffened. "Never!"

"You have no idea what it takes to succeed in this world. No one will do anything for you without getting something in return, and you don't have what it takes to handle any kind of pressure.

You won't survive. You'll be back, and when that happens you'll do things my way."

Her father turned, opened the door, and stepped into the house. Tyler followed him inside and the door closed.

Chapter Nine

Georgette stood, facing the closed door, unable to move.

The reflection of the moon on the smooth wood mocked her with its silence.

Everything she had taken for granted was gone.

Her car. Her computer. The furniture. Her jewelry. Her tools.

She still had her cell phone in her purse, but she was positive that by morning, that account would be terminated too.

She tried to imagine the contents of her closet, her dresser and the racks of shoes. She couldn't imagine everything stuffed into only a dozen boxes, but that was all that remained. Her life had been reduced to a dozen boxes, sitting on the lawn.

Money can't buy happiness.

She didn't need so much money. All that money certainly hadn't bought her a trouble-free life.

But love doesn't pay the rent.

Georgette squeezed her eyes shut. She didn't have to worry about paying the rent. She didn't have a home to pay rent on.

But she would. She refused to go crawling back to her father, and do the wrong thing for the wrong reasons.

For years, she'd wanted to become independent, and now she was going to do it.

She pulled her keyring out of her purse, removed the key to her father's car and the key to the front door, and left them on the doormat, which she would never cross again. She kicked off her high-heeled shoes and loaded the boxes into the back of her truck, one at a time.

The truck didn't start easily, but it did start. Fortunately she'd insured it so she could take it on test drives as she continued to work on it. The insurance was one thing her father couldn't cancel.

She drove away from her father's home without looking back.

She didn't know where to go. Without looking, she knew she had under five dollars in her wallet.

Her first impulse was to go to the bank machine, but by the time she got there, her father's threats had indeed come to pass. He'd gone into the account online and transferred out all the money he'd given her, just as he'd said he would. Of course, since she'd counted on her allowance, she'd spent more than what she'd received in her pay. The account now held exactly one dollar, which was probably the minimum requirement to keep the account open.

She couldn't seek shelter at the homes of any of her current friends. She wasn't even sure she could call them friends. She hadn't seen a single one of them since she'd started her job, and not one of them cared enough to ask about her. Not one of them would ever do anything to cross her father.

The people she called friends were the guys at the race track. Yet those friendships were minor ones, not true personal relationships. No one there knew her background, and she worked hard to keep it that way. Many of them lived from paycheck to paycheck, and she didn't want to intimidate them. Besides, most of them were married and so she couldn't very well show up at the home of a married man on Friday night, asking to spend the night. She certainly wouldn't ask any of the single men that question.

Another option would have been the people she knew from church, but she didn't know anyone well enough to impose. The only people she'd had minimal contact with were those in the family from whom she'd bought the truck, and they had enough problems of their own without adding hers. Lately she hadn't even been going to her own church. Instead, she'd been sneaking into Bob's church, arriving late because of the long drive, and leaving right at the close of the service. Bob never even knew she was there, but she needed to get home before her father became too angry with her for going to church at all.

For lack of anywhere else to go, Georgette drove to her sister's house. Her sister wouldn't agree with what she'd done, but she would certainly understand. Whatever Terri thought, Georgette needed someplace safe and warm to retreat for the night, a quiet place to think about her future.

She knocked softly at the door and heard shuffling, then silence. Georgette waited for a significant amount of time, and when no one answered, she knocked again.

"Terri? Are you there? Byron? It's me. Georgette. Please let me in."

More shuffling sounded on the other side of the door, and then it opened.

Her brother-in-law stood in the doorway, his clothing disheveled. "What are you doing here at this hour?"

She looked down at her watch, then back up

again. "It's not really that late, but..." Georgette's voice trailed off.

Romantic music echoed in the background, but Terri was nowhere to be seen. A bottle of wine sat on the coffee table, with two half-empty glasses beside it. A pair of ladies' shoes lay on the carpet beside the couch. Pretty shoes, but they were big. Not her sister's size fives.

"Terri isn't home. Is there something you need?"

"Where is she?"

"She was out with Melissa, shopping all day. They went out for dinner and the evening, and she's spending the night downtown with Melissa."

A sick feeling gripped her stomach. Georgette glanced from side to side. Along with the faint smell of the wine, she could smell a woman's perfume.

"May I come in?"

"Actually, I'm really tired, so this isn't a good time. I'll tell Terri you were here."

For the second time that night, a door closed in her face.

This time, instead of standing there and staring at the closed door, Georgette turned and ran straight for her truck. She drove away quickly, without thinking of where she was going.

She found herself in the parking lot of the repair shop.

She slid out of the cab and stood in the lot,

empty except for her pickup, and stared up at the decidedly non-glamorous, board sign, lit up by a pair of colored spotlights. In the darkness, the old building looked even more drab than usual, but at least the night hid the marred surface where vandals had once written crude words, though Bart had cleaned most of it off.

It wasn't much, but she had nowhere else to go. Payday was six days away. She had less than half a tank of gas, almost no money in her wallet, no credit cards, and no one left to turn to.

A cool breeze caused her to shiver.

Without digging through the boxes, she wasn't sure she even had a jacket.

She ran her fingers along the keys in her hand. About a week ago, Bob had given her a key and the alarm code, saying that in case of an emergency, she might need to come in early, or lock up one night.

This might not be an emergency in the strictest sense of the word, but the shop was her only safe haven for shelter and warmth for the night.

She said a quick prayer that she'd remembered the code correctly, and opened the door. Just as Bob had warned her, the system started with a series of beeps. She quickly pushed the code into the buttons on the keypad, and the building went silent.

While the shop was located on a commercial

roadway, in this end of town it wasn't exactly a major thoroughfare. She stood still, experiencing the silence as never before. Her father's house was often silent when her father and all the staff were sleeping at night, but she was always comforted by knowing they were there.

Here, though everything was familiar, she felt truly alone.

She turned and stared outside. A few cars were lined up along the fence, waiting their turn to be fitted into the work schedule, but her old truck was the only vehicle in the parking lot. She trusted the neighborhood in the daytime, when everything was bustling with activity, but at night, if someone came by and wanted to steal the last of her worldly belongings, from the back of the truck, she would be helpless to do anything. By the time she could call the police, they would be gone.

She caught the reflection of herself in the large window. She was still wearing her new dress, the one the same color as Bob's eyes. She could do nothing about that. But she could do something about her footwear. She kicked off her high-heeled shoes, retrieved her safety workboots and an extra pair of wool socks from beneath the counter, and slipped them on.

Depending only on the muted light from the streetlamps, Georgette hauled all twelve boxes into the corner of the private office without turning on the light so anyone passing by wouldn't think she was taking things out instead of moving things in, and call the police. Once all the boxes were inside, she moved her truck to the lineup of vehicles along the fence.

When she was done, Georgette locked the door behind her and sank down on the worn couch.

She'd couldn't remember ever being so tired. It was now Saturday, 4:48 a.m. She'd been up at 6:15 a.m. on Friday morning in order to get ready and be at work for 8:00 a.m. She'd put in a full eight hours on the job, and then when she got off, she'd gone shopping for the new dress she'd worn to that fateful Chamber of Commerce banquet. Then she'd moved whatever remained of her material possessions twice, first lifting everything into the back of her truck, then carrying everything inside the building.

The chill of the night started to set into her bones now that she was sitting still. Being tired made everything feel worse. She hoped that whoever threw her things into the boxes had included a jacket or a sweater. If she couldn't find a sweater, then she could grab any article of clothing and throw it around her shoulders like a shawl.

Except she didn't have the energy to move to find out.

Georgette wrapped her arms around herself, and let her head fall back on the couch.

Her life was a disaster. But, for now, she had a roof over her head and a clean washroom nearby, which was all that mattered until daylight.

When the sun began to rise, that would be her signal to leave. Like most people, she worked Monday to Friday, but Bob worked six days a week, including Saturdays and since it was now officially Saturday morning, Bob would soon be in to open for business though a little later than the weekday opening.

Not bothering to fight back a yawn, she tried to figure out what she could do until it was time to sneak off. No thoughts would form, so she did the only thing she could think of, which was to ask God for help.

No answer came.

Slowly, the world faded to black.

Bob tucked the morning newspaper under his arm while he unlocked the door, then pushed it open. He stepped inside and flipped the panel covering to turn off the alarm, ready to punch in the code, but his hand froze in mid-air.

There was no tell-tale beeping that the door had been opened or that the motion detector had caught his presence.

He blinked and stared at the panel. The green light was on, not the red.

Slowly, he tapped his chin with the rolled-up newspaper as he continued to stare at the panel. He had been the last one out on Friday night. If he'd forgotten to set the alarm in his hurry to get home and change for the banquet, then this was another sign that he was working too hard. That was the reason they'd hired George, but they'd obviously hired her too late. He was already losing it.

He began to turn around, then stopped. As if she'd materialized from his thoughts, George lay on the couch in the lobby.

Bob shook his head, but the image didn't clear.

Still in a sitting position, she was sprawled on the couch, her head resting at what had to be a painful angle, her blond hair spread like a halo around her face. She still wore her dress from Friday night, a close-fitting, silky green number that proved there was more to George under those coveralls than just a mechanic.

But the worn workboots on her feet shouted exactly that.

She gave a little snort, her head jerked slightly as if to awaken, then sagged once more.

Bob ran his fingers though his hair and looked outside. The parking lot was empty at 7:30 a.m., except for his own car. So he wasn't totally losing his mind by not realizing she was there before he stepped inside. But that only added to the mystery of how she got there, especially since George was dressed as though she hadn't been home.

Very quietly, he approached her until he was only one step away. He waited, but she didn't awaken.

Bob leaned forward and sniffed the air. He didn't detect the smell of alcohol, only her perfume.

He closed his eyes as he inhaled the faint but heady scent more deeply. He knew it was only the expensive perfumes that could linger for hours and hours and remain sweet, but now that he knew who she was, that she could spend so much money on perfume didn't surprise him.

Bob quickly stepped backward and opened his eyes at the memory.

She was no longer just George the mechanic. This was Georgette Ecklington, daughter of William Ecklington, billionaire magnate of the biggest chain of retail discount stores in the country.

And she was sleeping on his couch. His old, beat-up, dirty couch that he'd repaired with duct tape.

Suddenly, her eyes opened. She blinked a few times, gasped and scrambled to her feet.

Her eyes lost their focus, and she began to sway.

Without thinking, Bob grasped her shoulders to keep her from falling.

After a few seconds, she raised one hand and pressed her fingers between her brows. "I think I stood up too fast."

"Are you okay?"

She nodded, so Bob released her, and stepped back once more. "What are you doing here? Where's your car?" He looked down at the work-boots on her feet. And your shoes…

Her lower lip trembled. "I don't have a car. But I have a truck…" She turned her head and Bob followed her motion with his. Parked in the row of vehicles waiting their turn for repairs, was an old, decrepit pickup truck he didn't recognize.

Her voice shook as she spoke. "That truck is mine."

"But it's so…" he let his voice trail off. He really didn't care about what she drove, although the condition surprised him. His main concern was George. "You didn't tell me what you're doing here." He knew she'd been to the banquet with Tyler, and an urge to protect George boiled to the surface. Bob clenched his fists. If Tyler had hurt her or threatened her to cause her to hide, Bob didn't care who Tyler was, or where he lived. Bob would force him to make it right.

George's voice came out in a choked volume barely above a whisper. "I had nowhere else to go."

"I don't understand."

"I told Daddy I wouldn't marry Tyler."

Bob shook his head. "Now I really don't understand. I think I've missed something."

"It started at the banquet, after you left. Tyler told Daddy everything. Daddy didn't take it very well."

While she paused, Bob looked down at her. Despite the snug fit, George's dress was wrinkled. Besides that, it was smudged with dirt, almost as if she'd been rolling on the ground. He followed a run in her pantyhose that extended from beneath the rolled edge of the wool socks visible above her workboots, upwards, disappearing past the hemline of her dress.

Bob quickly raised his eyes. "Tyler asked you to marry him?"

"Not really. But he discussed it with Daddy. Daddy told me I had to marry Tyler because I had ruined the family name and his reputation. Daddy actually approved of what Tyler was doing."

"Now I know I'm confused. Maybe you should go back to the beginning."

"After you met my father, Tyler told him what you really do, and what I really do for you. Daddy was mortified, to put it mildly. He said that his reputation would be ruined, and the only way to save it was for me to marry Tyler. But I refused. So Daddy kicked me out."

"He kicked you out because you won't marry

someone you don't love?" Suddenly he didn't want to be looking into her face, just in case she said she did love Tyler. It shouldn't have made a difference to him, but it did.

He lowered his head, intending simply to stare at the floor, but he found himself staring again at her workboots. The workboots belonged to George the mechanic. The woman before him was wealthy beyond anything he could ever imagine. At the banquet, he'd thought she looked spectacular in that dress, but now he knew why. That dress was probably worth an entire month's mortgage payment. Yet now, with it, she was wearing dirty, worn workboots.

He didn't know which was the real George—the one wearing the workboots, or the one wearing the expensive dress.

"Of course I don't love Tyler. I don't know if this is a very Christian thing to say, but I think I actually hate him. Although I can't blame him entirely for what happened. I had planned to tell my father about what I really do here at some point, but I would have used better timing. In a different setting, he still would have been angry about my job, but I don't think he would have kicked me out."

"Your father kicked you out because you have a job?" Bob knew many families where the parents were ready to kick out lazy grown children because they *didn't* have a job.

"He was fine with me having a job, as long as it was the job I led him to believe, which is something with a title." She grinned. "Administrative assistant sounds good, don't you think?"

He couldn't help but grin back. "I guess. But I still don't know what one does."

Her playful grin dropped. "Not working with your hands and getting dirty, that's for sure. I love my job, but more than the job, I love doing what I want to do. I don't know if I'm being ungrateful for all my father has given me, but I want to make my own choices, especially when lately he's been trying to push everything down my throat. Not just getting married to Tyler, but his antiquated ideas of what I'm allowed to do and what I should be doing to make him look good. I just never realized being independent would come at such a high cost." Her voice lowered. "I don't think marrying Tyler, especially this way, is what God wants me to do with my life."

"What are you going to do?"

"I don't know. I'm so sorry, I know I shouldn't be here, but I had nowhere else to go, and I didn't know what to do."

"I think the first thing you need to do is start looking for an apartment."

"I can't. I don't have anything."

He unrolled the newspaper, which had been in his hand for so long some of the ink had come off on his skin. "Then a room-and-board situation would probably suit you. You could take your time buying new furniture if you don't mind smaller living quarters and sharing a bathroom." Although, knowing now the moneyed background from which she'd come, he had no doubt she'd lived in quite a mansion. Not only were the grounds probably like living in a park, the house itself must have been huge and luxurious. Her bedroom was probably bigger than the living room in his humble house. Between carrying the mortgage on the house and half the mortgage payment on the business, he could afford to live comfortably no matter how small his house was in comparison to hers. That was all that mattered.

He walked to the coffee table, opened the newspaper and started paging through to the classified section. "I know how much you make, so I know what you can afford. I'm sure we can find something for you." He paused for a second, halting on his own words. He'd said *we,* and as soon as the word had come out of his mouth, he'd realized he meant it. Besides the fact that he liked her as a person, he felt somewhat responsible for her having been kicked out.

"I don't think you understand. I don't have any money until payday."

Bob looked up. "I don't know how personal I should get here, but let's define 'no money.' Just how low should I start looking? Some of these places aren't in the best neighborhoods, and you don't want to be there."

"I have $4.37."

"Anyplace will take a check, George. That's how most people pay the rent."

"No, you really don't understand. I have $3.37 in my wallet and exactly one dollar in my bank account. Daddy took back my allowance. I didn't see this coming, and I had lots of money last week when I went shopping. Daddy took out everything except for what I deposited myself, and he didn't leave anything to cover what I'd spent. That means everything I bought came out of my paychecks. My credit cards have been cancelled. Even my cell phone doesn't work anymore." She buried her face in her hands. "It's really starting to hit me now. Everything is gone. I don't even know what's in the boxes, I'm too afraid to look."

"Boxes?"

"The staff tossed my personal things in boxes, and dragged them outside. Everything I have left that my father doesn't think is rightfully his is in twelve boxes, which are stored in the corner of the private office until I can figure out what to do." Her stomach growled, causing her to cover her stomach with her arms. "I'm hungry, and I don't even have enough money for breakfast."

"Actually, you can buy a loaf of bread and a small jar of peanut butter with what you've got in your wallet, so technically, you do. But that doesn't solve your problems."

Bob raised his hand and ran his fingers through his hair again. He'd never been without support. His family didn't have much money, but they'd always had enough food to eat, a roof over their heads, each other, and God watching over them, and that was all that mattered.

When he'd started his business, his parents had co-signed the mortgage for the shop because the bank had turned him down. His family had been there to help when he needed it. By the time he bought his house, the business was stable enough that he could get a mortgage as a single person without a cosigner.

He studied George. By her drawn expression, he could tell she hadn't had enough sleep. The dark color of the dress made her look even paler.

Her stomach growled again. Instead of blushing, as most women did, her eyes became glassy. She blinked repeatedly, then swiped the back of her hand over them.

Bob's throat tightened. He reached into his back pocket, pulled out his wallet, and handed her some money. "Here. Go to the deli and bring back a couple of breakfast sandwiches."

"I can't accept your money."

"Don't worry about it. I said to buy two, one for you and one for me. It's just two friends sharing brunch together. You can pay next time." He really didn't want her to repay him, but he had a feeling that she would, even though she wouldn't be able to save the money for extras any time soon.

"Thank you," she muttered as she accepted his money. She took one step toward the door and skidded to a halt. She looked down at herself. "I can't go like this. Excuse me." She spun around and ran into the private office, and the door closed.

Instead of standing and staring at the door, Bob turned on the lights, flipped the sign to Open and booted up the computer. Just as he started to type in his password, George emerged from the office dressed in what he was more accustomed to seeing her wear—jeans and a T-shirt...and the workboots.

She looked down at her feet, and tapped her toes. "I couldn't find my sneakers, but I'm not about to wear dress shoes with jeans. I'll be right back." As Bob watched, she nearly skipped out the door, despite the heaviness of the steel-toed safety boots.

Instead of starting the day's projects, he returned to the newspaper and started looking for a room-and-board rental in a respectable neighborhood. He could only find a few vacancies that he considered reasonable, but none of them were in a neighborhood he approved of, especially knowing her background.

By the time she returned, Bart had arrived and Bob had joined him to work in the shop.

"She's back. I gotta go for a sec."

Bart straightened and rested his fists on his hips. "Who's back? George? What's she doing here on Saturday? You didn't tell me she was coming in. Is she taking time off another day, or are we paying her overtime?"

"Neither. It's personal."

A smile lit Bart's face. "Wow. I knew it."

"Don't even think about it. It's not that kind of personal. I'll be right back."

He could feel Bart's eyes on his back as he exited the shop and joined George in the office. She already had both sandwiches, complete with napkins, spread out on the counter.

Just as they did when they went out for dinner on Thursday nights, Bob led with a short prayer. George immediately bit into her sandwich as Bob took a glance at the logo on the wrapper. "I see you went to the deli, after all. You were gone so long I thought you took a trip across town."

She shook her head, then swallowed her mouthful with a big gulp. "I decided to walk in order to save gas. Also, while I was walking it gave me some time to think. If I could find a place to rent that's close to here, I could walk to work and cancel the insurance on my truck. I could use the refund to pay for a damage deposit, and maybe the rest for the balance of this month's rent. Did you find anything in the paper?"

"No, I didn't. Maybe I can get my mother to ask around and see if anyone she knows wants to take in a boarder—just until you can get on your feet financially. I'm sure that in a few months..." His words trailed off as a thought struck him.

"Bob? Is something wrong?"

"You're going to need a place to stay tonight, and my mother will never come up with something that quickly. But I may have another solution, at least a temporary one. A couple of years ago I fixed up my garage into a small apartment for when my cousin Jason was going to college. I've been using it for storage lately, but I'm sure it wouldn't take much to get it livable again. There's just one thing."

"It sounds perfect!"

Bob raised one hand. "I'm not finished explaining yet. When I said small, I meant really small. It's a regular single garage, but narrower inside because I insulated it and put up wallboard. It's basically one room with a living space on one end, and a utility kitchen on the other, outfitted like a camper. I made a small bathroom in one corner. There isn't even room for a bathtub, just a shower. Jason used a wardrobe in the corner to hang his clothes. You'd have to sleep on the futon which serves as a couch during the day and pulls out into a bed at night. It's not glamorous, but Jason liked it that way. It's easy to keep clean and besides, the biggest factor for him as a student was that it was free. If you want it, it's free to you, too, for as long as you want to use it."

George's eyes narrowed, and one corner of her mouth turned up. Bob could tell she was trying to imagine the garage apartment as he'd described it, except he doubted she really was aware of how small *small* could be. While she was on her way to the deli, he had pulled out her personnel file to look up her address. He hadn't known where she lived because George's first duty was to handle the paperwork and get the accounting caught up, so she had entered her own records into the computer, with their payroll of one.

The second he saw her father's address, he could picture the neighborhood. They weren't just homes. They were estates. Not a one would have a single-car garage. He wondered if she'd even ever *seen* a single-car garage.

"I still think it sounds perfect. Thank you so much. I don't know how I'll ever repay you."

Bob cleared his throat. "Don't worry about it, but maybe you should see it before you make up your mind."

Chapter Ten

Georgette followed Bob's car through the neighborhood to his house.

The homes were older and were all small and similar in design and structure. Yet, despite their age none were run down. Bob had explained to her that many of the residents were couples like his parents, who had bought the homes many years ago when they were first married, and had remained after their children were grown and gone. Lawn care had replaced child care for them over time.

Other residents were like Bob—first-time home buyers who purchased a small, older home because that was what they could afford.

Still, the neighborhood had a charm of its own, and Georgette didn't feel threatened, only out of place.

At the end of the block, Bob turned into a lane, and she followed.

With the age of the neighborhood, instead of built-in garages like her father's these homes had detached garages, accessible via a back lane.

Bob turned to park on a slightly raised cement pad beside a very small garage. Georgette slid out of her truck at the same time as he exited his own car, and she joined him.

"Here we are. Welcome home."

All Georgette could do was stare. The building was small. She couldn't see that there would be much room inside it for anything besides an average-sized vehicle. The gardener's shed on her father's property was bigger than Bob's garage.

She struggled to think of living in such a tiny building, but Bob's cousin had done exactly that for an entire school year. Therefore, so could she. Besides, beggars couldn't be choosers. It was either this, or go back to being a prisoner for the rest of her life. Like her father, Tyler would do everything in his power to limit her exposure to church and to other believers, and would do everything he could to squelch her faith in order to mold her into what he wanted her to be. She couldn't live like that.

Living in a building smaller than her bedroom at her father's house was fine, if it gave her the freedom to live her own life and make her own choices. She had to live the way God wanted her to live, not the way Tyler wanted.

Bob's ears turned red. "I'd like to say it looks better from the inside than from outside, but since I didn't have any notice, today it probably doesn't."

Georgette forced herself to smile graciously and told herself the same thing she'd thought just before she fell asleep on the couch in the lobby of the shop. It was a roof over her head and it had a clean washroom. At least she hoped the washroom was clean.

"I'm sure it's fine. I don't know what to say, you're being so generous."

His ears turned even redder. "Don't give credit where it isn't due. It's not going to cost me anything for you to live here. I just have to find someplace else to put my junk."

She knew he was wrong, but she didn't want to argue with him and diminish his graciousness. At the very least, he would be paying more on his utility bill for the electricity she used.

He led her away from the roll-up door to a small, painted door on the side of the building, the entrance to her new home. No polished, carved mahogany double doors here.

"You don't have to worry about anyone getting

in by opening the main garage door," Bob mumbled while he picked through his keyring. "The roll-up door opens, but I built a small storage area there. From the inside, it's a solid wall."

Georgette turned her head and looked from one end of the garage to the other. It was already small enough without taking away interior space for storage accessible only from the outside.

The door opened with a creak.

"I guess I'll have to oil that. Come on in. Just remember that I wasn't expecting anyone actually to be here."

"Oh!" she exclaimed, then slapped her hands over her big mouth. It was even smaller inside than she had imagined, although Bob had been perfectly honest about its shortcomings.

"Yeah. I know. It's really small."

Besides a number of boxes piled up, the only furniture inside was a futon, the smallest wardrobe unit she'd ever seen, a desk, a half-size kitchen table with two chairs and a small stand with a thirteen-inch television on top. It wasn't much furniture, but nothing else would fit and still leave room to walk. "It's okay. It's…cozy."

"It won't look so bad once all my extra stuff is out of here." He picked up a box and carried it outside, so Georgette did the same. When all the boxes were outside, they moved her twelve boxes from the back of her truck inside, making it look exactly the same, except that this time, the boxes were hers.

Bob swiped one finger through the layer of dust on the desktop. "This isn't bad, considering that no one has lived here for a year. You'll probably want to clean up before you start unpacking. Just let me stack my boxes in the storage area, and I'll go into my place and see what I can find. This will give you some time to check the place out on your own."

Before Georgette could protest, he was gone.

This was it. Her new home.

It felt like a closet with furniture. And lots of dirt.

She walked to what could loosely be defined as the kitchen. The refrigerator and stove were miniature versions, like those that might be found in a child's playhouse. Yet as small as they seemed, the size was appropriate to the rest of the dwelling. For the balance of the kitchen, one double-sized upper cabinet hung on the wall, and a double-sized lower cabinet with a countertop on it had been installed beside the fridge, half of the surface was taken up by a small sink. Even combined, the usable cupboard space wouldn't hold much, but Georgette had no idea what to put in them, anyway. She didn't know how to cook anything without a microwave oven, which was glaringly absent from the facilities. She didn't want to think about there being no dishwasher. But it didn't really matter. She didn't have any dishes.

A few steps further, she stepped into the doorway of what had to be the bathroom, if the word *room* could be applied to a space so small.

Aside from the layer of dust, it looked relatively clean. To her surprise and delight, it was in much better condition than the washroom at the gas station where she changed her clothes every day.

"Well? What do you think?" Bob's voice echoed from behind her.

Her breath caught. She spun around, pressing her hands over her pounding heart.

"Oops. I didn't mean to scare you. I thought you heard me coming."

"No, I didn't. Everything looks good, except the toilet is broken. There's no water in it."

Bob grinned, then squeezed past her and knelt beside the toilet. He reached between it and the small vanity and turned a small chrome tap.

The trickling sound of running water resounded throughout the small room.

"That's because I turned the water off when Jason moved out. I didn't want it to stain."

"Stain?" She suppressed a shudder. "Is there something wrong with your water?"

"No, but if no one is using the toilet, the water

would go stagnant from not being flushed for months, and would stain the bowl as it slowly evaporated over time. So it was just best to leave it dry."

The water stopped running. Bob turned and pushed the toilet handle, making it flush. She stared, fascinated, as the dry, empty bowl filled with clean water.

Georgette tried to stop the sinking feeling that threatened to envelop her. Her life had deteriorated to the point where she was happy to see a toilet flush.

"See? It works just fine. All this place needs is a good wipe-down and it'll be as good as new. I brought over a box of cleaning stuff and my vacuum cleaner for you to use. Now, if you'll excuse me, I should get back to work. I'll see you in a couple of hours."

Bob parked his car on the cement pad beside the garage where he always parked, but today he looked at it from a different perspective.

There was a second vehicle parked here.

George's.

By now, George was probably nearly finished making his garage into her home.

He grabbed the bag with the two burgers he'd picked up at the drive-through on his way home, and slid out of the car. As he did, Bart's words of caution came back to haunt him.

Earlier, when he got back to the shop, he'd had a long talk with Bart. Bart had reminded him that it wasn't a great idea to have their employee living on his property. Bob had agreed, but he couldn't put her out on the street. George was a Christian sister who needed help, and he had the means to provide it. This also changed everything about their relationship, the parameters of which he still hadn't fully considered.

He pushed the car door closed and started walking toward the garage. Now that she was living closer than next door, he wondered if she would be attending church with him in the morning; he wanted her to be there with him. So far she'd been attending the evening services, but he thought she'd been continuing to attend at her home church for the morning services, though someone had mentioned to him they'd seen her at his church. Now that she was so close, things could be different. However, he wasn't sure that would be wise. In his current position, he should have been setting firm lines to distance himself. Instead, the lines were becoming more fuzzy. Yet, he couldn't not take her if she asked, even if the only reason to go to his church, the closer one, was because she didn't have any money for gas.

As he approached the side door, he noticed that it was wide open. When he stepped into the opening, the scent of pine cleaner was so strong it made his eyes water.

Bob stepped back to give himself some air.

"George?"

She didn't reply, but he could hear splashing coming from the bathroom, as well as the noise of the fan. Since the bathroom door was also wide open, he considered it safe to continue inside.

The closer he got, the stronger the onslaught of pine became, until his eyes wouldn't stop watering. He swiped his eyes with the back of his hand, and stepped into the opening for the bathroom.

He found George wringing out the sponge in the bathroom sink.

"What are you doing in here?"

"I'm finally done. What do you think?"

He blinked repeatedly, but his eyes still burned. "It looks good, but I think the smell of the cleaner is a bit overpowering."

"The label said it would make everything fresh and clean. It's antibacterial."

Bob swiped his hand over his eyes again, and resisted the urge to cough. "That could be, but I think you used a little too much."

George looked up at him, her eyes as red as his felt. "The label said to use full strength on bathroom fixtures, and then diluted on wood and painted surfaces. So I did."

He looked at the bottle, which was on the floor next to the toilet. Before today, he'd only used it once. It was now half empty.

He turned toward the shower stall. Part of him wanted to see how shiny she'd scrubbed the inside, but part of him didn't want to open it, for fear of getting knocked out by the fumes.

Bob cleared his throat. "I brought supper. We should eat before it gets cold." Or permeated with pine. He would never again feel the same about walking through an evergreen forest.

They walked to the kitchen area. The sink, counters and appliances were so clean they sparkled, but the smell of pine wasn't diminished enough for Bob to want to expose his food to it. "Let's go into my house. I have ketchup."

He didn't give her a chance to respond. He simply walked out, expecting her to follow, which she did. Once outside, he inhaled deeply. When he did, the sudden ability to draw in unscented oxygen made his head spin.

"We should leave the door open, to air the place out while we're gone. We can keep an eye on everything from the kitchen."

All she did was nod, so Bob continued into his house. "It's kind of messy. I know I already said this earlier, but I wasn't exactly expecting company today. It's been a long, busy week, and housework isn't my first priority."

"That's okay."

Fortunately for Bob, he didn't have to lead her past his bedroom. The only time he made the bed was when he knew in advance that his mother was coming. The first thing she did when she arrived was march to his bedroom to check that he'd made the bed. When he hadn't, which was every time he wasn't expecting her, she promptly lectured him. Now, he wished he'd listened to her.

George wiped her hands down the sides of her jeans. "If you don't mind, I need to wash my hands. I can still smell that cleaner."

He pointed down the hall, hoping she wouldn't look into other rooms as she walked by. When she returned, she still smelled as if she'd been attacked by a pine tree, but he kept that thought to himself.

She joined him at the table, where he had already set a burger and fries in front of each of them, and poured them both a glass of milk. "I hope you're hungry."

George smiled weakly. "Actually, I'm not sure how I feel. I was so busy cleaning I didn't think about eating. I hope I did it right."

"I'm sure you did fine. Let's pray now, before

this gets completely cold." He bowed his head, and said a short prayer, thanking God for both the meal and George's new home, and he began to eat.

George sat there glassy-eyed staring at the burger.

Bob stopped chewing. "What's wrong?"

She blinked and picked up the burger. "I feel so strange about this. You bought me lunch and now supper, and I don't have any way to repay you. More than that, you've given me a place to stay, rent-free. I've never had to accept someone's charity before, and I can't say I like it very much. I wish there was something I could do to repay you."

He shrugged his shoulders. "Don't worry about it. I already told you it's not a big deal. It's not costing me anything for you to stay in my garage. Although, now that you've cleaned it up, we should call it an apartment." He smiled.

She didn't smile back.

"It's okay, George. I'm sure there's something you can do for me. How about if we make it your job to sweep up the shop at the end of the day?"

She shook her head. "No. You already pay me a wage for stuff like that. I want to do something else for you."

"It looks like you did a good job cleaning the, uh, apartment. How about if you did some housecleaning for me?"

"Are you sure? I've never done this kind of thing before. I'm still not sure I did a good job."

"I'm sure you did." Even if she did use a double dose of the pine cleaner. Or maybe even a quadruple dose. They'd been away from the garage for ten minutes, and the pine forest still surrounded her. "Now eat your dinner. Good food makes everything better." He grimaced. "My mother always says that. I can't believe I'm repeating something my mother said."

She gave him a weak smile, and finally took a bite out of her burger. "Is your mother a good cook?"

"Yeah. She makes the best osso buco in the world. My brother Tony runs an Italian restaurant, and even he can't make osso buco like Mama. When she goes to his restaurant, she always ends up in the kitchen improving the recipes. I know that probably doesn't sound very good, but once you meet my mother, you'll understand." As soon as he realized what he'd said, he snapped his mouth shut.

He had already crossed the line between business and personal too many times. He didn't need to expound on his mother and her quirks. It was bad enough that he was with George now, in his home.

After eating half the burger, George laid it on the wrapper. "I'm sorry, but I can't finish this." She paused and pushed the burger away. "Actually, I don't feel very good. At first I thought I was hungry, but now that I've eaten, I think I feel worse." She covered her mouth with her hand, and made a little cough.

Bob frowned. "I wonder if it's because you've inhaled too many fumes today. Maybe you should lie down."

She shook her head and took a long sip of milk. "I shouldn't need to do that. Josephine never has to lie down."

"Josephine?"

"Our housekeeper. She's very thorough. The house smells so nice and clean when she's finished every day. She always has Daddy's clothes freshly pressed so they're ready for him in the morning. Daddy likes to get into a warm shirt in the morning."

"Morning? She irons in the morning? You mean you had a live-in housekeeper?"

She blinked a few times. "Of course..."

Bob ran his fingers through his hair. He felt as though he'd been living in another universe light years away from George's world. "George, I've never even had a housekeeper, never mind a live-in person. I also wash my own floors and clean my own bathroom and do my own laundry."

"Why don't you send your laundry to the service that does the shop?"

"We don't *have* a service. On Saturday, Bart takes the bag of dirty coveralls home, and his wife washes everything for us. If you were wondering about who empties the garbage cans and washes down the bathrooms, Bart and I take turns. We alternate weekends."

Her face paled suddenly. As much as he didn't like housecleaning, Bob didn't think the concept was that abhorrent. He accepted it as something that had to be done. He and Bart saved quite a lot of money doing what they did, because both tasks were expensive to contract out.

George covered her mouth with her hand, and her complexion turned gray. "I really don't feel well."

Before Bob could blink, she turned and ran down the hall. The bathroom door slammed, and she started to retch.

Bob pushed the remainder of his burger into the center of the table. Suddenly he wasn't hungry anymore, either.

When everything became quiet in the bathroom, Bob walked down the hall and tapped softly on the door. "George? Are you okay now? Can I come in?"

The door didn't open. "I'm so sorry. Please go away."

Bob didn't go away. He couldn't remember the last time he'd been sick as an adult, but he clearly remembered his mother taking care of him when he'd had the flu as a child. Having someone who loved him care for him when he was down made the experience a little less horrible.

He seriously doubted George's father would have taken care of her. And while Josephine sounded like an efficient housekeeper, that's exactly what she was—paid help. For now, George didn't have the option of either one of them. The only one she had was him.

He wiggled the knob, and it turned. "At the count of ten, I'm coming in. Ten. Nine." Shuffling echoed from the other side of the door. "Eight. Seven." The doorknob moved, but since he was holding it firmly, he knew the lock button wouldn't work. A grumble came from the other side of the door.

"Six." He slowed his counting.

The toilet flushed.

"Five."

The water ran, and he could hear splashing and the frantic pumping of the soap dispenser, which reminded him that it was almost empty.

"Four."

"I give up. Come in. But you're not going to like what you see."

He opened the door.

George stood beside the sink, her arms crossed

tightly over her chest, her shoulders hunched, and her eyes big and wide as she stared up at him.

"Are you okay?"

Her lower lip quivered. "No, I'm not okay. I don't think I've ever been less okay in my life." Her eyes welled up, and one tear spilled over onto her cheek. "I'm such a failure. I can't even do something simple like clean a bathroom without making myself sick. How pathetic is that?"

Bob stared at George. He pictured her as she had been on the day she walked in to apply for the job—poised and self-confident.

She wasn't like that now. Not only did she look defeated, she looked alone, and she was. Her father had abandoned her. He knew George had a sister, but she hadn't gone to her for help. As a tomboy, George probably didn't fit in with the other single women in her social circle, it hadn't appeared so at the banquet.

She really had no one to turn to besides him. The revelation was startling and heartbreaking. The expression *poor little rich girl* had never meant anything to Bob until now, and it put the verse, "What you do for the least of these, you also do for me" in perspective.

He'd given her shelter, but it was only his garage, which he wasn't even using. In a way, having her live there gave him the benefit of added security. No one would break into his storage area in the middle of the night with someone in the building.

He fully intended to buy her meals until payday, but that was as much for his benefit as for George's. Spending time together away from work when they went out for dinner together every Thursday night had made him realize how much he missed female companionship. George, unlike the other woman he'd dated, understood what he meant when he talked a little shop. He also could enjoy himself with no risk that anything more was going to happen than a pleasant evening. She knew his schedule and his obligations, and knew that the reason they were together was simply a weekly escape from routine. Thursday nights had become another routine, but one he enjoyed.

It suddenly hit him that they would no longer be enjoying Thursday dinners together. Up until now, George had insisted on paying every second time. Now, he refused to accept her money. She couldn't afford it, and he doubted she would accept more charity from him.

In a way, he was almost working on Tyler's manipulative scale. Bob was her boss. And a happy employee was a productive one. So helping George out ultimately helped him financially.

What George really needed right now was a

friend who had nothing to gain by knowing her, and he couldn't make that claim. But he supposed that anyone else in his current position would probably give the poor girl a hug.

He started to step forward, but stopped. He didn't want to frighten her and he had her cornered in the small bathroom.

Bob remained in the doorway and extended his arms toward George. "Come here," he said softly.

Her lower lip quivered, and she came forward, but instead of throwing herself into him the way he expected a distraught woman would, she only leaned her forehead against the center of his chest. Fortunately, she didn't cry, which was good. If she had, he didn't know what he was supposed to do.

The only thing he could think of was to rest his hands on her shoulders, which he did. "Everything will be fine," he mumbled. "You just need to give yourself more time."

He felt her shake her head. "I don't know what I'm doing. Everything I do is wrong. And then when I think I'm doing something right, it backfires in my face. I can't even clean up without getting sick from the cleaner."

He massaged her shoulders with his thumbs. "That's just inexperience. You didn't know and you used too much. Next time, put only a little on the sponge, and you'll see that it goes a long way.

You also picked the worst job first. I don't know why you didn't do the dusting and vacuuming before the bathroom."

"The bathroom was smaller, so it looked easier."

"Actually, it's not. Vacuuming is probably the easiest household chore."

"I don't know. I've never done it before."

Bob froze his movements. "You've never vacuumed?"

"Well, once. When I was a child, one day I thought it would be fun to help Josephine, but Daddy saw me with the vacuum and took it away. He told me never to do that again, that I wasn't a housekeeper, I was an Ecklington. And of course, when I was a teenager, I grew out of wanting to help Josephine really quickly."

"Uh…do you at least make your own bed?"

"Of course not. But I wouldn't talk about not making the bed, if I were you."

A smile started to tug at the corner of Bob's mouth. The George he knew was back. "You'll do fine. You just need some help to get started. If you want, I can show you what to do."

He felt her nod again. "I'd really like that," she said, and as she spoke, she moved forward. Her hands fell to the sides of his waist, then started to inch to his back, but suddenly she stepped backward, covering her mouth with both hands. "I'm so disgusting!" she said between her fingers. "I have to go brush my teeth. One day, I'll pay you back for everything you're doing for me. I promise."

Before Bob could tell her that wasn't necessary, she squeezed between him and the door, and ran down the hall. The back door opened, closed and all was silent.

Chapter Eleven

Georgette slathered a layer of Bob's mother's homemade strawberry jam on her toast and took a big bite.

"Did you sleep okay last night? Most people don't sleep very well the first night in a new place."

She swallowed while she nodded, then sipped her coffee. "This is so delicious! Yes, I did. I slept great."

She'd truly slept like a log. Last night she'd wiped down the bathroom with water four times to get rid of the residue of pine cleaner, but this time, she went outside to clear out her lungs periodically. With the door open to air the place out, she'd vacuumed, dusted and even scrubbed out the insides of all the cupboards with dish soap.

At midnight, she dug through the boxes only long enough to find what she was going to wear to church that wouldn't need to be ironed, then dropped herself on the futon, more exhausted than she'd ever been in her life. She wasn't aware of a thing from that point on until Bob knocked on the door and told her it was time to get up for church.

Georgette checked her watch, knowing that they had to leave in a few minutes for Bob to be on time to practice with his friends before the service started.

She sipped her coffee quickly, enjoying common coffee as she never had in her life. More than feeling awkward in new surroundings when she woke up, she keenly felt the absence of a coffeemaker. And coffee filters. And coffee. And cream. And food.

The only thing she did have was a mug, but it was at work, which didn't do her any good.

There were so many things she needed, but the $3.37 in her wallet wasn't going to go very far.

She would have to pawn her expensive watch, even though she knew she would only get a fraction of its original price. The only other thing she owned of any value was the truck, and it would take too long to sell in its present condition. She could have money in her pocket from the watch Monday morning.

"Were you warm enough with that blanket I left for you? When we get back from church I'll give you some dishes and stuff out of my cupboard this afternoon, to get you started."

"I can't take your dishes."

Bob grinned. Georgette nearly choked on her current bite of her breakfast. The little crinkles that appeared at the sides of his eyes made him so attractive she stopped breathing. He always looked good in his customary attire of jeans and T-shirt, but today, dressed in black slacks and a neatly pressed blue cotton shirt for the more formal service, he was handsome in a different way.

"Sure you can. Technically, I really only need one plate, and so do you, if the dishes are washed and put away after every meal. I have a set of eight, so I can certainly spare a couple of sets of plates and cutlery. Besides, it's only a loan."

She didn't want to accept any more charity from him, but she was helpless not to. "Only if you're sure."

"I'm sure. Except you'll still be very limited as to what you can do. I only have one toaster, so if you like toast for breakfast, I'll give you a key for my house and you can come in after I leave in the morning. There are probably a number of other things you need that can't wait until payday on Friday, so I'm going to give you an advance on your paycheck."

"Are you sure?"

"Yes. I won't advance the whole thing, but I can give you a portion."

She looked again at her watch, which she now could keep, at least temporarily. "You have no idea how much I appreciate that."

"I know. Monday morning, pay yourself out three days. That should keep you going until Friday, when you can have the balance."

She finished the rest of the coffee in her mug, then set it down on the table, keeping her hands clasped around it. "I don't understand why you're being so nice to me. Not that I don't appreciate it, because I do. It's just that no one has ever treated me like this before." Not wanting to say so, she didn't understand his motives. Everyone always wanted something, and she was actually costing him money, with little or no chance of repayment, at least not for a very long time.

He shrugged his shoulders. "Do I need a reason? You need help, I have what you need and God put you in my path. I don't think it's any more complicated than that." He stood. "If you're finished, we really should go."

The drive to the church only took a few minutes, just as he'd said. There were only three other cars in the parking lot.

"It looks like Randy and Adrian beat me. Paul and Celeste aren't here yet."

"But there are three cars."

"That's Pastor Ron's car. He has to be here first to open up the building. Then he goes into his office to pray while everything is quiet, before everyone starts setting up for the service."

"Oh..." She'd never thought about what happened before a Sunday-morning service.

Georgette followed Bob onto the stage area. She stood to the side and watched as he started putting the drum set together. Adrian and Randy waved, then continued laying out cords and monitors.

"Is there something I can do?"

Adrian pointed to a carrying case beside the stairs. "You can assemble the microphone stands if you want. Everyone gets one except Bob.

She turned to Bob. "Why not?"

"I can't sing while I'm playing drums, nor would you want me to. I don't sing all that well."

Celeste arrived as Georgette finished assembling the last stand and Georgette went over to watch her set up the piano. "Have I told you how much I enjoy listening to you play? I took lessons for a year when I was a kid, but I wasn't very good. One day I took the keyboard off and was trying to figure out how the hammers were constructed and how everything worked together with the pedals, when my father discovered what I was doing and sent me to my room." Georgette grinned. "That was the end of piano lessons for me. They had to get a technician to put the piano back together, and he sold it a few days later."

Celeste smiled back. "The electric pianos aren't quite as interesting inside, but they are portable." She patted the corner of the unit.

Georgette turned to Randy. "Is there anything else I can do?"

"Nope. But I'm sure Pastor Ron would like some help setting up chairs."

Georgette gasped. "The pastor sets up chairs!?"

"Somebody's gotta do it—unless the congregation wants to stand or sit on the floor. That's the way it is in most organizations. Ten percent of the people do ninety percent of the work."

"Then I think I'll go set up chairs." She turned to Bob, who smiled his approval.

She expected Pastor Ron to be surprised at her offer, but he didn't refuse. However, when more people started arriving to help, the men took over and sent her away.

Since she no longer had anything to do, she stood to the side and watched the practice while the room started to take shape as a sanctuary. She'd never thought much about drums as an instrument, but watching the musicians go over selected parts until they got it right, she saw just how important it was for the drummer to give them the framework they needed.

When all the chairs were set up, she found a seat and waited for the service to begin.

It was very similar to the evening service, only more formal—except when the children were dismissed. They walked quietly out of the main sanctuary, but as soon as they crossed the threshold into the lobby, the running and screaming began, fading as the horde made their way downstairs to the classrooms.

Up on the stage, Paul smiled and shook his head, and the congregation sang one more song. As Pastor Ron started speaking, the worship team quietly left the stage, and shuffled into their seats; Bob sat beside her. Just as they did in the evening service, the worship team returned to the stage during the closing prayer so they could play the last song, and then the congregation was dismissed.

The instruments and equipment were left on the stage for the evening service so Georgette joined Bob on the stage, waiting beside him while the worship team picked up their music and put everything in order. Bob's cell phone rang, and he left the noise and walked to the back, where he spoke facing the wall for some privacy. The conversation was short, which Georgette was learning was typical of Bob. Within two minutes, he had returned.

"That was my mother," he said to the group in general. "I have to go to my parents' house for lunch. My mother wants to throw a big surprise party for my father's sixty-ninth birthday. I need to run over there for lunch, while he's out. My mother's called the family together to discuss the details, so I can't go out for lunch today." He turned to Georgette. "When I told her that you were with me, she invited you along too."

Georgette frowned. "A big party for his sixty-ninth? Why wouldn't she wait for a year and have something bigger for his seventieth?"

Bob grinned. "Because that's what Papa expects. Far be it from Mama to do what is expected of her."

Celeste remained straight-faced, but Adrian, Randy and Paul all grinned, as if they knew something she didn't. Georgette turned to Celeste.

Celeste shrugged her shoulders. "I've never met Bob's mom. But I will at the wedding. Oh, that's right, I nearly forgot. We need your address, Georgette."

"What? Why?"

Adrian slipped his arm around Celeste's waist. "Yes. We'd like to send you an invitation to the wedding, but I guess we can get your address from Bob."

Bob's movements froze. "Yeah. Or you can just

give it to me when the time comes. You've got a few months still."

"I know," Adrian said, "but it's best to be prepared." He smiled down at Celeste. "I think we should get going so we can get a good table." He turned back to Bob. "See you tonight at the evening service."

Bob shifted into Park, and turned off the engine. The house blinds flickered when the car stopped, but he chose to ignore it. "This is it, my parents' house."

"This isn't far from your house, is it? Your house is about a mile and a half that way."

"Yes. Bart's parents live on the next block, and Bart and his wife Anna live two blocks that way. All close to work." He pointed to the left. "Our days are long enough without adding even more driving time."

He turned and put his hand on the door handle, but before he could open the door, George's hand on his other arm stopped him. "Why didn't you tell your friends that I've moved into your garage apartment? It was obvious they didn't know."

He released the door handle, and turned to her. "With those guys, I have to wait until the timing is right. I figured I'd tell them on Wednesday, at practice." Celeste wouldn't have thought anything special of it, but when he told the guys, especially Randy, he knew he would be in for the razzing of his life.

"Does your mother know?"

"George, no one knows. It all happened so quickly, and remember, I spent most of the day on Saturday at work, like I do every Saturday. It's just that I haven't had time." Not that he couldn't predict his mother's reaction. He had a woman living on his property. Regardless of the fact that George was living in a separate building across the entire yard, his mother would point out every possible and potential moral infraction imaginable. He knew he couldn't avoid the confrontation, however, so better sooner than later. He hoped his mother would at least lecture him in private, where George wouldn't witness it. After all, he was her boss, and he needed to maintain *some* dignity in front of her. "Let's go in. I saw the blinds move." For the second time since the car had stopped. "Just one more thing. Sometimes my family can be a little overwhelming, so don't take anything that happens too personally."

One eyebrow quirked, but George said nothing, so he led her up the walkway. The door opened the second his foot touched the first step.

"Hey, Rose! How's it going?" He turned to George as he stepped onto the porch near Rose. "This is my sister, Rose. Rose, this is George."

Rose's eyes widened, she blinked a few times and backed up to allow them to enter. "Hi," she said as they passed. "Mama is in the kitchen."

He took Rose's hint, and walked toward the kitchen. "Hi, Tony, Gene," he said to his two brothers, who were sitting on the couch in the living room, as he walked by. "This is George. We have to talk to Mama. We'll be right back."

They smiled and waved without speaking, and George did the same. Bob slowed his pace and turned his head to speak to George over his shoulder. "I guess my other sisters aren't here yet. Gene's wife, Michelle, is probably in the kitchen with Mama."

In the background, Rose called Michelle, and as Bob and George stepped into the kitchen, Michelle passed them, nodding a greeting without stopping.

Bob's mother was stirring something on the stove.

"Hi, Mama."

His mother turned around, smiling. She looked up at Bob, her smile fell and her gaze lowered to rest on George, all five foot four of her.

"Roberto, you told me you were bringing your new mechanic, George. I think you need to get eyeglasses with your age. You have brought a woman."

"Mama, this *is* my new mechanic. Her name

is George. George, this is my mama, Angelina Delanio."

George stepped forward. "Hello, Mrs. Delanio," she said smiling, as she extended one hand to his mother. Her voice dropped in pitch; she spoke evenly and in a friendly, conversational tone. Bob could see her years of fine upbringing being put to good use. "My name is really Georgette, but my friends call me George. I'd like to count you as a friend, so please, call me George. And I really am Bob's new mechanic."

His mother reached forward and slipped her hand into George's, but instead of a handshake, George covered his mother's hand with her other, gave it a gentle squeeze, and smiled.

Bob's mother returned George's smile. "Now I have seen everything. But this is good my son has seen a woman can do such a job." Her eyes narrowed slightly. "You are doing a good job for him?"

George released his mother's hands, but the two woman remained facing each other, neither of them acknowledging Bob. He might as well have been invisible. "I like to think so," she said.

"He and Bartholomew started that business many years ago. My son, he works too many long hours. This must stop or he will drive himself to an early grave. It is good to see they have hired you."

Bob cleared his throat, wondering when he'd

lost control. "Mama, there's something else. In addition to being my new mechanic, George is also my new tenant."

His mother's eyebrows knotted, and she planted her fists on her hips. "Tenant?"

"Yes. She moved into the garage apartment."

"For how long has this been going on?"

"George moved in yesterday."

Her eyes narrowed even more, and Bob nearly shivered with the ice in her glare, making him wish he were invisible. "How could you do a thing like that? It is so small. There is no room for clothes. And the kitchen! There is no kitchen! Jason could live on Antonio's pizza, but a woman needs a place to cook!"

"But..." Bob let his voice trail off. He'd thought all the same things, and he didn't have an answer. For George, the price was right, so that was all that mattered.

"Really, it's fine," George interjected. "In fact, I've never lived on my own before, so it's perfect. A small apartment is easier to keep clean."

"It is too small. Where are you going to put all your things?"

"I don't have very much. I actually have to go shopping tomorrow so I don't have to borrow so much from Bob. The garage apartment is just perfect for me."

"Well, if you are happy, then it is good to have someone new living there." She turned back to Bob "It has been a waste to have the apartment empty. Jason moved back home nearly a year ago. After all that work, and so much money you spent to fix it."

"I've been using it for storage. And you just said it was too small a few minutes ago. *"Mama! Mi fa la testa cosi!"*

She waved one hand in the air to dismiss his frustration. "Come, George. Come meet our family. Especially now that you are my son's tenant." She rested her hand on George's forearm and guided her back into the living room.

"Mama, I've already introduced them," Bob muttered, following behind.

His mother ignored him, and continued walking. When they arrived in the living room, he saw that his other sisters had shown up while he was in the kitchen. She stopped in front of the couch where Gene and Tony were sitting, and guided George to stand beside her. Bob shuffled to stand on George's other side while the introductions were repeated.

"George, this is my oldest son, Eugenio."

Bob leaned down to the height of George's ear, knowing his brothers could see what he was doing, but his mother could not. "Pst. He prefers 'Gene,'" Bob whispered, then straightened.

"And his wife, Michelle. Over here, this is Antonio."

Bob leaned to her ear again. "Pst. Tony."

"And his wife, Kathy. Here is one of my daughters, Rosabella."

"Rose."

"This is Maria."

"We couldn't shorten that one."

"This is my youngest child, Giovannetta."

"Gina," Bob whispered.

His mother leaned forward around George and glared up at Bob, obviously fully aware of what he'd been doing. "And of course you know my third son, Roberto," she said, rolling the *R*s, which she always did when she wanted to make a point or remind him of his heritage.

Bob stepped forward, grinned, pointedly cleared his throat and pounded his fist into his chest. "Me, Bob," he said, deepening his voice.

His mother picked up a section of the newspaper from the coffee table, and whacked him lightly on the head. "Respect your Mama. Your birth certificate, it says *Roberto.*"

George grinned.

"Don't you dare take her side," Bob grumbled.

"Enough of this. It is time to eat."

Everyone filed into the kitchen and sat at the table while his mother and Rose set the food on the table. The room went silent while Gene said a short prayer over the food. At his closing *Amen,* everything erupted into the usual Delanio family get-together. At least three conversations were going on at the same time, with everyone involved in more than one. Rose and Tony started arguing about something Bob knew nothing about, and even Michelle started waving her arms in the air as she spoke to Gina about future party details.

Through it all, George was silent. She listened politely and responded when someone spoke to her, but she added nothing to the myriad conversations around her unless addressed directly. With friendly bickering, they agreed on enough details to begin planning the party.

After an hour, the timer on the oven began dinging.

"You must all go, except for Eugenio and Michelle. Your father will be returning soon with little Eddie after their fishing trip. He must not become suspicious. But we have a little time yet, George, would you like to come with me? I would like you to see some things."

"Of course, Mrs. Delanio."

Bob stood to accompany them, but his mother waved one hand in the air, halting him in his tracks. "Roberto, I need you to go to the garage and bring me four boxes. Hurry. Big boxes. Like this." She motioned the size with her hands, and he knew he was dismissed.

Bob sighed and went to the garage. His father regularly flattened boxes, *every* box they'd ever received, and stored them in the garage. For more years than he could remember, the entire neighborhood came to his mother when someone needed a box, and she always had just the right one, which of course, only made her worse.

By the time he returned, fifteen minutes later, he found a pile of miscellaneous household items piled at the back door.

"What's going on?"

"These things are for George. They are extra. I do not need them. Hurry and pack them into the boxes and carry them to your car before your father gets home."

"If this isn't going to be okay with Papa, then I think we should wait."

"Your papa will not even notice."

He scanned the pile. "This is a lot of stuff." But the more he thought about it, he thought that probably his father would be pleased to see it gone if he knew, as it lessened the volume of "valuable" things his mother stored in the basement.

"Hurry! Pack these things and go. Eugenio and Michelle are cleaning the mess in the kitchen, and I must help."

Before he could say anything more, his mother was gone. "I give up," he muttered.

Beside him, George giggled as she hurriedly began ramming things into the boxes. "I like your mother. I hope she manages to pull this birthday party off without your father finding out."

"If she doesn't, he'll still pretend to be surprised. He'd never do anything to hurt her feelings."

Bob picked up an old toaster he remembered using as a child. "I remember when this broke. Papa fixed it, but Mama had already bought a new one and used it, so she couldn't take it back. It's just like her to keep it all these years, just in case."

"Yes. She told me about that toaster. I'm just so stunned that she's given me all these things." She held up a towel. "Look at this! It's so soft! I can't believe she wasn't using it. She said she didn't like the color."

"Mama may seem pushy at times, but she has a good heart."

"Yes. She seems very sweet, and I love listening to her accent. Does your father have an accent, too? You don't."

"My parents immigrated right after they were married. In order to preserve the language, we always spoke Italian at home, and English when we were in school or out with others. We stopped speaking Italian as frequently when Gene married

Michelle, because we didn't want to be rude when she couldn't understand us."

"So you speak Italian fluently?"

"Yes, but I don't use it as much as I used to."

"You said something in Italian when we were in the kitchen. What did you say?"

Bob blushed. "*Mi fa la testa cosi.* It's just an expression of frustration."

"But what does it mean? It sounded so regal."

"It's not. It means 'you're going to make my head explode.' Mama sometimes does that to me."

George started to laugh. The heat in Bob's face extended to his neck.

"That's so funny! What a way to put it."

"It's just an expression. You can't translate these things literally. Now come on, we have to hurry if you want to unpack and still have time to eat supper before we have to leave for the evening service."

Chapter Twelve

Georgette smiled broadly as she closed the cupboard door. All of the cooking utensils and supplementary things Bob's mother had given her were put away properly, including a few miscellaneous kitchen items whose purpose was still murky. The one thing she definitely knew how to use—a coffeemaker with a mismatched pot, was washed and sitting on the counter, ready for its first use—when she could finally buy some coffee.

Bob's mother had been so thorough that Georgette's remaining list of things to buy was now short and affordable. Exactly as promised, first thing that morning at work, Bob had given her an advance on her paycheck, which would be enough to buy the critical items on the list and enough groceries to last her until payday. She could still drive to work too, if that was the only place she went.

She even had a phone to use. Bob had given her one of the phones from his house, and pointed out a phone jack in the wall that was connected to his own line at his house. Not that anyone she knew would call her. Listening to Bob's private phone ringing felt odd to her, but he had wanted her to have a phone available in case of an emergency.

A knock sounded. Georgette grabbed her purse with a light heart. The only other time she'd felt so free was the day she got her job.

She opened the door and stepped outside. "I really appreciate you taking me shopping. I never really thought of how long your days are. You start before I do in the morning, then you close up more than an hour and a half after I'm gone. I see what your mother said about you working too much."

He sighed. "My mother means well, but sometimes she gets carried away."

Georgette tried to stop the wistful feeling that sneaked up on her. "Your mother seems like a wonderful person, and I'm sure she's only doing it because she loves you. I miss that."

Bob stopped walking. "I'm sorry, George, I didn't think. Don't get me wrong, I love Mama, and there isn't anything I wouldn't do for her. But when she has a point to make, nothing stops her from making it. I know I work too much. In fact, today Bart and I decided to cut back our hours.

We're finally at a point where we're able to keep everything current. Starting tomorrow, I'll go home at the same time as you. Bart will arrive later, the same time as you, and he'll stay to close up at six. We even talked about each taking a day off midweek in addition to Sunday, because we both need to be here Saturdays; it's our busiest day. It hasn't been easy for us, but I think we can finally cut back to both of us working five days instead of six, and the business won't suffer."

Georgette smiled. In her own way, Bob's mother had made her point and got what she wanted, which was the best for her children. One day, Georgette wanted to be that kind of mother, only she hoped she could make her point a little more delicately.

She looked up at Bob, whose face had softened while he thought of his mother. Before Georgette thought of being a mother, according to God's direction, a husband came first. She wondered what it would be like to be married to Bob. He was a considerate and generous man, a good son, and he would make a good father as well as a good husband. He respected his mother, regardless of her quirks.

Georgette shook her head. As much as she liked him, she could never forget that he was her boss—as he often reminded her.

Georgette forced her thoughts back to that working relationship. "What day do you think you'll take off?"

"Neither of us can take Monday because it's always really busy. Bart wants to be off Tuesday, so I'll take Thursday off. That way the shop won't be one person short two days in a row." He smiled and stared off into space. "It's been so long since I've taken more than one day off in a week. I've never even had a vacation in all the time we've been running the business."

Georgette couldn't imagine that. As busy as her father was, he always traveled twice a year, once in peak summer vacation season, and someplace exotic in February. "That sounds great. What do you think you're going to do?"

"I don't know. First I might catch up on a little sleep." He turned and grinned at her. "I certainly don't sleep in on Sunday morning. If I take Thursday off, I'll finally have some time to practice drums on my own during the daytime, when my neighbors aren't home. I think I might spend a little money and buy a spare drum set to keep at home. You have no idea how much work it is to lug a drum set back and forth every week between home, the church and Adrian's house. I don't want to move them any more than I have to."

"Or maybe you can buy one of those small electronic sets, with headphones to practice at home."

His grin widened. "Yeah. That's a great idea."

She wondered if one day, Bob's neighbors would thank her. The smile didn't leave Bob's face as he drove them to the big supermarket.

Once inside, she tried not to gape at the scope of the building. She stared up to the open ceiling and its metal rafters in which birds could nest without anyone being the wiser.

"George? What are you looking at? We should get moving. It's getting late."

She caught up with Bob, who was pushing one buggy for the two of them, since he only needed a couple of small items.

"How do you find what you need in a place like this?" The place had dozens of aisles that seemed to go on for miles.

One eyebrow quirked. "You learn the layout. I know where everything is, at least the things I buy. I guess this is bigger than what you're used to."

"You've got that right. We had groceries delivered."

Their first stop was the bakery aisle. She put a couple of loaves of bread in the buggy, along with a package of muffins that looked good, before she remembered that she had to make every purchase count.

She put the muffins back.

The next stop was the meat counter.

She stood, staring at the packages of…raw meat. Her stomach churned when she looked at a huge ugly mass labeled Beef Tongue.

"Not over there, George. Over here they sell single portions. It's a little more expensive per pound, but this way you don't waste anything and you don't have enough fridge space for more. Those pork chops look good." He picked up a package, and handed it to her. "What do you think?"

Georgette took in a few deep breaths to help force the picture of the mutilated cow parts out of her head, then turned the package over. "There aren't any directions."

"You don't need directions. It's just a plain pork chop. You fry it."

"Is that hard?"

Bob's mouth opened, but no sound came out.

"I don't think you understand. I've never done this before."

"You've never cooked a pork chop?"

"Not only have I never cooked a pork chop, I've never cooked anything. I've certainly never bought raw food."

Bob shook his head. "I don't understand. I've seen you bring some wonderful homemade things for lunch. Stroganoff. Chowders." His eyes brightened, and he smiled. "Lasagna. You even brought an extra piece for me. It was delicious."

"Josephine made all those things for me. She took care of all the meals and groceries. Besides, my father would never let me do anything so mundane as food shopping."

She held out the pork chop for him to put back. "I wouldn't be able to use this."

"Then what do you know how to cook?"

"I know how to make macaroni and cheese in the microwave."

Bob shook his head. "There's no room for a microwave in that apartment. You'd have to make your macaroni in a pot."

"You can make macaroni in a pot?"

Bob lowered his head and pinched the bridge of his nose. He mumbled something in Italian that she wasn't sure she wanted translated.

"I told you. If it's not something I've gotten at our deli or from Josephine, I don't know how to do it."

"You can make a sandwich, I hope? You know. Two pieces of bread, condiments, meat and maybe some lettuce and cheese?"

She couldn't tell if he was being sarcastic. All she knew was that people were starting to stare.

"Can we go someplace else to talk about this?"

He waved one hand in the air, the hand that held the packaged pork chop. "There is no place else to talk! This is the supermarket! Where people go to buy food! Which is what we're supposed to be doing!"

She lowered her voice. "You're shouting."

The volume of his voice lowered, but it was still tight. "What did you think you were going to buy here?"

"Besides the things on the list you said I had to buy, I need coffee. Maybe some cans of soup. I could probably do that without a microwave, too, couldn't I?"

"How did you think you were going to live on your own if you can't cook?"

"I never thought about it. No one really gave me the chance to learn, and now I don't have much choice. I'll figure it out." She extended her hand. "So give me back that pork chop."

Bob sighed, but instead of handing her the pork chop, he tossed it into the buggy, along with another one for himself. "I should have figured something was amiss when you didn't know what that chopping board my mother gave you was for. I can get you started with a few basic techniques. I certainly can't let you starve to death."

"Maybe cooking will turn out to be a hidden talent for me."

"Talented or not, you've got to eat. We'd better get moving. We have to get everything you need and be out of here before they close for the night."

Bob shuffled the bags he was carrying to balance on one arm, knocked on the door of the garage apartment, and waited.

He hadn't made it out the door at work as early as he'd hoped. Today he had promised George he would show her how to cook her own supper, which was supposed to be the pork chop they'd bought last night. With her questionable level of domestic ability, he feared for their safety if she were to start cooking without him.

The door opened.

"Sorry I'm so late, I..." Bob's voice trailed off as he looked at George's face. "You've been crying." He dumped everything he'd been carrying onto the futon, and grasped her hands. "Did you burn yourself? Are you okay?"

He turned and looked at the table, which was set for two. A pot and a frying pan were on the stove, empty and unused. It wasn't injury.

"What's wrong?" he asked, not releasing her.

"I've been thinking about my sister, Terri," she sniffled. "I tried to call her, but she wasn't home and now I can't stop thinking about her. I went to her house first when Daddy kicked me out, before

I showed up at the shop. Her husband Byron was there, but he wouldn't let me in. I need to talk to her. Just in case I'm wrong. Or maybe just in case I'm right."

"I'm afraid I'm not following you."

George gulped. "I think another woman was there, that night and I want to talk to Terri about it, because if I'm right, this is something she should know. Everyone would tell me to mind my own business, probably her too, but I can't. I've picked up the phone a hundred times today. Then, when I finally got the nerve to finish dialing the number, Byron answered, and I hung up without saying anything. I'm such a coward." A tear rolled down her cheek.

Bob's gut clenched. He'd heard comments about watching a woman cry from his brothers and his friends. Joking aside, his stomach really did feel strange. He wanted to hold George and soothe away the tears, but he wasn't in a position to do that. Even though they were going to be spending a lot of time in each other's personal space while he helped her get back on her feet, he certainly didn't want to get in any deeper by getting involved with her family. The woman needed some privacy.

He ran his thumbs gently over the insides of her wrists, and she sniffled again. The lump in his stomach turned to a rock.

It might have made sense before, but his position made him feel like a hypocrite. His own family had pretty much adopted George in just one visit. After their lunch with his mother and siblings, Gene had called and asked if Bob was bringing her to his father's birthday party, since she'd already heard most of the preliminary plans. He only hung up for about ten seconds before his mother had called, offering to teach George how to make his favorite three-cheese lasagna. He didn't want to go there.

But he couldn't stand the thought of George facing her sister's marital problems without anyone to stand by her. With his large family, he'd never had to face a problem alone, unless he wanted to. He also had always had the support of his best friend Randy, as well as Paul and Adrian, and, of course, his partner, Bart.

Even though he'd lived by himself for over five years, Bob had never felt alone.

He didn't know what he could do, but if George tried to handle this herself, he felt as if he'd be sending her alone to face the wolves.

"Is there something I can do?"

"No. I don't even know if there's anything I can do." She cleared her throat. "I really think Byron is cheating on Terri, and I think she should be told. I don't even care if she hates me for saying something, which she probably will. But I can't say nothing. That's not the way God wanted marriage to be."

"Then I think you're right, you should talk to her."

"I want to, but I don't know what to say. Do I just knock on her door and say 'Hi, Terri, how's it going? By the way I think your husband is having an affair?' I don't know if I can do that. Besides, if I see Byron, I think I might just fall to pieces."

"I think you're stronger than that."

She said nothing. All she did was stare up at him.

He knew that her parents had separated when she was a child. Now with her sister's husband having an affair, Bob suspected that George had never seen the workings of a good marriage. On the other hand, Bob's parents had been wonderful examples. They were approaching their fortieth year together. When an issue came between them, they were often loud, but they always followed God's direction and worked it out.

One day, George would have someone to stand beside her, but for now, all she had was him.

"How about if I go with you?"

"Would you do that?"

"I wouldn't have asked if I didn't mean it."

"When?"

He turned to look at the pile of stuff he'd come with, strewn on the futon. He couldn't believe how much his life had changed in only a few days. He didn't want to deal with any more on an empty stomach. "After supper would probably be good."

She pulled her hands out of his, and swiped her eyes. "Of course. I'm so sorry. If it helps, I'm ready to start as soon as you are."

"For the first meal, I thought we could do something really simple and just fry the pork chops and have mashed potatoes. Let's start."

Bob showed her how to peel one potato, then he let her do the second one. He passed on his mother's instructions to use only enough water to barely cover any vegetable, including potatoes, and moved on to preparing the pork chops. He used the cooking spray he'd brought on the frying pan, and when the pork chops were sizzling, he spread on some of his barbecue sauce. He showed her how to slice into the chops to see if they were done, then had George heat up a can of corn, and their supper was ready.

He knew his mother liked to put everything in separate bowls and set them on the table when serving more than one, but Bob only thought of having to wash more dishes. He placed the food directly and set the plates on the table.

"This is it. Let's eat."

George checked her wristwatch. "That took an awful long time for just one allegedly simple supper. Isn't there any way of doing it faster?"

"I'm afraid not. This is nothing. There are some things my mother cooks that take hours to prepare." He grinned as he thought of mealtimes when she served pasta asciutta, another family favorite. "Takes us only ten minutes to eat, though."

George planted her fists on her hips. "That doesn't seem worth it."

He shrugged his shoulders. "That's life. A person's gotta eat. Might as well make it good."

As hostess, George said the blessing. When she thanked God for his presence in her life, and then said what a blessing he'd been to her, Bob could barely choke out an answering *"Amen."*

"Do you think I'll be able to do this by myself?" she asked after taking a few mouthfuls.

"I don't see why not."

"I guess I'll have to buy some sauce and stuff, won't I?"

He nodded. "Yes. But remember, that was only your first grocery shopping trip, only for the barest of basics. Next time, you'll have more money to spend."

They didn't rush but they finished quickly. Perhaps George had been as hungry as he was, but it was probably the errand looming over both of them, and without much more fussing around, they left to face Terri.

Chapter Thirteen

Bob followed George's directions to her sister's house, which was, as he had expected, in an area of the city where he could never afford to live. It made him embarrassed that his renovated garage was the best he could offer George, and his house wasn't much better than his garage.

He followed George to the door and stood to the side when she knocked. A woman who was unquestionably George's sister answered. Terri was taller than George, and her figure much more womanly, although he suspected her attributes were surgically enhanced. Still, George's blue eyes stared at him out of that heavily made-up face.

"Georgette? What are you doing here?" Terri glanced at Bob, then back to her sister.

"I need to talk to you. Is Byron home?"

Terri glanced to the street, then back to Bob. "No, but he shouldn't be too much longer."

"What I have to say won't take long. May we come in?"

"I suppose."

The second he was inside, Bob wanted to turn back and leave. White carpeting throughout, was the crowning glory of a pristine decor that shouted adults only. The uncomfortably sterile atmosphere also reminded him that he hadn't yet showered after a long day at the shop.

"To say I'm surprised to see you would be an understatement. Daddy told me that you ran away with some guy he didn't know. I'm assuming that's *you*." She spared Bob a rude glance before continuing. "He's been very upset. He told me that Tyler was going to ask you to marry him, but you left the banquet early, and when he got home all your things were gone. Where did you go? "Have you eloped? Daddy is very, very angry with you. You know how he's always wanted you to have a big wedding like mine."

Bob squirmed, not knowing if he should tell George's sister what had really happened, or if he should keep silent.

George stared down at the floor and cleared her throat. "No, I didn't elope, and that's not exactly the way it went. But I'm not here to talk about me. I'm here to talk about you."

Terri's eyes widened. "Me? Whatever for?"

"Terri, are you happy?"

She backed up a step. "Of course I'm happy."

"What about Byron?"

"Byron is fine."

"But does he love you? Do you love him?"

Terri stiffened. "I think maybe you should leave."

George shook her head. "I can't leave until I say what I came to tell you. Terri, I came here on Friday night, and you weren't home, but Byron was. I could be mistaken, but I think he had another woman here."

Terri's face paled. "You mean he had *her* here?"

George's face paled as well. "You mean you already knew?"

"Did anyone see her besides you? I told him not to bring her here."

Bob stood stunned, unable to believe what he was hearing.

"I don't understand. Aren't you going to do something about this?" Georgette asked her sister.

Terri blinked and stared George in the eye. "I'm going to tell him not to embarrass me, and to keep her away from our house."

Bob knew George's sister and brother-in-law

weren't Christians, but that was no reason to accept infidelity in a marriage. He could no longer keep silent. "Excuse me, but are you going to counseling about this? There are things you can do."

She turned and stared at him. "This is none of your business. You two aren't even married."

Bob opened his mouth, but no sound came out. He wanted to say he was George's boss, but his reason for being there had nothing to do George's job. He was there because he wanted to help her and be there for her when she needed him. And that was wrong. He was supposed to be pulling back, not getting more entrenched in her personal life. George didn't need that complication and neither did he.

The most effective thing to say was that he was a friend, but he didn't want to go there. He couldn't cross that line.

"I'm Bob," he said, hoping he didn't have to clarify it with more, and felt George's fingers intertwining with his.

Terri stared down at their joined hands, and then turned back to George. "Don't lecture me about right and wrong. I can't believe you ran away with someone Daddy didn't even know." She sniffed the air, telling Bob that what he suspected was true. Even though he always wore coveralls over his clothes all day, he still smelled like a grease pit. "Daddy doesn't approve of this at all."

"Daddy and I don't follow the same standards. He approves of things I would never do."

"And running off isn't wrong? What does your God say about what you did to Daddy?"

Since their arms were touching, he could feel more than hear George's quick intake of breath.

Bob gave her hand a gentle squeeze. He lowered his voice, trying to sound gentle, even though he could feel his anger building inside. "She didn't exactly run away. Your father kicked her out."

Terri stared at George, and backed up another step. "If Daddy kicked you out, then I don't want you here, either. And how dare you lecture me about what's right and wrong and all that religious nonsense, particularly with *him* here." She waved one hand in the air in Bob's direction.

Bob continued speaking, even though Terri wasn't looking at him. "We're not living together, and we're certainly not doing anything wrong. But we didn't come here to talk about us. We came to talk about you. You don't have to live like that. Fidelity in marriage is something everyone deserves. If you want, I can recommend a counselor."

Terri stepped around them, and opened the door. "I'm fine the way things are. It's time for you to leave. If you hurry and Byron doesn't see you, I won't tell Daddy you've been here."

"But..." George stammered.

"Get out."

Bob knew no progress would be made by arguing. It was time for Terri to mull over what they said. Maybe one day she would take him up on his offer of counseling, but that day wasn't today.

They left quietly, and not a word was said the entire drive home.

When Bob reached to turn off the motor he turned to George, but remained seated in the car. "You did your best. All you can do now is wait, pray for her, and hope she calls you."

"I know."

They left the car, and he walked George to the door of the garage apartment.

She unlocked the door, but instead of pushing it open, she turned to him. "Not that I didn't appreciate you going with me, because I know I would have fallen apart without you there, but I need to know why you came. Are you doing this because you feel sorry for me?"

Bob gazed into her wide eyes as he ran through a mental list of everything that had happened since he'd met George. Of course he felt bad that her family was rejecting her, but she'd acted honorably. He was proud of her for giving Terri that bad news. But he wasn't helping her because he felt sorry for her.

She was efficient and capable, and she just needed a little help to get over the hump. George always accomplished what she set out to do, even if it was the hard way. She'd earned the respect of his customers, and likewise, by her hard work and dedication, she'd also earned his respect.

Yet Bob wasn't at peace with what was happening between them. He couldn't help it, but he sometimes felt twinges of jealousy because of the privileges she'd grown up with and taken for granted—things he would never know. Nothing had ever been out of her budget. She'd told him she had had all the latest and the greatest stuff, including a state-of-the-art computer and big-screen television, two things he really wanted but couldn't afford. She could have gone to the best university, if she had chosen her courses from her father's selected list. She'd always had the best clothes, any car in the world she wanted, and had lived in a home bigger than anything he could ever dream of with an indoor pool, sauna, and a private tennis court. She didn't merely play tennis, she'd taken private lessons on her own court.

The men she dated also had always known the same privileged life. Only in the last few years had Bob not had to worry about budgeting in the price of dinner and a movie if he wanted to take a woman out—if he could even take the time for a date from his work schedule.

Now, finally, he was able to work only five days a week. Still, he had to work, and he had to work hard in order to survive.

Until now, George hadn't had to work if she didn't want to. She could have lived a life of leisure, and it wouldn't have been wrong.

And now, all that was gone.

But as to her question, no, he didn't feel sorry for her. Still, he knew it wasn't smart to have gone with her, given what his presence with her implied to Terri especially when Georgette had grabbed his hand. She came from another world, a world where he was considered little more than the hired help. In hindsight, he supposed, her culture and refinement had been evident from the day he had hired her, in everything she said and did.

That a person like him could be the employer of a person like her was what he would have called one of life's cruel jokes. If the same thing had happened to someone else, Bob might even have considered it funny.

But Bob wasn't laughing.

Learning to make do with a modest income was something George had never had to do. For now, having to work and save money to get what she wanted, or even the necessities of daily life, was a novelty. Very soon, that would wear off and she would experience the frustration that came when sometimes, no matter how hard a person worked for something they wanted, the answer was still no.

He'd lived with a lot of no's in his life, and he knew how difficult it could be. He couldn't deal with the hurt and disappointment when he was unable to live up to her expectations. He certainly didn't want her to live down to his. Falling in love with someone from the other side of the tracks only worked in fairy tales.

"I don't feel sorry for you. You're my employee and you need help, so I'm here. I'll see you tomorrow, at work. Good night."

Georgette cut the last piece of meat, then picked up the cutting board to scrape the pieces into the pan in with a knife.

She shuddered as she picked up a slimy hunk that had fallen onto the counter, and tossed it in with the rest of the raw meat. "This is so disgusting," she muttered, then immediately went to the sink to wash her hands with the dish soap. The only thing that made her feel any better was the aroma of the meat frying as it started to cook.

"It's just stewing beef, George. It's the same as any other piece of beef."

She dried her hands on the dishtowel, then turned to Bob. "I didn't have to hack at the steak yesterday. I only had to make a few slices in it, pour that brown sauce on it, and let it sit."

He sighed, and she immediately felt ashamed of herself for her outburst. "We were marinating a less tender cut of meat. Today we have meat that needs more work. If you simmer it for a couple of hours, it will just melt in your mouth. Otherwise, it will be tough. These are things you have to do when you're living on a budget. You can't eat New York Cut steaks every day any more."

A wave of guilt washed through her. "I'm sorry. I know you're sacrificing your time to show me how to do this, and I really appreciate it. It's just that I never thought handling raw food would be like this. It's..." She shuddered again. "Not exactly pleasant."

Bob snickered and then his smile straightened with a visible effort, although Georgette could still see the corners of his mouth twitching. "Maybe tomorrow I should show you how to stuff and roast a chicken. There's nothing to cut when you roast a chicken."

He spoke with a straight face, but his lower lip wouldn't stop quivering.

Georgette narrowed one eye. "Is that hard?"

"No."

"Is there a catch?"

"Maybe."

Both eyes narrowed. "What?"

"You don't have to do anything from the outside, but when you buy a chicken, there's a bag inside the cavity, you know, the hollow part where the guts were."

Her stomach churned. "I'm not sure I understand. Why would there be a bag?"

"They save the heart and liver, and put them in a bag, and put the bag in the cavity. You have to take it out before you cook the chicken."

If she didn't feel sick enough thinking about it before, the queasy sensation quadrupled at the thought of reaching inside a disemboweled animal and touching the internal organs. "If they're in a bag, then I don't have to look. I don't have to reach inside, do I? Can't I just shake the chicken, and everything will drop right into the garbage can and I don't have to watch?"

"You don't want to waste it. Mama cooks the liver and chops it up then she adds bread, onions, celery and spices to make the best stuffing you've ever tasted in your life."

Georgette held back her comments and turned her attention to the small counter and the table, both strewn with dishes and utensils. A pile of potatoes and vegetables lay on the counter, which she would cut up and throw in later, after the meat had cooked for a while. "I had no idea this was going to be so much work, and look at the mess already! Do you go through all this every day, when you're cooking for yourself?"

Bob pressed both palms over his stomach, which was quite tight and flat, and grinned. "I love to eat, so unless I go home to Mama every day, that means I have to cook. But I will tell you a secret. When I make a chicken, I do exactly just what you were saying. I throw the innards out, and use the instant stuffing you buy in a box and make it in a pot. I don't mind cooking, but usually I don't make anything fancy and I like to have left-overs. Now, my brother, Tony, he loves to cook even more than he loves to eat. He can cook as good as Mama, even better on some things. But don't ever tell her I said that."

"Tony owns and operates a restaurant, doesn't he?"

"Yes. God has really blessed our family. Tony loves to work with food as much as I love to work with motors. We've each managed to run a business doing what we love the most. God really opened the doors for both of us."

Georgette wasn't sure she agreed. Over time, she'd seen how hard Bob worked, and she knew the long hours he put in. He also hadn't always run a good profit margin. God had certainly made it possible, but He hadn't made it easy.

She didn't understand why men like her father had it easy, when good men like Bob didn't. Her grandfather had passed the chain of stores on to her father, so her father didn't have to put his heart and soul into building the business; it was already very successful when he took over. That hadn't stopped him from doing many things she considered questionable, if not downright unethical to increase his profits.

Bob, on the other hand, sometimes barely broke even in a transaction, simply because he honored his estimates, even if the situation wasn't in his favor.

Lately she'd been finding that when she came home from work, she missed him, especially now that she had reminders of him everywhere. She heard the minute he came home, because he parked his car on the cement pad next to the garage. Today, she had stopped what she was doing and listened to him as he cut the engine and walked past the garage to get to his house.

Her heart pounded sharply until he showed up back at her door, ready to demonstrate the meal of the day.

It was foolishness. He had been more than obvious in his professional feelings, yet she couldn't help but compare Bob favorably to every other man she'd ever known. Despite the privations of his youth, Bob was satisfied with his life. He was who he was, and that was a nice, honest man who put God and his family first in his life. It made him easy to love, and one day, when he decided to settle down and get married, he would make a good husband to a very fortunate woman.

A twinge of jealousy for a woman who didn't exist yet flashed through Georgette's mind.

Bob walked to the fridge, opened it, and began rummaging through the meager contents. "Now is the time for you to put in an onion. I know we bought some."

She couldn't help but watch him. Bob was physically fit because he worked hard all day, but she didn't often see him without his baggy coveralls. Up until now, his coking lessons had kept her running around too much to notice, but at this moment she had nothing else to do but watch.

Georgette blinked, and forced herself to get her mind back on cooking, and away from how good Bob looked, especially from the back. "I think they're on the second shelf, behind the yogurt."

He reached in further, then backed up, an onion in his hand. "You're supposed to put the onions in the bin marked for vegetables."

"But I didn't want the carrots to smell like onions."

"Don't worry, that won't happen. Although, you should have kept the onions in the bag."

"Really? But they weren't in a bag in the store, so I thought you weren't supposed to keep them in the bag at home."

He shook his head. "Nope. It's best left in the bag. Now it's time to cut it up and put it in with the meat as it cooks."

She accepted the onion, and searched in the drawer for her one and only chef's knife, which had been given to her by Bob's mother. "Is it true what they say about onions, that they make you cry? I've never dealt with one raw."

"Then you're in for a bit of an education, George."

She had received more education in the last three days than she'd had in the last three years, but Georgette held her tongue.

He stepped closer when she placed the onion on the cutting board. "There are a number of old wives' tales about cutting an onion, but I think it's just best to do it quickly. First cut the ends off, peel it and then cut it up into bite-sized pieces."

Georgette did as instructed, and soon she had half the onion cut. At first, the strong smell was just annoying, but the more she cut, the worse it became, and soon, her eyes were burning and watering.

She looked up at Bob and smiled. "I see what everyone means."

"You'd better stop talking and hurry up. I don't want to end up like you!" As if to emphasize his point, he chuckled and stepped back.

"Coward," she sniffled. "This isn't so bad. It burns, but I can take it." Except that her nose was getting increasingly stuffed-up, and her eyes were overflowing. She cut a little more, and the burn worsened, making her want to close her eyes, which she couldn't do if she was going to finish cutting up the onion. The tears became more irritating as they dribbled down her cheeks.

She sniffled again, and raised one hand to swipe away the tears.

"No! George! Don't wipe your eyes with your..."

Using the back of her hand, she rubbed over her left eye.

"...hands..."

"Ow! Ow!" The sensation changed from a burn to a stab of pain. Her eyes squeezed shut of their own accord, and she dropped the knife to raise her hands, but stopped them in midair, trying to overcome the urge to rub her eyes. "I can't see! It hurts!"

A warmth enclosed both wrists. "Come to the sink. Quickly."

She followed Bob as he dragged her to the sink. He enclosed both wrists with one hand, and the water started running. She heard splashing, and he pulled both her hands under the water. "Bend down so your face is over the sink. Keep your hands under the water." He released her wrists, and one wet hand pressed into the back of her head. A gush of warm water splashed over her eyes, followed by another. "Try to open your eyes now."

She managed to open both, but the left eye wouldn't open more than a slit.

"Keep them open."

Before she could respond, a couple more splashes of water hit her.

"That helped," she sputtered, spitting out some water that had splashed into her mouth before she straightened.

"Good. Now wash your hands with dish soap, and you'll be able to finish what you were doing."

She dribbled some soap onto her hands, rinsed them and returned to the chopping board with the half-processed onion. Working quickly, she swiped the cut pieces into the pot and swiped the remainder of the onion into the garbage. "Forget it. That's enough. I don't need so much onion anyway."

"That's cheating."

"Too bad," she muttered as she ran water over the chopping board and knife, standing back as far as she could while doing so. When the board was sufficiently rinsed, she knew she should turn around, but she didn't want to. Without looking, she knew her eyes were red and puffy, her face was streaked and blotchy, and she would have unsightly splashes of water down the front of her T-shirt.

She'd never looked so bad in her life, not even on the day her father had kicked her out of the house.

It shouldn't have mattered, but she'd already lost everything; all she had left was her appearance, as silly as that might seem. The harshness of her new reality smacked her between the eyes. How ridiculous to be brought so low by a lowly onion, but there it was. She stood before Bob rejected by her family, homeless and ugly.

She didn't understand why everything was happening to her this way. She hadn't led a bad life, even before she became a Christian, yet God allowed everything to be stripped painfully away.

She turned around, only because she couldn't keep her back to him all night.

Bob lifted his wrist and checked his watch. "I think you have everything under control now. I have to go, I'm already late for practice. Cut up the carrots and celery and throw them in, then in an hour, cut up the potatoes and add them, too. When the potatoes are cooked, you'll have made your very first batch of beef stew."

"But there's so much here. Will you be back in time to help me eat it?"

"Sorry. Worship team practice won't be over in time. I'm going to grab something quick on the way to Adrian's. We were supposed to start early tonight because Paul has to be at the school afterwards for some kind of competition." He began walking to the door, hesitated, then turned around. "I feel so strange. I almost said that I have to get up early in the morning, too, but I don't." He grinned from ear to ear. "I get to sleep in."

"I hope the noise of my truck starting in the morning won't wake you up."

"Don't worry, it won't. By the way, when I was talking to Adrian earlier today he said he's going to have some time to stop by and go over the books with you tomorrow, to get a start on what he needs for our corporate taxes. I think you'll be fine without me, so I told him it was okay." He checked his watch again. "You'll have enough leftovers here to last you through supper tomorrow, so I guess I'll just see you Friday at work. Bye."

Chapter Fourteen

Bob missed his timing with the cymbal, then hit the lower tom harder than he should have. Completely losing the beat, he paused, intending to listen to everyone else and regain his bearings. Instead, without him keeping tempo, the music ground to a slow and painful halt.

Paul shifted his bass guitar so he wouldn't hit Adrian with it as he turned, and stepped toward Bob. "Is something wrong? You've been having trouble keeping it together all night."

"Nothing's wrong," Bob muttered. "I just have a lot on my mind."

Adrian turned around to face him. "I hope it doesn't have anything to do with tomorrow. If you're not ready, I can do it another day."

Bob shook his head. "It's not that. In fact, I'm not even going to be there. George has been doing a really good job. The bookkeeping is as ready as it's ever going to be."

"You mean you won't be there? Where are you going to be?"

"I don't know yet."

All of his friends turned and stared at him.

Randy left the sound board, walked right up to him, and stared him in the face, not breaking eye contact as he spoke. "You mean you're taking a day off? Midweek? And you don't have specific plans? Is everything okay?"

Bob cleared his throat. "Things have never been better. That's one of the reasons Bart and I hired George in the first place, so that we could work only five days like everybody else. Now that we're finally at that point, I have to admit I don't even know what I'm going to do with myself. What do you guys do when you have a day off?"

Adrian shrugged his shoulders. "I've never taken one off midweek. But if I did, I'd probably go to the library and get a new book to read. I'd practice learning something new on my guitar, too, probably."

Randy grinned. "I'd go shopping."

Bob turned to his best friend. "Are you nuts? You work at the mall. Don't you see enough of it during the week?"

"That's different. I don't get enough time to do

real shopping. Maybe instead I'd go online and play games with whoever else is on at the time."

Bob shook his head. "Computer games," he muttered. "Don't you think you're getting a little old for that? You really are crazy. What about you, Celeste?"

"I'd probably do the same as Adrian. Read. Practice my piano for a while. Play some of my favorite songs. Work on some new ones. Stuff like that."

"What about you, Paul?"

"I don't get days off one at a time. When the kids aren't in school, we have workshops and seminars to keep current with what's going on. If I were to have a few days together, like in the summer, I would go somewhere I've never been. See the sights."

Bob nodded. "Well, maybe I can come up with something. Let's finish up practicing these last couple of songs before it gets too late."

"This is great, much better than I expected," Adrian said to George. "Bob's transactions are usually so disorganized it takes me weeks to sort through them. You've got it all balanced, and it's reconciled, too."

George smiled up at him. "Thanks. I've worked hard to get it to this point. I finally got them to give me a written record of every transaction, including what they buy online. It's much easier to enter everything and balance it when I can follow a paper trail."

Adrian nodded. The last time he'd balanced Bob's books had been the worst. He hadn't been looking forward to it at all this time, but George had surprised him. "They really needed a professional bookkeeper. You've done a great job."

"Thanks. I do my best."

While George typed in the command to call up a journal of the payroll taxes that were due to be paid the next day, Adrian looked through the window into the shop, where Bart was working, all alone. "It's so strange to be here, and not see Bob."

"I know. But it's been something we've all been striving for."

"Yeah. Last night he was trying to think of what to do today. Do you have any idea what he decided?"

George shook her head, and hit the key to print the screen. "No. Last I talked to him, his only goal was to sleep in. I made sure I was really quiet when I left this morning, so I wouldn't wake him."

Adrian nearly dropped his pen onto the floor. "Wake him?" he sputtered.

"Yes. He's always gone before me. In fact, it's been kind of my cue to get up. He's like clockwork. I don't even need my alarm clock. I just get up and start getting ready when Bob starts his car.

It was just so strange today, trying to be quiet because I knew he wanted to sleep in, particularly since I really need to fix my muffler."

"Let's back up. What's going on?"

She sighed. "New things like the muffler keep coming up all the time—I just don't know where the money will come from. I know I need a new one, but Bob is teaching me how to prioritize my expenses. We figure if I let it warm up for only a minute, then the noise shouldn't annoy his neighbors too much. By the time the muffler blows completely, I should have saved enough money to fix it." She turned and grinned at him. "Bob said I only have to pay the wholesale cost on the parts, and I can do the work myself in the shop after hours, which will save me a lot of money. I should be able to get it done in a couple of weeks."

"I'm still not getting this. Annoy Bob's neighbors?"

"Yes. The muffler noise is annoying to any of the neighbors with windows open, or thin walls, for that matter."

Adrian stared at George, at a loss for words. Last night everyone had noticed Bob's strange behavior. They had all assumed Bob was obsessing about taking time off, and Adrian had thought it quite amusing, as did the others. Everyone had had their little laugh, brushed it off and moved on.

Apparently, they'd been wrong. There had been more going on than any of them could ever have guessed.

George walked to the printer and pulled out the printed sheet. "It sure is different than what I'm used to, actually depending on an older vehicle for transportation, rather than just playing around and fixing it up as a hobby."

Adrian raised his palms in the air. "You'll have to forgive my bluntness, but have you, uh..." Adrian stammered, trying to think of how to say what he wanted without sounding like he was making an accusation, when actually, he was.

He shook his head. "Forget it. I'll just come right out and ask. Have you moved in with him?"

George's face paled, which Adrian wasn't sure was a good sign. He didn't know her well enough to know if she was shocked by what he'd asked or by being caught.

"You mean he didn't tell everyone at practice last night?"

"Tell everyone what?"

George sighed. "I've been having some troubles with my family. I needed a place to stay, so Bob is letting me live in his garage apartment."

"Garage apartment?" Adrian crossed his arms over his chest while he gathered his thoughts. "Oh, that's right. That's where his cousin stayed.

Are you saying that you've moved into Bob's garage?"

Her cheeks darkened. "It's really quite a nice apartment. It's a little small, but the longer I'm there, the more I like it."

Adrian narrowed one eye while he studied George. Randy had cornered him after Paul, Bob and Celeste left. He had insisted that something was going on between Bob and his new mechanic. Adrian had brushed it off at the time, but it seemed as though, for once, one of Randy's crazy hunches was right. In hindsight, Bob really had been far too distracted to be thinking only about taking a simple day off work. If George had been having family problems, it was just like Bob to be concerned and try to figure out a solution.

George looked down to the floor. "Adrian, you've been friends with Bob for years, haven't you?"

He nodded. "Yes. We grew up together. All four of us have."

"So you know him pretty well, then?"

"Yes, I like to think so."

"He told me on Sunday he was going to tell everyone at practice that I had moved into his garage apartment. Yet now, I find out he didn't. Do you think he didn't say anything because he regrets letting me stay there?"

"No, I don't think so at all. Bob wouldn't have

made such an offer if he didn't mean it. But he kept zoning out on us all night, and now I know why. Bob works best when he can focus on one thing at a time and he's obviously got a lot to think about. That's how he built that business from nothing. One step at a time. It's just the way Bob is. Bob doesn't multitask. Randy, now there's a man who multitasks." Adrian shook his head.

"Pardon?"

He turned back to George. "None of us can figure out how Bob and Randy can be in the same room together sometimes. Randy can't function unless he's doing fifteen things at once. Bob grabs one thing at a time and worries at it like a dog with a bone, before moving on to the next thing. Yet they've been inseparable since we were kids."

"I don't think I know what you're trying to say."

"I'm not sure I can explain it. Bob is a very linear thinker. He's got to have something all figured out before he can talk about it. So while something *is* bothering him, it's probably not exactly you living in his garage. It's more." Adrian paused to think of Randy's suspicions. Randy had it figured out, but the more Adrian thought about it, the more he also thought that Bob hadn't figured it out yet.

Adrian bit back a grin. In the future, he'd have to give Randy more credit.

"Don't tell anyone I said this, *especially* not

Bob, but I think he likes you. I'm not the only one who thinks that, either. He likes you so much it's distracting him."

It was awhile before George finally spoke. "I don't think it's that. Bob is teaching me to cook, and he's helping me learn how to manage a budget and balance my checkbook. He's so good at showing me what to do, and how to do it. He's so patient, no matter how many mistakes I make."

"Remember Bob is the youngest boy in his family, so he knows what it's like to be the underdog. At the same time, his sisters are all younger and he helped care for them when they were little. Bob's got the ultimate middle-child syndrome."

George's eyes widened, but she didn't say anything.

The more Adrian thought about it, the more he could see why Bob was having difficulty making everything fit together. He would have to deal with George one way at work, and another way on their shared property. Again, it would be a different set of rules when he was in her home, or when she was in his.

"Do you have any advice for me?"

"I'm afraid I don't. All I know is what it was like for me, before Celeste and I were engaged. There were things I wish I'd known sooner, but I guess it all worked out. I like to be prepared, but life doesn't always work that way."

Georgette smiled. "See, there's some advice for me, after all."

Chapter Fifteen

"Bye, Bart!" Georgette called out. "See you tomorrow!"

"Bye, George!"

The entire trip home in her truck, Adrian's words echoed through Georgette's head. *I think he likes you.*

She couldn't help it, but she liked Bob too. Yet just as Bob needed time to think about what was happening, so did she. Above all, she had to be realistic. Bob was her boss, her landlord, her tutor, and recently he'd become somewhat of a spiritual mentor. She didn't want to think that he was acting like a big brother just because he had three younger sisters.

As she turned into Bob's back lane, she saw the garage door was open, displaying the storage area

Bob had built. Bob, wearing coveralls, stood on the pad, next to something she'd never seen him with before.

A big, big motorcycle.

Georgette drove up, parked her truck and approached Bob. "What in the world is that?"

"It's my baby. Isn't she a beauty?"

Georgette ran one hand over the chrome handlebars. She didn't know much about motorcycles, but she could tell it was old. "What year?"

"She's a 1949 Harley-Davidson Series F Hydra-Glide Solo, a real classic. It was the first year they introduced the hydraulic front forks." He paused to run his hands down the chrome plating of one of the forks. "She used to belong to my father, but he wasn't really interested in motorcycles, so he gave her to me when I got old enough to drive one responsibly. Of course, I had to get her running first."

"If he wasn't interested in motorcycles, what was he doing with it?"

"Someone gave it to him. A friend didn't have any money to pay for some work Papa did, so he bartered the motorcycle instead. It wasn't in very good condition, but Papa felt obligated to take it."

Georgette had a feeling that Bob had learned many of his kind ways from his father, whether they were good business practices or not. "It looks like you've done a good job fixing it up."

He ran one hand lovingly over the leather seat. "Thanks. It took me a long time to get her to look like this. I thought today would be a good day to take her out—with all the work I've been doing, I haven't been able to lately."

A slow grin began to spread on his face. "Do you want to go for a ride when I'm done?"

Georgette's heart pounded so hard, she thought Bob would be able to see the movement through her T-shirt. For years, it had been her secret fantasy to ride a motorcycle, but she didn't know anyone who owned one, nor did she have a motorcycle license.

She hugged her purse as she studied Bob's bike. The burgundy paint shone in the sunlight, and when she moved, the reflection of the sun off the polished chrome nearly blinded her. The motorcycle was big and proud, it would be noisy, and it would turn heads. The force of the wind would be exhilarating in the rush of the speed.

She steeled herself. "Have you got an extra helmet?"

"Of course." He pointed to two helmets, exactly the same color as the bike on one of the shelves in his storage area.

Her voice quivered as she spoke, and she couldn't stop it. "Need some help getting it in shape to go?"

He bent down, picked up a wrench and handed it to her. "Here you go."

They worked in silence for a few minutes, but it didn't take long before Georgette couldn't stand it anymore. "I didn't know you had a motorcycle. Why didn't you tell me?"

He shrugged his shoulders. "There isn't much to tell. I own a motorcycle. So what?"

"I haven't seen it or even known about it in all the time I've known you."

"It's a noisy thing to start up early in the morning, so I can't take her to work. Like I said, I had a few things to fix up before I put her on the road again. I belong to a Christian motorcycle group, and it's our annual camping trip soon, so I need to get her in good shape."

"Camping trip?"

"Yeah. Usually we head up into the mountains, but this year so many people are going, we rented a couple of acres on a ranch. We head up Saturday, have a big barbecue together for supper, and camp out Saturday night. Sunday we have a worship time and short service, then have a big picnic to finish up the leftovers before everyone goes home."

"You like doing that?"

Bob nodded. "Yeah. We go in groups of twenty or thirty bikes, and we all meet there. There's nothing like being in the middle of a bike caravan.

This year I think they're expecting five hundred people."

"Where do they put everyone? Where do you sleep?"

"I told you, George. It's camping. Everyone brings a tent and a sleeping bag and one change of clothes. There's not a lot of room to carry stuff on a motorcycle."

"A tent? You mean you sleep—" George gulped "—on the ground?"

"Yup. That's what camping means. Sleeping on the ground in the great outdoors. Haven't you ever gone camping before?"

She shuddered just thinking about lying on the ground with the bugs and whatever else was down there. "No."

He sighed. "I forgot. You've probably traveled around to all the great cities of the world, where you only stay in the best hotels. You've probably never not had running water."

Georgette pressed one hand over her heart. "No running water? Where do you…uh…"

Bob sighed again. "The people who do the organizing rent chemical toilets that don't need flushing."

"Ew."

"It's not as bad as you think. It's actually a nice break to get away from a busy life. We sing songs by the light of the moon, under the starry sky. You can't see the scope of the heavens or the number of stars under the city lights. I think you'd really be amazed. If you came, I bet you'd enjoy yourself."

"But I don't have a motorcycle. I've never even been on one before."

"Lots of couples come, and not everyone has their own bike. A motorcycle seats two."

"But you and I... We're not...you know."

He shrugged his shoulders. "It's a Christian campout, George. Not every couple that comes is married. It's well-chaperoned, and at night, it's divided into three sections. One for families and married couples, one for the single men, and one for the single women. And let me tell you, the single men *far* outnumber the single women. You've still got lots of time to decide. It's not this coming weekend, it's next weekend."

"That's only ten days away."

"Like I said. Lots of time."

"What about the shop?"

"I do this once a year, and Bart runs things by himself for a day."

George stared at Bob. She wanted to think he'd invited her because he cared for her in a special way, but Bob's deliberate reference to the abundant supply of single men contradicted that. Still, it was something she'd never done. "Let me think about it."

"Sure. We're done. Are you ready to go?"

She studied the bike. Suddenly, instead of looking like fun, it felt intimidating, now that she was so close to it. "I don't know."

"We can make your first ride a short one. How about if we just go to the grocery store, and come back with something to cook for supper."

She looked down at the saddlebags attached over the rear tire. They were as small as Bob said, but they would certainly hold enough for one meal.

"Okay. Let's go."

He handed her a helmet, then helped her fasten the chin strap so it was positioned securely. Satisfied, he closed the garage door and locked it, put on his own helmet, then slid onto the motorcycle. "Come on, George. Hop on." He patted the seat behind him.

Suddenly her doubts pressed in on her like a wall. The motorcycle didn't have a seatbelt. The only way to stay on and not fall off was to hold something, and that something would be Bob.

But now that she had the helmet on, it was too late to change her mind.

"Don't be nervous. I'm a safe driver, and I'll take the corners carefully. All you have to do is hold on tight, and lean with me. I haven't dumped it in five years."

"Dumped it?"

"That's when something happens and you lose your balance and the bike lands on its side. With a bike this size and weight, it takes two men to get it upright again. That only has to happen once, and it's a lesson learned for life. It's really embarrassing." He patted the seat again. "Up you go."

Inhaling deeply, Georgette walked stiffly to the motorcycle and slid on behind Bob.

The seat was surprisingly soft. For a short trip, it would be fine, but she couldn't imagine sitting on it for hours and still being able to walk with any sort of dignity afterward.

Beneath her, the motorcycle roared to life.

She stiffened from head to toe.

Bob twisted around to look at her. "This is it. Hang on."

When he turned so he was once again facing forward, she gently rested her hands on the sides of his waist.

He twisted slightly, flipped the visor up once more, and looked into her eyes. "Not like that. You'll never be comfortable enough to enjoy the ride if you're not holding on properly. Like this."

Before she could think of what he was doing, his hands pulled hers forward and pressed her palms onto his stomach. The unexpected movement sent her front into Bob's back, her head landing between his shoulder blades.

He patted her hands, then let go. "Just remember to lean with me."

Without waiting for her response, he took off.

Georgette squeezed her eyes shut and hung on for dear life. She pressed herself into Bob's back, and didn't move. When they came to the first corner, it took every piece of strength within her to lean into the curve with him, feeling the pavement approach the tender flesh of her leg.

Bob slowed as they approached a red light, and she could feel his body shift as he extended one leg to support the bike while they waited for it to turn green.

Georgette opened one eye. Nothing seemed abnormal as they sat in the traffic. She opened the other just as Bob revved the motor, which she took as the cue that they would be moving in another second or two.

From behind him, she watched as the world went by in a glorious rush.

She didn't feel entirely safe being so open to the elements, but she was starting to feel more comfortable.

Not moving her hands from the security of Bob's stomach, she straightened her back so she could see better. Riding on the back of the motorcycle was fun. Kind of like the scariest ride at the fair.

Too soon, Bob turned into the supermarket parking lot.

She slid off the bike first, then Bob followed. He engaged the kickstand, pulled off his helmet, and smiled down at her. "Did you enjoy the ride?"

She pulled off her own helmet. "Yes! I can hardly wait for the ride home."

"First, we have to buy something to make for supper."

"What do I do with this?" She held out the helmet.

"I'm afraid we have to carry them. I don't have a lock to keep them on the bike and if we don't take them inside, someone will steal them. Sad but true."

She followed Bob inside and through the store, selecting some vegetables and a package of chicken fillets. The ride home was much more enjoyable than the ride to the store, and when they pulled onto the pad beside the garage, Georgette was sorry it was over so soon. The only reason she didn't ask Bob to keep going was that she was so hungry.

"What are we making today?"

"A stir-fry. Only because I'm really hungry, I'll cut up the chicken, and leave you to cut up the vegetables, so we can get it done faster."

She remembered the disgusting process of cutting the beef. She didn't imagine cutting raw chicken was any different. "You won't get any argument from me on that one."

When they were done, she followed Bob to the stove. "First you put a little oil into the pan, let it heat up a bit, and before you add the chicken you test the heat. Mama showed me how to do this. Splash a few drops of water in the pan. If the water rolls in a little ball for a second before it evaporates, the oil is ready."

With Bob standing and watching, she did exactly as he said, and strangely, the drops of water did stay in a little ball rather than a puddle when he splashed some in. Bob tossed in the chicken, stirring and showed her what to look for to tell when it was time to add the vegetables.

Leaving Georgette in charge of the stir-fry, Bob began rummaging through her fridge.

"Don't you have any soy sauce?"

"No. We haven't ordered Chinese food because I didn't have enough money."

Bob stood. "Soy sauce doesn't only come in those little packets, you can buy it in a bottle. I have some at home. I'll be right back. Just remember to stir this in a couple of minutes, so it doesn't burn."

"Will do."

Instead of staying by the stove, she walked over to the window to watch Bob as he dug his keys out of his pocket and went into his house. She pictured him walking to his kitchen, since she now knew the layout. The phone rang, causing Georgette to flinch and breaking her reverie. So she returned to the stove and stirred the cooking chicken, as instructed.

She waited for a minute, then gave it another stir. A watched pot might never boil, but a watched stir-fry was making her restless.

Georgette walked to the television and flipped it on to listen to the news. Then it was time for another stir, so she walked back to the stove, tended to their dinner, and went back to the television where the theme had changed from world news to local, and a reporter came on with a live broadcast of a boat accident under one of the city bridges that had tied up rush-hour traffic when the boat hit one of the bridge supports.

Just as a city engineer started describing the steps it would take to ascertain that no permanent damage was done, Georgette smelled smoke.

She ran back to the pan, which had started smoking. Time seemed—slow. Just as she reached for the spoon to stir everything again, the smoke alarm in the center of the room began to screech. Her hand continued its course and the exact second she touched the spoon, the contents of the pan burst into flame.

Time snapped back into focus. Georgette backed up, unable to believe what was happening. She ran to the cupboard, grabbed a glass, then ran to the sink to fill the glass with water. She had just filled the glass and aimed it at the flames, when the door burst open.

"What are you doing?!" Bob exclaimed as he ran for the stove. He grabbed the lid for the pot and threw it on top of the flames. It landed crooked, but he made a quick jab at it to push it so it fit squarely. He blew on his fingers, turned off the heat, then stuck his fingers in his mouth.

"How did this happen?" he yelled around his fingers. "I thought I told you to stay there and stir it every couple of minutes." He pulled his fingers out of his mouth, looked at the reddened tips, then shook his hand in the air.

Georgette couldn't answer, not that it would have made any difference. The screeching of the smoke alarm would have drowned out anything she said.

Bob reached forward and pushed the button to turn the fan above the stove on, then ran some water over his fingers in the sink. After a few seconds, he muttered something else under his breath, dragged a chair under the smoke alarm and took out the battery.

The only sound remaining was whirring of the fan above the stove.

It was still too silent.

Bob returned to the stove, and using a towel, he lifted the lid to confirm that the fire had been extinguished. "It's out," he grumbled.

Georgette felt her lower lip quivering, but she refused to cry. After everything that had happened, and after everything she'd done, she didn't want to give in to the last sign of weakness and defeat.

"I'm so sorry," she mumbled. Her eyes burned, but she blinked a few times to fight it back. If she said any more, she knew she would lose control, so she remained quiet.

Bob waved one hand in the direction of the stove. A black smear marred the stove hood, and a cloud of smoke hovered next to the ceiling over the space of the entire apartment. "How could you let this happen? I told you not to leave it."

She stiffened and tried to be brave, but her voice came out in a squeak. "You didn't exactly say that. You told me to stir it in a couple of minutes. When I heard the phone ring, I knew you'd be gone longer, so I actually stirred it a few more times."

His arm dropped to his side. "And what were you doing with a glass of water? You of all people should know better. That was a grease fire. It was the oil that was flaming, not the meat. Water spreads a grease fire."

"There isn't a fire extinguisher here, so I didn't know what else to do. It didn't occur to me to smother it."

The sound of canned laughter drifted from the corner of the apartment that was officially the living room.

Bob's eyebrows knotted, and his eyes narrowed. "Were you watching television?"

"I got bored, and then I got distracted. I'm so sorry." She bit into her lower lip, to keep it still.

Bob ran one hand down his face. "No, I'm the one who should be sorry. I should have come straight back. I also shouldn't have yelled at you."

Georgette stared at Bob, waiting, although she didn't know exactly what it was she wanted. It felt like a moment from a TV commercial, where Bob would open his arms, welcoming her. Then, in slow motion, she would glide across the room into them and they would close around her. His kiss would make it all better, and end their first fight.

Bob sighed, disturbing her thoughts. "I guess we'd better clean up, and decide what else we can make for supper. I have a fan that I can put it in the door to see if we can get more air circulating to clear out the smoke."

Without waiting for her to comment, which would have been pointless anyway, he turned and walked out, leaving her all alone.

The stove fan continued to whir, reminding her of how stupid she'd been.

She'd failed again.

Georgette looked at the charred meat inside the pot, and swept her hand over the top to check the temperature. It was still warm, so she set it aside to cool completely before she threw it out.

Her father had been right when he said she could never live on her own. She couldn't even cook an edible meal by herself.

Rather than do nothing, she retrieved the pine cleaner and a sponge, two things she had come to know quite well, and began scrubbing the black spot, standing on a chair to reach. She didn't even bother to turn around when clunking behind her signified Bob's return.

The noise level increased significantly when the second fan started.

"If you're interested, we can eat the leftover stew from yesterday," she said as she wrung out the sponge. "I think there's enough for both of us."

"No, I think I'll leave that for you for tomorrow night, because I'm not going to be here. I'm going out with Randy." He paused for a few seconds. "You do know how to heat something up without a microwave, don't you?"

She dipped the sponge in the water again, and

resumed scrubbing. "I've never done it before, but I'm sure it's not difficult."

The pause before he spoke was almost tangible. "Tell you what. Tomorrow at lunch time, I'll go out and make an extra house key for you, and you can use my microwave. It's probably a good idea for you to have a key for my house, anyway."

Georgette felt herself sinking to an aptitude level below that of the common earthworm.

She kept scrubbing, not trusting herself to speak.

"For today, I have a solution for supper." Bob picked up the phone and dialed. "Hey, Tony. It's me. Bob. Can you send over a house special pizza to my garage?" Bob paused. "Yes, I said the garage, very funny. Jason used to order pizza all the time. Thanks."

Georgette felt herself sinking lower, if that was possible. Even Bob's brother knew how hopeless she was.

Her father was right. She would never survive. Even her boss's family knew it. Unless she could live on peanut butter sandwiches. *Those* she could make without setting anything on fire or doing anything else potentially fatal. Of course, she could always cut off her fingers in the process.

"George? I don't think you're going to get that any cleaner. Pretty soon you're going to take the paint off."

She froze, staring at the stove hood. Bob was right. No black remained. The surface was back to its original luster.

She turned around and smiled weakly. "This pine cleaner and I, we have a history together."

Bob approached her, standing in front of her as she remained standing on the chair. It felt strange to look down at him. She'd never seen the top of his head before. His hair was dark, thick and slightly wavy. She wanted to run her fingers through it, to see if it was as coarse as it looked.

He tipped his head up and trapped her with his vivid olive-green eyes, eyes that were the only criteria for that dress she'd purchased, a dress she would keep for the rest of her life, simply because of those eyes.

"It's okay, George. Everyone makes mistakes. You're still learning. I just keep forgetting how little you've done before."

"It's not okay. I can't do anything right. The only thing I can do without some disaster happening is my job. Someone has to do everything else for me, or I mess it up."

"That's just inexperience, not lack of ability. There's a big difference. You have loads of ability. It's just… never been tested."

"That's not true. Every time I do a test drive

on my abilities, something needs to go back for repairs."

She glared down at him, daring him to differ.

"Will you get down from there? I can't talk to you like that."

Before she could refuse, his hands circled her waist, and he lifted her down from the chair.

Her heart pounded in her chest. Don't let go. Don't let go, she chanted inwardly.

His hands remained fixed on her waist. "I've never seen you make the same mistake twice, so that means you're learning, and you're teachable. That's the first thing I thought when I hired you. You were anxious and willing to learn, and sometimes that's almost as important as ability."

She went to raise her free hand almost as if in a dream, but discovered the hard way that it was too confining to rest her hand on his shoulder, which had been her intention. Rather than let her hand drop, she positioned her palm on his chest, over his heart.

She opened her mouth to tell him that his kind words meant a lot to her, but no sound came out. His body heat warmed her hand, and his heart beat accelerated beneath her palm. All coherent thought deserted her.

His grip on her waist tightened slightly as he drew he closer. One eyebrow quirked as he looked down at her.

She couldn't help herself, she let her eyes drift shut and tipped up her chin.

His lips brushed hers in the lightest of kisses. Not wanting to let the moment end, Georgette leaned forward, just enough to increase the contact slightly, to savor the softness of his gentle kiss.

She felt a soft sigh escape from Bob under her palm. His hands drifted slightly so they were more to her back, and his mouth came fully into contact with hers.

The sponge dropped from her hand.

Bob's kiss deepened, and he kissed her in a way she'd never been kissed before, as if he meant it.

Fool that she was, she kissed him back in equal measure.

A gentle rapping came from the doorway. "Bob? I got your pizza."

In a split second, Bob stepped back, breaking all contact. A shiver of cold coursed through her at the loss.

"That shouldn't have happened. I have to go. Keep the pizza. I'll see you at work tomorrow."

He stumbled around the fan, past the boy with the pizza in his hand, and was gone.

Chapter Sixteen

"I am an idiot," Bob muttered to himself as he reached up to the muffler of the car on the hoist above him and pulled on the tail pipe.

He picked up his hammer and began to hit at the muffler to loosen it, when out of the corner of his eye, he saw George through the window, dealing with a customer. She was as efficient as always. Polite. Cheerful. Proficient. Capable. Soft. Warm. A great kisser.

Bob took a harder swing at the muffler and missed shattering the exhaust pipe mounting bolts instead. The pipe itself hit the frame, then bounced back, narrowly missing his head.

"I'm a *total* idiot," he grumbled as he yanked it off, then stomped to the parts area for a new one.

"You're talking to yourself again," Bart said as Bob walked by.

"Ma fatti affari tuoi," he grumbled.

Before he could walk two more steps, Bart was beside him.

"I remember what that means, and you're wrong. It *is* my business when you walk around talking to yourself. What's going on with you and George? And don't try to deny it. She's been acting funny today, too."

Bob sighed. "I lost it last night, and things went further than I wanted them to go."

Bart stiffened. Bob had never seen Bart's eyes open so wide.

"Don't look at me like that," Bob muttered. "Her honor is fully intact."

"Then what's the problem?"

Bob waved one hand in the air toward her. "She's our employee, for crying out loud! What would happen if we got personally involved?"

"I dunno. The business would turn into a three-way partnership?"

"Not funny, Bart."

"I wasn't trying to be funny. I really like George, but if you're doing something that's going to cause her to stumble…"

Bob swiped one hand down his face. "It's not that at all. It's just that she's got too much going on in her life to start something, even if she wasn't our employee. The fact that I personally hired her makes it even worse."

"I know she's got a few things to deal with. Everybody does. That's life."

Bob made a mental list of all the things that had gone wrong in George's life in the past few weeks, from Tyler to the situation with her father and then her sister, to her complete lack of experience in looking after her own daily needs, for starters. "You don't know the half of it," he mumbled.

And yet, as much as he knew it wasn't wise to get involved, he still wanted to help her be the person God wanted her to be. It wasn't likely God meant that to include kissing her.

"Earth to Bob. Hello, Bob. Put the landing gear down."

"Sorry. I was thinking about something. What did you say?"

"I said, I think you two should go out for coffee and talk, and get things back to normal. If that's not possible, at least make some kind of agreement that will allow things to go on the way they were before around here. I'll hold down the fort while you're both gone."

"No, that won't be necessary. I actually don't have much to say. It might even be a good idea to do it now, before the rush starts. Can you watch the front?"

Bart nodded and followed him into the lobby.

"George, I think we need to talk. Let's go into the office. Bart's going to run interference for us."

Her face paled. "Uh, sure…"

The second the door closed behind her, she spoke, her voice coming out barely above a squeak. "Am I fired?"

"No, of course not. But if you're worried about that, then it *is* best that we talk." He sat behind the desk and clasped his hands together on the desktop in front of him, trying to get himself into "boss mode" when he really felt more like a teenager.

When she was seated, Bob cleared his throat. "First of all, I need to apologize for yesterday."

Her face paled even further. "Apologize? But—"

Bob held up one hand to silence her. "Please. I'm finding this really difficult, so I'll just come right out and say it. I'm not sure what's happening between us, but what comes first is that I'm your boss, and I can't do anything to jeopardize that relationship. I've heard and seen too many times when people who work together start dating, and then the relationship ends. There are only three of us here, and we work together too closely to risk that kind of thing, so I think it's best to stop right now, before things get out of control. I think we can stay friends, and if we both keep that in mind, I think we'll be fine."

"Are you still going to show me how to cook and help me figure out a budget and all that stuff?"

"Of course. I said I would, and I have no intention of breaking a promise."

Her eyes widened. Bob felt as if he'd been poleaxed. He'd never seen a woman with eyes like George's. She sat before him, dressed as unwomanly as possible in her coveralls and safety workboots, complete with a streak of grease across her left cheek. Yet he'd been fighting the urge to gently wipe the smudge off ever since she'd come into the office. He knew that if he touched her, everything he was trying so hard to do would be lost in an instant.

Even though he'd been fighting his feelings toward her all day, now that they were together, her eyes held him like a deer in the headlights. He couldn't look away. Sincerity, hope, innocence and trust, all shone through right at him. He knew the difficult turns her life had taken. He wanted to move mountains for her, and it hurt him deep inside to know he was just a mechanic.

"What about next weekend? The campout with all your biker friends. Am I still invited? I was thinking about it all night, and I really want to go."

Bob's breath caught in his throat. The campout

was his one break in the year—for two short days, his motorcycle took him to a place where no one could reach him, and he couldn't reach anyone else. This year, the organizers had encouraged everyone to leave their cell phones at home, or keep them turned off and pretend they wouldn't work on the wide-open ranchland the same as in the mountains, which blocked the signals. This was where Bob could retreat into rest and quiet, put all his problems and worries in a box for the weekend and listen to God talk.

Except he'd already promised George she could go with him.

But then, the quiet retreat would probably be good for her, too. It would be selfish if he didn't let her go.

"Of course you're still invited," he said, forcing himself to smile. He reached into his pocket. "Before I forget, I went out on my lunch break and made this key for you, like I said I would. Feel free to go in and use the microwave any time you want."

"I don't want to intrude. When will you be home?"

"Not until late. I'm going to the mall as soon as I get off, to meet Randy. As soon as he gets off, we're going shopping."

"Shopping? What are you going to buy?"

Bob's grin reached from ear to ear. "He's going to help me buy an electronic drum set. I can hardly wait."

Bob steered his motorcycle into the row of other motorcycles, and cut the engine. Supporting the weight of the bike with his leg until he could get off and engage the kickstand, he pulled the helmet off his head and turned around, still seated. "Here we are, George. It's time to dismount."

George pulled off her helmet, but remained on the bike. "I don't think I can move."

He grinned. "You'll only be stiff for a few seconds, and then you'll be right as rain."

"What a stupid saying. Who made that up, anyway? When it rains, I don't feel very 'right.' All I feel is cold and wet."

"There's only one way to get limber and that's to quit stalling. Just do it."

Before she had a chance to attempt to get her joints working again, a voice came from Bob's right side. "Hey, Bob! Good to see you."

He turned. "Hey, Brad. Good to see you, too."

Brad turned to George and smiled at her. "Care to introduce me to your friend?"

Bob squirmed invisibly on his seat. The entire trip, he'd been telling himself that it would be a good thing for George to meet eligible men, nonetheless, what he kept *feeling* were her arms around him as she rode behind. Now that he had someone to whom he could introduce her, Bob wanted to punch him in the nose.

He eked out a smile. "George, this is Brad. He's a wimp. His bike is one of those foreign makes."

Brad grinned. "Yeah. My bike actually lets people hear each other talking when they ride. I can demonstrate if you want to come for a ride with me."

"I'm sorry, I'm not sure I can get off *this* motorcycle, never mind get on another one."

"Some guys get all the luck," Brad said. "When you decide that he's not your type, have Bob give you my phone number."

Her face turned ten shades of red. "Uh...yeah... sure..."

At her reply, Brad moved on in the direction of the barbecue, from which Bob detected the aroma of roasting hot dogs. He mentally kicked himself for not being sorry to see Brad leave.

Finally, George slid off the seat, allowing Bob to slide off as well. He engaged the kickstand, and turned to George.

"What did you think of the ride?"

She rubbed her backside, obviously not caring if anyone around them was watching. "It was fun until it was time to move. How does anyone sit on those things for so long?"

"I guess we get used to it. Are you hungry? They have the barbecue going already."

"Yeah..." She inhaled deeply, grinning as her voice trailed off. "I sure am."

"Don't get too excited. It's just hot dogs. They have to keep the costs down."

"No, you don't understand. Daddy never barbecued anything, certainly not hot dogs, and neither did Josephine. I once had a hot dog from a vendor, but it was pretty gross, to say the least."

He supposed hot dogs, like meat loaf, for example lacked upper-class appeal. His family, on the other hand, loved meat loaf, even though it wasn't on a typical Italian menu. And when they all got together in the summer time, they always had barbecued hot dogs because his father could put more of them on the barbecue at once than anything else.

He led her to the barbecue, where she ate two hot dogs, loaded with onions, mustard and ketchup, then gave him half of the third one when she couldn't finish it.

He noticed a few raised eyebrows, and he did feel strange eating the rest of her hot dog—it spoke of a closeness that they didn't have. People seemed to move beyond that, though and during the course of the day, he introduced Georgette to as many people as he could, men and women.

The group varied in age and background, but she connected with them all.

He helped her with the small dome tent he'd brought for her, and they set it up together in the area designated for the single women. She merely stood back and watched as he set up his own tent in the area for single men, as he claimed it wouldn't be good for his male ego if she helped him.

By the time the sun had set, about five hundred people had arrived, as expected. A number of campfires had been started, and about a dozen people with guitars scattered themselves throughout the site, all wearing battery-operated headsets so they could hear the leader and play the same thing at the same time.

"They're going to start in a few minutes. This is going to be really fantastic." Bob spread out a blanket over the grass, and they sat.

"Why aren't you playing something with them?"

"I play drums, not guitar."

"Drums aren't electric. At least not your old ones. You could play them here."

He grinned. "A drum set doesn't easily fit on the back of a motorcycle."

"Oops. I never thought of that."

The strumming guitars halted their conversation, and soon the rich sound of five hundred voices carried songs of praise throughout their own gathering, echoing off into the distance to whatever animals lived on the land.

Bob preferred a small congregation to a large one, but the combined effect of so many people singing and worshiping together was like nothing else, especially outside, where there were no boundaries. He wondered if this was a small sampling of what it would have been like during the journey of the twelve tribes of Israel in the desert, except those people would have been walking, not arriving on motorcycles of course.

Though George didn't know all the songs, unlike him, she participated where she could, and a few times he thought he saw tears shimmering in her eyes.

At the end of the worship time, everyone broke into small groups to pray, to catch up on events since the last time they saw each other, or simply to spend time with a friend.

As more people crawled into their tents for the night, Bob eventually found himself alone with George. He led her away from the brightness of the fire and pointed to the sky. "Look at the stars. You don't see this from the city."

She tipped her head up. "I've never seen anything like it. It's breathtaking."

"This time of year you see more shooting stars. They're fascinating to watch. This is the only time

I can forget about everything and just be quiet in God's presence. Looking up at the big, wide-open sky reminds of how little I really am, and how big God is. Big enough for all our burdens."

George sighed. "I have to admit that I've never had so much to deal with as I have in the last few months. But when I'm busy all day, and so tired at night, I can push it aside. Here, though, I feel like God is telling me to make some decisions."

He turned and looked down at her. At work, and even in the kitchen with one notable exception, he didn't stand particularly close to her. Yet now, in the quiet of the dark, open field, with nothing and no one else nearby, her small size made him want to get as close as he could, wrap his arms around her, and shelter her from the world.

Instead, he picked up one hand, linked her fingers in his, and gave a gentle squeeze. "Then this is probably a good time to be quiet, pray and let God speak. Care to join me?"

"Yes, I'd like that."

He regretted the loss, but he had to release her hand to flip open the blanket he'd been carrying, and spread it on the ground.

He sat, and patted the blanket beside him in invitation. Once she was sitting, he lay flat on his back to look up at the night sky, his hands linked behind his head in contentment.

"This is the best way to see everything. Don't be shy."

"You know I'm not shy," she said as she flopped down on her back and assumed an identical position.

They lay in silence, looking up. Bob tried not to let her proximity distract him from God's leading. He turned his thoughts to how to pray.

Things were going well for his business, Bart was enjoying fatherhood, and in one short week, Adrian and Celeste were getting married. All in his own life was good. George, however, needed a lot of help and even more prayer.

He cleared his throat and tried to sound casual, but his insides churned. "Is there anything you'd like me to pray about for you?" As if he didn't pray for her every day already.

"I don't know. I think things have been pretty good. I have a good job, a nice place to stay. I'm making new friends." Even though Bob remained with his head facing straight up, he sensed George turning to look at him as she continued. "I have you helping me with everything. I thank God for you and all you've done for me every day."

Fortunately, the dark night hid his blush. "Thanks," he mumbled.

"I'm learning so much, I think it won't be long before I'll be able to manage on my own. So really, everything is good except for two things."

She sighed, and her voice lowered in pitch to barely above a whisper. "Daddy, and my sister."

He hated himself for asking, but he had to know. "What about Tyler?"

"I've thought a lot about him. I still think that the way it played out was his fault, but I have to be realistic. Daddy would have found out what I was doing sooner or later. I can't say anything would have happened any differently if I told him instead of Tyler. I've been doing a lot of reading on forgiveness. If I don't forgive those who wrong me, it doesn't hurt them. It hurts me and my relationship with God. I've got to let it go. It's past, there's nothing I can do, so I have to move on."

As much as everything George said made sense, Bob didn't know if he would have been as gracious in the same situation. His own family accepted him unconditionally, of course, if he did something they didn't approve of, he heard about it for months. But still they forgave him, just as God forgave him for past wrongs and even future ones. The unqualified forgiveness made him eager to please God.

"That's great. I'm glad you can think of it in that way."

"There's actually a little more. Tyler was just being true to his own nature, which is to do anything to get ahead. It's simply the way he is, and

I've always known that about him. He didn't even mean it personally—I was just a means to an end. He'll have to answer for that one day, but I can't judge him. That's not up to me. It's up to God to judge."

"Wow. I'm impressed."

She made a short, humorless laugh. "Don't be. There's so much junk on television that I've been doing a lot of reading. Celeste loaned me a few books, and what I was talking about came from one of them. That doesn't mean I have everything worked out. I haven't been able to fully forgive my father. I knew I was spoiled, but Daddy didn't give me everything because he loved me. He used it all to control me. And I let him because I was too much of a wimp."

This time Bob couldn't remain still. He rolled onto his side, and propped his head up with his arm, resting his elbow on the ground. "You're certainly not a wimp. You took the job knowing your father wouldn't approve. You went to church and worshiped God knowing he wouldn't approve. Then when push came to shove, you didn't cave in, but sacrificed everything you knew and took on a world of unknowns rather than do something you knew wasn't right."

She rolled onto her side and also propped her head up. "That's not exactly true. I knew you."

Bob opened his mouth, but no words came out. Not wanting to look too stupid, he rolled onto his back again.

He heard the movement as George also rolled onto her back. "I know it's something I have to work out, and I know I have to keep praying about that. But I really would like it if right now we could pray for Terri. I've phoned her a few times over the past few weeks, and she wouldn't talk to me. But yesterday when I phoned, she finally eased up a little and we talked. I think she'd been crying. She said that even though she wasn't happy with Byron, at least she could do what she wanted, which was more than she could do when she was living back at home. She won't do anything about Byron, because she doesn't want to have to go back. I tried to tell her that God would help her if she would only let Him, but she hung up on me again."

"That's so sad. It's easy for us to say, but you're right. She really could do something about it if she wanted to. I think it all comes down to how much a person is willing to sacrifice in order to do what they feel is right."

Thinking of George's sister, who preferred to remain miserable in order to keep her privileged lifestyle, emphasized for Bob how much George had given up to be free.

He liked to think that if the same thing happened to him, he would be able to do what George had done, but he'd never had to face something so hard. All his life, Bob had lived with very distinct guidelines of right and wrong. He'd never known a time when God wasn't acknowledged and obeyed in their home. As an adult, he lived the same way his parents had raised him, which was to try to love other people as God loved them, warts and all.

He knew he was a sucker for the underdog, but George wasn't an underdog at all. Despite her struggles, she was emerging victorious. Very soon she wouldn't need him any more, and they would go back to the way things had been before, whether she lived in his garage or not. He supposed her indomitability was one of the reasons he'd fallen in love with her so quickly.

Love.

Bob squeezed his eyes shut. All this time, he'd refused to consider that his feelings toward George were anything other than sheer altruism, but he'd been fooling himself. He did love her. He didn't know when it had started, but that didn't make it any less real.

What also was a reality was that he could never provide the things she was used to. For now, scrubbing toilets and cooking onions was a new experience, even a novelty. Very soon, it would become drudgery. She would become bored, feel trapped and resentful of having to do those things.

While the partnership in the auto shop with Bart was successful enough, neither of them would ever be rich. Up until now he'd been perfectly content. His life plan was to have a wife and children and raise his family the same way he had been raised, although Bob had no intention of having six children. Four would be good enough.

But George had grown up with an army of staff—a nanny, a housekeeper, gardeners, chauffeurs—so she didn't have to lift a finger, if she didn't want to. He couldn't see George being happy slaving over a hot stove while children tugged at her legs to go outside to play ball and the laundry piled up, and then he came home tired and dirty after a hard day at work and fell asleep on the couch.

He knew she would say it didn't matter, and maybe it wouldn't for the short term. But Bob needed someone who could be content in that atmosphere for a lifetime.

When George's warm hand rested on top of his, Bob sucked in a deep breath and tried to rein in his thoughts.

"Can we pray now?"

"Sure."

He led with a few words of praise to start, but their prayers drifted off to silence as they prayed individually, their hands still joined. Bob's prayers were mixed between concerns for George's sister, her father, for George herself, and even for Tyler. In praying for himself, all he could do was ask for guidance and promise to be open to God's leading.

He was startled when George pulled her hand out of his and sat up. "I don't think anyone else is awake except for us," she whispered. "We should probably get to our tents."

He sat up, and sure enough, everything in the huge expanse of the campsite was dark. "Yes. Tomorrow we're going to have another morning worship time, finish up all the leftovers for lunch, and then everyone will head home."

"I have a feeling tomorrow is going to go fast."

"Yup. Before we know it, we'll be back at work on Monday."

Using the flashlight sparingly, he led George to her tent, then went quietly to his.

Monday was going to come much too quickly.

Chapter Seventeen

"Hi, George. I see the counter's full. Where would you like today's mail?"

Georgette hit Enter on the keyboard, and stuck out her hand. "I'll take it..."

As the mail carrier left out the main door, Bob walked in from the shop door. "I'm expecting a letter about some warranty work. Is it in there?"

Georgette picked through the pile of envelopes, but stopped before she made it all the way through the pile.

"What's wrong? Is there something that isn't for us?"

"No. There's something here with my name on it. Something marked Personal and Confidential." Her heart nearly stopped when she recognized the company name on the return address. "This is from Tyler." She grasped the envelope by the corner, and immediately marched to the shredder in the corner.

Bob appeared beside her and snatched the envelope from her hand just as the corner touched the mechanism to activate it.

"Wait. Aren't you going to look at it?"

"No."

"What if it's something important? If you want to shred it after you've read it, fine, but you should see what it says."

She almost started to argue, but her words caught in her throat. No one knew where she lived. Even if they had, Bob's garage didn't have a separate street address. She didn't have a phone listing that could be traced through directory assistance. She'd tried to give Bob's phone number to Terri, but Terri wouldn't even write it down.

Her only tie to her former life was that Tyler knew where she worked.

If something had gone wrong or if her father or her sister were sick, no one had any way of contacting her except through Tyler.

"Maybe you're right." She accepted the envelope, opened it and began to read.

Dear Georgette,

I'm sorry to be sending this to you at work, but I couldn't find any other way to contact you. I want to tell you how deeply I regret what happened. Before you feed this through the shredder, I want you to know that I think about you every day, and wish we could start over under different circumstances.

Unfortunately, I can only beg you to speak to me. I would like it if you would meet me for dinner one evening soon. I know I will never be able to make up to you for what I've done, but please let me try.

Your father doesn't know I'm sending you this message, and quite frankly, I no longer care. I now understand your conviction to follow your own path, and your own heart. If your father fires me for attempting to contact you, then so be it. There are other jobs and other corporations, but there is only one Georgette Eckington, and I miss her.

Fondly, Tyler

Georgette's hand shook as she tucked the paper back into the envelope.

"What's wrong? Is it bad news?"

She shook her head. "Tyler says he misses me, and he wants to get together and talk."

Bob's face turned strangely pale. "Are you going to?"

She ran her fingers over the envelope and

skimmed through the letter once more. Despite Tyler's lovely words, she wasn't sure if she could trust him. He'd hurt her badly, and his actions had changed her life forever. The Bible told her to forgive Tyler, which she had, but the Bible didn't tell her to let him do the same thing to her a second time. But if he was sincere, and if things did go well, a union between them would see her gain back everything she had lost, without the roadblocks her father had set before her.

If he was sincere. It was a big *if.* The only way to know would be to see him in person and hope she could be discerning enough to tell the difference.

She looked up at Bob to see that he'd been watching her.

She wished she could read what was in his mind, but she couldn't. She wanted to see sadness, loss, even fear that she would actually call Tyler, but she saw nothing. It was as if he'd turned to stone.

Georgette stared back. "What should I do?" she asked, hoping, praying that Bob would tell her Tyler was completely wrong for her, that he could give her more than Tyler ever could, that his love was worth more than any material goods Tyler could ever provide, and to put the letter through the shredder after all.

"Do what you want. It's your life, and your decision."

Her heart sank. But, contacting Tyler would either give her closure, or a way to start again.

Before she could respond, Bob turned and disappeared into the shop, the door closing harder than usual behind him.

Work couldn't still her mind, she could only think about what could be. At first, she hadn't cared that she'd lost every piece of her past, but it didn't take long before she felt a distinct lack of roots. Bob's roots were a large part of his personality. Seeing Tyler wouldn't restore her relationship with her father, but it would either give her back a piece of who she was, or allow her to make the decision to make the break complete on her own.

Partway into the afternoon, she couldn't stand it anymore. She called Tyler to set up a dinner date.

Bob walked in just as she finished the conversation.

"I see you decided to go."

"Yes," she said, her hand still resting on the phone. "It will bug me if I don't. If it works, fine, and if it doesn't, at least it will give me a sense of closure. We're going out tonight."

He looked down at the floor, not facing her as he spoke. "I guess we won't be making dinner together, then."

"No."

"Then I'll see you Wednesday. Bart and I switched days off this week. I've got tomorrow off, and he's got Thursday off."

"Oh." Her heart sank. Whether things went well or badly, it had comforted her to know that Bob would be there for her the next morning, but it was not to be. She didn't want to wait until Wednesday to see him again. "What about dinner tomorrow?"

He shrugged his shoulders. "Dunno," he mumbled as he turned his head back toward the shop. "I have to get back to work."

"Wait. Didn't you come in here for something?"

He shrugged his shoulders with a grimace. "I forgot what it was. If it was important, it'll come back to me. Have fun tonight."

Georgette watched as Tyler sipped his wine, then spoke to her over the top of the flute. "I don't know how you managed to get in and out of that truck in that dress. I could have picked you up or called a cab."

She smiled weakly. It wasn't the dress that was the hard part. It was the shoes. She hadn't worn heels for so long, her ankles wobbled. When she'd slid out of the truck, she'd nearly fallen down when she landed.

Dinner with Bob every Thursday had been different. She had the money to pay her own way. They both wore jeans, and chose places where a meal didn't cost a whole day's salary.

"Let's just say the truck keeps me humble."

"I'm so glad you decided to come. There are so many things I want to say to you."

She noticed that he hadn't given her any time to say anything that *she* might have wanted to say. He didn't ask her how she was coping, how she liked working for a living or even if she was happy. Even though she was the one wronged, the conversation was still about Tyler.

Bob would have made sure she was comfortable first, and he always let her vent if something was bothering her, even if it had nothing to do with him. Bob always listened before he talked.

"I've missed you, Georgette. I didn't notice until I wasn't seeing you any more how much your smile helped whatever had gone wrong that day. And you always understood what I was talking about when I talked business. No other woman I dated cared much about the workings of my day. They only cared when it meant I couldn't take them where they wanted to go."

Georgette held back a sigh. The alleged apology centered around Tyler. She couldn't believe she was hearing about his dates with other women, *he* was the one who'd set up this "special time."

Bob never talked about other women. The one time she'd asked about a woman he'd dated, he'd quickly changed the subject.

"You're always happy, no matter where we go or what we do."

Every time they'd gone out, it had been to a place of Tyler's choosing. Many times, he'd picked the last place on earth she wanted to be. Tyler's word meant nothing. No matter what he promised, she knew she would never trust him fully, not after he'd betrayed her so badly at the first opportunity for his own gain.

Bob never went back on his word. For a short time, she could tell that Bob wasn't sure if he'd made the right decision to let her move into his garage. But he'd given her his word, and that was final. He was a true man of honor.

"I guess what I'm trying to say is that I think we're a good match. I think it would suit us both to get married."

Georgette choked on her tea. "Married! Are you serious?"

He smiled a nice, corporate businessman's smile. No warmth, no personal connection. It looked as if it was painted on. "Of course I'm serious. We'd both get what we want, and each of us would benefit."

She set the cup on the saucer, before she

dropped it and broke it. "How do you know what I want?"

The phony smile stuck to his face, but didn't reach his eyes. "I know you want the good life back. You can't possibly be happy having to work every day and then go home and bury yourself in chores. But if you wanted to keep working, that would be fine with me. I wouldn't even mind if you wanted to go to church every once in a while. It's a noble thing to do, and it looks good, too."

She was so flustered she could barely talk. "What—what about you? Would you go to church with me?" She didn't want him to go to church with her just to sit beside her. She wanted to marry a man who shared her faith. Like Bob.

He shrugged his shoulders. "I would probably go a few times a year, like Christmas, Easter and probably Mother's Day. After we had children and you became a mother, of course."

The thought of having children with Tyler made Georgette gag. Rather than losing the meal that had cost more than the brake job she'd been saving for, she stood. "You know, I have to get up early for work tomorrow. I think it's time to go."

He reached for her hand, but she pulled it away before he made contact.

"Wait, Georgette, there's something else. After you called me, I talked to your father. He wasn't exactly pleased, but I did manage to convince him to take you back. He said he would restore your credit cards and give you back the car. I realize I sprung this on you rather quickly. Moving back home would give you more time to think about it."

She backed up a step, unable to speak. She'd always imagined a proposal would be a little more personal. Even romantic. Fat chance.

Tyler took another sip of his wine and again spoke to her over the glass. "Marriage isn't a bad thing, you know."

Marriage. She still didn't know whether her mother had deserted her two young daughters because she couldn't stay married to a man who treated her badly, or if her mother had been thrown out for not measuring up.

The last time she'd spoken to her sister, Terri had been crying because Byron was cheating on her. Yet Terri stayed in a marriage where there was no love rather than going back to their father's emotional abuse.

She couldn't imagine being married to Tyler, who always thought of himself first.

She wouldn't marry a man like Byron, who'd only married her sister for her assets.

The only man she would ever marry would be Bob.

Georgette froze.

Bob.

She wanted to marry Bob.

She was in love with Bob.

She didn't know when it had happened, but they could talk about anything and everything. They both could get mad and then laugh about it afterward. And then there was the kiss…

He couldn't have kissed her like that if he didn't mean it.

Georgette struggled not to close her eyes at the memory. She'd sure meant it. But she wasn't with Bob now. She was with Tyler.

"I'm really sorry, but this was a mistake. I can't marry you, and I'm certainly not going to go back to living under Daddy's terms and conditions for the sake of a little money." Not that it was a "little money," but she had learned the hard way that it really didn't buy happiness. "Thank you for dinner, it was lovely. In case I never see you again, have a good life, Tyler. I hope you find the woman who will be right for you one day. I know I'm not her."

Georgette drove home as quickly as she could without getting a speeding ticket. When she pulled onto the cement pad beside Bob's car, not a single light was on in his house.

She closed the truck's door as quietly as she could, and retreated into the apartment.

Tonight she wouldn't wake him, and tomorrow

during the day, she wouldn't see him because she had to work. But after work she intended to make use of her newfound discovery.

When they were together, Bob only saw "George the Mechanic." Now that she was aware of her own desires for a future with Bob, Adrian's words came back to her, and now she believed them to be true. However, something was holding him back.

Regardless, Georgette smiled to herself as she got ready for bed. Tomorrow things would change, because tomorrow, she had a plan.

Chapter Eighteen

"Hey! George!"

Georgette spun around, then tried to determine who in the crowded mall had called to her.

A man seated on one of the benches next to the planter stood, with a hot dog in one hand and a drink in the other. "What are you doing here?"

"Randy," she said, sighing as she pressed one palm over her heart. "You startled me. I guess you're on your supper break."

"Sorry," he said and nodded as he bit into the hot dog and swallowed. "Is something wrong with Bob?"

"I assume he's fine. He traded days off with Bart, so I think he's at home. Why do you ask?"

"I've never seen you here shopping without him, that's all."

Georgette smiled. She was shopping alone because she didn't want Bob to see her purchases. Not yet. "Actually, this isn't the kind of trip he would enjoy. I'm going to buy some girl stuff. You must know the mall well. Where would be a good place to buy a nice dress? I don't want to spend too much money, but I want something nice."

"There's a ladies' clothing boutique beside where I work. It must be good. There's always women going out with big bags in their hands. Try that one."

"That's great. I'll do that."

The first thing that caught Georgette's attention was a big sign stating Summer Clearance.

She headed straight for the sale rack of dresses.

A woman a few years older than her approached. "Can I help you?"

"I don't know. I want to wear something special for tonight, but I don't have a lot of money to spend."

She hadn't originally even planned to go to the mall. She'd gone grocery shopping on the way home, and gone way over budget in order to cook Bob a very special meal. She'd already phoned him to invite him over, but how she would serve it would be a surprise. Her plan wouldn't work if she was wearing the same old jeans and T-shirt he saw her in every day. When their supper was in the oven, she'd gone to change into her beloved green dress. Her heart sank when she discovered a big rip in the bottom. She must have caught her heel in the hem when sliding out of her truck after the non-date with Tyler but in the dark outside, she hadn't seen the damage.

"The dress I wanted to wear has a hole in it, so now I have to buy something new. I'm kinda out of time."

The woman smiled. "Then let's find something nice in your price range."

Together they picked out a flattering style that was just on the edge of Georgette's meager budget, which meant her muffler and a few other repairs on her truck would have to wait. Randy was walking into the electronics store next door just as she ran out. He looked down to the bag under her arm, winked and waved as she ran past him and headed back home.

She was just doing up the zipper when she heard a knock on the door. She yanked on a slip, stuffed her jeans and T-shirt into the armoire, ran her fingers through her hair to tidy it, and ran to the door.

Bob's eyes grew as big as saucers when he saw her. "Did I get the day mixed up? I thought you went out with Tyler yesterday."

He took one step backward, but Georgette grabbed his arm to stop him. "I thought that if I can dress up for Tyler, I can certainly dress up for you."

He looked again at the dress, which fitted her to perfection, even though the style wouldn't have been her first choice. It was a deep blue that went well with her eyes, though the top was too low. But she couldn't argue with the price. He cleared his throat, and wiped his palms on his jeans. "Okay… But then I'm really underdressed."

"You're fine. It was supposed to be a surprise."

He glanced to the table, where she'd set a red candle in the center, something Bob's mother had given her, which she thought gave everything a romantic touch.

"Uh… Yeah… I'm surprised."

She led him to the table and sat him down. "I made you something special."

He turned toward the stove expectantly even though everything she was cooking was back in the oven after her secret last-minute errand—except the salad of course. "Why?"

Because I love you, she thought. "Because you deserve a special evening," she said.

According to the clock, everything should be cooked, so she donned the oven mitts and bent over to take the food out of the oven.

When she turned around, Bob's eyes averted quickly to her face and his ears darkened, telling her that when she'd bent over, he'd been watching. If it had been anyone else, she would have smacked him. But since it was Bob, she smiled inwardly, knowing he appreciated the view. That was one of the reasons she'd worn the dress. She gently plated their meal and carried the plates to the table, then set the potato casserole on the trivet, and retrieved the salad from the fridge.

"Wow. Chicken cordon bleu. And this potato casserole is my favorite. How did you know?"

Actually, she'd asked his mother, who had e-mailed the recipe to her at work that afternoon. That extra work meant she'd had to buy the chicken cordon bleu at the supermarket, ready-made. Knowing her skills, though, that was probably for the best. "Let's just say it's my little secret."

"I don't know what to say."

"Then say grace, so we can eat before it gets cold."

He said what she thought might have been the world's shortest prayer of thanks, and dug in to the chicken.

Bob closed his eyes and sighed. "This is so good. You're a better cook than you think."

She had to laugh at that. "Bob, you can still say that after the Great Stir-fry Fire? All right I'll admit it, I bought the chicken already made up."

He savored another morsel and smiled. "Well, you did a fine job of heating it up without a microwave."

She smiled at him, hoping her nervousness didn't show. Who knew if her hair and makeup would withstand the heat of the small kitchen.

"I made dessert, too." Even though it was just a mixture of pudding, gelatin and whipped cream, she'd still put it together herself.

His eyebrows raised. "I don't understand. Are you going to tell me something bad?" His fork froze halfway to his mouth. "You're not quitting, are you?" His face paled. "You were out with Tyler last night…."

"Yes, I was," Georgette cut in finally. "I'm glad you convinced me to read that letter. It helped me come to a few decisions about my future."

Bob's face paled further. He had a death grip on that poor fork.

She tipped her head and studied him. "Are you feeling okay? Was this a bad night?"

He lowered the fork and dabbed at his mouth with the napkin. "No, I'm fine. I skipped lunch. That must be it. What did you decide?"

"I decided that I was right all along. Tyler is a jerk, and events, as unpleasant as they were, did work out for the best. I also decided that it's about time I started dating."

Bob's eyes flitted to the candle, then to her low-cut dress, and back to her face. "And tonight?"

"Tonight is for you."

His confusion registered in his eyes. She'd been evasive on purpose, for fear of eliciting a decisive but negative response. Tonight, she needed to show him that she no longer wanted to be George. From now on, for Bob, she was going to be Georgette, and not just as an employee either. She wanted to be Mrs. Georgette Delanio.

"Okay..." he muttered, and resumed eating. "So how was work today? Did that guy say anything about that 4X4?"

"It was more than he thought it would cost, but he seemed happy after I showed him what was wrong with the old oil pump. I explained how if we didn't replace it now, it would cost him double to have to take the engine apart in just a few months again."

"And what about that old station wagon?

She hadn't intended to talk about work, but she couldn't not answer. Although, when the conversation drifted to his motorcycle and what he wanted to do with it, she forgot all about her previous conviction not to talk shop, and lost herself in the discussion of the restoration process.

They spent far more time at the table than she had intended, but then again she hadn't thought to plan beyond the meal. She couldn't even rent a movie, because she no longer had a DVD player.

For now, buying one didn't fit into her budget. *Especially* not after buying the dress.

"Can I help with the dishes?"

She looked at the mess on the counter. It wasn't much, but the counter was so small that even a few utensils out of place made it look messy. She was dressed to go out, but her plan to make the evening a romantic event had already taken a dramatic nosedive from all the shop talk.

"Sure. You wash, and I'll dry."

Bob nodded, rolled up his sleeves, and began rinsing the residue off the baking sheet while Georgette spooned the leftover casserole into a plastic container and put it into the fridge. When she turned around, Bob was already up to his elbows in the soapy water, softly humming a song they'd sung at the weekend retreat.

It was no wonder she loved him so much.

By the time the dishes were done, she could no longer hold herself back. She had to touch him. To hold him. To tell him she loved him.

She watched him wring out the dishrag, and just as he began to turn around, Georgette stepped in front of him, with very little distance between them. In order to prevent him from moving away, she rested her hands at the sides of his waist. "Thank you for a lovely evening," she said, surprised at the rough timbre of her own voice.

He smiled down at her. “I think that’s my line. You’re the one who made supper. Which was great, by the way. Thank you.”

“Isn’t the way to a man’s heart through his stomach?” With that thought in mind, she raised one hand and pressed her palm over his heart. The steady rhythm thumping against her hand was strangely comforting.

He pressed one hand over hers. As he did so, the speed of his heartbeat increased just a little. “George, I don’t think this is a good idea.”

“Why not?” she asked as she covered his hand with her remaining one.

In a flash, his other hand covered hers, completing the connection. “It just isn’t.”

She leaned into him, tipping up her chin, making it easy for him to kiss her if he wanted to, because she sure wanted to kiss him. “Then what would be the way to your heart?”

“I…uh…”

Everything she’d learned about how to attract a man flew out the window. She didn’t want to play coy or cunning, but she didn’t care how it happened, as long as it happened.

She raised herself up on her tiptoes, leaning into him so much she could feel his knuckles digging into her chest and stomach. “Kiss me, Bob,” she whispered huskily, her mouth only inches from his.

Time stood still, and just as she began to wish the earth would open and swallow her up, Bob's lips touched hers. It was nothing like the first time. This time, he kissed her as if he couldn't stop.

So, of course, she kissed him right back.

He pulled his hands out from between them, and held her tight as he kissed her again and again until she was breathless and her heart was pounding so hard she knew he had to feel it, because she could certainly feel his heart pounding beneath her palms, which were still trapped between them.

He lifted his mouth from hers, muttered her name, buried his face in her hair then hugged her even closer.

Georgette's heart soared as she pressed her cheek into his chest. A kiss like this could only mean one thing. Confirmation.

"This won't work, you know," he said softly.

She stiffened from head to toe. She couldn't believe he would say such a thing when she was still enclosed in his embrace. "What do you mean?"

"For now, we're both charged. This thing, whatever it is, is new and exciting. But as time goes on, that novelty will wear off and you'll start to feel trapped. I can't offer you what you've left behind. Not even close. You're better off on your own. You should find a man who can treat you the way you'd like to be treated, and then you can live the way you want to live. I've seen it before. It's one thing to marry into money. It's quite another to marry out of it. I don't want you to come to hate me. When I get married, it's going to be for life, just as God dictates."

"You're wrong. I'm finished with that kind of life. Money isn't where true happiness is. It can't even promise stability if there's too much worry about losing it. It can be evil."

"It's not wrong to be rich, George. People get it wrong all the time, but God doesn't say that money is the root of all evil. He says it's the *love* of money that's the root of all evil. It's very different. But the bottom line is that you don't belong here. I won't keep you. It's not right, and I really don't believe you would be happy being stuck here for the next fifty years. I'm a mechanic, and that's all I'll ever be. And I'm okay with that. But you were made for better things."

"But I..." she let her voice trail off. She nearly said she loved him, but she didn't want to beg him to take her, when he was pushing her away.

He released her and stepped back. Ice pervaded her soul.

"I have to go. We rescheduled worship team practice for tonight, and even though Adrian and Celeste won't be there on Sunday, we're still practicing at his house."

"They won't be there?" she echoed weakly.

"They're getting married this weekend, remember? The rehearsal is Thursday night, Friday we have a bunch of setup and other wedding-type stuff to do, and then the wedding is on Saturday. I'll be really busy, so it would be better if you went by yourself, because then at least you can come and go with the rest of the guests."

"Oh, uh, I guess."

He backed up another step. "So I'll see you around, or something."

The door opened and closed before she had a chance to respond.

Georgette refused to break down and cry or throw things. Bob was right. She had been raised better than that. But some things were worth breaking rules for.

Seeing red, she stomped to the door, and kicked it so hard she hurt her toes.

"Love stinks!" she yelled at the top of her voice and limped off to bed. There was breaking the rules, and then there was nearly breaking a foot. There had to be a better way.

Chapter Nineteen

"You may now kiss the bride."

Bob watched his friend kiss his new bride.

Of course he was happy for Adrian and Celeste, but watching them kiss only reminded him of kissing George a few days ago.

It felt like a lifetime ago.

At work nothing had changed, but everything was different.

George had been avoiding him, and he supposed if the situation had been reversed, he would have felt the same. Between the dress, the wonderful dinner and the way she'd initiated their kiss, it was obvious that she had strong feelings for him. That left the decision in his lap. Even though it wasn't what he wanted, he had to back off. He was realistic enough to know that what they had couldn't last a lifetime.

Bob smiled for the cameras as he escorted a

bridesmaid down the aisle behind Adrian and Celeste.

He should have been happy, but he wasn't. Watching Adrian and Celeste only reminded him of what he couldn't have.

He couldn't have Georgette.

Bob shook his head, then forced himself to smile for another camera.

For the first time, he'd thought of her by her real name, not her mannish nickname. He didn't know if he could ever look her in the face and think of her as George again.

It was the way she'd inched herself into kissing him, the dress hadn't hurt, either. He loved her so much. She did everything she could to get him to kiss her; when she'd flat out told him to, he could no longer hold himself back. He'd felt a connection between them like nothing he'd experienced in his life. And now, if the dress she'd worn Wednesday night hadn't been enough to send his brain into outer space, tonight she was wearing the very memorable green dress.

Georgette Ecklington was definitely all woman.

Unfortunately, she was too expensive a woman for him.

By the time he was seated at his place at the head table, he felt utterly miserable. He was at a point in his life where he wanted to settle down and get married, and he'd fallen in love with the wrong person.

When everyone else closed their eyes to pray for their meal, Bob prayed for God to help him deal with his situation. The ceremony had kept him busy, and then there were wedding pictures in the park. For twenty minutes, the guests watched a video that Randy had made of Adrian and Celeste's courtship and the time leading up to the wedding, which provided a good comic relief. But, that was over too quickly. They were having dinner now, and before long that would be over, too. Soon, it would be time to mingle with all the guests including Georgette.

Mentally, Bob shook his head. *George.* In the green dress. But she was still George. A mechanic. His employee. A woman who had lived with the best the world could offer, when he could offer nothing.

The woman he loved, and would love until his dying day.

Bob's heart clenched every time someone new started tinkling glasses for the bride and groom to kiss. He couldn't help himself. Every once in a while, he glanced at George. She didn't look as if she was having a better time than he was.

When dinner was over, he made his way around the floor. Without realizing how he got there, he found himself at George's table, where she sat talking with his mother, of all people. The second the two of them noticed him, his mother got up to leave without saying a word. He didn't know if that was good or bad.

"Hi," he mumbled, for lack of anything better to say as he slid into the chair beside George.

"I'm glad you're here," she said, although her voice was anything but cheerful. She sounded as sad as he felt. "I have to talk to you, and I suppose this is as good a time as any. I need to know how much notice to give you."

Bob's heart stopped beating. "Notice?"

"Yes. I think I've found another place to live, and they need to know when I can move in. I assume that the sooner I leave, the better, so you can find a paying renter."

"I don't understand."

"I've also started looking for another job. I haven't found anything yet, but I thought it would be fair to let you know."

His heart nearly stopped, and he had to force himself to breathe. "Do you need more money? I can give you a raise."

She sighed, and something about her looked even more sad than she already was. "This isn't about money. In fact, if the next job I find pays less money, I'll still take it. I can't handle only seeing you at work, and knowing that's all it will ever be. You've shown me how to budget, how to cook and how to take care of a home. I think it's time for me to put all that practice into use and function on my own."

"But—"

She held up one palm to interrupt him. "You suggested it, Bob, not me. I think you know what I want. Without that, it's torture to work with you all day and go home to your garage at night. It's time."

Bob's head spun.

She was leaving.

He'd been telling himself for months that it wouldn't work, and he should have seen this as the solution, but it felt as if his world was coming crashing down around him.

"What about Tyler? And your father?"

She sighed and looked away, staring at a blank spot on the wall. "They will never change, and I've changed too much to go back. I'll keep praying for them, and one day, I'll contact Daddy and see if he's ready to accept me as I am. But until that happens, I guess I'll just keep working and plugging along. I'm not unhappy. In fact, I've been more content in the last few months than I have been at any time in my whole life."

"You say that now, but it hasn't been very

long. Life sometimes has a way of beating a person down."

"God is always with me. Hasn't He always been with you?"

"Of course He has."

"What about when you started your business with Bart? Didn't people warn you that it might not work?"

He let out a humorless laugh. "George, we were both nineteen years old and we started out of my parents' garage. Nearly everyone we knew told us it wouldn't work. There were times when Bart and I were the only ones who thought it would. And sometimes we weren't even sure ourselves."

"And what about now? Hasn't God been faithful?"

"Of course."

"I believe God will be faithful to me. I may not always have the biggest and the best, but that doesn't mean I'll be unhappy. I know I'll have struggles. Everyone does. I'll face them, and I'll become stronger. I've just done that, Bob, and I'll do it again."

Bob stared at her, her words finally sinking in. She *had* made it through before.

The bright spot in his day was the minute George arrived at work, and the bright spot in his evening was when they sat down together to eat supper. On the weekends, he even enjoyed doing simple housework with her and then working on his old Harley.

She was the answer to all his prayers for the perfect life partner. If she left, his life would not only be empty, it would be meaningless.

He stood. "Stay with me."

"I can't. It hurts too much. I know it could work between us, but it won't if I'm the only one who believes it."

"But I do believe it. I was wrong." He stood and held out one hand toward her. When she gently put her hand in his, he pulled her to her feet, then cupped her face with his hands. "I'd like you to stay in the garage until we can get married. George, will you marry me? If you're willing to give me a second chance. A second chance for forever."

She rested her palms on his shoulders. "Are you sure?"

"I've never been more sure of anything in my life." He finally knew what he had, and he prayed it wasn't too late for him to keep it.

"Then of course I will," she said, then snuggled closer. *"Ti amo."*

He smiled, and slowly ran one finger down her cheek. "I love you, too. How did you know how to say that in Italian?"

Her cheeks darkened. "Your mother taught me."

Just as Bob leaned down to kiss her, the flash of a camera glared.

He opened his eyes, glanced to the side, and lowered his hands to her shoulders. "Randy," he mumbled.

"Whoo-hoo!" Randy exclaimed, waving his digital camera in the air. His movements stilled, he took one more picture of the two of them gaping at him, did a short two-step dance, twirled around, and sauntered away.

"He's going to be the best man, isn't he?"

Bob sighed. "Yup. I hope you know what you're in for."

George's arms slid around to his back, she tucked her head under his chin and embraced him fully. "I sure do, and I can hardly wait.

* * * * *

Watch for Randy's story,
CHANGING HER HEART,
next in the MEN OF PRAISE *miniseries*
in February 2006.

Dear Reader,

Welcome once again to Faith Community Fellowship!

Many people work hard all their lives. Many of us work too hard, and need to slow down before it's too late. Sometimes we need to work harder than those around us to get what we want, or even what we need. In both these times, often God sends messages, or messengers, in likely and unlikely forms, for our own good, whether we like it, or not.

The hardest part can be meeting in the middle. It is human nature to keep going the same way, just because we know what to expect. I've often heard it said that the greatest fear is the fear of the unknown. In this story, Bob didn't know what it would be like not to work…*hard.* Georgette didn't know what it was like to work at all. Of course, the best place is somewhere in the middle, and I hope you enjoyed the story of how Bob and Georgette met each other, with God's guidance, in that middle ground.

With the closing of *His Uptown Girl* we move next to Randy, who sometimes marches to the beat of a different drummer.

I look forward to seeing you again, when we see what God has in store for Randy.

Until then, may God bless you in your daily journeys.

gail sattler

And now, turn the page for a sneak preview of
DIE BEFORE NIGHTFALL
by Shirlee McCoy,
part of Steeple Hill's exciting new line,
Love Inspired Suspense!
On sale in September 2005
from Steeple Hill Books.

Chapter One

She'd never hung wash out to dry, but that wouldn't keep her from trying. Raven Stevenson eyed the basket of sopping white sheets and the small bucket of clothes pins sitting at her feet. How hard could it be?

Five minutes later she'd managed to trample one sheet into the mud. The other two were hanging, lopsided and drooping, from the line. "It could be worse, I suppose."

"Could be better, too." A pie in one hand, a grocery bag in the other, Nora Freedman came around the side of the house, her eyes lined with laughter as she eyed the muddy sheet. "Never had to dry laundry the old-fashioned way, I see."

"I'm afraid not. Hopefully it won't take me long to get better at it."

"It won't. You wouldn't believe how many renters have turned away from this property just because I don't have a clothes dryer."

"Their loss. My gain."

Nora beamed at the words. "I knew it, knew the minute I saw you, you were the person for this place. Here, I've brought you a welcome gift. Pecan pie and some things to stock your cupboards."

"You didn't have to—"

"Of course I didn't. I *wanted* to. I'll leave everything in the kitchen. Gotta scoot. Prayer meeting in a half hour. Call me if you need something."

"I will. Thank you."

"See you at church Sunday? You did say you planned to attend Grace Christian?"

The nerves that Raven had held at bay for a week clawed at her stomach. "Yes. I'll see you then."

"I knew it. Just knew this would work out." Then she was gone as quickly as she'd come, her squat, squarish figure disappearing around the corner of the house.

In the wake of her departure the morning silence seemed almost deafening. Raven hummed a tune to block out the emptiness, bending to lift the dirty sheet, her gaze caught and held by a strange print in the barren, muddy earth. A footprint—each toe clearly defined, the arch and heel obvious. Small, but not a child's foot. Someone had walked barefoot through the yard on a day when winter still chilled the air.

Who? Why? Raven searched for another print and found one at the edge of the lawn. From there, a narrow footpath meandered through sparse trees, the prints obvious on earth still wet from last night's rain. She followed the path until it widened and Smith Mountain Lake appeared, vast and blue, the water barely rippling. And there, on a rickety dock that jutted toward the center of the lake, her quarry—white hair, white skin, a bathing suit covering a thin back.

Raven hurried forward. "Are you all right?"

"Thea?" The woman turned, wispy hair settling in a cloud around a face lined with age. "I've been waiting forever. Didn't we agree to meet at ten?"

Ten? It was past noon. Two hours was a long time to sit half clad in a chilly breeze. Raven's concern grew, the nurse in her cataloguing what she saw—pale skin, goose bumps, a slight tremor. "Actually, I'm Raven. I live in the cottage up the hill."

"Not Thea's cottage? She didn't tell me she had guests."

"She probably forgot. Were you planning a swim?"

"Thea and I always swim at this time of year. Though usually it's not quite so cold."

"It *is* chilly today. Here, put this on." Raven slid

out of her jacket and placed it around the woman's shoulders.

"Do I know you?"

"No, we haven't met. I'm Raven Stevenson."

"I'm Abigail Montgomery. Abby to my friends."

"It's nice to meet you, Abby. Would you like to join me for tea? I've got a wonderful chamomile up at the house." Raven held out her hand and was relieved when Abby allowed herself to be pulled to her feet.

"Chamomile? It's been years since I've had that."

"Then let's go." Raven linked her arm through Abby's and led her toward the footpath, grimacing as she caught sight of her companion's scraped feet. Another walk through the brambles would only make things worse. "It looks like you've forgotten your shoes."

Abby glanced down at her feet, confusion drawing her brows together. Then she looked at Raven and something shifted behind her eyes as past gave way to present. Raven had seen it many times, knew the moment Abby realized what had happened. She waited a heartbeat, watching as the frail, vague woman transformed into someone stronger and much more aware.

"I've done it again, haven't I?" The words were firm but Abby's eyes reflected her fear.

"Nothing so bad. Just a walk to the lake."

"Dressed in a bathing suit? In..." Her voice trailed off, confusion marring her face once again.

"It's April. A lovely day, but a bit too cold for a swim."

"What was I thinking?" Frustration and despair laced the words.

"You were thinking about summer. Perhaps a summer long ago."

"Do I know you?"

"My name is Raven. I live up the hill at the Freedman cottage."

"Raven. A blackbird. Common. You're more the exotic type I'd think, with that wild hair and flowing dress."

Raven laughed in agreement. "I've been fighting my name my whole life. You're the first to notice."

"Am I? Then I guess I'm not as far gone as I'd thought." Despite the brave words, the tears behind Abby's eyes were obvious, the slight trembling of her jaw giving away her emotions.

Raven let her have the moment. Watched as she took a deep shuddering breath and glanced down at her bathing suit. "I suppose it could be worse. At least I wore clothes this time. Now, tell me, where are we headed?"

"To the cottage for tea."

"Let's go, then."

"Here, slip my shoes on first."

"Oh, I couldn't. What about you?"

"I've got tough skin." Raven slid her feet out of open heeled sneakers and knelt to help Abby slide her feet into them.

They made their way up the steep incline, Raven's hand steady against Abby's arm. It hurt to see the woman beside her. Hurt to know that a vital, lively woman was being consumed by a disease that would steal her essence and leave nothing behind but an empty shell. Why? It was a question she asked often in her job as a geriatric nurse. There was no answer. At least none that she could find, no matter how hard she prayed for understanding.

"Sometimes it just doesn't happen the way we want."

"What?" Startled, Raven glanced at Abby.

"Life. It doesn't always work out the way we want it to. Sad really. Don't you think?"

Yes. Yes, she did think it was sad. Her own life a sorry testament to the way things could go wrong. Raven wouldn't say as much. Not to Abby with her stiff spine and desperate eyes. Not to anyone. "It can be, yes. But usually good comes from our struggles."

"And just what good will come of me losing my marbles, I'd like to know?"

"We've met each other. That's one good thing."

"That's true. I've got to admit I'm getting tired of not having another woman around the house."

"Do you live alone?"

"Good Heavens, no. I forget things, you know. I live with… I can't seem to remember who's staying with me."

"It's all right. The name will come to you."

Abby gestured to the cottage that was coming into view. "There it is. I haven't been inside in ages. Have you lived here long?"

"I moved in this morning."

"You remind me of the woman who used to live here."

"Do I?"

"Thea. Such a lovely person. It's sad what happened. So sad…"